SHADO

Glover Wright has written five previous novels including *The Hound of Heaven*, *Blood Enemies* and *Eighth Day*. He has worked in advertising and entertainment and has travelled extensively. He lives in Jersey with his wife and daughter.

Also by Glover Wright

Eighth Day

SHADOW OF BABEL

Glover Wright

PAN BOOKS
IN ASSOCIATION WITH MACMILLAN LONDON

First published 1993 by Macmillan London Limited

This edition published 1994 by Pan Books
a division of Macmillan General Books
Cavaye Place London SW10 9PG
and Basingstoke
in association with Macmillan London

Associated companies throughout the world

ISBN 0 330 32612 0

1 3 5 7 9 8 6 4 2

A CIP catalogue record for this book is available from
the British Library

Typeset by Cambridge Composing (UK) Limited, Cambridge
Printed and bound in Great Britain by
Cox & Wyman Ltd, Reading, Berkshire

For Jack, in loving memory

ACKNOWLEDGEMENTS

My very special thanks go to Carl Meyer of the United States Secret Service in Washington, to Carolyn Mays in New York and Andrew Nurnberg in London. My thanks go too to Guiseppe Calvani and Camilo de Padova. Finally I happily acknowledge the contribution made by my dear friend Jack Clarke to whose memory this book is dedicated.

And they said, 'Let us build a city and a tower whose top may reach unto Heaven' . . . And the Lord came down to see the city and the tower which the children of men built and said, 'Behold the people are one and have a single language . . . now nothing they have in mind to do will be beyond their reach . . .'

Genesis

And you shall know the truth, and the truth shall set you free . . .

St John

PROLOGUE

Mojave Desert
California 1986

The driver sprawled too loosely on the seat, his expression stunned, a man relieved or condemned: a great weight lifted from him or the promise of life withdrawn.

He had one positive action left in him.

Two, he thought, lifting the bottle stiffly to his mouth, breaking blisters of sweat on his face.

Two.

He put the car into gear.

He had nowhere to go but forward.

Crossing himself he flicked his Zippo lighter alight, tossed it on to the gasoline-doused rear seats, jammed his foot to the floor, the Chevy's tyres biting, squealing, as, trailing fire, he bore down like hell's breath on the oncoming Buick that filled his windscreen as solid as an ebony coffin, and as punctual as death. His last thought was of his children, his last feeling guilt, his last cry Maria.

The fireball matched the sinking orange sun but lingered longer, exploded fragments from it burning in the sudden desert night like camp-fires around a battlefield.

A speeding car approached from the same direction as the Buick, slowing well short of the wreck, the driver exiting and moving forward cautiously, arms raised against the fierce heat, circling the wreck uncertainly before stopping abruptly, staring at something lying in the scrub by the side of the road, barely visible in the light of the flames. He moved closer, knelt, and lowered his head to the twisted blackened shape. For a long moment he remained kneeling, staring down, before finally backing away.

He returned to his car as though dreaming, turned it around and retreated the way he had come; at first slowly, almost reluctantly, but his speed building as the desert night and his own fears swallowed him whole.

The flames died slowly, crackling down to silence with short-lived defiant flurries of sparks trailing tracers into the desert, while within the mangled, ticking black mass a dull red glow lingered. Finally this, too, died.

A figure staggered from the scrub on to the road, crystals from the Buick's windscreen glinting in his blackened face and singed hair. He fell, screamed, dragged himself up again, then made for the smoking wreckage.

In the rear of the Buick, between two charred bodies, he found the leather attaché case he had supplied them with, its exposed lead-lined steel shell still too hot to touch. He kicked it out on to the blacktop then collapsed beside it, his pain locked out of his mind. Inside, he found the container they had promised him – still sealed, hot, but undamaged. *Safe.* He closed his scorched eyelids.

He regained consciousness still on the road, not remembering the explosion nor being thrown from the car and only half-remembering crawling back into the wreckage. He would remember the pain always but that was bearable as long as he had the recording. He lay waiting. His schedule was known. He had prepared the way. It was only a matter of time. He stared at the wreck, staying awake to stay alive.

He needed to stay alive.

CHAPTER
ONE

Tomorrow

'What's behind that?' asked John Cornell, indicating a steel security door with an electronic ID panel and a firm warning prohibiting entrance to unauthorized persons.

'New technology, sir,' answered Harden, the NSA station-chief. 'Experimental. I barely understand it myself.'

Meaning I've no chance, thought Cornell. 'Explain as much as you do understand,' he said, evenly.

Cornell distrusted everything NSA. Not because that Intelligence organization's astonishing electronic eyes and ears could spy on anything, anywhere, from their orbital satellites – including, he had no illusions, his own bedroom if they really wanted to – but because he had been forced to inherit its cold, arrogant, practically invisible chief, when he, John Patrick Cornell – grandson of an Irish immigrant railroad labourer originally named O'Connell – was sworn in as President of the United States of America.

Nearing the end of his first year in the White House, he had spent no more than an hour face to face with the legendary spymaster, William Bradley Kent.

Long enough, he thought, recalling the studied, subdued lighting of the office at Fort Meade, NSA's HQ between Washington and Baltimore, Maryland, and the silent, still figure behind the bare desk as he, a fledgeling president, expounded his views on foreign policy and the dangers of intelligence gathering without strict – he had meant presidential – control to a man who, reputedly, acknowledged no control over his organization except his own.

3

It had been a fraught, negative meeting, with Defence Secretary Lester Stansfield, NSA's direct boss – a normally forceful personality who some predicted would succeed Cornell – virtually mute. Direct light had not touched Kent's face once, and though forewarned of the man's disfigurement, Cornell had found himself conceding almost everything he had planned to stick on; starting the downward slide in an effort to put the man at ease and ending, he never quite knew how, in near abdication of his power over him.

Throughout, Kent had not uttered a forceful word in argument, protest, or opinion, yet somehow had won.

Cornell learned later that this was a master interrogator's technique: calculated silence at the correct moment allowing a subject to talk himself into his own grave.

Grave, good metaphor, he decided, trapped still in the chill, depressing room with the shadowed figure sitting too stiffly in his chair, as if pain lay just beneath one thin damaged layer of skin and every movement had its cost.

Afterwards, he felt as if he had been talking to a spectre.

Now, almost one year later, Kent was still in place and continued to take no apparent notice of the views of the President. That was how it seemed to Cornell. And probably, he decided, to too many of the people that mattered. It was a situation that could not continue, a running battle he was weary of, and he knew that soon he must concede defeat or swing the hatchet. If he could.

The Mark of Kent, as his wife acidly put it, pervaded every NSA installation from its massive headquarters in Baltimore, Maryland, to its smallest outposts across the globe; evidenced by obsessive secrecy and patronizing, intimidatory attitudes – as though they were saying: Mr President, you don't know *shit* about what's going on and without us couldn't keep this country as a world power. Meaning, you don't, we do.

Cornell needed no reminding how near this was to the truth, and, given the chaotic dangerous state of world order at that moment in history and NSA's proven ability to monitor, manipulate, even escalate events, knew this was too much power for any unelected body – or its ruler. It was perilously close to a case of the guard dog cornering his master inside the wire while overtly performing duties as his protector.

4

Paranoia? wondered Cornell, glancing away down a long row of blinking and whirring machines whose operators moved silently like white-coated priests performing mass at the altar of high technology. He hoped he was honest enough to recognize it in himself if it were.

'I'd like to see inside,' he said.

'Excuse me, sir?'

Cornell ducked his head at the security door.

'I'm afraid that isn't possible, Mr President.'

He felt blood rise to his face. Keep cool. Control it. You're the man. He has to do what you want. 'Open it up.'

'There's a timed procedure for that area. The duty-shift won't be out for another five hours. They're working with extremely sensitive equipment. A new breed of artificial-intelligence computers. Operating conditions are about the same as in a surgical-transplant theatre. That critical, sir. Even the air is scrubbed. Of course if you'd given us warning . . .'

'I didn't know it existed.' *Like too damn much of Kent's empire.*

'The work being carried out in there will be of great benefit for the future,' Harden assured.

Whose future? Mine? The American people? Humankind? Or your kind? Kent's kind? The steel-eyed ones who talk a language few understand, nor I suspect are meant to. 'I'd like to see personnel data for that facility. I want an idea of the numbers we're discussing here.'

'That's highly classified information, sir. Ultra-secret.'

Cornell was stunned by the sheer confidence in the man's barely veiled refusal. His voice tightened. 'Harden, let me inform you there isn't an Intelligence operation running that doesn't need presidential permission. It's known as a *Finding*, if you're not aware already? I hope you're not telling me that what you got going behind closed doors in there hasn't reached my desk?' He glared at the flabby face. *Too much, too wordy, just tell the son of a bitch to move his ass.*

'As I said, Mr President, we're talking experimental work here – not an operation. You have to be snowed under with Intelligence information already? You don't need to know. Not right now, anyway.'

When? Some future stage? Then only maybe? 'Just give me sight of that personnel list – or get on to your boss and ask him if he wants to do this the hard way?'

'I need to make a phone call – sir.'

'You don't need to do anything except obey my order.'

Harden hesitated momentarily, then hustled away.

Cornell watched his fat backside disappear into an office. *He'll call Kent. Let him. I can over rule anything Kent says. Goddamn it! I'm the fucking President of these United States. I can overrule* anybody.

Except Madelaine.

If she was here she'd have said: You handled it well but you took too long getting him to jump, *and she'd be right.*

Harden returned, thrusting a computer read-out forward.

Maybe he didn't call Kent? thought Cornell, pleased, and – he wondered, uncomfortably – relieved?

He scanned the list vaguely, not really interested, feeling Harden's eyes on him. *You're playing power games and he knows it. That's why he didn't call Kent. He knows you're out of your depth in their world. You're an irritation. A timewaster.* A familiar name caught his eye. 'How long have you had Greg Lewelyn with you?'

Harden seemed startled. 'You know him, sir?'

'I know his father from college days. We roomed together. Greg's a very bright young man. I didn't realize he'd followed his father into NSA? I thought he was still Air Force? I was there when President Bush decorated him after the Gulf War.'

Harden seemed eager to limit any damage. 'He's in good shape now, sir. Just fine. Real fit, runs every day in the desert. Been with the agency some months now. Computer whiz, like the others in there. Experimenting with deep-space radio signals – part of an evaluation programme of the equipment. He's doing real well. I'll tell him you said hello.'

'Do that.' Cornell scanned the meagre list on the read-out. 'Doesn't appear to be many people working on the programme?'

'You're talking highly specialized skills, Mr President. There's not too many of the calibre we need available to us.'

Don't ask for more, Cornell thought, and folded the read-out.

Harden held out his hand. 'That can't leave the station, sir. Security.'

Back on the surface, darkness had cloaked the Mojave desert. The silhouetted circle of thick metal masts, cross members, and dishes that were the eyes and ears of the underground station looked primeval and threatening against the stars.

The waiting Sikorsky S-61 from Edwards Air Force Base had its rotors swinging as Cornell ducked below them, an arm raised to his face against the whipped sand. Inside, buckled in, he gazed down as the helicopter lifted, the massive black circular construction falling away below reminding him of a dare he had undertaken when visiting England as a student: sitting at midnight in the centre of the great ring of Stonehenge on Salisbury Plain.

Maybe Stone Age man listened to the stars too?

He closed his eyes. He knew he would tell Madelaine about the restricted area. He knew she would have him call Sam Lewelyn and put strain on an old friendship. He wished he could be as tough with her as he had been with world leaders since he had taken office. He had banged heads, trying to make them see sense, and was beginning, he hoped, to make them understand and face their responsibilities in a fragmented, unpredictable, changed, and downright dangerous world.

And yet with Madelaine . . .

You don't love world leaders, you don't make love to them, they don't see you naked with your vanities stripped away and your insecurities hanging out as plain as impotence. They don't see you ageing.

He shook his head angrily. Maybe you're not the youngest president that ever took office but you've *achieved*. You're *it*. Number One. And there's more to do. A hell of a lot more before we can all sleep safely. Get some sleep yourself or you'll look like shit. He wished he was already in the presidential jet, comfortable in soft glove leather, lights dimmed, lifting off from Edwards for Washington.

She lay unmoving as he entered their bedroom in the White House, exhausted, determined to avoid inspection tours of remote secret installations for at least another year.

He knew she was awake. She always was.

He undressed in the dark, dumping his clothes over a chair back, then slipped beneath the covers, feeling her warmth.

'How was it?' she asked, clear voiced, any effects of sleep gone.

He wondered what time she had returned from whatever

7

function from that week's calendar she had chosen to grace. He wondered also – fleetingly, shutting down fast – *who* was there? Who had interested her? Dark questions he never allowed into the forefront of his mind. He had every reason for jealousy and more reasons than most for never admitting it.

'Don't ask. Not until my head clears of this damned cotton wool.'

'You need your ears seeing to. I've told you before. I'll fix the appointment.'

'It's only flying. Pressurization.'

'It's only deafness. You want to risk that?'

Welcome home.

'No problems? John?'

He shrugged and she caught the movement. 'Kent?'

'You know the situation.'

She turned over. 'So how did you handle it?'

He was too tired for interrogation. 'Talk about it tomorrow.'

'It is tomorrow. And if you don't start handling Kent *hard* you won't have a tomorrow. Not in the White House. And nor will I.'

He hated talking in the dark. With her, anyway. For a second he imagined he was with another woman. Anyone. But someone who exerted no pressure. The reverse. Lifted it from him. Would make him feel that just lying there was enough. Was everything. He smiled and she couldn't see it and that pleased him because at least he had one secret from both her and William Bradley Kent.

'What went wrong?'

'I didn't say anything went wrong.'

'You didn't have to.'

He wanted desperately to sleep but his nerves jangled with anxieties that he had forced down and she drew out. The darkness felt oppressive. He closed his eyes. He might have been back in the desert, deep underground. He listened to the whisper of the air-conditioning; sometimes he found it soothing.

'There was a door. A security door. Warnings posted. No guard. High-tech electronics. You know the sort of thing. Call it intuition, call it the Irish in me. I just wasn't convinced. That's all.'

'Of what?'

'That the station-chief was telling the truth. The whole truth, anyway. He was defensive.'

He felt her rise to one elbow, her face close in the dark, her breath on his skin. He smelled mouthwash and a hint of garlic.

French cooking, he thought. Their embassy. He avoided French *men*. An informal dinner. He remembered seeing the invitation. She had said she wanted to go – because of the food – but wouldn't, of course, without him.

Yesterday's promises are worse than lies.

'Aren't you listening?' she said.

'I'm sorry – I'm really beat.'

'Could it be something unauthorized? Illegal? Christ, if only!'

'Kent isn't stupid.'

'He's over-confident. Face it, he doesn't see *you* as being a problem and he might just overstretch himself because of that. Might finance something from some slush fund he's set up somewhere – knowing it wouldn't get through the watch-dog committee. Something unconstitutional. If it's covert he'd need authorization from you and it sounds like he may not have it.'

'You're making too much of it.'

He heard her breathing change, sharpen, as it did when she made love. Her excitement was clear. He knew she would not let go now.

'So what did you say? You had this gut feeling and you did what? Shook the man by the hand and left? *What?*'

'I asked to see inside.'

'And?'

'There's a time-lock. Duty shift-workers get sealed in. They're testing advanced computers – that's their story – so working conditions have to be sterile. Hell, I don't know enough to argue! There was no way I was going to get in there right then and I couldn't wait five hours for the shift to end. You saw my schedule.'

'So you left?'

'I asked to see the personnel list.'

'Why?'

'To see how many were in there. Get an idea of scale.'

'Good. Very good. But they could easily lie.'

'Of course. I got a computer read-out just the same. I guess they thought it wouldn't make any difference me seeing it.'

'What's new? And?'

'There were twenty-three people listed. Computer whizzes apparently. Greg Lewelyn was one.'

The bedside light snapped on. She was sitting up, naked; younger than him by ten years but looking twenty. And he knew it.

'He's Air Force,' she protested. 'I remember his uniform.'

'He's NSA now. Like Sam.'

'Greg married that unsuitable girl? There was a problem with her family? Religion? Some cult or other?'

'Unsuitable by whose standards? Yours? Because she was raised in West Virginian mountains and not on rolled East Coast lawns? Elizabeth and Sam thought she was just fine. I remember her as bright – a little highly strung maybe. And no *girl*. She was a damn good-looking young woman.'

Her mouth was ugly. 'So what's he doing there?'

'Greg? I've no idea.'

'Get it from Sam. He'd know if there are any rumours circulating – he *should* as head of their Office of Security.'

'I haven't seen or talked with him since. I should have done. I feel bad calling him with this after so long.'

'You're the president now, personal lives suffer, he knows that.'

'I really want to avoid using Sam.'

'There's plenty you avoid doing already. Like dealing with Kent, directly.'

He hadn't the fight in him. 'I'll call.'

'Don't discuss it on the telephone. Arrange to meet him. Somewhere Kent can't hear or see you.'

'Where do you suggest? The bottom of the Potomac?'

'Leave that to me.'

Somewhere you know already, he thought, sickeningly.

He reached for her but she turned out the light leaving him the darkness and her back for comfort.

Cornell swung in his chair and gazed out of the Oval Office windows at the Washington morning, his eyes gritty. 'Sam? This is John – John Cornell.'

'Mr President?' enquired a deep, suspicious voice.

'It's all right, Sam, this isn't some TV hoax show. And drop the formality – you've seen me in my underwear.'

The voice opened up and Cornell could almost see the broad smile with the familiar football-field breaks in two upper front teeth. 'Out of them too,' reminded Sam Lewelyn.

Cornell laughed. 'Some days!'

'You bet.'

An aide entered and hovered with material for attention. Cornell turned, pointed impatiently at the desk, and swung back to the windows. 'Sam, it gets pretty stressful up here, I need to get away – meet real people once in a while.'

'You offering to buy me a drink?'

'Damn right. It's been a long time.'

'Not so long. We had a few moments together when Greg was up for the presentation. At your present address – before you took up residence.'

'That was three years ago, Sam.'

'Was it? My God. Where does it all go?'

'I know the feeling. How's Elizabeth? Over in England again, I suppose?'

The line fell silent.

'Sam?'

'She died, John. In England. Cancer. It was a long-time thing she'd kept to herself. You know how she was. I found out toward the end, of course. Couldn't help it. I spent the last few months with her – over there.'

'*Christ*, I didn't know. Sam, I'm sorry. So sorry. I should have been told. I should have made it my *business* to know.'

'You're the President of these United States – you've a million things on your mind every day of the week. It doesn't matter. To tell the truth she was glad when it was over. In a way I was too. The pain was worse than death, John.'

Cornell sat silently remembering a tall Englishwoman with a sharp laugh, biting wit, and mind to match. *Half an aristocrat, half a washerwoman's brat*, was how Elizabeth Lewelyn enjoyed describing herself: her father modestly titled, her mother a below-stairs domestic whose own modesty had slipped under her master's attentions.

'About this drink?' reminded Lewelyn.

'Right. Away from here, OK? Nothing public. Do you mind? You still have that gas-guzzling Lincoln?'

'Nothing else fits.'

'Feel like driving over from Baltimore to Falls Church?'

'Sure.'

Cornell gave an address.

'Something wrong, John?'

Cornell had forgotten how quick Sam could be. 'Just shaken by the news of Elizabeth. Maybe a little tense. The job. Not exactly nine to five with a zero stress-rating.'

'You're doing well. When?' enquired Lewelyn.

'Tonight? Anything arranged?'

'Nothing that can't be dumped.' Lewelyn chuckled. 'You can always make it an Executive Order.'

I could, thought Cornell, but don't let it come to that. 'Make it nine thirty. There's a cocktail I have to attend here first. I need an excuse to get away and you're it.'

'Just make sure they don't think you're cheating on the First Lady.'

Cornell laughed and replaced the receiver. He stared at it. *Just using an old friendship.*

The house was red brick and wood, set back from a small clinically trimmed front lawn bearing neither wounds nor debris from children and boxed in by a razor-cut hedge that shut off the view from and of the road.

'Pull right up in there, Jim,' Cornell ordered the owner of the plain Ford sedan whose – reluctant – co-operation had enabled him to escape the White House without the heavyweight presence that generally accompanied presidential movement.

Jim Bentley stopped the car before a single closed garage.

'Take a couple of hours,' said Cornell, not moving. 'Catch a movie if you like.'

'I'm staying right here, sir. After I've checked the house.'

'The house is just fine. Belongs to a friend. I appreciate you've a job to do, Jim, but it's OK. Relax.'

'I'll be right here, Mr President,' repeated Bentley, firmly.

Cornell glanced around. 'There'll be a caller coming soon. Male, white, big, looks military but isn't. Name's Lewelyn. Samuel. Don't search him, he's a friend.'

'Will he be armed, sir?'

'He's a friend, Jim.'

Bentley's black face dipped glumly.

A door opened in the house and a chic, petite woman of around thirty-five stepped outside, a newly clipped poodle under her arm, its face alert, ready to bark. She placed one hand around the dog's mouth and tickled its head with the other, then walked off down the driveway. The Ford might not have existed.

Cornell climbed out.

'Anyone else in there, Mr President?'

Cornell smiled.

Bentley tipped the rear-view mirror to a better angle and slumped lower in the seat, his fingers reaching down to check for the compact powerful machine-pistol underneath, his heart rate lifting a little against the revolver holstered to his ribs. He did not like surprises, he did not like strange neighbourhoods – no matter if they employed their own watch and tended their lawns like putting-greens – he did not like the idea of the President of the United States visiting houses that hadn't been checked from roof to foundations first. Most of all he did *not* like being the only – maybe the last – thing between the President and the worst kind of historical event.

Shit! If his boss could see this situation he'd be *freaking*.

Your ultimate boss just walked right in there through an open door after saying everything's cool, he told himself, but it was no consolation.

The old Lincoln Continental lurched to a halt just inches behind the sedan, its long bonnet dipping slowly like a carrier's prow, huge in the Ford's rear-view mirror.

Sam Lewelyn got out and rapped on Bentley's window. 'Where's the heavy artillery?' he asked as the glass dropped.

Bentley saw shrewd, cold blue eyes set in a heavy, blunt face. 'Came without them – sir.'

'Not your happiest day then?'

'Not hardly. You're Mr Lewelyn.'

'Right. He's in there?'

'Expecting you, sir.'

'He'll be OK with me. What's your name, son?'

'Jim Bentley.'

'All right, Jim. Don't worry about inside because I'm there. Understood? You just stay sharp out here.'

Lewelyn slapped the roof and walked away.

So the President wasn't having a fling on the side, thought Bentley. Good, made his job easier and kept his conscience clean. He watched the big man raise his fist to the knocker just as the door opened. Pro, he decided. Not one step taken without his eyes doing the walking first. Not a cop, not military 'cause the man said so – so from one of the spook outfits. Pushing sixty, but I wouldn't bet my life against him. I wouldn't even bet my mortgage.

Inside the house, Cornell let his hand be enveloped in Lewelyn's meaty grasp. 'Great to see you, Sam. You're looking good. Rested.'

Lewelyn accepted the light beer offered from a small bar in the scrupulously clean living room, sipped, grimaced, then moved around the room, examining. 'John, I was never fooled back then and I'm certainly not fooled now. Who runs this place? CIA? State?'

'Nothing like that. Belongs to a friend of my wife. From college days – like us. Executive with one of the banks. Don't know her myself.'

Play it straight, don't lie, Cornell had warned himself. He'll have thought this through before he got here. Sam believes everything has a motive.

Lewelyn glanced around. 'Woman's world. No man in it.' He tilted the weak beer each way as proof. 'So why are we here?'

'I've a favour to ask.'

'You could have done that on the phone. Why the safe-house routine?'

'I wanted to see you. Especially after Elizabeth . . .'

Lewelyn took out a browned meerschaum, looked in vain for an ashtray, and repocketed it. He gazed at Cornell. 'Maybe that's half of it – now. I doubt if it was the start of it.'

'It's Kent,' admitted Cornell.

Lewelyn lowered himself into a beige leather armchair, grimacing at its grip around his big frame. 'You want him dumped.'

'No.'

'Sure you do. He doesn't kow-tow to you. Kent's worse than J. Edgar Hoover and James Jesus Angleton together. And cares less about his reputation. His reputation in others' eyes, that is – not his professional reputation. That's sacrosanct. He'd kill to preserve it.'

Cornell gestured frustratedly and sat opposite. 'Sam, I need to feel I can control – that I have control – of my major Intelligence-gathering organization.'

Lewelyn heaved himself up, discarded his beer, found a bottle of good bourbon whiskey behind the bar and poured two stiff measures. 'We're here because NSA doesn't know about this place, right?'

'You do,' said Cornell, steadily. 'Now.'

Lewelyn cast him a hard glance. 'Meaning I report back to Kent? You're the President of these United States and I'm a superannuated spook paid on your say-so. That's real life.' He drank. 'OK?'

'You've retired?' Cornell was clearly shocked.

'I cut early because of Elizabeth. Had to. Had to be with her.' He gazed at his drink. 'I'm easing the new man in so I've still got some *inside* privileges – if that's what's on your mind.'

'I'm not pulling rank, Sam.'

'No, you're relying on friendship and I don't know which I prefer as a means of coercion.'

'I'm not forcing you into anything. I swear to God.'

'But you planned on asking?'

Cornell swallowed bourbon. 'I need to know what Greg is working on.'

'My Greg? Stuck in the Mojave desert listening to radio emissions from black holes or wherever. Beats the hell out of me the technology they've got these days. You want his job description, ask his station-chief.'

'They wouldn't let me into Greg's area. It was restricted – heavily restricted. I wanted in, they gave excuses. I don't trust them. I think there's more to it. Something they – Kent – hasn't declared.'

'What?'

'Listening in or watching somewhere sensitive – somewhere they don't have clearance for.'

'You're looking for an excuse, John. You want Kent's ass – fire him! You're the President.'

'Naïvety doesn't suit you.'

'Conspiracy doesn't you, John. You're straight, that's always been your pitch and I've always believed it to be true.'

'I'll say it again. All I want is to feel safe when I make foreign-policy decisions. I do not want to feel that I might have a rogue at the head of my – hell! – the most powerful intelligence service in the entire goddamn world doing things *his* way behind my back! *Deliberately* behind my back.' Cornell's finger stabbed out. 'And that's behind the back of the presidency, Sam! We're living in critical times: Langley's paranoid – with reason – that the East European republics are shaping up to take a swing at each other with the heavier nukes left in the deep silos; the Arabs are about to turn all of the Middle East into a desert with old Soviet bin-ends, and maybe us too if we don't bow down to Allah . . . and Federated Europe is either about to sink under the weight of refugees or swing so far right we won't be talking the same political language any more! Remember that nightmare scenario they used to specu-late about back in George Bush's day? It's here and I'm the one facing the reality. That's what being the President of the United States means. You hear what I'm saying. I have to be *damn* certain I'm getting the whole picture of what's happening out there. Certain that the pictures, the transcripts and the goddamn analyses that come out of NSA are good – and not what *Kent* thinks are good! I'm sorry to get hard-nosed, Sam, but you've got to see this my way. Let me put it this way: Kent may be the cameraman – up there with all that space hardware – making like he's doing a great job for me – but what if he's decided he's the director too?'

Lewelyn drained his bourbon. 'I avoid going to Greg – OK? That's reasonable? If I get stonewalled I'll use him, otherwise he's a no-no. Best I'm prepared to do – as a favour to a friend. You want to make this anything more that's your prerogative.' His hard blue eyes rested on Cornell.

'I'll appreciate anything you can do. As a favour. Nothing more.'

'You got it.' Lewelyn stood. 'I'll be getting along. And maybe you should be getting back to the White House – your man outside is ageing by the second.' He looked at a large carefully positioned silver-framed photograph of two women: one attractive, grasping a poodle close to her face as if for comfort, the other beautiful, head turned, offering her half-profile as a gift to the photographer, her tawny eyes smiling calculatedly.

'Madelaine enjoying the life?'

'The life *style*. Hates politics.' Cornell smiled, feeling wretched, believing a long-held friendship had disintegrated.

He stood by the window watching Lewelyn go, then poured himself another drink, sipping slowly until it was finished.

He needed a friend who understood. He needed love that had no price tag, no wounding barbs, no emptiness. He needed to believe in himself again – not in the position, not the trappings. Where does a man turn with the avenues of friendship and love ruined or barricaded? To God? God had given up listening long ago. Or maybe *he* had given up listening to God?

He took the glasses to the kitchen and washed them. It was almost like being back home. Home, before he was married. Family. All gone now. He wondered if he would ever be truly happy again before his own time came. Happy for himself – not from pleasure in his achievements. And there had been real achievements. That was pride. Vanity even. Not happiness. For his achievements there would be testimonials. Memorials. He really believed that. However negative his words to Sam, he knew that his was a momentous time to be president of the greatest power the world had ever known. There were no limits to what he might achieve. The world was changing fast and he stood over it, the master of change. He could halt those changes or let them flow. He had more control of the world's destiny than any other human in history. He had to be strong and decisive. Yet here he stood, in a stranger's house, washing away the dregs of old friendship; not trusting his wife, nor those who served him. Perhaps not even trusting himself, any more.

CHAPTER
TWO

The chattering woke her and for once it was not her *voices*.

Gathering up the goose-down duvet she had bought as protection against the station accommodation unit's chill air-conditioning, she arose and moved down the narrow corridor toward the sound.

Greg Lewelyn's concentration was split between a lap-top computer and the oscilloscope beside it, completely oblivious to her presence, his dark head clasped by large headphones while his sun-browned hands adjusted sound equipment to his right.

She touched his shoulder, feeling hard muscle toned by weights and punishing dawn and dusk desert runs beneath his MIT sweat shirt.

He pulled off the headphones and made to bite her half-uncovered breast.

She clasped his ears, tugging his head back. 'Hey! I couldn't keep you in bed this morning?'

'Let's catch up on lost time.'

'I thought you're not supposed to take anything out from down there? Greg?'

He looked at her. 'I didn't. It's you. Last night.'

She pulled away.

'I couldn't wake you.'

'So you recorded me instead? I want to hear it. Now.'

He slowed the tape-recorder operating speed to normal and handed her the headphones.

She listened for a few seconds then snatched them off, glaring at the computer screen. 'You're *using* me.'

'I'm using the wave-forms your voice produces. That isn't you.'

'Why? What for?'

'You won't understand.'

'Don't patronize me.'

'All right. I'm searching for a key. A mathematical key. Your voice patterns are unique.'

'When I'm out of my *head*?' She pushed him away, angrily.

'Carolyn, you have to come to terms with your—'

'*Problem?*'

'Gift. It's part of you. You can't deny it. It's something that happens to you. You can't cut yourself off because of it. There are good people here, you have to try and fit in.'

'I know what they think.'

'What do they think? They don't know!'

'Does it matter?' She swung her head at the tape. 'They'll know soon enough.'

'When I'm through your voice won't exist. I swear. No one could identify you.'

'It isn't fair.'

He smiled and held her and she let him. 'Sure it's fair. A wife is supposed to support her husband in his career.'

'Career? I married an Air Force pilot and all I see is desert, that steel cage out there, and you disappearing under it every day!'

'We've been through this. I'm making five times my flight pay. I'd have been crazy to turn the project down.'

'Locked underground all day? Sometimes all *night*. When do we get to spend it?'

He released her.

'Greg, I didn't mean that. You know I don't care about the money. It's this place!'

'The choice was yours. You could have lived off-station.'

'And see you *when*?'

'It's tough, OK, I know that.' He looked out at the desert beyond the high-security fence, imagining what it was like for her. 'Listen, I've got seven straight days' leave due. We could fly to Washington, see Dad, hit the stores? Maybe drive up and see your folks . . . if that's what you want?'

'Great!'

'So?'

'So what's *down there* got that I haven't?'

The tape came to its end, whipping viciously. He turned to shut it down but she held him. 'You don't commit yourself to something as difficult – as destructive – for us as this without knowing what's hooked you. I'm not stupid, why don't you talk to me?'

He switched off the machine. 'I've told you as much as I can.'

'That you listen to outer space? I thought people *looked* at outer space? Through *telescopes*? Maybe I am dumb.'

He could see the massive circle of masts and white dishes shimmering in the growing morning heat. There were no answers he could give her. His entire purpose in being there was to gain answers. All he had were questions.

'Greg, every woman wants to know what keeps her man away from her.'

He sat down. 'You know why I quit flying?'

'Of course I know.'

'You don't. I was ready to quit before the Gulf blew up. Once the war started I had to see it through—'

He stopped and she could almost see the shutters come down, knowing she could never enter the black space he kept inside, knowing, too, that she would never come to terms with her ignorance of what had been done to him – even though half of her did not want to know.

He stared at the computer screen. 'I was already becoming more interested in the on-board computers than I was in flying the aircraft. I knew that, soon, computers will be doing the real flying and pilots will only be there to make taxpayers feel safe.' He pressed keys and watched complex patterns form. 'Space is full of sound. There's a great invisible sea of radio waves breaking over our world. Maybe the answer to why we exist is fixed in one of those waves: one signal from the furthest end of the universe sent by some intelligence superior of ours? We've got a chance of receiving it – decoding it, understanding it – right here. We've the best people, the best equipment. Better than anyone. We're at the leading edge and there's nowhere else I want to be.' He looked up. 'But I need you here with me.'

She was scared and as so often in her life there seemed no reason for her fear – only that dreadful feeling of *knowing*; as though blind yet aware of an abyss some unknown distance ahead. She wished her voices would fall silent and let her live her life – let her love – in peace.

'What's the matter?'

She kissed him. 'Let's go to Washington. Did you mean what you said about my folks?'

'I'll take you if that's what you want.'

'It's been a long while.'

Thank God, he thought, but said: 'We can get to the mountains by Saturday morning.'

She kissed him again then held him close. 'With ten days we could even fly to England and visit your mom. It's been almost a year.'

She felt his tight nod and smiled.

'Cardus wants you,' said Larry Maine as Greg exited the electronic high-security lock that protected both secrets and sensitive equipment of the NSA station's restricted area.

'Know why?'

'I don't even know what I'm doing here!'

'You're solving the mysteries of the universe.'

'I'm solving shit.'

'You need a break.'

Maine tilted his head toward the door at the furthest end of the stark white and stainless steel corridor. 'Tell God.'

'Hang in there, we'll crack it.'

'If it doesn't crack us first. You want to know how high the personnel turnover is on this project? OK, don't remind me: *Restricted Information*.' Maine jerked a thumb at the security lock. 'The proles outside see the changes and they talk. I fraternize – you don't. It's *high*, take my word for it. Way too high. Burn-out. That's prime cause. Trust me.'

'We get paid burn-out rates.'

'So where do they go after here? A rest home somewhere? Sunshine? Women! Tell Cardus I'm ready.'

Greg walked the passage to the project-head's door and knocked.

'Sit,' said Cardus.

Greg obeyed and watched him make his habitual, speed-written notes, the pale face dipping emphatically with each stop of his pen, one hand lightly tending his swept-back grey-blond hair, the back and sides cut brutally short.

Cardus controlled the project by penetrating analysis of each member of the team's individual efforts, shift by shift, seemingly tireless, nothing escaping him. Greg imagined him constantly behind his shoulder, monitoring, peering at his work, or somewhere above, omnipotent, staring down vacantly but absorbing everything.

'I'm told you know the President?' enquired Cardus, head still down.

Greg cross his arms. 'I knew him *before* he became president.'

'Through your father.' Cardus's eyes lifted a little, as if to note body language.

'And mother. I haven't seen or spoken to John Cornell since his inauguration – except on that.' He pointed at a TV screen mounted in a console behind the desk.

'Do I detect bitterness?'

'Personal.'

'You know he was here? In the station?'

'Only after he left. I was on duty. The visit wasn't announced.'

'Inspections never are.'

Greg disliked Cardus's method of firing questions like arrows, arched high, seemingly random missiles, some targeted and barbed – but which? He also disliked Cardus. Small, petty reasons. His over-correctness jarred, his perfect desk top annoyed. He pictured his own mildly chaotic work space and felt guilt. He remembered Larry Maine's warning upon his arrival at the Mojave Desert station: *Cardus is an automaton posing as a human, with a mind like an ice pick – and yours is the face he's ascending; yours and mine. He uses people.*

'You're settled in well enough?' enquired Cardus, now looking up fully, wanting to see the answers.

'It's been three months.'

'Of course. One loses all sense of time down here. Your wife? We don't see much of her. She finds the conditions difficult?'

'Carolyn's fine.'

'We know her background of course for her security clearance. I would have thought a closed community such as this might suit her very well? Of course religion does have a very strong hold on people.'

'She's broken free of all that.'

'Really? Because of you? *For* you? Religion and parental influence – powerful emotions involved there. Not easy to break away from that kind of influence.'

'Maybe she's still fighting the battle,' Greg admitted, annoyed.

'And the marriage is strong enough to take the attrition?'

'We'll make it,' said Greg, tightly, his rising anger derived as much from guilt as Cardus's probing.

'Good. You have much to give to the project. And have the dedication – and the mind – to rise with us. I don't want your work adversely affected.'

'It won't be.'

Cardus studied him for a long moment as if expecting more.

'That's it?'

'Regarding the President. Your father and he really were very close – at college?'

'Ask them.'

'You object to my question?'

'My father's personal relationship with the President is irrelevant to my position here.'

'You misunderstand. There's been no *pressure* regarding your status here. We're not influenced by outsiders.'

Greg looked at him. 'The President of the United States is hardly an *outsider*?'

Cardus gave a rare smile. 'My underground mentality is showing. Of course I meant outside this facility. But, realistically, even the President has limits to his knowledge of secret projects. Ours for example. As far as the technology is concerned, he *is* an outsider. He knows the basis of our work but does not need to know more. He's hardly a scientist, is he? The poor man's head must ring with the amount of information he's already asked to absorb.' He paused. 'However – and let me be completely frank here – the more information a president, or anyone in high office for that matter, is given, the more they want. That is in the nature of ambition. This widens the circle of knowledge on any secret, because whatever the President knows, given time, his aides and confidants will also know. Thus security risks are heightened. Sometimes unacceptably so.' He waved a hand. 'We are way ahead of our – I was about to say, enemies, but that is a difficult term these days so let's call them *competitors* – and we don't want to lose that advantage.'

'You think I'm a security risk?'

'You might discuss matters with your father. Perfectly natural. He was one of us. Technically still is, until his successor takes over fully.'

'And he might tell the President?'

'It is possible.'

'It isn't. Dad and I have a strict understanding. We never discuss NSA business.'

'I'm pleased to hear it.'

Greg pushed himself up. 'I'm starting shift.'

Cardus seemed unaware of his anger. 'Work going well? Any breakthrough you want to discuss?'

Greg faltered at the door. 'There is a . . . new direction . . . I've been exploring.'

'I'll look forward to results.'

'It's just an idea I've been working on. I'll need more time.'

'Questions of the universe aren't settled in a day,' smiled Cardus, writing again. 'You have leave due. Where do you plan on going?'

'Washington.'

Cardus frowned.

'To see my father – not the President. Then to West Virginia – the mountains. Maybe England for a couple of days. My mother is buried there.'

Cardus's pen had stopped, poised. 'I thought you said your wife stayed away from that – community?'

'It's been a long time. I promised I'd take her up.'

'You're leaving' – Cardus checked a table swiftly – 'tomorrow. Going where first? We like to know – in case of emergencies.'

'The mountains first. Washington after the weekend.'

Cardus laid down the pen. 'I'll wait to hear news of this *new direction* of yours.'

In his darkened cubicle Greg leaned back into the acoustic hood that formed an integral part of the special seat each of the team used and watched the row of small oscillating screens before him,

24

feeling, as usual, as if he were back in the cockpit of his F15. But the sound he heard as he worked controls embedded in the seat's padded arms was not the roar of jet engines, was not any sound he had heard before entering the depths of the Mojave station the first time three months before; was not, he was certain, a sound produced on Earth, although his task was to prove that supposition. It filled his every waking moment and often his dreams. It was the roaring heart of the underground, ultra-secret project and, if the whispered scare stories inside the sealed unit were to be believed, had driven some who had sought to analyse it to the edge of their sanity – even beyond.

Greg Lewelyn had decided it was, in its complex immensity, like listening to the mind of God.

He believed he was hearing His language.

All he had to do was understand.

And not go mad.

John Cornell pushed away his breakfast plate as the first call of the day came though on his private line. He sighed and arose to take it.

'Sam? I didn't expect to hear from you so soon. Sounds like you had a rough night? I see. Maybe we should talk?' He scanned the note his wife thrust under his eyes. 'Come up to the White House. Dinner tonight? Informal. A few other friends will be here but we'll have time to talk privately. Madelaine really wants to see you . . . tell you how bad she feels about Elizabeth. She gave me hell for not knowing. We both feel terrible.'

Madelaine Cornell, sitting opposite, winced.

'Say you get here by seven thirty? Gives us time for a drink and a chat before the others arrive. How's that sound? Fit your schedule? Fine. We look forward to seeing you. You know White House routine, I'm sure. Security will have your name.'

He put down the receiver. 'What's the matter?'

'That *damned* Irish in you. Sam Lewelyn isn't the kind of man who wants a friend gushing tears over him – real or crocodile. And he knows what Elizabeth thought of *me*.'

'He doesn't know what you might have felt for her?'

'When God doled out naïvety you played Oliver Twist.'

And who made first in line for venom?

'Don't think it – say it.'

He looked down from the window to the lawn where two secret-servicemen produced weapons as if from thin air before slipping them beneath their light raincoats and repeating their deadly wizardry, the flat silence making the act chilling. *They swear to give their lives for mine, I swore to live for millions. Which is the higher price?*

'I don't know how much friendship remains,' he said. 'Sam and me.'

'Does it really matter? Maybe it's outlived itself? Neither of you are the young lions you were once. Just make sure you get the most out of what's left.'

'Go to hell.'

'That option didn't come with this marriage. You're stuck with me. Live with it. Unless you *want* to lose the presidency.' She sighed and arose. 'I'll have to rearrange the table. We're a woman short. Doesn't matter. He's probably off them after months watching one decay.' She caught his murderous glance. 'Prolonged death *is* debilitating for the living, you know.'

He looked out across the gardens. 'Who else is invited tonight?'

'Don't you ever read your social diary? Why do I bother? Social events may not be your forte but the effort costs nothing and pays dividends when it matters. Like winning a second term?'

'I'm too old.'

'You're pitiful,' she said, walking from the room. 'Reagan had years over you and rode back on a cloud.'

He caught sight of himself in a dark mirror, one of the many antiques she had usurped ruthlessly from historic rooms in the White House and had transferred to their second-floor private apartments.

He was tall, iron-grey, heavy, but carried little surplus poundage despite minimal exercise. His broad big-toothed open smile topped by bright Irish-green eyes made men trust him and did wonders with women. He liked to think he had an academic's mind, a lawyer's logic, a street-fighter's balls, and a patriot's heart – and hoped most of it was true. He definitely gave all of himself – if he was allowed to. He drew his shoulders back. She was right, he could do it again. She was right too often. He needed *something*, though. An edge. An event. An accelerator. Bush had the Gulf but no one – except the lunatics, and they existed – wanted another war.

Absently, he lit a cigar.

What he did not want was a rocked boat. So best tread carefully with William Bradley Kent. A rogue elephant doing its thing in its own pen was controllable, but released, unchecked, it could destroy the zoo. The country was half-way zoo already, the rest circus, and he controlled all of it – or liked to believe he did. Which half was he in? Was he head keeper? Ringmaster? Both? Sometimes he felt more like the shit collector. And sometimes, with her, the clown.

On the lawn, one of the secret-servicemen looked up, saw him and raised a pink-palmed black hand. Cornell nodded, recognizing Jim Bentley.

Would I give my life for you, Jim?

'Can't you do that in your own space?' Madelaine Cornell complained, returning, crushing out his cigar.

This is my space, said his silent heart.

Greg Lewelyn ran toward the sinking red ball on the horizon, feeling its dying rays on his skin.

'That's it!' protested Larry Maine. 'Enough, already.' He collapsed on to the cooling sand. 'How the heck do you *do* this every day!'

Greg sprinted hard, then turned and jogged back. 'I know if I don't I'll end up like you.' He dropped to his haunches, trickling sand through his fingers. 'Sand has its own sound,' he said. 'The world has its own sound. We just don't hear it.'

'Don't you ever stop?' complained Maine. 'Going all Greek, are we? Listen, Mother Earth doesn't coo at us – and if she could I doubt if she'd have anything maternal to say the way we've screwed her. There's no life in inert material. Wind moving across the sand creates infrasonic sound waves – deeper than anything we can hear. Birds navigate by it. That's *it* and you know it. If there were any truth in mythology and we *could* hear anything it would probably be raucous laughter at crazies like us spending what's left of our youth buried under a pile of hot sand. Quit worrying.' He jabbed a finger at the sand. 'Leave it in down there. Best advice you'll get this year.'

'Larry, we're only hearing what we're capable of hearing.'

'Where have you been these last three months? We've got equipment that'll pick up the sound of a flea scratching its backside.'

'Given. But we still have to understand what that sound is.'

'You're in danger of going in spirals up your own ass. What do you think we're doing here? Our sole purpose in life is trying to understand!' Maine spread his arms wide. 'Of course we have to separate all the frequency-spaghetti first but that's only going to take a million years or so!'

Greg squinted at the huge circular metal cage on the horizon wavering in the evening heat. 'What's the nearest analogy you can think of to describe the noise?'

'Easy. Worst hangover in the world.'

'I'm serious.'

'So am I, you don't drink. OK, I remember being about five and my dad holding this great conch shell up against my head. Sounded weird, echoey – unworldly – scared the shit out of me. I was the original wimp. The noise is like that. Unreal.'

'Chaos.'

'What?'

'The sound of chaos. The concept of a confused and formless mass – primeval emptiness – out of which the ordered universe was created.'

'*Erebus*, *Tartarus*, *Eros*: darkness, the underworld, and desire? You're back with the Greek mythology. Come on, I majored in Classics. You've been out here too long. I warned you what this project does to people.'

'Ever heard of *tongues*, Larry?'

'Jesus! What is this – an exercise in lateral thinking? It's too early. You're not being Born Again, are you? I couldn't stand it.'

'Speaking in tongues. Glossolalia. Supposed communication between Man and God. Vocal communication.'

'Humankind, please. Haven't you heard that Man is defunct? Like I feel right now.'

'There's that same chaotic element: unintelligible sounds, gibberish. In the noise it's multiplied a billion times. That's why there's no pattern. No way of reducing redundancies. Why we never get anywhere – why all the burn-out cases before us never got anywhere.'

'What is this – an overnight quantum leap? Where's the basis? The inspiration? What kicked it off?'

Greg shrugged. 'I've been fooling around with crowd sounds: ball games, conventions, anything involving massed voices, speaking, shouting – but nothing in unison, nothing chorused. A completely random mix – which gives the element of chaos. Ever seen a commodity exchange working? Sounds chaotic, right? But there's form, understanding – order. We can take one voice out of any crowd and make it audible – and intelligible – you know that. We could do the same with varying degrees of success – given time – with every voice in the crowd.'

Maine tucked his hands behind his head and lay back on the sand. 'Well, since they've delivered the data-compression equipment and the neural networks let's really use the stuff. You want to go the Chaos Theory route? Let's take in image transformations while we're there. Fractals? Barnsley's iterated functions systems to reduce space? We'll need all we can get if you're really taking *random*. You'll need Gibsonian cyberspace to handle that quantity of information! The noise is *huge*. Is this extracurricular, by the way? Does Cardus know?'

'I told him I was trying a new direction. Nothing specific. I'll tell him when I'm ready.'

'When's that going to be?'

'Maybe when I get back. I've got to check some things out first.'

'In Washington?'

'No.'

'Don't be coy.'

'It's sensitive.'

'Sensitive meaning secret? Listen, don't screw around behind Cardus's back.'

'It's personal. Leave it, OK?'

Maine sat up, untied his trainers, and poured sand out slowly. 'All right, I'll ride your brainstorm a while longer. Why tongues? Regular crowd sounds don't give you enough chaos?'

'Ever heard tongues spoken?'

'No.'

'I have. There's a sensation of being on the verge of something unexplained, something powerful. If you could cut through the gibberish ... something world-shaking maybe.' Greg shook his head. 'It only needs understanding. I get the same feeling when I hear the noise.'

Larry Maine grinned. 'You think God is trying to communicate with us? It's finally got to you!'

'This is a straight scientific problem. A door we can unlock once we find the key. And I mean to find it. *God* doesn't enter into it.'

'Maybe we *need* to find God to survive this place.' Maine heaved himself out of the sand. 'I guess Cardus will have to do for now.'

Greg stood. 'All we need to survive this place is a little time away from it. Which is exactly what I'm going to do starting first thing tomorrow.'

'And the noise goes with you,' warned Maine, heaving himself up.

'What I've got is rumour,' stated Sam Lewelyn. 'Some might call it legend. We'll call it fantasy, all right?'

'No facts?' questioned Cornell.

'In my world *facts* are usually someone's evaluation of someone else's observations.'

'So evaluate.'

'Let me say this first, John. This is your hunt and you've certainly got the firepower ... but some jungles are murky, some animals don't die easily, some take you with them. You're sure?'

They were in Cornell's study that evening, in the White House west wing, seated like chess players faced off over a low, carved mahogany table; fine single-malt Scotch whisky in thick crystal between them.

'Genesis?' pressed Cornell, his green eyes sharp.

Lewelyn smiled. 'That's the secret of your success. You always want it all. No half-routes, no short-cuts. I bet your working day is longer than any president in history.'

Cornell raised his glass. 'I've missed you, Sam. I'm sorry we had to get back together under these circumstances.'

Lewelyn lit his meerschaum. 'I've done some thinking since yesterday. In your place I'd feel pretty much the same way you do about Kent. About *anyone* I felt was holding out on me. I'd need to know what's going on right down the line. I don't think you have any choice but to act if you want to function as president. It's a *my way or the highway* situation – but you have to make damn sure your way is right and that any action you take doesn't come back and bite you in the ass. Hard.'

'That's why I need you, Sam.'

Lewelyn pulled on his pipe and settled back. 'Once upon a time there was the Evil Empire. Remember? And there was us. Black hats, white hats. We all knew where we stood, what we stood for, who we stood against. Sometimes someone from over there wanted out. Wanted all the good things we could offer: liberals, pay-medicine, open pornography, AIDS.'

'Still the same old dinosaur?'

Lewelyn sipped whisky. 'I'm old-fashioned enough to think that over-liberal thinking doesn't push barriers back, it lifts them for the mob to come rampaging through and take everything you've got. If that makes me a dinosaur so be it.'

'We've got plenty going for us these days, Sam – don't dismiss all of it.'

'I don't. Sometimes though I wake up and it seems like it's gone.'

'The American Dream?'

'American reality. The dream is what we're creating now. I just have this bad gut feeling we're building ourselves a nightmare.'

'You're still living back in the fifties, Sam. Those days are gone.'

'You bet they have. John, the enemy may have physically disintegrated – but don't believe their *thinking* is dead. Their power didn't come out of military might alone; it was their *creed* which changed the world – and there's plenty who still believe. And not all of them all over *there*. They're bent on slapping us into their – failed – shape, John, whatever it takes and whatever the consequences. Elizabeth once told me – after I made some crass self-satisfied statement about being a secret warrior who had defeated his enemy: *They're not beaten – they'll simply move the goal posts.* Very British, but she was right. They couldn't breach our military defences, couldn't match our economic success, so they're attacking our minds, our morals, our traditions, and good old American freedom of speech – so *screw* the First Amendment unless it works to their benefit. Controlled Godless mediocrity, that's their future for us.' Lewelyn leaned forward. '*You* could stop the slide. No one ever told you how to think and got away with it. Not the way I remember it.'

'Sam. Ninety-nine point nine per cent of this job is spent walking a political tightrope with every self-seeking son-of-a-bitch in the world trying to grab the balancing pole.'

'I'm aware of that.'

'Being aware isn't being president.'

Lewelyn sucked noisily, then shrugged. 'What the hell do I know?'

'So someone jumped from the East?' Cornell reminded. 'That's immediately Langley territory, surely?'

'Wait. You wanted it all, you're getting it. *Two* jumped. Male and female.'

'They approached us? Or did we hold out the apple?'

'Unknown.'

'*Fantasies* don't have a date, I suppose?'

'Nineteen eighty-six. June.'

'Some fantasy. Go on.'

'Whatever they were offering involved Signals Intelligence, so NSA not CIA answered the fire-call. It was hot enough for a senior officer to take over.'

'Wouldn't a senior man take charge anyway?'

'I said take over. Not sitting on high pulling strings – there on the ground doing the coaxing and maybe some serious pushing too. Broke all the rules. Worked without back-up. Worked direct to them. Showed his face. Broke his cover.'

Cornell cut the end of a cigar and inspected it. 'Must have finished his career as a spook? If Moscow *made* him, you'd back-room him. Even if you only *thought* they had. No choice. That's how your world works. Right?'

'You might think so.'

'I don't need to think, I've seen the results: empty-eyed, slack-jawed middle-agers pulling courier duty out of your Sensitive Materials Centre. All right, more.'

'He arranged their lift-out face to face. They were working on some *glasnost* cultural-exchange programme, so it was easy.'

'Europe?'

'Israel.'

Cornell grimaced.

Lewelyn nodded. 'I know, could have been cover and should have been read that way.' He held flame to Cornell's cigar. 'He preceded them back to the US. They followed: scheduled flight, travelling on genuine US passports, no special handling, everything straight, no NSA involvement, not even the passport – or so I'm told the records show.'

'Risky – for the bad old days?'

Lewelyn shook his head. 'Sharp decision. You have any idea how many Americans visit Israel every year? Sometimes, given a clear run, with the opposition missing the initial break-out, the simplest way is safest.'

'They made it safely?'

'As far as California.'

'Then?'

'Choose you own ending except for lived happily ever after.'

'What's yours?'

'Maybe your beginning?'

'Lost you?'

'Mojave Desert, right route for one of the agency's remote stations – between the Solar One power plant and the Naval Weapons Centre B range. They're riding it, another car comes out of nowhere, wrong side of the road – *bam* – fire finishes what the impact started. Maybe a drunk, maybe a KGB hit that went wrong – for the perpetrators.'

'The defectors died?'

'Charcoaled.'

'And the senior NSA officer?'

'Highway patrol report listed three bodies from two vehicles. No survivors.'

'William Bradley Kent,' said Cornell.

Lewelyn smiled. 'It's a great story.'

'Explains his burns.'

Lewelyn drained his glass. 'Don't need explaining. The record had him surviving a chopper crash at Edwards Air Force Base. You know that.'

Cornell reached for the decanter and poured more whisky. 'I have a wild imagination, Sam. Let's say the record is a lie and your fantasy, truth? What did the defectors have that made Kent forsake his usual professionalism, risk his career, almost lose his life and certainly his looks? He was a handsome man once by all accounts – though I've never seen a photograph.'

'None exist. He purged agency and public records and he's as well protected now from photographers as you are from assassins.' Lewelyn lifted his glass and looked appreciatively at the mellow-gold liquid. 'No one knows what the defectors had but whatever it was, once he was out of hospital his rise was meteoric.'

'When he should have been sidelined at the very least?'

'That's how it usually runs.'

'So he's got something to hide.'

Lewelyn sipped, silent.

'Sam, the desert project – Greg's – has something to do with the defection operation. That's what you're implying? You said the route they were taking was right for an NSA station.'

'I never trust the obvious.'

'You also said that often the simplest way is the best.'

'I said the simplest way could be the *safest*.'

Cornell tapped an inch of ash from his cigar. 'The defectors' identities? Too much to ask for? If we had those it might point toward whatever they were offering. You mentioned Highway Patrol? That means an accident report exists.'

Lewelyn leaned back. 'Up to now we've been talking the kind of stuff that maybe gets kicked around when old spooks get together in the dark corner of some safe bar. Most of it is plain old bitching. *How'd that son of a bitch make it instead of me?* There's always someone ready to put the number one man down. Make up some reason for him having made it: illegal, immoral, or both.' He sucked hard on his pipe, grimaced, then tapped black ash out into a tray. 'I've done some listening, a bit of coaxing, and way too much drinking to get this. Up to now it's been kept tight. In the family. If you want Highway Patrol records . . .' He looked up. 'John, if any of this is fact and a cover-up took place there might be a standing order for Kent to be informed? You light that fuse you better be damn sure you know where the rocket's going to explode.'

'Would Kent have been powerful enough – back at the time of his accident – to order a police cover-up?'

'Maybe he'd been *given* the power, or the leverage to gain

34

power. In that case others he may have involved, more senior, might have acted for him.'

'You've got to check out Highway Patrol, Sam. If there were bodies, records were kept. Had to be.'

Lewelyn's eyes measured Cornell. 'John, he had powerful friends and a long reach. Right into this room if he wants. You can sweep for bugs as long as you like, won't do you any good, he'll get you from outside. You wouldn't believe what can be done these days. Back at that house last night you talked about the nightmare scenario they used to speculate on in Bush's day being here? Well, here's one for you: that scary future world writers used to scare us with . . . ?' He smiled and pocketed his meerschaum.

'You mean I may be president but I'm also a politician with enemies?'

'*That's* American reality.'

'Who told you all this, Sam?'

'A man who might have been your Director of NSA instead of Kent.'

'Why isn't he?'

'That's the big question.'

'I want all of it, Sam.'

'I'll tell what he told me.'

'He believes this story?'

'He believes something happened to Kent. Changed him irrevocably. Saul on the Road to Damascus is how he put it. He tends toward God when he isn't leaning on the bottle.'

'Changed how?'

Lewelyn looked up in warning. 'Keep this in mind: he may have been looking too hard at Kent for his own reasons.'

'Understood.'

'He thought he recognized the glint of fanaticism – of conversion – in Kent's eye. Thought Marx had defeated Mammon in the battle for his heart and mind. Remember, this is before the East went west. He'd seen it happen before, of course. We all have to some degree in the Intelligence community. There's always a danger in our world that you can be so steeped in cynicism you'll willingly climb the slimiest wall if it promises a way out.'

'And?'

'He suspected Kent might have doubled. He was senior to him

back then. Pulled more strings. He had MOSSAD watch Kent when he made the Jerusalem trip.'

Cornell reacted. 'MOSSAD? Why not use our own?'

'Irrevocable step. Like serving divorce papers, like signing a death warrant. Any internal, or worse, *external* investigation could have proved terminal for Kent's career – whether he was innocent or guilty. It's like AIDS; you only have to look like you've got it to be branded a victim.'

'He was under suspicion, Sam?'

'Everyone is under suspicion. It's only when you start *acting* suspiciously that action is taken.'

'And Kent did? How?'

'Unreported meetings; making field-trips to destinations he hadn't listed on his itinerary; acting like he had his own secrets and wasn't prepared to share them.'

'And you believe him. Your contact I mean.'

'Kent destroyed him,' warned Lewelyn once more.

'So all this could be malicious? Straight revenge?'

'I don't think he has the lucidity to focus on revenge. Not any more.'

'He was lucid enough to relate the story!'

'Bitter memories keep longer.'

'You wouldn't be here if it were just memories. Or if you believed it was complete fantasy.'

Lewelyn settled back on his chair, big arms behind his grizzled head. 'MOSSAD videotaped Kent meeting with a man and a woman in a church in Jerusalem.'

'And your contact has a copy?'

'Wouldn't let me view it. Maybe he thinks I'm Kent's man.'

'You're *my* man. Will he believe that?'

'If you tell him.'

'I'll call him now.'

'No call. Face to face.'

'Difficult. My movements are not really my own.'

'You found a way to see me without dragging around the entire circus.'

'Name?'

'Clair Morrison.'

'Never heard of him.'

'Before your time – here. Old-school academic, not nearly hard enough for our world. But brilliant, once.'

Cornell nodded. 'Arrange it. Tomorrow. Have to be well after midnight, I've got something formal on. I can make, say, one thirty? Will that be too late for him?'

'You're the President. You say one thirty he better stay awake. I'll tell him to leave the hooch alone.'

'What about the Highway Patrol records? Hold on those for now?'

'You know what I think.'

'What do you think about Morrison? Gut think?'

'Hiding something, deep down, deeper than the liquor reaches. I think he may have recognized who – or what – the man and the woman on the tape were. Or MOSSAD did, and told him.'

'Will he tell me?'

'I'm going to break this up,' trilled Madelaine Cornell, entering, waving elegant fingers across her face. 'I've held dinner as long as I can but there is a limit! Informal or not. How can you two *breathe* in here! Sam, you look *terrific*. You know I've never realized just how alike you two are. A pair of greying grizzly bears! Come on, there are people to entertain.' She laid her hand gently on Lewelyn's arm as he stood. 'About Elizabeth. Don't blame John. It was my fault. I'd heard on the Washington lunch circuit she hadn't looked well for a while. I should have told John but the poor man barely has enough time to worry about himself. You understand, I'm sure. If only I'd known how serious it was . . .?'

Lewelyn towered over her. 'I'm surprised anyone noticed. Elizabeth wasn't one for lunching much.'

'But she was an *aristo*, Sam. You have to remember that. I've never believed that silly backstairs-conception story of hers. Anyhow, this is Washington! Even being *half* a blue-blooded Brit immediately makes you fair pickings for the luncheon crowd.'

'Liz would have put it another way.'

'Really! How?'

'Fair *game*.'

Madelaine Cornell smiled her perfect, hollow, smile.

CHAPTER
THREE

In Rome the sun was well up over the Basilica as the motorcade drove at speed into St Peter's Square, swerving to the left of the obelisk, then straightening, before swinging around to allow its important passenger to alight, bodyguards tight beside him.

The crowd numbered hundreds of thousands, the chant from a great swath of them clear now outside the bomb-proof Mercedes. *Bestia! Bestia! Bestia!*

He stopped, momentarily thrown at seeing the frail, stooped figure in simple white robes waiting to greet him. He had expected pomp and circumstance and was being shown humility. He sought the reason in the old face – *there was always a reason* – but saw nothing except warmth of greeting.

He gave a curt, almost mocking bow just as the *whip* of the shot was heard and recognized by the closest bodyguard who leapt forward, ignorant of the bloody mess already on his clothes and seconds too slow to collect the fast-falling body in the safety of his arms.

Somewhere high above the scene in a dusty forgotten part of the colonnade, the assassin peeled off thin rubber gloves, dumped them by the high-powered scoped and silenced sniper's rifle and walked out, straightening his worn cassock as he made his way down, fingering his rosary.

He saw rushing figures, lay staff from the Vatican offices, and called out in enquiry.

They shot him! Didn't you hear the crowd?

The assassin had prepared himself. He cried: 'The *Papa!*'

'Praise God, no. *La Bestia*. He'll have time for God now!' one called backward as they ran off.

But will God have time for the Beast? asked the assassin silently and walked on.

At the chosen exit he found the waiting police Alfa Romeo, a uniformed driver at the wheel. He entered the rear beside an older man wearing civilian clothes whose gaze was fixed rigidly but coolly out of the back window, his hand resting on a scuffed travel-bag.

The man turned and handed over a plastic Alitalia wallet. He spoke in English. 'Your route is Rome, Paris, Dublin. You will have one hour and thirty-five minutes to wait at Charles de Gaulle. They'll be watching, so stay inconspicuous. Read this.'

The assassin took the well-used black Bible and smiled. 'Thank you, *Commandatore*.'

In Baltimore, Maryland, it was just about 2.00 a.m. and Clair Morrison needed a drink. There was no way he could relate the story of his downfall without one – with or without the President of the United States in his neglected home.

He poured the first one since falling into bed the previous night, after Sam Lewelyn's late call warning him to stay sober on pain of death. He looked once more at the dusty clock face on the wall of his living room. More than twenty-four hours, he realized. *A whole day*. The longest he had gone without alcohol in twelve years.

He drank, and any pride in his achievement slid into shame as the clear neat spirit drew the warm quilt of conscious oblivion over him: shame compounded by self-pitying tears which filled his reddened eyes, not spilling but hovering, like his own day to day existence, on the brink of self-destruction. Only some inner core of steel – worn over the years to a slender thread but still holding – saved him from outright degradation, for no matter what or how much he drank, he could always walk, swaying slightly, to answer any caller at his peeling front door. This he did now, a handkerchief – miraculously still laundered, taken from a forgotten drawer – dabbing his wet eyes as he walked down the hall.

He paused by a mirror, tightened the bow of his Harvard tie, breathed deeply once then pulled open the door. 'An honour, Mr President, a great honour. Sam.' He stood aside and waved the two men through with a gracious, dated gesture made a little extravagant by the effects of the stiff measure of vodka.

'You have the tape, Clair?' asked Lewelyn, gently.

'Took some finding, I'm afraid,' lied Morrison, for the search had taken only seconds. *Beginning* the search was where his effort had lain. Sitting, staring, dry and slightly feverish, at his abandoned but never forgotten attaché case where the videotape lay like the final letter in a love affair that had died on one side only: too real to reject, too painful to view, the shadowed images bringing too many others forward from the dark spaces he had filed them.

'May I offer you something?' He made for a dark wood carved oriental cabinet.

Cornell glanced at Lewelyn.

'We're fine for the moment, Clair,' replied Lewelyn, easily.

'Of course. Oh! Please sit, make yourselves comfortable. I apologize for the state of my home. I'm afraid I no longer have my housekeeper . . .'

Cornell shuffled uncomfortably then sat, acutely aware he was never at his best with failure; his own or others.

'Clair?' Lewelyn prompted, knowing Morrison would procrastinate for as long as he was allowed to.

The lean, jaundiced face dipped in acknowledgement, long fingers raising a remote-control unit toward a television screen buried in a massive casket of walnut, the only item in the room recently cleaned, a discarded duster beside it as evidence. 'Would you care for me talk you through it, Mr President?'

'I'd like to gain my own first impressions, if you wouldn't mind?' Cornell answered, responding to Morrison's genteel, donnish manner.

'Certainly. The location is Jerusalem.'

'Thank you.'

'There's no soundtrack, just a terrible noise – either Kent using a jamming device to stop eavesdropping or perhaps interference from the electronic equipment you'll see being used. MOSSAD did what they could to enhance it – to no avail I'm afraid. I'll keep the sound turned off. It really is quite unbearable.'

Cornell watched the large silent screen intently as shadowy images revealed the interior of a church. He had been there before.

Not *déjà vu*; reality. A lifetime ago. As the young man he was once: a committed believer and pilgrim; a Christian who practised what his heart felt. The distance of the memory shook him. Dear God, was it so long ago? He stared at the screen and he might have been there again, the first time, his thoughts then – written down in a young man's self-conscious hand – still clear now: *It had been a place of horror named Golgotha, the skull. Men had died here, horrifically, nailed to rough timber: hanging, legs broken, asphyxiated by their own dead weight; the statue of Our Lord above the altar as testament.*

It was a moment of wonder. There, in the Church of the Holy Sepulchre, the most sacred shrine in Christendom, built on the traditional site of Christ's crucifixion, he had found his God. The memory was indelible. He had truly felt He was with him, touchable, utterly believable, *real.*

Now, He was almost forgotten. The world had stripped away that certainty and though he might pray for its return, he knew any affirmation he made of unreserved faith would ring hollow. He had slipped from the spiritual to the material: content to believe in His existence because it was safe but terrified to turn and face Him in case there was nothing there but the vanishing wisps of his faith. He felt the claws of his own mortality grip as they did too often these days and hurled that black creature back into the pit.

He put on spectacles and leaned forward to the tableau unfolding on the screen, back in the present, nailed to his own cross.

A swarthy man who but for his beard might have been the close-cropped woman beside him – so close was their resemblance to each other – spoke to a third, shadowed, figure before turning and adjusting electronic equipment on his right. The shadowed figure moved into the light, revealing himself to be a Roman Catholic priest. He spoke to a fourth: a fair, handsome man with hungry eyes. All of this in complete silence, broken only by Morrison's laboured breathing.

'Kent,' murmured Lewelyn, indicating the fair man. 'This must be the only surviving image of him in existence.'

Now the woman spoke, again directly to the priest, indicating the statue of Christ Crucified over the altar; her smile mocking.

Cornell turned to Lewelyn. 'We must have the technology now to clean up the sound?'

'We're field-leaders.'

'*We* being NSA? Back to Kent.' Cornell grunted and returned to the screen.

The silent exchange continued at length until, abruptly, the priest uttered something then stalked away, revealing a pronounced limp on his right side, the woman's cruel smile following him. Her twin – for there was little doubt that was what he was – shrugged and returned to his equipment. Kent looked casually about him, as though interested in the antiquity of his surroundings, the camera instantly shifting smoothly to the adjacent altar, holding there for a long moment, then quickly arching upward to the ceiling and panning across it before coming down to the entrance where sudden bright sunlight flared and killed the image.

'What happened there?' Cornell asked Morrison.

'Handover. Then Kent left. The camera couldn't – securely – stay with the action. Another member of MOSSAD's team confirmed Kent made the pass.'

'Passed what?'

'Travel documents, identities, money?'

Cornell studied his hands. 'MOSSAD's co-operation seems surprising? I've heard they don't get involved unless there's a percentage for themselves?'

Morrison nodded. 'Kent knew an awful lot about Israeli defences from our satellite reconnaissance. If he jumped East that knowledge went with him. Which meant it would end up in Syria. MOSSAD *had* to pick up the hand once I'd dealt it. But they were cautious and played it lightly. I really had very little to offer – or to frighten them with. Frankly, they didn't believe me. Kent had been good to them. He admired their ruthlessness, as did many in the Intelligence community – still do, I imagine. They used a small team: tourist cover for the video operator and partner in the church – outside, local or pilgrim.'

'The priest? Who was he? He appeared to be part of it?'

Morrison shook his head, firmly. 'Jesuits were running the restoration work at the time. Still are, I imagine. Never stops.'

'He seemed angry?'

'The Russians had been there for two weeks. Perhaps their electronic equipment had become a hindrance? Jesuits can be blunt when the need arises. I know, I almost became one myself,

42

once.' Morrison coloured. 'Another lifetime,' he murmured, seemingly ashamed either by his confession or his failure.

'He was speaking to Kent,' pressed Cornell. 'How did that start?'

Morrison shrugged narrow shoulders. 'An irrelevance. Kent entered the church alone – playing tourist – the priest and the Russians were already inside, each dealing with their own projects. The priest came over, perhaps to complain? Kent became involved because he was talking to the Russians.'

'Couldn't MOSSAD's people hear – physically – what was being said? Wasn't there a transcript?'

'People murmur in churches and churches echo – the worst combination for eavesdropping, live or electronic. MOSSAD wouldn't go in close. As I said, they weren't committed, they wanted it over without damage.'

'What happened next?'

'Kent left Israel immediately: private jet to Cyprus, then God alone knows? Something fast and private – or our air force, if he'd pulled strings I didn't know about.'

'The Russians left when?'

'Four days later.'

'MOSSAD saw them board the plane?'

Morrison nodded. 'Practically helped them aboard – then sighed with relief.'

'I don't doubt it. By then they must have realized they were observing a double-defection operation to the West – not a highly placed American Signals Intelligence officer bolting East.'

'The second that plane lifted off the runway and turned toward the United States my career was over,' said Morrison, his bitterness clear.

'Could there be a chance,' Cornell began, carefully, 'Kent engineered the whole thing to get rid of you? *Knew* you had mounted surveillance on him? Was aware of your suspicions and used them to destroy you? You *were* senior to him and I understand a real threat to his advancement in NSA?'

'I was very careful.'

'Not careful enough, as it turned out?'

Morrison coloured, his eyes flicking involuntarily toward the oriental cabinet.

Cornell looked at his watch. It was past 3 a.m. He had to have it all. And Morrison had not given it yet. He dipped his head at the cabinet. 'OK, Sam.'

Morrison took out cigarettes, his hands shaking wildly, spilling some on to the unkempt carpet.

Cornell retrieved them, and struck his lighter. 'Fine rug. Persian?'

'I was in Iran for a time.'

'I know. Caught in the middle of the revolution. Not too long before all this happened. They gave you a rough time? The revolutionary guards?'

'Our listening posts tend to be located out in the wilds. Even though we knew what had happened there was still the problem of getting out. It wasn't pleasant. We were the target for a lot of anger, yes.'

'And you returned feeling you might perhaps have been passed over? Missed the promotion boat? Kent was rising fast beneath you – that's on record.'

'Those weren't my motives.'

'But you were in pretty poor shape, physically – and mentally. Emotionally too? Your judgement might easily – and understandably – have been clouded.'

Morrison's shoulders squared. 'I saw ruthless ambition in Kent, I admit that. I feared it because I don't have it. Perhaps I envied it. But I also believed that he was capable of selling us out to further his own ends. I believed his driving force was derived from some other allegiance. For God's sake, we've seen it happen before!'

Cornell nodded. 'To our cost.' He paused. 'I think we need to make sure the quality of your life improves. You've done much for your country. It should repay that debt.'

'I've done as much as any man in my position, Mr President. I've done my duty.' Morrison's eyes filled. 'I'm grateful for your concern.'

Lewelyn placed a generous measure of vodka in the trembling hands.

'Who *were* they?' asked Cornell. 'The man and the woman? Is there any doubt they were from the Soviet Union?'

Morrison was transformed as the effects of alcohol swept through him. His sagging, yellowed skin seemed to become firmer, to gain colour. He became positive. 'None. They were scientists working on one of those quirky projects the Soviets used to fund heavily. Paranormal studies: telekinesis, telepathy, that sort of thing.'

'Known to us?' asked Cornell, intrigued.

'To MOSSAD through the worldwide Zionist network. They were Russian Jews. Not known to the Intelligence community here. We tend not to take their field very seriously.'

'Names?'

'Markarov. Brother and sister. Identical twins – apart from sex – as you saw. Ilya and Irina.'

'What would Kent want from them? *Paranormal studies?* Seems to me to be a complete contradiction? NSA's entire existence is based on advanced technology. These Markarovs were experimenting with . . . intangibles?'

Lewelyn interrupted. 'They interested Kent enough to risk his career and his neck. Whatever they were selling couldn't have been that intangible. He wasn't going to give them a free ride. He'd expect them to deliver. If they were jumping from a funded programme – which means they already had privileges so life wasn't bad – then I'd guess whatever it was needed something we had? Something the Soviets could not deliver and had no hope of delivering? That could only be one thing – and NSA had it in spades. Microchip technology.'

Cornell nodded. 'All right, I'll buy that. But would Kent be drawn into such a prospect, Sam? I mean, the paranormal? He's a technocrat!'

'And an atheist,' said Lewelyn, pointing at the television screen. 'Hates religion. Any religion. Hates anything that causes people to be dependent. He'd have hated that meet in that church yet he agreed to it. *Their* ground, remember – Kent would have hated that too. Risky. Could have been terminal. The Markarovs had something he wanted very badly. Something he could use.'

Cornell turned to Morrison. 'That equipment the Markarovs had set up? Someone check the video? The picture's not great but an expert might spot something?'

'What does it matter?' Morrison muttered, defeatedly, slipping downhill again. 'The tape doesn't exist, Jerusalem never happened, no defection operation ever occurred, the Markarovs never existed,

William Bradley Kent is all-powerful and I'm . . . I'm here!' His hand flopped vaguely around him. 'The tape can't damage Kent.'

Cornell's patience deserted him. 'It's not a matter of what it might do to him but what it did *for* him. Sometimes to destroy a man you don't attack his weakness, you attack his strength. Did the Markarovs give Kent his strength? Give him something, or promise him something in exchange for his getting them out, that made his star rise? Something connected with whatever they were doing in the church?'

'That was cover,' stated Morrison.

'In your world because something is overt it has to be cover – I accept that is the norm – but they would only need cover if they were acting on Moscow's orders. They were *defecting*. You told Sam yesterday they were on some *glasnost* exchange? If that was cover then what were they *really* doing in Jerusalem? Spying? Do you really think MOSSAD could be fooled that easily?'

Lewelyn said, carefully: 'Unless the whole thing was a Moscow Centre operation in the first place? To get Kent into the driving seat at NSA? Which would make him one of theirs from day one.'

Cornell stared at him, the possibility shocking. 'You believe that?'

Morrison said, wearily: 'Mr President, if it were true it makes little difference any more. Who would he be reporting to? Moscow Centre doesn't exist – none of the old *apparat* does. Not as it did then. Not the same control, nor the motives, certainly not the power. Kent would be dead in the water today.' He smiled. 'There's no one more redundant than a master spy with no masters.'

Cornell retorted, brutally: 'The difference it would make is that we could hang him out to dry.'

'Careful,' warned Lewelyn. 'We're running ahead too fast. As I see it, the truth of any of this is hidden behind a lie. One specific lie.' He looked hard at Morrison. 'Clair, why do you say he was in that desert car wreck and not where the official record states he was: at Edwards Air Force Base in a helicopter aborting take off in flames?'

Morrison stood, shakily. He poured himself more vodka, a lot of it.

'We need it *all*, Clair,' warned Lewelyn.

46

Morrison turned, swaying. 'I don't think he was in that car. I *know* he was.'

'How can you be so certain?' insisted Cornell.

'Because I followed him.'

'To the *Mojave*?'

Morrison drank deeply. He might have nodded.

'You were on that road?'

This time the nod was positive, jerked, the vodka splashing over the rim of the glass.

'You saw the crash?'

'Let me tell it all. In my own way. Please. I knew the time of their arrival – the Markarovs. I was there at Kennedy. I watched Kent meet them. He'd bought tickets – cash – while he was waiting. Internal flight to Los Angeles. My ID got me details. I took the same flight.'

'He must have seen you?' objected Cornell.

Morrison's mouth twisted. 'I boarded with the flight crew and rode the jump-seat.'

'So in LA?' prompted Lewelyn.

'He rented a Buick. Markarovs sat in the back – they wouldn't separate, it seemed. Kent drove; no escort, no one riding shot-gun, no tail – apart from myself.'

'Certain?'

'As death,' stated Morrison, close, very close, to breaking down.

'What happened?' asked Lewelyn, gently.

'I had to lay well back on that desert road because he'd have picked me up in no time. I couldn't lose him – there was nowhere else to go apart from the desert and the Buick wasn't made for it. Besides, I'd already worked out where he was going. One of our new desert stations. I remember thinking that whatever the Markarovs had got they needed space because we'd built that station big, deep, and purposely way oversized. The speed our technology was advancing then we knew we'd need all the room we could get to house it.'

He gulped vodka and choked, but kept on speaking, his voice raw; barely there. 'I saw the explosion from a mile back. It was just sundown. By the time I reached the wreck it was an inferno. I made out two cars but couldn't see past the flames. It was so hot I couldn't get close anyway. There was nothing I could do. *Nothing*.'

He drifted away for a moment. 'Night falls fast in the desert. I was in near darkness within minutes – except for the flames.'

'Where was Kent?' pressed Lewelyn.

'In the scrub by the roadside. He'd been thrown out. He was dead.' Morrison looked up, grey-faced. 'I *truly* believed he was dead. I swear it. I could see him in the light from the flames. He was terribly burned. Black. His face seemed to be set with diamonds. I picked one out. It was glass from the windshield.' He looked, hopelessly, at Cornell. 'Nothing would have convinced me that he was alive. *Nothing.* I put my face close to his but I felt nothing, I heard nothing. All I could hear were the flames. I wanted him to be dead.'

'You left him?'

Morrison nodded mutely. 'Drove back the way I came. Just kept on going. Absent without leave for a month. I think I was absent from my mind as well. When I finally reported in, I was told there had been a full alert out for me across the entire world.' He showed neglected, brown teeth. 'I knew rather a lot about NSA. I was suspended pending an investigation. The investigation finished me.'

'You told them about the Mojave?'

'I told them I couldn't remember anything of where I'd been.'

'Why?' demanded Cornell. 'When you *did* remember?'

'What differences would it have made? Kent was a hero who had miraculously survived a chopper crash and I was . . . I was finished.'

'You should have told them, Clair,' said Lewelyn. 'At least to find out what the mystery was, what all the lying was about?'

'Admit I'd abandoned a fellow officer in the desert, horrifically burned, and with God only knew what other injuries? That I'd just driven away and got drunk for a month? I'd behaved appallingly. Perhaps my guilt, my weakness, my dishonour was self-evident? They didn't press, they hardly needed to – but I knew they wanted me out of the way quickly. I was history and the future had already risen from the flames in the desert. It was me who burned that night. The investigation just finished the job.'

Cornell took a small sip of the whisky that Lewelyn had placed at his elbow. 'Who did you tell?'

'I don't understand?'

'You told someone you were going to be on that desert road.'

'No. How could I? I didn't know myself until I was there. I had no idea what Kent's plans were for the Markarovs.'

'You called no one at NSA from Kennedy, saying you were going to California?'

'No one. I was hunting alone.'

'Then if the crash was no accident, who gave the assassin the route? The Markarovs themselves? If they were plants they would pass on any information Kent gave them of course, but that presupposes Moscow wanted them dead and that makes no sense whatsoever? Why *place* them, then kill them?'

Lewelyn interrupted, shaking his head, firmly. 'Kent could tell them nothing. If they pressured him for a location it would be out by a thousand miles. If he believed he had struck gold why tell anyone where he was stashing it? Or how he'd get it there?'

'So the car wreck *was* an accident? That's what you're saying, Sam?'

'No way it could have been an accident. The cover-up afterwards confirms that.'

'So who was the third party?' Cornell persisted. 'Someone knew that route, knew the correct car. *Someone* arranged the assassin? An assassin whose luck ran out.'

'*All of it*, Clair,' growled Lewelyn.

Morrison murmured, 'The car that hit Kent's rented Buick was already on fire.'

'You said you were a mile back?' Cornell questioned.

'The road was straight but undulating. Every time I came to the crown of a rise I saw the Buick. The final time I saw a speeding car trailing fire coming from the opposite direction – not exhaust gases from some hot-rod – flames, a long tongue of flames. Kent saw it too, swerved all over the road but it was too late, the car drove at him, deliberately, suicidally, there was nothing he could do.' Morrison shook his head. 'No one should have survived. Even now I barely believe he did.' He looked at his glass. 'Sometimes I can forget if I really try.'

Cornell looked at Lewelyn. 'KGB never went in for suicide hits, Sam. They were professionals, not fanatics. The Markarovs were

Russian Jews – had just spent time in Israel. So some Islamic terror group?' He turned to Morrison. 'This was around the time of the raid on Libya?'

Morrison nodded. 'Libya was April eighty-six, yes. Kent's Jerusalem trip was three months later.'

'It's astonishing that he was prepared to travel to the Middle East during the period? *Glasnost* may have been flowering in the Soviet Union but the KGB was still financing every terror group willing to take their money. NSA pin-pointed the targets for the Libyan air-strike, for Heaven's sake! Wouldn't he have immediately thought *trap*? Snatching – or killing – a senior NSA officer would have been a bigger coup than the kidnap of CIA station-chief William Buckley in Lebanon. And potentially more damaging: damn it, Kent must have seen satellite photographs of every Israeli position at the time!'

'Obviously the stakes were high enough,' said Lewelyn.

Morrison said, thickly, '*Could* have been the Arabs. Their style, certainly.'

Cornell frowned. 'The best thing that could have happened to Kent after exposing himself as he did was to be "dead". Adopting another identity would have been child's play in his position. Yet he fabricates a non-fatal helicopter crash at Edwards and confirms he survived? Makes no sense? Sam?'

'It does if it drew attention away from the Markarovs. By switching the story he effectively made the Markarovs vanish. Never existed – *here*. Never set foot in the USA. Leaving him clear to do whatever he wanted with—'

'With *what*?'

The door bell chimed. Morrison drew himself up and walked stiffly, deliberately, toward the sound.

Cornell leaned forward, ejected the videotape, and pocketed it.

Jim Bentley came in fast, propelling Morrison before him.

'Jim! What the hell—!'

'Got to get you back to the White House *now*, Mr President.'

'Take it slow. What's happened?'

'Just came through – European leader's been shot.'

Cornell leapt up. '*Sazarin!* The Federation President? Shot dead?'

'Head wound. Bad, they said. We got to go, sir. Now. The press corps see you arriving back at the White House near enough four in the morning with something like this going down they're going to be asking questions maybe you don't want to answer.' Bentley looked pointedly at Lewelyn and Morrison.

Cornell glanced at his watch. 'He'd have been arriving at the Vatican. *Dear God, the Pope!*'

'Not harmed, sir. They said you'd ask.'

Morrison crossed himself.

Cornell's own hand came up to genuflect but faltered and instead was thrust forward to Morrison. 'I keep my promises. Do yourself some good and empty the hooch down the sink. Sam, I'll be in touch. I'm sorry, you may have to talk to Greg.'

CHAPTER
FOUR

The sound of the music was clear, the distinctive pounding four-in-the-bar beat defeating both Merle Haggard's country-radio lament on America's decline and the Corvette's powerful engine.

Greg Lewelyn remembered their music well. And the manifestation it heralded.

'They're really *up*,' he grunted, worn by the night drive on poor roads, aware he should have rented a more suitable vehicle after their wearying flights from Phoenix to arrive at Roanoke, Virginia, but the Corvette had proven irresistible. Now, the thought of having to start the visit this way was too much.

'If they've got the snakes out I'm not going in,' he warned.

Carolyn gazed out at the mist hanging over the tiny, damp township, the mountains looming behind, throwing the straggling clapboard houses out of perspective, reducing them to toys, making her a child again against her will.

She was puzzled by the music so early in the morning. It wasn't Sunday? Or any holy day?

A pick-up truck roared toward them, too fast for the dirt road, the driver suddenly braking, skidding wildly on loose gravel then crunching gears as he backed up at speed, horn blaring.

'Greg, stop!' Carolyn yelled.

'What's going on?'

'Just wait, please.'

He braked and pulled over, the pick-up squealing painfully toward them, almost clipping the rear of the Corvette as it weaved alongside.

Greg swore.

Carolyn leaned across him. 'Mr Harper?'

'It's happened!' the driver blurted, almost falling out of the pick-up, his years unable to match his fervour. 'The Holy Spirit came down. It's the *time*.'

'Jesus,' murmured Greg.

'Don't,' she rebuked him.

'It's *your* folks!' cried the old man, his dust-smeared face streaked by tears of joy. 'They got chose first. Child, you should have stayed with your own people.'

'Where are they?' she asked, fearfully.

Greg jumped out. 'OK, that's it. Do your preaching somewhere else.'

The old man held his ground. 'The time for preaching's done. The Holy Spirit's come down and we're the chosen ones. Her folks are only the beginning. You took her away, son – stole her chance to be on high with the Lord. It's not too late – you stay with us and your time will come, real soon.' He tilted his head to the rising, manic music. 'You go on up there and sing your praises to Jesus. Listen to it! They're waitin' on *their* time. It's going to happen. The signs are right. There'll be folks comin' for miles!'

Carolyn was out of the car now, placing herself between Greg and the old man, her eyes desperate. 'It's not possible!'

'Where's your faith, child? You lost it out there? We warned you. I tell you it's *happened*.'

'*No*.'

'What the fuck's going on?' snapped Greg.

Harper glared. 'Profanity has no place on this Holy ground.'

Greg fought his frustration; bad memories from the last time, rising. 'I'm sorry. Just tell us, what's happened?'

Carolyn stared up at the mountains, seemingly dazed, fear still in her eyes but now there was something else: wonder.

The old man intoned: '*For the Lord himself shall descend from heaven with a shout, with the voice of the archangel and with the trump of God and the dead in Christ shall rise first . . .*'

She took up the Gospel words: '*Then we which are alive and remain shall be caught up in the clouds to meet the Lord in the air and so shall we ever be with the Lord.*'

'Carolyn!'

She turned. 'It's the time of the Rapture, Greg.'

'Listen to yourself! You left all this *superstition* behind!'

'They've been chosen,' announced the old man triumphantly. 'She's next for sure.'

'She's not next for *anything* here. Where are they? What have you done with them, you old fool?'

The old man prised Greg's powerful hands from his dungarees with a miner's strength. 'If you need to ask, son, you'll never know. And for sure you'll never see Jesus.'

'You lunatics have got them hidden away somewhere. It's those goddam snakes, right? They got bitten? Damn you people!'

Harper glared, his eyes alight: '*He that believed and is baptized shall be saved but he that believed not shall be damned. They shall take up serpents and if they drink any deadly thing it shall not hurt them and they shall lay hands on the sick and they shall recover.*'

Greg had had enough. He pushed Harper back firmly and took hold of Carolyn. 'Your folks are being kept somewhere. Not in heaven. *Here*. They're stopping them from getting medical attention. They're *praying* them to death, for Chrissake!' He stabbed a finger at the throbbing white clapboard meeting-hall. 'Listen! They're going crazy!'

'Greg, I want you to leave me here. I'll find out what's happened. You go on to Washington. I'll call you.'

'No way.'

'It's the *only* way.'

'That's not good enough. These people aren't safe to be with. Don't you know that? You left all this behind, Carolyn!'

'They're my people. I have to stay. You have to understand that. If you love me you must go.'

'Bullshit! I'm staying.'

'You know that won't work. You can't take it and they won't accept it. Please go, I'll find the truth.'

'Best do as she says, son. You don't fit here.'

'Greg, I'll call you, I swear to God. Just leave me be for a while.'

'This is *crazy*.'

'To you maybe it is. I've lived in your world and found that crazy sometimes — but I did all you asked. Just do this one thing for me now.'

'Something's happened here. The police ought to be told.'

'I'll tell you if there's any need.' The music suddenly grew louder as the doors to the meeting-hall opened. A group of people stared out at them from the entrance steps, hair and clothes wet with sweat from their exertions. 'Please go now,' she said, urgently.

Greg could see gyrating bodies inside the hall grasping deadly rattlesnakes and copper-heads with bare hands, the raw music driving upward to a crescendo.

It was all he needed. 'You've got it!' he snapped. He opened the trunk of the Corvette and dumped her suitcase in the rear of the pick-up. 'Your problem,' he told Harper, got into the car, and spun it around, wheels showering dirt in a cloud.

He could see her in the rear-view mirror, shrouded in dust and mist, her head down into the old man's shoulder, sobbing. He kept going, already regretting his actions but unable to turn back. He knew he could not get her to leave without using force and that would make things worse and could even become dangerous. If she was going to leave she would do it on her own; take the first step herself as she had done when she walked down the mountain away from their fundamentalist madness to gain herself a college education, then moving further from them when she had become his wife. And what a struggle that had been! It seemed now he was about to fight that battle over again. He should never have suggested coming back here. *God damn it!* Except the lunacy was supposed to be in His name – just as most of the world's madness was.

He smacked down on the accelerator, the big tyres biting harder, the heavy beat of the music far back now, yet still in his ears; the spectre of serpents released from their boxes and held, writhing, fangs exposed, mesmerized by the music and flailing bodies, terrifying for him. He felt cold sweat break over him, followed by nausea, and he was back in the airless cell he had never quite escaped from: thousands of miles away, with a man to whom cruelty was a craft, perhaps even an art, who had scoured his being until he had found his deepest fears in his childhood; in his English public schooling where cruelty was fostered as a means of building character, where children were allowed the power of fear and used it ruthlessly; where an act of extreme cruelty and crass stupidity had him falling into a zoo's reptile pit, leaving him transfixed in a dim near eternity of stark terror, ended only by the inevitable snakebite which almost killed him and scarred his mind for ever – but which, at least, brought the gift of oblivion.

He drove hard and fast. Speed killed terror for him and always had done. Flying the F-16 guaranteed he left all his fears in its wake. He wondered if that made him the most cowardly hero in America.

He lost track of time, driving in silence with the deep power of the engine for comfort, finally rolling into Roanoke airport dazed, the sound of the big jets soothing him. He missed Carolyn desperately, fought the urge to drive back, told himself she would return once she awoke from the spell they put on her. She was bright, she'd seen through them before, she would again.

He swung the Corvette into the lot, dumped the keys at the hire desk, phoned his father's number, and boarded a flight for Washington, wishing she was with him. At that moment he would even have faced their serpents if it meant taking her from them.

He slept deeply on the plane, trapped in a dream that had him facing a gleaming, dark angel in absolute silence, unmoving, locked in terror. He awoke with Washington spread below his window and – too long for his peace of mind – was unsure where or who he was. He knew that some day soon he would need real help to clear his mind of shadows.

Carolyn Lewelyn had one hope fixed in her mind, carried over from her childhood. Jesus had come then too – or so they had let her believe – taking two of their number, newly-weds, *into the air* to meet with God. The truth – overheard later in her parents' muted tones – was that the *disappeared* young couple, far from joining Jesus in the air, had in fact gone to burn with Satan in a place called Philadelphia, which city for ever afterwards became, for her, synonymous with hell.

As she climbed the ragged path up the mountain to her parents' house, she remembered running barefoot with Rebecca May Garrett to the window of the young couple's abandoned shack and straining upward to peer, pop-eyed, inside to see where angels had stepped, praying in small gasps to Jesus that silver footprints would still be visible.

Her disappointment had been cruel but at least with revelation of the truth short-lived. But more than anything, even above expectant awe, above fear too, she remembered her sense of betrayal: Jesus in heaven had failed; and Satan in Philadelphia had won. Jesus was supposed to win *always*.

Now as she opened the door to her childhood home she instinctively looked downward. Nothing. Just scrubbed floor. Wholesome cleanliness. Neatness. Order. Not poverty, but a step or two above it. Barely.

Enough to get by, Carolyn, that's all we need – all any of us need. Her mother's voice, so clearly recollected she might have been right there in the room. And perhaps she was?

Carolyn moved, knowing she must, knowing she could not let fear freeze her to the spot like a frightened rabbit or doe. She was a woman, a woman with strength, a woman with intellect, trained intellect; she refused to let herself be towed under by the wash of religious mania.

But it was in her soul. She could not escape it. She was how she was formed. Formed so very young. All that had happened since was reshaping. The original mould would never be broken.

'Shut up!' she told herself, aloud. '*Now!*'

It was then she noticed the odour – as she had sucked in breath to scold herself; faint, but real, more real than she wanted it to be. She backed against the wall. 'Mr Harper!' Her voice sounded like her grandmother's had a half-breath from dying.

The old man had waited outside, fearful to enter, the house already a shrine.

'*Mr Harper!*'

He put his face to the bug-mesh on the door.

'You have to come in.'

Hesitantly, he entered. 'They said there was something,' he murmured, sniffing.

'What did they say?'

'Something in the air.'

'What is it?'

'*Angel's breath.*'

She believed him because she was trapped by her beliefs, held even by its most outrageous utterings; yet, deep inside, part of her fought back weakly but valiantly, allowing Greg's voice – and her sublimated rationale – through. *Carolyn, if angels exist and are as good as they say, they breathe air like the rest of us. Not gas. Gas is for devils. Or humans.*

The bedroom was where it had happened. No signs of struggle. To the contrary, the bedclothes were turned back lightly, almost caringly, the indentations from the two bodies still visible on the scrubbed sheet and pillows. Carolyn reached out her hand, expecting somehow to feel their body heat, then drew back from the cool touch of lightly starched worn cotton.

'*Mama*,' she whispered.

'Don't fret,' said Harper, poised at the bedroom door, not entering, torn between compassion and fear. 'They're waitin' on you right now. Just a matter of time, child.'

The percussive thump of the music rose up the mountainside like distant heavy guns in a rolling barrage. Carolyn felt herself slip out of time and it might easily have been an earlier century with battles raging on Virginian soil, blood against blood, families ripped apart as the cost of beliefs. Like she from her own.

She turned to the old man. 'How can you be so *sure*?'

'It's just *knowin'*. You lose it if you live *their* way. Outsiders.'

'He's my husband.'

'You should have thought about this.' Harper nodded at the empty bed.

'*This*?' Carolyn pointed, afraid – and angry. 'No one thought this would happen *now*.' She wept. 'This was for some other time – someone else's lifetime. Not mine?'

'When the Lord comes he comes like a thief in the night and there'll be no knowin' beforehand. You should read the Holy Gospel as if your life depends on it – for it surely does. This is the time. The signs are all there.'

She stared at the bed, tears streaming down her face. 'I can't believe it. I won't.'

'You will, child. You believe in the Word of God?'

'I wouldn't be here if I didn't – I'd be with my husband!'

'Then believe this is His Will, the start of His Glory. Prepare for all that will come. You must be ready.'

She knelt by the bed, hearing him shuffle away. She called: 'Mr Harper! Where were you going when we saw you?'

'To spread the word, of course!'

'By yourself?'

Harper came back and pointed at the small outdated television set on the dresser. 'One man can spread the word throughout the world without even raisin' his voice, child – just as the good Lord Jesus did.'

Carolyn knew his name. Robert Maddox.

'Greg!' Sam Lewelyn called as his son came into view at Washington National. 'I had your phone message from Roanoke. Where's Carolyn?'

'Let's talk in the car.' Greg caught his look. 'There's a problem but it'll work out OK.'

'We can talk in the car. It's right outside.'

'It'll get towed.'

'There's a security guard sitting on it.'

'You used agency ID? That's cheating.'

'Not really. You could say I'm here on important agency business.'

'What's that supposed to mean?'

'Later. First I want to hear what you've done with your wife.'

'Not me – God.'

The airport security guard was running his hand admiringly over the sculpted metal wheel-cover at the continental rear of Sam's sixties Lincoln. 'Don't make 'em this way any more. Want to sell?'

Sam grinned, pleased. 'Not hardly.'

'I guess when you've had a car this long you may as well keep it.'

'They can bury me in it,' Sam said as he settled himself inside and drove the massive automobile away from the concourse, its engine virtually silent with only a trace of oil-smoke giving away its age.

'A real dinosaur,' said Greg, enjoying the smooth power. He grinned. 'I meant the car.'

Sam stuck his meerschaum in his mouth and lit it one-handed. 'The President called *me* one just yesterday.'

Greg stared fixedly ahead. 'So he finally got in touch?'

'The man's barely been in the White House a year – and done a heck of a lot in that time. Don't think we're the only people he has to care about.'

'It needed a phone call – that's all. "Sam, I'm sorry Elizabeth's

59

dead, I can't make it over but I'm thinking about you." Not a hell of a lot to ask from a friend?'

'He didn't know.'

'He should have made it his business to know.'

'That's what he said.'

'He was right.'

'I think she knew and kept it from him.'

'Superbitch?'

'Hey! You watch that mouth, son,' Sam growled.

'You know what they say about her on station?'

Sam turned, angry. 'I don't care to hear. She's the First Lady – don't you forget it!'

'Your loyalty always does you credit, Dad. You just need to see things as they really are a bit more.'

'You mean with the cynicism of modern youth? Goddamnit! At your age I was still filled with the wonder of things. All I seem to hear now is how boring everything is today. Values? Forget it. Nothing's worth a damn any more. Not family, not money – you ever see an advertisement now that doesn't mark its prices "only"? *Only* so much. Hell! someone has to earn that money.'

Greg grinned. 'You're finally getting there, Dad. That's how old folks talk: yesterday was great – today is shit.'

'Today *isn't* shit, it's how your generation view today that makes it seem worthless. Can't you see that an attitude like that is offensive to people like me?'

'We're living what you handed down to us. Ever thought of that?'

'Well, somehow it got changed in the passing – and don't ask me how because I've no idea.' He sucked frustratedly on his dead pipe. 'Forget it, we're not about to agree. What did you mean by God being responsible for Carolyn not being here?'

Greg sunk lower in the armchair-sized leather seat. 'She just can't get that stuff out of her soul. She thinks straight when she's away from there but . . . Hell, I don't want to talk about it, just makes me mad.'

'They must have got their hooks back into her damn fast? You couldn't have been there any time at all?'

'Minutes, that's all it took. Maybe ten minutes.'

Sam frowned. 'I thought she was stronger than that?'

'Not when you get told your parents have gone up to meet God in the air! Exactly what's been predicted for as long as you can remember.'

'She believed that?'

'I'm here, she's there, her folks *weren't*. What do you think?'

'Take it easy. So where are they? Couldn't you convince her there's a logical explanation?'

'When she starts thinking their way, logic goes out the window.'

'So you just left her?'

'I told her what happened to them but it made no difference.' Sam glanced quickly at him. 'You know what happened to them?'

'You've never seen them, Dad. Not for real.'

'I saw that TV programme.' He raised thick eyebrows. 'Dangerous. Takes some faith to do that! They take the Bible's word literally: "They shall take up serpents". Right?'

'They're not the only ones who do that with snakes – but for sure they're the most extreme. And they get bitten. They don't get medical help – they pray. Sooner or later someone had to die. The law of averages guarantees that. But they don't see things that way. Maybe they don't care.'

'So they've got Carolyn's folks locked away somewhere – snake-bitten and dying – or maybe dead already? That's what you're saying. Sounds like police business to me.'

'That's what I told her. She told me to leave. To come here and wait. She'd call. Whoever said religion is the opiate of the masses was dead wrong. It's a stimulant that turns rational human beings into psychopaths. Turn on your TV news any day of the week!'

'She'll call, son. Once they let her see her folks. Just cool down.'

'I just can't take this regression. I thought it was over.'

'You can't expect her to give up her belief in God?'

'It's the way she *sees* God. Right now she's being convinced – probably is already – that the *Rapture* is happening. You familiar with that crazy fundamentalist notion? The time when certain chosen people disappear and rise to sit with God while the rest of us go down the tube. Very Christian.'

'Come on, that's just another version of the Day of Judgement. Kids' view, really.'

'Is it, hell! Its pre-judgement. They believe they'll rise up *still alive* – nothing to do with the earth and the waters giving up their dead. Just selected people, rising up to sit with Jesus and watch the rest of us who don't think their way screw up some more?'

'Come on, you knew what you married. You faced the responsibility – or you should have done. The beliefs came with the woman. You were warned. Your mother was—'

'What? Understanding but cautious?'

'No. Worried about the differences between the two of you.'

'That was the English *class* thing.'

Sam snapped: 'Was it, hell! She knew that Carolyn was bright – that she could – *had* – overcome an underprivileged background.'

'Trashy, say it.'

'I don't mean trashy, damn it! I mean *poor*. Carolyn pulled herself out of that, made it through college by her own talents, her own efforts, her single-minded determination. Your mother admired her.'

'I know that.'

'Do you?'

'Of course I do.'

'Then when she calls be as understanding as you can. Tell her you'll wait here for her.'

'I've only got a couple of weeks at the most. She could be there for all of that. I planned on visiting England. Mom's grave. I promised Cardus – my boss – a breakthrough when I got back. There's no way he'll let me extend.'

Sam glanced at him. 'Breakthrough?'

Greg shifted and gazed out of the window. 'Forget it. Security's so hot I'm surprised I'm allowed to breathe outside the station – never mind discuss what goes on.'

'I'm going to have to ask you to do just that.'

Greg turned. 'I don't understand.'

'I need to know what's going on down there.'

Greg laughed. 'You know exactly what goes on in an NSA station.'

'Not in your section, I don't. Seems very few do. I understand there's a security lock? Sealed? Like a space station. Must take some room? I checked the original plans for the station. It doesn't exist. No special security. So what goes on?'

Greg sat mutely.

'I need some answers from you, Greg.'

'Oh no. Not from me. Anyway, why? What's your interest?'

'Directly, none.'

'Don't play games.'

'No game. Fact. I need the answers for someone I can't say no to. Nor can you.'

'You're talking about John Cornell? Is this connected with his inspection trip? What's going on here? The President wants information from the Director of NSA he picks up a phone and asks – he doesn't ask an old friend to pump his son. An old friend he conveniently forgot when he got elected. I'm sorry, Dad – but you know how I feel.'

Sam waved a big hand dismissively. 'OK, Mr Correct, what if the President doesn't get answers? Real answers?'

'Ridiculous.'

'Say he's getting the runaround? Or answers that are straight fabrication? Bloody-minded technical hocus-pocus made up by your grey wizards to confound the likes of us. And I don't mean you. You know how easy that can be in your world!'

'John Cornell can get the truth whenever he wants – if he's got the balls to press for it or the mind to understand it. Frankly I doubt it.'

'That's arrogant – it's also quite enough! Now you listen to me. Whatever the President wants to know you'd better be damn ready to give him answers and you tell him sir while you do it.'

'No, sir. I'm not in that position. I report to my boss, he reports to Director Kent who reports to the President. I'm at the wrong end of that chain – the nearest to being flushed down the pan. Leave me out of this, Dad. I mean it.'

'Too late. Haven't you noticed this isn't the quickest route to Baltimore?'

They were stopped in traffic. Ahead was Washington Circle and Pennsylvania Avenue.

'The White House? This isn't fair. Drive me to Fort Meade.'

'You'll never get near Kent. No one gets near him unless they're from right there on Mahogany Row – and sometimes they get to wait a week to touch the hem. You must know that by now?'

'Let me call my boss then.'

'Speak to the President first.'

'No!'

'What are you people hiding down there? What are you keeping from the President?'

Greg shook his head, disbelievingly. 'Dad, you ever see that movie, *Seven Days in May*? A military plot to take over the government? Topple the president? No, that's not what we're doing – but it sure as hell sounds like the kind of paranoiac thinking that's going on in the White House.' He leaned back for his bag and opened the car door. 'Sorry, Dad, Cornell's the president so he should know there's protocol to obey here – and this violates it. He can't shoot me for refusing to talk. Tell him to get Director Kent's consent and I'll give you all I know – which isn't much. Better he asks him directly, that's my advice. He'll learn more.'

Horns began blaring. 'Get back in,' ordered Sam.

'Can't do that. Sorry. Tell John Cornell I'm not screwing up my career by getting involved in politics. That is what all this is about, isn't it? I'm not stupid. He's using you. Call you later, Dad.' Greg pushed the door closed and darted through the angry traffic.

Sam Lewelyn cursed and pulled the big Lincoln away hard, the blare of horns dying behind him.

Greg took a cab and headed north-east across the capital, held it until he got an answer to his buzz at a house on the Seventh Street end of Orleans Place on the north-east side of the city, then paid him off.

Georgia Rowntree lectured in philosophy at Gallaudet and was the nearest Greg had ever had to a sister. She viewed him in an entirely different way but kept *that* buttoned down tight.

'I know why you're here,' she told him, taking his bag and frantically checking through it as they climbed to her first-floor apartment.

'There's none there,' he told her.

'How the hell do you know what I'm looking for?'

'Because every time I see you you're giving up smoking.'

'Shows how little you see me. I give up once a year!'

Inside, he dropped on to an enormous ancient over-stuffed sofa draped in hand-woven African rugs. 'I'm beat.'

'She's left you. For Jesus. Right?'

He sat up. 'Dad called you?'

'No. I saw her on that.' Georgia pointed at a television set shrouded by a small jungle of exotic plants. 'News break from the Smoky Mountains—'

'Appalachians, Smokies are in Tennessee.'

'You're so heartbroken you can lecture in geography?'

'How did the TV station get on to it?'

'They called them, I guess? Her people.'

Greg frowned. 'I thought they'd want to keep things quiet?'

'Why? They've got the Second Coming to publicize! Hey, that's no short order. It's bumper-sticker time: *Jesus is back and boy is he mad!*'

'Carolyn's folks got bitten by those snakes they handle. That's the truth of it. You saw that TV story on them last fall?'

'Ugh.'

'They're being hidden somewhere. Until they recover. Or don't. Whatever else is being said is just crazy.'

She flicked a TV-remote unit. 'Robert Maddox doesn't think so. He's bought their story and he's selling it hard.'

The face of the powerful TV evangelist filled the screen, his tanned face, white teeth and gently greying hair, perfect.

'. . . the significance of this event is beyond measure. It was prophesied in the Gospels and it has occurred. More will follow. I shall be praying nonstop and I ask you all to join me so that we too may be chosen to sit beside our Lord Jesus Christ. It is the time of *Rapture.* I ask you to come to me here—'

Greg stabbed the remote off. 'And bring me your money,' he intoned in the evangelist's, deep, earnest tones.

'You should try show-biz,' Georgia snapped. 'Don't you want to see pictures of your wife?'

'Doing what? Praying? Bowing down to Maddox?'

'Looking like a refugee. That's real poor country up there. I never realized. Some of those shanties – and the vehicles! Makes my old VW look like it just rolled off the production line. Hey, don't you care any more? What happened to all that love you talked about incessantly? You had these problems before – you can handle it again. Say you'd married me? A Catholic, trying to convert you dawn till dusk? Mass twice on Sundays, kids point

65

toward Rome or you don't get to make any! You didn't do so bad.'

'Rome doesn't expect you to put your life on the line every time the *Holy Spirit* moves you. Rome expects you to be taken to hospital if your life is in danger. Rome demands a lot – but all of it is within reason. That's how I understand it, anyway.'

She shrugged, mixing drinks. 'Can't argue with that. You still on the health kick? Juice? No wonder you look so damn good. Maybe I'll really give up smoking this time. And booze. OK, so Carolyn got re-converted? What are you going to do about it?'

'Wait.'

'What does your father think?'

Greg accepted the offered drink and glared at the glass.

'What's wrong?'

'We've got a problem. Dad and me. Not Carolyn – professional.'

'Shouldn't work for the same organization. So you're not communicating?'

'He met me off the plane at National. I jumped ship at Washington Circle. He'd turned heavy on something.'

'It's not your day. Call him, make up, you don't need more family troubles than you have already.'

'He's not home. Right now I'd say he's where he was taking me.'

'The zoo?'

'The White House. And, no, I'm not calling there.'

She sipped her drink. 'You want to talk about it?'

'I can't.'

'Secrets?'

'Ethics.'

She laughed. 'Ethics! In your world? How can people who spend their life snooping on the rest of the world have any ethics. Come on!'

'He wanted me to report directly to the President.'

She raised her eyebrows. 'You mean without your own boss knowing? Sounds a little . . . ?' She tilted her glass, side to side. 'Politics? Or has someone been bad and you're expected to play Deep Throat?'

'Politics. Inside NSA it's accepted there's a problem between the Director and the President. Personalities, lack of communication – whatever – I don't fly at that altitude.'

She sat down, intrigued. 'Maybe you do? Maybe that's why you were asked? Maybe you don't know it. I imagine your world is full of maybes.'

'I'm an analyst – that's all.'

'Ananlysing what?'

'That's what I'm not telling the President. Anyway, I don't know. Not precisely.'

'Then you're a magician, not an analyst. You can't analyse without information.'

'I know only the part I deal with. Drop it, OK.'

She flicked on the television again. 'Watch the news and think about what you're going to do. You're not really going to leave her be, are you? *Wife.*'

'I did that already. She told me to go.'

'That was then, this is now. Bedtime's coming up and she's going to be wishing she could rewrite the script. Trust me, I know.'

He stared at the TV set. 'The news said she was going to Maddox?'

'In Austin, Texas,' she said with a broad drawl and tossed him an airline schedule. 'Get outa here!'

CHAPTER
FIVE

While her husband had sat in emergency session with foreign-policy advisers in the Oval Office considering the political implications of the assassination attempt on the newly appointed President of Federal Europe through most of that Friday – Madelaine Cornell had worried, frustratedly, over the identity of the priest on the videotape he had returned with late the night before.

She was convinced she knew him and that he was *involved*. His shadowed positioning, his body language, suggested conspiracy; his apparent anger as he stalked away from the man and woman tending the electronic equipment, confirmed for her that he was no unwitting bystander. She was convinced that he wasn't standing by Kent, he was *with* Kent.

For once her exceptional faculty of recall, a critical factor in her husband's successful campaign for the presidency – he being embarrassingly forgetful with names and faces – seemed beaten, until her gaze halted on a photograph on the Steinway of Cornell taken a decade before, which displayed clearly how time and the strain of growing political responsibility had taken their toll.

No one escapes, she thought. And some suffer more because of the weight they add to their lives.

She worked the remote control, froze the priest's shadowed, black-bearded face, mentally adding years and the ravages wrought by a selfless calling, his elusive identity close enough now for his breath to be on her face.

She halted the tape as her own words, spoken during those cruel heart-in-the-mouth final campaigning days, flowed back: *He'll help get you the bleeding hearts and the ethnic minority vote you need badly. He's in* Time, Newsweek, *and the networks love him, so he's got the movers and shakers on his side, not just the great unwashed. And they say he got that limp from combat and not from kneeling and giving the last rites to dying high-school boys in Vietnam, so he's even got credibility for the red-necks. He's hot, John, so are you, and there's a lot of goodwill going his way that can spill over.*

She had not added: and he's sexy in a haggard, brutalized, intense sort of way – because that was counter-productive.

In the event Father David Kolchak had not been persuadable – one of her few failures – firmly stating his position of being politically aware but non-aligned. She had not believed him. God had simply got there first.

She had dismissed Kolchak, casting him aside with disdain, utterly forgotten, as only sunken political stepping-stones can be.

Now, relishing the renewed challenge, she crossed her very good legs and smiled in anticipation as the telephone line purred, for intense committed men gave her chills that only their *heat* could warm.

She closed her eyes. Life was cold within the presidency, *affaires* absolutely out of the question. She could put up with that. No one needed to tell her that power was the most potent aphrodisiac of all. If she hadn't the constant, nagging fear that at any time her husband's dangerous, basic honesty would cause him to lose all she had gained for him, she felt she might happily be experiencing a five-year-long orgasm.

She pictured Kolchak in his Chicago ministry, offering God and other more practical aid besides, to the great wash of human debris from the wreck of Eastern Europe while still finding time to attack those who disrupted or disapproved of his work. The once rapacious media pack, however, had moved their attentions to feed on fresher, less domestically upheaving, causes.

The White House press office had supplied her with his current telephone number and a photocopy of a recent inside-page news story with photograph captioned THE FIGHTING FATHER showing his release following a night – reportedly unashamed – in police custody for using his fists as well as words to defend his displayed charges from ultra-right orchestrated violence.

She sipped coffee delicately from an exquisite bone china cup bearing her own design for the Cornell presidency.

Ten years hard ageing, she thought, laying the photocopy on the cold marble table-top before her, the tape running silently in the background. Is that God's price, Father? Sacrificed youth? Is that why He's eternal? An ageless vampire? She sighed. So sad, all that delicious black hair turned tired grey. Heredity, or pain, Father? Or your humanity showing?

She touched her own hair, feeling that small but daily increasing lurch inside which warned the time was nearing when even the most sycophantic hairdresser would advise, coyly: 'Time to let it show, my dear.'

'David Kolchak,' said a tired, hard, voice, prepared for argument.

'Father?' She sought confirmation, thrown by his brusqueness.

'Who is this, please? Are you in trouble? May I help?'

She smiled. *Oh yes.* 'This is Madelaine Cornell. You may recall we talked briefly – oh! a little more than a year ago? Before my husband won the presidency?'

The line fell silent.

She worried that she'd put emphasis on won, then dismissed the thought: he wouldn't care, there'd be no wound to rub salt into. This was not going to be easy. Do it or lose it! she ordered herself. She would brief her husband later, the important thing was to get Kolchak to Washington.

'I'm really sorry to call you out of the blue this way.'

'How can I help, Mrs Cornell?'

'You can help *yourself*, Father. That is to say your cause, your fine work. The President is becoming increasingly concerned with the problems faced over here by refugees from Eastern Europe. He showed me a recent newspaper story concerning you. An attack by . . . well, I have to say they sounded like *fascists*.'

'A global problem, Mrs Cornell, we face only one small part of it here in the United States. The President is right to be concerned.'

'Would you be willing to come to Washington? I know he's eager to speak with people who have first-hand experience of the problem.'

'Coffee-table discussion with concerned Washington liberals will solve nothing – even with the President present. If you could see the number of people who rely on the work we do you'd understand why I can't leave.'

'Father, all you need to do is get on a plane and spend an hour in the White House. I'm sure you're able to delegate for such a short period? The benefits to your work will surely make up for any temporary lapse in the service you offer these people?'

'We don't offer a *service*, Mrs Cornell. Just the necessities for survival – with Christian compassion.'

'My poor choice of words. I apologize. I realize how arduous and, in these times, how important, your work is. I certainly didn't mean to trivialize it. The proposition was for serious, *constructive* discussion with the President himself. I'm calling on his behalf. If it's a question of funds for the air-ticket that's not a problem. Please try? Father?'

Kolchak hesitated. 'Very well. Please tell the President I'll be honoured to come. Next week some time?'

'Well . . . he may have to leave any time for Europe – you're aware of course of the news from over there?'

'An act symbolic of our times, I'm afraid. Too much wealth – and influence – in one part of the world while others collapse, politically and economically bankrupt. A reactionary act – and not the last, I'm certain. The revisionist trend is growing in Europe – brutal history is in very real danger of being sanitized. The displacement of Eastern European peoples is nothing new, Mrs Cornell, nor is assassination to achieve political ends. The next world war will not be fought between countries, it will be fought between those who have and those who have not. I fear it has already begun.'

She raised her perfectly drawn eyebrows. *Here endeth the first lesson.* 'The President is in a meeting with advisers right now, otherwise he would have called you himself. Today may be the last opportunity he has to talk with you before leaving for Europe.'

'Surely with all that's going on he won't have time?'

'It's because of what has happened in Europe and what has *been* happening concerning refugees that he feels it imperative he speaks to people at – may I say – *ground* level? Those who really understand. Who see the way things are going and are having to deal with the after-effects. He'll make time, I guarantee it. I've taken the liberty of arranging a return flight out of O'Hare. It leaves at thirteen fifteen. Can you make that?'

'I'll leave right away.'

'Good. Oh! On a lighter note – I understand you were involved some years ago with the Church of the Holy Sepulchre in Jerusalem? My husband made a pilgrimage there during his college days. An important event in his life, I know. I'm trying to give him something back of that time. Do you own copies of any recordings made in the church? Perhaps the choir? A full mass would be too much to ask, I suppose? It would be a wonderful gift for his coming birthday.'

She expected hesitation but the hard voice came directly back. 'How did you know about my time there, Mrs Cornell?'

She sensed anger, the same anger she had sensed from him on the silent videotape. 'An acquaintance of my husband informed me. Does it matter?'

'A priest?'

She laughed. 'Hardly. I suppose I shouldn't admit this but he's part of what they like to call the Intelligence community up here. Specifically, the National Security Agency out in Baltimore? I can't imagine you having connections in that field!'

'I regret I have no recordings – only memories of my time in Jerusalem.'

'But recordings were made there?'

'Radio and television broadcasts were made from the Church of the Holy Sepulchre – especially around Christmas and, of course, Easter. Sometimes these were recorded.'

'There was a particular recording you might recall – as the people involved were from Eastern Europe. Actually, from Russia. You're half Russian, aren't you?'

Tension came down the line like electricity. 'My father was from the Ukraine. I was born in the United States.'

'Then you speak Russian?'

'It would be hard – impossible – to do the work I do without it, Mrs Cornell.'

'Of course. Well, goodbye for the time being. There'll be a car to meet you on arrival and get you through security here at the White House. *Bon voyage*, Father.'

She put down the receiver, frowning. Had she overdone it? Damn it! She had to make certain he came. And if that meant making him run scared a little . . . well so be it! She began the video again, reaching forward for the coffee pot.

The sudden, explosion of sound was almost physical, tearing at her brain and shattering fine china across Italian marble. She stabbed frantically at the remote-control she had brushed against.

Silence fell. More complete than she had ever known. She gasped in relief. A wave of nausea arose, then ebbed. She stared at the dead screen. She'd been warned about the electronic jamming on the videotape and had pressed the mute control, but no warning could have prepared her for what she had heard. There's *madness* in there, she thought, still shaken: *bedlam, with the door locked behind*.

She summoned staff to clear the debris, gave herself a stiff drink when they had gone, then settled herself and watched the video through again until every movement, every nuance, was imprinted in her mind and only the lack of sound denied her knowledge of what was occurring, taunting her – as, she pondered, the almond eyes of the woman on the screen taunted David Kolchak.

'Fool!' she snapped suddenly, snatched up the telephone and stabbed in a Georgetown number. '*Hello*, is that Felicity? Hi, darling, is Mommy there? You know who this is? Of course you do. Sweetheart, I want you to *sign* Mommy that I'm coming over right now and is that a problem? Do it *now*, Felicity.' She waited. 'It's not a problem? Wonderful. She wants to know why? *Sign* that I've got a video I want her to see. Of course you can watch it too. Who's in it? Why, *Jesus*, sweetheart! No, not in His crib, on His cross. Felicity, don't be a baby, it's only a statue. See you *real* soon, darling.'

John Cornell broke his emergency meeting in the West Wing Cabinet Room with dusk falling over the John F. Kennedy Rose Garden outside, and immediately made for the South Portico ground-floor Map Room which was set aside as a convenient, presidential, private meeting place.

'Problem, Sam?' he asked, finding Lewelyn pacing the colourful Heriz Persian rug. 'They called me but I couldn't get away right then. Sorry to keep you waiting so long.' He indicated the Chippendale-style chairs. 'Sit. Don't worry, they've lasted since the eighteenth century and bigger men than you or I – in every sense – have sat in them. Where's Greg? Your message said he was flying in to Washington?'

'Greg's behaving like a fool.'

'Tell me.'

'He refuses to talk about the project unless he's given clearance by Kent. Even to you, John.'

'Admirable loyalty.'

'His loyalty should be to his President. His behaviour is inexcusable. I feel ashamed.'

'Don't. There'll be another way. It's a pity you brought up the subject before he saw me, he may not have felt able to refuse in these surroundings?'

'I have to be frank, John. Greg's opinion of you is a little coloured right now.'

'Elizabeth? Can't undo it, Sam.'

Lewelyn nodded.

'Where's Greg now?'

'Took off. Left me sitting in the Lincoln in the middle of a traffic jam about an hour ago.'

'The Lewelyn temper at work? I remember—' Cornell smiled. 'Never mind. Where might he go? Friend? Hotel? Bar to cool off?'

'Doesn't drink – not since Iraq. They fed him some real cocktails. He won't touch any kind of stimulant any more – and don't tell me alcohol is a depressant not a stimulant. Won't even drink coffee. Sometimes I wonder just how deep the scar goes. He's not the Greg I reared, that's for sure. The change is subtle – but it's there.'

'Maybe he's just grown, Sam?'

'He's twenty-eight!'

'You think you were through growing at twenty-eight? I sure as hell wasn't. *Forty*-eight, maybe. I meant the war. *His* war would have broken most men. Maybe it broke him but it doesn't show? I understand he quit flying to join NSA. Any stress involved in that decision?'

'Not on any medical report I've seen.'

'You've had sight of NSA's report?'

'Not officially, but I made sure I saw it all the same. He was in great shape. On the outside. I saw enough of what can happen on the inside after 'Nam. It's a worry.'

'He certainly looked good the day President Bush made the

74

presentation. You must have been real proud, Sam. I sure would have been.' Cornell smiled, regretfully. 'I'd have been proud to have either son or daughter – with or without the decoration.'

Lewelyn nodded.

Cornell grinned. 'Sorry. So where's Greg?'

'Georgia.'

'He must have a private rocket!'

'Georgia Rowntree. Family were neighbours of ours from way back. You met them. Georgia lectures at Gallaudet, now.'

'I remember. Greg got problems at home?'

'Georgia's not one of them,' answered Sam, sternly.

Cornell indicated a telephone on a blockfront desk, under a portrait of Benjamin Franklin. 'Call her now, Sam. I may have to leave for Europe at any time. If Kent gets word of my interest, he'll shut things down tight and I may never get a clean bite at him again.'

An aide knocked and entered, glancing pointedly at Lewelyn speaking on the telephone. 'Go ahead, Walter,' said Cornell.

'Mrs Cornell has returned, Mr President. She asks if you'll please join her in the West Sitting Hall. She asked that the message be conveyed urgently.'

'Thank you. I'll be right along.'

'I'll inform the First Lady, sir.'

Lewelyn put down the receiver. 'He was there but he's gone. Headed for Austin. Just made the last flight out of National – going after his wife. Georgia said to watch the news, that'll explain quicker. Greg told her what happened in the car with me. He said I'd probably be here. And she told me to make sure you watch the Robert Maddox channel. The evangelist?'

'That charlatan? Why?'

'He's spouting off about you wasting your time going to Europe. Sazarin isn't going to die – Bible says so. He's going to recover and become the most dangerous man alive. Book of Revelations stuff. Maddox's big number. He's picked up on that chant the Italian crowds have been giving Sazarin all week since his election. See it on CNN? La Bestia. The Beast. That's prime meat for Maddox. Makes for high ratings. People like being scared. Especially the kind that watches him. He's got a Gospel telethon going right now, really whipping up the airwaves.'

'I'm surprised an intelligent woman like Georgia could be bothered to watch a manipulator like Maddox. What's this to do with Greg?'

'Greg's wife's folks are part of a fundamentalist sect up there in the Appalachians? Pentecostalists? Whatever? *Signs*, *tongues*, all that. They're prime-time news. The networks are running some crazy story on them. Whole communities are making for Austin – that's where Maddox has his TV ministry.'

Cornell nodded. 'Thirty storeys leased out at premium rents. I know all about Maddox – and others like him. I've got a commission looking at the way these people operate – and I'm going to nail them good, when the time comes. And I've made my intention clear. So Greg's chasing his wife?'

'I'm afraid so.'

'I need to speak with him, Sam.'

'There's not a lot I can do about that. If he calls I'll tell him he gets back here and that's an Executive Order direct from you – or else!'

'If reason doesn't work that's what you may have to do. But it could blow this thing wide open – and you know how stories spread in this town. I don't want it made public I'm gunning for Kent. Try to make Greg see sense.'

'John, do you mind me saying something?'

'You're here to speak your mind.'

'This is more my gut rumbling.'

'So rumble.'

'This thing is rolling too fast. Every time we've moved there's been an escalation into something else, something bigger.'

Cornell grinned. 'Sam, if you're implying that Kent is connected with Sazarin being shot in Rome, remember that I'm supposed to be the mildly paranoid one here.'

'Forget it.'

'All this talk of signs and portents getting to you? You're not turning fey on me, Sam?'

'Maybe just old?'

'You and me both.' Cornell stood. 'Madelaine wants to see me. Come on up and have a drink, we'll watch the news and a bit of Maddox – though as far as I'm concerned he's just a bad side-show in this crazy circus we live in.'

Madelaine Cornell waited agitatedly in the West Sitting Hall which served as their private living room, sitting on a *chaise-longue* away from the large fan window, clutching a hand-written transcript, all satisfaction from her initiative defeated by a new uncertainty, even the beginnings of fear. Yet, still, her pride would not let her be cowed.

'Sam's joining us for a drink,' announced Cornell, entering. He dismissed hovering staff and began mixing drinks himself, a task he enjoyed. He worked the TV remote. 'Sam needs the news. I'm supposed to suffer that crook Maddox – the TV preacher. He's appointed himself presidential foreign-affairs adviser. I bet the SOB's never left Texas!'

He saw the transcript in his wife's hands. Her mood, her silence, stopped him. 'What's that?'

She glanced pointedly at Lewelyn.

Sam got up. 'I'll call you later, John.'

'Sam, stay where you are,' ordered Cornell. 'Whatever it is, Madelaine, say it.'

She looked at the transcript. 'Ruth Crayford is deaf.'

'I know, so?'

'She reads lips like I'd read a book.' She smoothed the transcript. 'The big problem was that half of the dialogue was in Russian. I should have realized that straight away, it wasted time. I called for a translator from the pool but by the time she arrived Ruth had it all worked out.'

Cornell raised a hand. 'Hold it! Worked what out?'

'Kolchak was *translating*, don't you see? Translating for Kent. Which meant by following him, we got the English text complete then had the translator lip-synch it back in Russian. It worked perfectly.'

'Madelaine, what are you talking about?'

'The dialogue from Morrison's tape,' said Lewelyn, studying her. 'She's got us the sound.'

Cornell raised his eyebrows. 'I'm impressed. Who the hell is Kolchak?'

'*Listen*,' she almost pleaded.

Cornell put drinks down and sat. 'I'm listening.'

She switched channels and let the video run. 'I'll read the lines as it plays. All right. Four people in the church, close to the altar, electronic equipment set up next to two of them: the Markarov twins, Ilya and Irina – according to what Morrison told you. The priest is barely visible here – he's David Kolchak, a Jesuit, remember him? Turned us down for the campaign? Doesn't matter, I'll explain later. Dialogue starts in a moment, half of it in Russian, as I said. Kolchak translates into English right through.' She looked at her husband. 'They're *explaining*, you see. For Kent's benefit.'

'Explaining what? What's the matter? Madelaine, are you OK?' She looked back at the screen. 'You'll hear. Ilya Markarov speaks first, Kolchak translates for Kent:

> *It's all around us. In the ether. Sound waves, reverberating for ever. The grunt of the first caveman, the Sermon on the Mount, the words I'm uttering now.*

'Irina Markarov takes it up. Kolchak translates:

> *The last cry of Jesus to his father in Heaven if you believe the New Testament. Which of course you do.*

'Then he adds:

> *She means me.*

'He now says something to the Markarovs in Russian that we can't get accurately because he turns and his face is in shadow. We assumed he says: "It isn't possible," because he gives Ilya Markarov's reply as:

> *It is possible. With resources, with commitment. The technology is almost there. We've told you already, priest.*

'Irina says:

> *It's certain. You just don't want to believe.*

Kolchak is translating this verbatim even when they're attacking him – or what he stands for. He's furious but he's doing it.
'Ilya again:

> *We could confirm history or discredit it.*

'Irina points at the altar statue of Christ crucified:

Prove His existence.

'Ilya:

Which to you means God, of course. The Trinity?

'Irina:

Or disprove it.

'She enjoys that, you can see it.

'Ilya Markarov plays with the equipment then turns and gives a lengthy discourse. It was hellish but we got most of it. Kolchak translates right through so I'll read across the dialogue.' She looked directly at her husband. 'This is the heart of it.'

She spoke slowly and carefully, the text virtually memorized now, her eyes on Kolchak's angered face on the screen.

> *Consider the stars. Many of them don't exist any longer, yet we see their light. If we had telescopes powerful enough we could, logically, see past events occurring on such a star as though they were occurring in the present. A person viewing us from that same star might be seeing Caesar's legions. Or perhaps on this very site, if it really happened, the crucifixion of Christ?*
>
> *We believe sound is no different, that it too projects itself virtually for ever, with only its frequencies – and therefore our perception of its existence – changing, with time. We are discovering these hidden frequencies, recording them, but the equipment we have, though the best the Soviet Union can supply, is too primitive for our needs.*
>
> *We need the best recording equipment linked to advanced computers to scan, log and retrieve these past sounds. Computers capable of processing and storing vast amounts of data. Greater than any data-intensive project now being conducted or even envisaged. Greater than your Mars manned-spacecraft programme, greater than your Genome DNA-mapping project, greater than Star Wars. We need total commitment. In return we will give you history. You can confirm what you choose to confirm, destroy what you choose to destroy. The past is composed of icons and you will have those in your hands to do as you will. There's only one thing more powerful than seeing the future: knowing the past. Whoever knows the past controls the future.*

She stopped and looked at Cornell who sat stunned. He barely murmured: 'My God.'

'No wonder Kent buried this thing in the desert,' breathed Lewelyn.

Cornell turned sharply. 'He hasn't *buried* it, Sam, he's working on it. Don't you see? I want that priest found. I want him here. He wasn't there on any restoration project, I don't care what Morrison said. And, Sam, I want Greg, and I want him *talking*. This isn't a head-to-head between me and Kent any longer. This is a threat to every value we have. If this *is* possible, the Markarovs were the most dangerous people ever born – and that's no exaggeration. I'm not surprised they were assassinated. I'd say it isn't a question of who did it – but who got there first. Don't you see that even if they *couldn't* do what they say, the very *thought* of it is dangerous. The old Soviet Union used to simply rewrite their history – dear God, the manipulation made possible by *this* is awesome! Kent can't be in this alone. He couldn't cover the finance needed in his budget. Not the way the Markarovs were talking. Where's the money coming from? How deep is this thing? Where are you going, Sam?'

'To Clair Morrison, for the truth.'

'I can't leave here, not with all that's going on.'

'I don't really think you want to be there.'

Cornell looked at him, measuredly. 'Do what you have to do. And Sam, be careful.'

After Lewelyn had gone, Cornell reminded her: 'Kolchak?'

Madelaine Cornell reached for the glass in front of her, sipping the chilled white wine, avoiding his eyes.

'Madelaine? You made some connection?'

'He was – oh, a newsworthy liberal priest who could have done us some good for the campaign.'

'All right, that's past. Tell me about now.'

'I recognized him on the tape. He's aged badly – but it's him. I called him in Chicago – that's where he operates from. Runs a refugee aid unit. I arranged for him to come here.'

'You spoke to him?'

'I told him you wanted to speak to him – made up an excuse about you being interested in his wretched refugees. I sent a car to the airport to meet him. He never arrived.'

Cornell placed the telephone on the table before her. 'Call him.'

'I did, earlier. Someone there told me he left Chicago for Washington on the flight I'd arranged.'

'Call again, now.'

She stared at the telephone, then lifted it, dialled, and made her enquiry. 'I see,' she said, after a moment. 'Please have him call Mrs Cornell at the White House. Yes, the White House, thank you.' She replaced the receiver, trepidation growing in her eyes. 'He never returned.'

The telephone rang. She snatched at it. The White House operator's voice informed: 'I have a call for the President from the Vatican Embassy here in Washington, ma'am. Archbishop Marchionni?'

David Kolchak had made the thirteen-fifteen flight out of Chicago O'Hare airport with only minutes to spare.

The instant the telephone call from Madelaine Cornell had ended he called a Washington number leaving his name and a message with the apologetic nun who answered saying he would be arriving later that afternoon. This done he removed his worn work-day cassock, put on heavy-soled brown brogues – the right built up an extra half-inch to compensate for the effects of his old Vietnam War injury – a pair of whipcords, a woollen shirt against the autumnal wind, and a sagging tweed sport-coat with leather patches, becoming immediately, with the addition of steel spectacles, the teacher the Jesuits had trained him to be and part of him still was.

Throwing a newer cassock and other necessary items into a leather grip, he stepped on to the street, immediately smelling chocolate from the candy manufacturers who provided much of the work for the neighbourhood. He had forgotten the odour was there, his nose blunted by years of exposure to it.

All his senses seemed sharper. *Waking from the dead*, he thought, and hailed a cab. *Or the final walk*. 'O'Hare, fast as you can,' he said.

'You got it, Professor. Nice day to fly. Where you headin'?'

'Washington.'

'Hey, the White House!'

Kolchak didn't respond, sitting hunched in the back. Just as he had started to believe he had finally cauterized his guilt, his torture was beginning again. He had strived to atone by hard work and selfless devotion to God and His broken displaced children, but it was clear – no matter how necessary the deed had been – he could not absolve himself from responsibility for it.

The cabby shrugged, smacked in a cassette, and played old Motown too loud all the way to O'Hare.

The United flight landed at Washington National on time, a little more than an hour and a half later, Kolchak leaving the plane with the main group of passengers and settling himself in their midst as they walked. At the exits he limped directly past a crisply uniformed chauffeur holding up a board displaying his name, then took a cab to an imposing address on Massachusetts Avenue, near the vice-presidential mansion. There, he announced himself and was shown into the magnificent library by a serene nun to await the return of the Papacy's representative in America from an official engagement.

He found Teilhard de Chardin's *The Phenomenon of Man* on the shelves, turned to the page already embedded in his mind and read again the words which were both the heart of his torture and the other face of the same crucial concept with which the Markarovs had taunted him. With them came the persistent, echoing question: Had he been right to preserve what was, or had he stopped, dead, the promise of what was to come? He closed his eyes, the words like branding irons in the darkness.

> *Thus from the grains of thought forming the veritable and indestructible atoms of its stuff . . . the universe goes on building itself above our heads in the inverse direction of matter which vanishes. The universe is a collector and conservator, not of mechanical energy . . . but of persons. All around us, one by one, like a continual exhalation, 'souls' break away, carrying upwards their incommunicable load of consciousness . . .*

He awoke to a firm shake of his shoulder. 'David?'

He shook himself. He felt half-drugged. It was the smothering atmosphere of the library. And sudden inactivity. His life seemed to be ruled by time and tiredness, with too little of the former and too much of the latter. He felt ill.

'Why are you here, David?'

Kolchak found his steel spectacles on his lap, curled them over his ears, and peered upward.

The saturnine face leaning over him came into focus and he was in Rome, ten years before, walking out of Fiumicino airport after a back-breaking flight out of Israel, in time to breathe the exhaust of a baking day laced with the stench of rotting garbage.

'Strike,' his greeter had explained, driving precisely and very fast through chaotic traffic; his car – unsurprisingly for Kolchak, who had known him from boyhood, washing the first of many such and being paid fairly for the task – a blood-red Ferrari. 'Garbage on every corner. One week and we're used to it. Rome! David, I need to hear accurately what you heard and saw.'

'You'll never get anyone to believe you,' he had replied. 'It might all be pure fantasy – or megalomania. It hardly seems real, here, now.'

'Megalomania is only dangerous when it's not recognized as such. As, for a time, Pius XI with Hitler. Fantasy is a lot more dangerous – it can become truth if enough people believe it. Today's science fiction is tomorrow's fact. Someone will believe. I'll make sure they do.'

The Vatican was already there, the Basilica's dome rising, the Swiss guards coming up fast, Kolchak watching the swift one-handed buttoning of the loosely opened cassock, a gesture he knew well, the practised trick of a man never caught out, always prepared, always ready – but always tempted to the edge.

'What if they don't believe? Or do – but won't act?'

'Then God will,' had been the stark reply.

Now he watched as that same short figure – thickened little by the years – opened a large globe and extracted a bottle of fine cognac.

'I've already had too much over lunch, but you look like you could do with one?'

Kolchak nodded, watching the cognac being poured with flair, the crystal balloon swirled before being handed over. 'Drink, then tell – the Devil's Welcome, as they're supposed to say in the old country. They make it all up for the tourists.'

Kolchak swallowed a mouthful and closed his eyes, letting the smooth golden fire flow over the chill in his belly.

'I hope you don't mind me saying, David, but you've aged more than is good for you. Ease up. Leave that purgatory you've built for yourself in Chicago and come here, I can use you. I'd like to.'

Kharkov wanted to laugh. Archbishop Ricardo Marchionni, Apostolic Delegate to the United States of America, socialite and multi-millionaire, and Father David Kolchak, derelict and pugnacious, attending Washington society lunches together? Instead he said: 'It didn't die with them, Ricardo, I'm sure of it.'

Marchionni positioned himself opposite on an equisitely carved seventeenth-century chair covered with the original, now faded, burgundy velvet. Kolchak wondered how many of his people he could feed – and for how long – for its value at auction. He knew the chair and all the other costly furnishings would not be found on the Washington Delegation's inventory – just as the Ferrari in Rome had not been from the Vatican motor pool. The Marchionni family paid their own way. They had to. Very few could afford their standards.

Marchionni said: 'From the beginning, David.' He paused. 'By the way, I think you're feverish.' He pointed a manicured fingernail at Kolchak's greying head.

Kolchak touched his brow and stared at the slick wetness on his fingers.

'It's over, David. Long gone. Except in your own mind, of course. You should have been born in medieval times, then you could flagellate yourself to the bone.'

'I'm serious.'

'You think I'm not? Take a look at yourself in the mirror!'

'Madelaine Cornell called me. Yes, that's right. She asked me to come to the White House. I'm supposed to be there now.'

'Why aren't you?'

'They know.'

Marchionni arose and pressed a button by the side of a perfect white marble mantel. 'You're going to bed.'

'For God's sake, listen to me!'

'Everything I do is for God's sake but in this case your need is greater than His. You need a decent bed, uninterrupted rest for about a week, and a doctor who isn't dealing daily with an overload of poverty-stricken displaced persons who speak little or no English. Jewish is best; they really understand stress from overwork and commitment – trust me. David, why don't you ever call me or return my calls? Don't suffer in silence. I'm your friend, we're brothers in Christ! We're supposed to *share*.'

'She asked me about Jerusalem.'

'Asked how?'

A pretty nun entered, cautiously. Marchionni glanced at her and shook his head. 'Wait!' he called. 'Prepare a bed for Father Kolcak. He'll be staying indefinitely. Now go.'

He sat again. 'That woman is a viper – Madelaine Cornell, not my nun – and nothing she does is without reason. And I mean reason as motive. She's easy enough to read because her motive is always advancement. Her own, through that dull Irishman who somehow got himself elected president. Oh, he's a *safe*, decent man with plenty of charm that smoothly covers both sexes, all colours, and most deviations and shades in between, but I don't sense any *steel* in that big frame. So, the First Lady called you? Every word, please, I trust your memory even though you've shredded your brain over the years.'

Kolchak repeated the conversation practically verbatim, remembering the false – he suspected, trained – modulation of the voice and the affected, European vowels. This done, he leaned back as if his race was run and exhaustion his only prize. 'What must I do now?'

'Regain your strength. Physical and spiritual. Don't worry about the White House, that's my problem. And forget Chicago for the time being. Your work there will not suffer, I promise you.'

'How can I forget Chicago!'

'You can and you will. You know you're only driving yourself so hard as a means of escape. You might as well stop and face yourself, right here, now.'

'I must know what you plan to do.'

'At this moment nothing, except ensure you are looked after. Finish your cognac then sleep well, my dear David – when I need you I shall ask for you.'

The pretty nun had returned silently. Kolchak wondered if she had remained outside throughout or whether Marchionni's power allowed him to summon her without physically touching the bell. Right then he was prepared to believe anything.

With Kolchak out of the room, Marchionni immediately placed two telephone calls. One was to the White House.

CHAPTER
SIX

Greg Lewelyn had scraped on board the flight out of Washington's Dulles airport, the television image fixed in his mind of Carolyn beside the old man Harper, as the mountain community's line of battered vehicles were driven hard into Roanoke airport then abandoned haphazardly.

He had never seen her to lost, so frightened, as she was swept by the jubilant crowd into the airport building, their banners unfurled to joyful shouts proclaiming: 'Jesus is now! Nothing can harm His chosen! We are prepared! *Rapture is here!*'

There was an air of no going back about all of it that scared him – and that was all it had taken to put him on the last flight out to Austin that Friday evening after a hurtling drive in Georgia's startling yellow VW Beetle – with her in the passenger seat, eyes shut.

He had thanked her at the barrier, she saying, sure, as he bent to kiss her on her forehead and was running for the boarding gate before she could bring her chin up for another on the lips. She had mouthed shit and had let him go. As always. Hating it. As always.

As the aircraft's nose had lifted and full thrust pushed him into his rear-end seat he heard singing and leaned out into the steeply angled aisle. The flight attendant seated on the pull-down close to him caught his eye, smiled and pointed upward. 'They're heading higher than we are!'

He raised his voice over the roar of the Super-Eight's twin tail-jets only feet behind him. 'What are they on?'

'*God!* Right across the country they've suddenly found religion. It's that creep Maddox. He's really sold them. Great for the airlines!'

'He didn't sell you?'

'He couldn't sell me underwear if I was naked on Fifth Avenue.'

The engine noise dropped as the climb angle stablized. Greg ducked his head up the aisle. 'It isn't just Maddox. It's bred into them, cradle to grave.'

She swallowed against the air-pressure change. 'You should have seen them at Dulles trying to buy their way further up the ticket-lines. It was like the place was sinking and we were the lifeboats.'

Greg shook his head. 'For them it's the world that's sinking. They're raised to believe that. They're always waiting for it to take the final plunge.'

'So God as last resort?'

'God as *everything*. That's their problem. It doesn't take too much to get a knee-jerk reaction if you're always tensed for the blow. That's what we're seeing now.'

'You seem to know a lot about them?'

He shrugged.

'Uh-oh, there goes another call.' She moved off up the aisle.

He closed his eyes.

He awoke to the crackle of the announcements for the forty-minute stop-over at Chicago before Austin, then dozed lightly until the same flight attendant came back to the rear offering magazines.

He shook his head.

'You won't believe what's happening out there,' she told him, excitedly. 'They're literally heading for the heights. Maddox is telling told them to get up high and wait. The baggage-handlers say there's a sit-in on top of the Sears Tower!'

He heard singing again. Gospel music.

She grimaced. 'More boarding.'

'You have a telephone on board?' he asked.

She grinned. 'God doesn't take complaints. Sure, follow me.' She showed him the instrument then said, 'We're going to need that aisle seat you're using. Yours is window. We're really crammed, this leg. Sorry. That a problem?'

He shook his head and called Georgia's number.

She answered on the first ring. '*Greg!* Where are you – some bar? I thought you didn't drink!'

'Chicago. Still on the plane. We'll be taking off soon for Austin.'

'Sounds like a party.'

'It is. Any more on TV? Carolyn?'

'Only Maddox talking like he's got a direct line to God. He's beginning to look that way too – really spaced out. He's on something for sure. Some of the stuff he's spouting is crazy. *Dangerous*.'

'Going for the roof-tops?'

'You heard? There's already been fatalities. Police don't seem to know what to do. They've got enough trouble handling the rubbernecks.'

'*Fatalities*, where?'

'New York. Where else?'

'I don't give a damn about New York!'

'Take it easy. She's been away from them for long enough for you to be her main influence now. She's going to be thinking about you. She won't get swept too far along their crazy ride. When you get there she'll see sense. Listen, your dad called – from the White House! He's really worried about you.'

'You mean pissed off with me. Did he say he'd spoken with John Cornell?'

'Do you know you never call him the President?'

'Did he?' Greg repeated, impatiently.

'Yes. He was with him – right there in the same room, real close to the telephone. I wanted to yell, *Hi, Mr President!*'

'You met him once.'

'I *did*?'

'He visited our house. You were hanging around somewhere out back – a gangly kid with a big Afro that made you look even skinnier.'

'I was thirteen and had breasts! Not that you noticed.'

'He wasn't the president of course – just made senator. I figured that was as high as he was going to get. I forgot about *her*. Lady Macbeth. She and Mom used to smile at each other with their teeth. Reminded me of a couple of tigresses squaring off. She was jealous of Mom's Englishness. Wanted that accent so bad she'd watch out the corner of her eye for the shape of the vowels on Mom's lips. She'd already stolen the sound. I always wanted to laugh.'

'Laughing days are gone. She's made where she was headed. The White House.'

'Yeah, but who's the President?' A take-off announcement came on. 'Did Dad say anything specific?' he asked urgently as an attendant signalled furiously.

'Wanted to know if you were with me. Safe bet, huh?'

'Better go now, Georgie, they're starting the engines.'

'Call me from Austin if there's a problem.' The whine of jets built to a roar. '*Greg! Call me anyway.*'

He returned to his seat quickly and strapped himself back in as the Super Eighty shuddered on its brakes then thundered down the runway before spearing up into the night, the lights of Chicago falling away beneath like a retreating galaxy.

The flight attendant brought him food and he stared at it, spearing meat with his fork and chewing absently, his face turned toward the port to avoid conversation with the fat Chicago-boarder who over-filled the empty seat beside him, cramping him as tight as in an F-16.

Outside, a sudden lightning flash froze the swept-back wing of the DC9 into a shining scimitar which sliced deep into his mind. He broke into a sweat as the rocking turbulence that followed added more blows to his reeling brain. He fought for control but knew there was no escape. His mind shut down and all he knew was then.

The triple-A was so heavy that through his night-vision headgear it was like a haze of uncountable green-tinged fireflies on the surface of an impossibly deep pool. It seemed harmless with only the threatening white-hot skeletal fingers of tracer shells appearing lethal amid the chaotic dance.

The hit when it came was reality, but reality in some other world. It took seconds for his mind to register that he had no control and very soon would have no life. He could not know that shrapnel had pierced his canopy and had struck his helmet, stunning him.

He ejected above the hell of exploding hot metal, knowing he must plunge back through it, braced for the inevitable piercing blows, any or all of which might, mercifully, prove fatal.

Just make it quick was his only wish, because survival seemed impossible, and what survival was there with a shattered body and damaged brain?

His velocity and his luck saved him. His parachute opened late, below the triple-A ceiling, and he floated down through the darkness toward the next hell.

He had a pistol. It even had a silencer if he needed to kill silently to save his life. He also had a lethal pill to kill himself silently.

Amidst all this noise, who hears anyone die?

They were waiting for him. And why not, he decided. He had after all been trying very hard to vaporize them. So, inevitably, they gave him a hard time. He had expected it, so the fact was milder than the expectation. The truth was they were less adept at beating than were his instructors during his survival and interrogation courses. He put that down to hate as much as lack of expertise. You can't inflict pain clinically when you're blind mad at someone. That's why the technique was to get them mad for as long as possible. It was when they started thinking about what they were going to do with you that the pain really began.

And it did begin.

The pain was survivable, he decided, almost coolly, when they started in earnest. While I hurt I'm still alive. They concentrated on his leg because he had cracked that on some part of the spinning aircraft. It might have been fractured but he could walk on it – poorly – and anyway they seemed singularly uninterested in either offering medical attention or obeying the Geneva Convention. He supposed the only deference they had toward Geneva was the fact that their leader had many billions stashed there.

They tried to frighten him with the usual expected horror stories of Muslims over-running the world, but he knew – he had seen – what kind, what depth, of lead the West had and laughed at them.

They beat him.

They preached Allah and Mohammed at him for hours until he made them understand he believed even less in their God than in the one he had already been force-fed at school – and by far more terrifying tormentors than they ever could be.

They beat him some more and he told them they were fairies who preferred boys to girls so go and jerk off in their latrine.

Then the overweight, sweating ones were changed for one slim one who spoke English with a South American accent and had the balanced good looks, fair hair, and blue eyes of a child's story-book illustration of the archangel Michael. His heart though was black, and like Lucifer he had fallen to the depths.

So the pain ended and the drugs began and his laughter ended.

For thirty-six hours, non-stop, the dark angel had probed for the greatest secret in Greg's world. The one which, found, unlocked every other.

Greg, hear me, his voice purred. Every man has his unspeakable fear. The thing that dries up the tongue, makes the skin of your scrotum crawl and contract, leaving you small and almost sexless. Emasculation does it for some. You? I think not, though it would not be your most favourite item on my menu. My friends here lean heavily on the very physical. The power drill into the eyeball. The right first, with a pause to let you get over the pain a little and believe you have some hope, some sight remaining for your old age. Then the left before you've answered all their questions because that's the way they are, cruel impulsive children without sophistication. So now you're no longer caring about surviving to old age anyway and your blind, hurting, screaming soul says, 'Fuck all of you,' and you kill yourself by simply not living any more. Waste! But we're sophisticates, you and I. And I shall find you out. Nothing can hide any more thanks to our wonderful medical researchers. Welcome to my world, Greg, I plan to open your soul.

It became for evermore in Greg's mind the time of the serpents. No wild screaming, no frantic trembling or lashing out; just still, silent fright which paralysed every inch and, seemingly, every cell, of his body – excepting his hair wherever it grew which rose like the swaying forked-tongued heads before him. It mattered not whether these were real or the result of suggestion and hallucinogens, his cell became the childhood zoo snake-pit and he the boy, frozen through the long night, waiting for the strike. Except this time there was no oblivion, no warm, safe bed, no starched uniforms, no soft caring hands. This was the nightmare without the waking.

*He knew it was simply escape or die. Even escape and die was
preferable.*

'You passing on the cheese?' asked the voice.

Greg turned.

'The cheese? You giving it a miss?' The squeezed-out eyes in the
dough-face beside him flicked to Greg's flat stomach. 'It's your
diet, right? Ha!'

'Go ahead.'

'You OK? That storm shook you up, huh? I figure, if it's your
time it's your time, know what I mean? Over now. You can relax.'

Greg reclined his seat and closed his eyes, keeping the image of
Carolyn in tight focus before him and letting the hum of the Pratt
and Whitneys numb him.

The Super-Eight touched down at Austin's Meuller Municipal
airport just before ten o'clock, delayed some twenty-three minutes
by the electrical storm.

Greg exited the aircraft fast and headed for the airport's
forecourt and the line of waiting cabs ahead of the crowd.

'Howdy! Maddox?' asked the driver, grinning widely.

Greg nodded.

The cab pulled away fast. 'Knew it. Great for the airlines, great
for me. I'm Chuck. You Christian or lion?'

Greg leaned forward. 'Pardon me?'

'With or agin him? Maddox?'

'Who's against him?'

'Plenty. Cops mostly. He's got 'em all strung out – building
barriers up around the TV station, all kinds of shit to keep these
assholes under control. Regular churches are saying he's a dick-
head but then they're missing out on the business. You Press?'

'Just visiting.'

'Heck, you sure picked your time! They're flying in by the
barrel-load to rip him up. Me I don't give a flying fuck as long as
. . .' Finger and thumb met and rubbed together.

'How close can you get to his TV station?'

'Mister, it's the only show in town. Block or two – maybe. It's
between Mardi Gras and a riot down there.'

Greg held up a twenty. 'Close as you can, OK?'

'You're not Press?' The man grinned. 'Shit!'

Greg looked out at the skyline of the city, seeing the Texas State Capitol dome, built purposely taller than the United States Capitol in Washington but dwarfed now by surrounding skyscrapers. He remembered the last time he had been here, flying himself into Bergstrom Air Force Base, a cool twenty-three year old Air Force pilot with a *whiz* reputation on a service-sponsored trip to IBM's Austin research facility. He had eaten breakfast of taco and *migas* – scrambled eggs, tortilla bits, tomatoes, and peppers – in the Officers' Club. He could taste it now. He could taste, too, what he had been then – most of which he was prepared to spit out, keeping only the steel will that could lock out everything except what he really needed. He would welcome the return of that right now.

'See that spotlight? Big *mother*? Police rigged it. That's the Maddox Tower. Won't be long now. You planning to get inside? Forget it. The place is fit to bust already. He's got his own security people working all the entrances and you don't mess with them, OK?'

'Why the spotlight?'

'You ain't heard?'

'Heard what?'

'Word is he's got people up there ready to step into space if he says so. Folks'll believe anything they're told on TV.'

'He's telling people to jump!'

'Jump? Hell no! If you're one of the chosen you just step off the edge and Jesus'll pick you right out the air. Son of a bitch, if they start that there's gonna be some ketchup on the sidewalk come mornin'!'

They turned on to Martin Luther King Jr. Boulevard and hit heavy crowds. A woman police officer broke from a group and waved them down angrily. The cab driver halted and turned around. 'Far as we go.' He looked at the twenty-dollar bill.

Greg paid him.

'You going to try for it?'

'My wife may be with Maddox. Up there.'

'Shit!'

Greg jumped out and approached the woman officer. He

pointed, having to shout over the crowd. 'My wife may be up there!'

'I'm real sorry to hear that.'

'Has anyone jumped?'

She pulled him close. 'Not yet. But they will if they let him stay on air much longer. They've got the lights burning in the Capitol right now.'

'They're *debating* whether to shut him down? Why don't they just pull the plug on the broadcast?'

'And have every liberal in the country screaming we'd violated the right of free speech? Anyway, he's got independent power – real big generators down in the basement. Got a fallout shelter down there too.'

'Not for the whole building,' said the male officer nearest her, turning away from the heaving crowds.

'Are you kidding?' she snorted. 'Maddox believes in *numero uno* – and a few little *unos* on the side.'

'Yeah, blonde with big tits.'

'Shut up, Frank, this guy's wife is in there.'

'Should have kept a tighter rein on her, buddy.'

She glared. 'Asshole.'

Greg walked away.

She came after him. 'Hey! Listen, I'll take you up to the doors – after that you're on your own, OK?' She stepped in front of him, forcing through the crowd with her nightstick, talking all the way in fast bursts, turning: 'Those security guards of his are all football-sized – they play too – but not football. Hardball! We got tied hands because he's got serious influence this part of the country – keeps the voters in line, *delivers* – know what I mean?'

They made it to the furthest barrier and ducked under it, the roadway kept clear by heavy police presence. Two fire tenders were drawn up, stationary, the men inside expectant but relaxed.

'What's going on?' she bawled up at one of them.

The fireman shook his helmeted head. 'We got orders to sit in case there's any jumpers.'

'You going to set up air-bags?'

'Sure, anyone gets out there and looks serious we'll go for it.'

'Why not now?' asked Greg, leaning back, looking up at the building.

'It's all talk. No one's that crazy!'

'It's happened in New York,' said Greg.

'You'd expect that. This is Texas. Anyhow we're stretched. We have to be ready in case there's fires someplace else. You want to try putting one of those air-bags back fast?'

Greg looked at him, hard. 'They're not all from Texas.'

The woman police officer said: 'How you gonna tell when they're serious?'

Another fire officer leaned across. 'When you see the whites of their eyes, angel.'

'I'm nobody's angel.'

'When you've seen a few jumpers you just *know*,' said the first.

She turned to Greg. 'I'm real sorry about your wife.' She held out her hand, her grip strong. 'There's the lobby. Hey, good luck – and watch those good ol' boys in there, OK?'

Greg nodded and made for the towering floodlit building, the rumbling of the expectant crowd all around him. *Christian or lion?* He knew which he felt like. His fingers gripped the tape-cassette he'd taken from his bag as he'd come through the crowd. He would use their own gullibility against them.

'Hold it right there,' growled a security guard weighing the bad side of two hundred and fifty pounds, meaty arm straight out in Greg's chest.

'I have to see Maddox.'

'That's *Mr* Maddox – or Reverend Maddox. If you're planning to donate, today we taking phone donations only. Use your credit card. Take a walk, find a call-box.'

'I think my wife's up there.'

The man laughed and turned to two others wearing the same tan uniforms. 'Another one can't hold his woman!'

One called across: 'Well, if she didn't come here for it she's surely had it by now!'

Greg felt the heat build inside and used it. 'Listen, you thick fuck!' He thrust the tape-cassette in the guard's startled face. 'Your boss wants this tape – hear me? He's not going to be pleased if he finds you sent me away.'

'You watch your mouth!' growled the man, his anger blunted by indecision. He waved the others back. 'I'll take care of this. What's on that tape?'

'What's he waiting for up there?' Greg stabbed a finger at the heavy gilt crucifix bearing Maddox's profiled image in relief at its apex, pinned to the tan uniform. '*Who* should be on there?' he snapped.

The guard's mouth opened. 'This some kind of gag?'

Greg pointed back at the crowd. 'You don't think all this started with just some crazy story told him by mountain folk? Had to be more than that, right?' He dug in his windcheater and came out with his NSA identification. 'They were part of a government programme – an investigation of the paranormal – I was part of it too but I broke free because I found Jesus.' He held up the tape again. 'Maybe I *heard* Jesus!'

'Holy shit!'

Hallelujah, brother.

'How—?' the guard began.

Greg cut him off: 'My wife is one of them. It's her folks who disappeared. We recorded them just before they went to the Lord. The tape was taken up to Washington. I stole it and flew straight here. Look – here's my ticket, OK? Hear what I'm saying?'

'Yeah!'

'OK, so check out you've got Carolyn Lewelyn up there. You have a list or something?'

'Sure. We're organized. Say that name again?'

'Lewelyn. Carolyn Lewelyn.'

'You want to spell that?'

Greg leaned over and stabbed the keyboard rapidly.

The guard peered at the screen. 'Yeah, she's here. Got picked up from the airport. Like you said, she was one of the first.' He looked up from the screen, impressed.

'Good. Now listen up. Reverend Maddox doesn't know we succeeded with the tape. He surely doesn't know I stole it. There's a whole bunch of people up there and he's not going to want the word out before he gets it. Right?'

'Right! He's on air right now. He'll be real mad if he doesn't hear it first. I'll call—'

'Listen—' Greg glanced at his name-tag. 'Robert. Is that Bob?'

'Bob's fine but folks here mainly call me Bubba.'

'Bubba, you want to try explaining all of this to someone up there? Over a telephone?'

The guard lifted his hand from the instrument. 'Yeah. OK, I'll take you.'

'You're needed down here, Bubba. That crowd out there is growing fast. I've just walked through it and there's talk of forcing their way . . .' Greg pointed upward.

'Hell, you can find it real easy. Just take that elevator all the way. There's a guy dressed just like me up top. You just tell him Bubba said it's OK. He'll take you to the producer. Got that?'

'Got it.'

Greg stepped inside the elevator. The touch panel for the penthouse on the twenty-first floor read express and meant it. The smooth upward tug was over in seconds. Through the steel doors he heard a rising, hauntingly familiar, garbled babble of noise. Tongues. Hundreds speaking tongues. His words to Larry Maine in the desert whispered: *When I hear it there's a feeling of being on the verge of something unexplained, something powerful, something – if you could cut through that jumble of unintelligible sounds – world-shaking. It only needs understanding.*

He stepped out into what could have been the Tower of Babel.

CHAPTER
SEVEN

Sam Lewelyn drove through the entrance to the walled neighbourhood estate comprised of low substantial bungalows, spotting a security guard smoking guiltily in a parked sedan, lights off, in the darkest space beneath trees. Circled Wagon Syndrome, he thought; we've never got over it: we've contracted, not expanded.

He halted the Lincoln outside the darkened, grubby windows of Clair Morrison's home. Never trust a drunk, he thought, heaving himself out – though in Morrison's case he was prepared to believe that his lies preceded his alcoholism.

He walked to the rear of the bungalow ready to flatten the back door if necessary, but found it unlocked.

Morrison was in the small box bedroom he had finally retreated to over the bad years, abandoning others as their condition deteriorated, like a soldier in a hopeless rearguard action. He lay visible in the spill from the passage light, facing the wall, bedclothes tucked up tight around him.

Sam noticed two things immediately: first there was no bottle by the bed – for which he might offer congratulations before opening business – next, almost simultaneously, the hint of cordite that instantly made the first redundant.

Using his handkerchief Sam switched on the bedside light and, leaning over Morrison's still head on the pillow, pulled the covers back carefully. The small burnt hole behind the ear was not made by any gun either of them might conceivably have owned. He sighed as he gazed down at the wasted face, thinking that death had already occurred for Clair Morrison years before and this was just the formality.

He touched nothing more, straightened up and stood in the

mean gloom of the bedside lamp, putting pieces together but finding nothing that would fit the hole that was as good as a signature to those who knew a professional hit with a mob weapon: .22 calibre un-jacketed soft-nosed round, fired point-blank through a fully silenced barrel – a custom-made executioner's pistol of little use beyond its purpose of silent, close-quarters killing when the assassin was likely to be known to the victim and the nudge of the fat barrel behind the ear felt perhaps as the touch of an affectionate hand. The report would have been less than Lewelyn's own sigh.

Did you know? Sam wondered, doubting it. What a cheating way to die: asleep, no chance to say what farewells there were to say, nor remember what was worth remembering. He swore.

'Sorry, Clair,' he said, meaning it, for if neither the deed nor the blame was his, the finger that had pointed the way for its execution surely was. Then he went to the living room to find the bug.

He found several. He even found the miniature voice-activated infra-red recording device, which, in its cold state-of-the-art way, told him more than he wanted to know. He nearly trashed it – along with his pride in his near-lifetime of duty with the agency – but lowered the heat in his blood and pocketed it instead. He left as he had come but carrying more anger.

He drove to where he had seen the security guard; found him asleep, so rapped his heavy gold wedding band on the sedan's glass.

The guard started, his hand reaching instantly for his holstered weapon but Sam had already raised both palms so they could be seen. Recognizing the Lincoln the man stepped quickly from his car. 'Jesus, one of us almost died! Me from a coronary or you from a bullet. *God-damn!*'

'Dangers of sleeping on the job, son.'

'Yeah.' He shook himself.

'Moonlighting?'

The guard grinned.

Sam could see now that he was barely out of his teens. 'Nothing happens most of the time?'

'Yeah.' The grin tilted.

'Did tonight, son. Sorry.'

'What d'you mean?'

Sam pointed into the sedan. 'That radio get the police-band?'

'Sure. What—?'

'Death. I hope you logged every non-resident vehicle that came through tonight because that's the first thing they're going to ask.'

'You mean *murder*?'

'Murder *One*, planned and executed with malice aforethought. Name of Morrison. Back there in four-oh-nine. You've seen me visit him before.'

'Shit!' The guard spun and slapped the sedan roof, hard. 'Why me?'

'Because you took the job. Tell me about strangers?'

'Hey, how do I know you didn't—'

Lewelyn held his NSA pass close to the scared face. 'He was one of ours. A lush – you should know that if you've even half-way been doing your job – but he still had things in his head we preferred remained there.'

'I've got to call the cops!'

'Get yourself straight first,' Sam advised. 'Check out you filled your sheet.'

'Yeah, OK. Thanks. You sound like you know security work real well.'

Sam barely smiled.

The guard ran his finger down a list of vehicle registrations. 'OK, we had five come in non-resident on this shift: three were kids dating, the other two were deliveries, one pizza, one flowers.'

'Flowers? This time of night?'

'I asked that. She said they get late orders and she does 'em after dinner.'

'Pizza? Where from?'

'Hut, up the road a-ways. He had''em stacked in the van. They eat pizza here like you wouldn't believe. I know the delivery guy, OK?'

Sam eyes flicked to the car. 'Maybe you slept though? Missed someone? You didn't hear me till I was right there.'

'I saw you some in. Logged your registration. You've been here before, I'd know that monster any time. I didn't sleep until just now, I swear to God.'

'You missed someone, son. Unless it was the florist or pizza guy who did it?'

The guard forced a laugh. 'That's only on TV!'

'Call the cops.'

The guard reached inside the sedan then turned, smiling hopefully, but scared. 'There was the breakdown truck for Mr Morrison. But that was real early, when I first came on.'

Sam closed his eyes. 'When did you last see him driving a car?'

'He takes cabs, sure – but there's a Merc 300 in his garage, I've seen it when he flips the door up. He's got his liquor store in there. I mean *really*, you should see it!'

'He hadn't had a driving licence in years. The last time he drove, it was up Pennsylvania the wrong way. I bailed him.'

'*Shit*.'

'The truck have a name on the panel?'

'No.'

'Sure?'

He dipped back into the car and scanned his clip-board. 'No name. Got the registration though. Gunked up to hell but I got it. See?'

Sam copied it. 'Describe the operator?'

'Hey, what's a mechanic look like? Oily, dirty, wearing coveralls. Never got out of the truck. I wasn't making ID, OK? Average.'

'Like the truck?'

'Yeah.'

'US or Jap: the truck?'

'US, definitely. GMC, right across the front.'

'Makes a change.' Sam closed his small diary and turned for the Lincoln.

'Hey? You're not leaving! They'll want to talk with you!'

'I'll talk to *them*, son.' He held up his ID again then hip-pocketed it. 'We do it a little different. Don't sleep on the job any more. One day you'll dream you're dying and it'll be happening. It's that kind of world. Do it or dump it. Hear me?'

'Yo.' Shoulders slumped, the guard reached for his radio.

Sam released the brake and pulled the Lincoln away.

He had two options as he saw it. Drive straight to NSA headquarters at Fort Meade, guns blazing, or exact the cost his anger demanded with his own weapons and on his own terms.

Discarding the first – despite its obvious stupidity – took a great deal of effort and a hefty *filet* washed down by the best part of a bottle of good Californian red and an invitation by telephone to Chief of Detectives Hugh Edwards at Washington Metropolitan Police headquarters on Indiana Avenue to join him when he completed his business.

Edwards arrived at the small downtown restaurant in time to help consign the wine bottle to its rest.

'You eating?' offered Sam.

Edwards shook his jowly black face and sat in the booth. He knew Sam from service days: Edwards, even then a cop, albeit military and uniformed keeping order in Saigon, while Sam was quite the other thing, causing havoc while swinging illegally with Long Range Patrol Groups in and out of Cambodia and Laos. 'What's eating *you*?' asked Edwards.

'How far off is your pension?'

'You know damn well. A year. *Less*. Ten months.'

'Want to collect?'

'Course not. I plan to live on my stock investments.'

Sam pointed a fork at the door. 'Best walk then.'

Edwards settled himself deeper into the tired buttoned leather. 'I'll stay for the laughs.'

'You'll be disappointed.'

'Do the best you can.'

'Right now I can't tell you much.'

'Right now, or never?'

Sam shrugged.

'But you'd like my help anyway.'

'Yes.'

'This to do with your Orwellian brothers out in Baltimore?'

Sam paused and looked at him. 'Big Brother may have gone off the rails.'

Edwards muttered an expletive then raised one finger for attention, then two, pointing at a very old bottle on the bar shelf. 'I've said it for years: you people have got too much power. You've left us all behind. You live in a different world. You're right. I don't want to hear.'

'You checked the registration I gave you?'

'No one remotely concerned with your people.'

'I knew that. You've just left the scene?'

Edwards nodded and accepted the dusty bottle of Armagnac

and two goblets from the proprietor. 'The question is, *is* it a mob hit or meant to look like one?'

'You're the detective, you work it out.'

Edwards poured, sipped, and shuddered with pleasure. 'I could haul you in for withholding information.'

'I need information, I don't have a damn thing to withhold.'

'Just tell me what you've got.'

'No. And you'll thank me for it. I have the feeling this is one of those where nobody comes out well – if they come out at all.'

Edwards peered gloomily into the aged liqueur. 'The last time I saw this town really running scared was – ' he looked up ' – back in the bad old days of Watergate.'

'Now, what makes you think this is political?'

'*Everything* here is political. Specifically, I'd say anything that involves the President is *for sure* political, wouldn't you?'

'I haven't mentioned the President.'

'You want to know how many phone calls we've had the last couple of days from good honest folks – and that makes a change – saying they'd seen the President sneaking around town in the small hours? Just had one old woman tell me face to face at the homicide scene. Swears she saw him across the street from her window. No motorcade, no Secret Service, no protection – except one miserable-looking black guy waiting in a family sedan and a big feller built like a football player but too old. Her words, sorry. I wouldn't have believed it except she ID'd this white Lincoln Conti parked on the street with the sedan. No mistake, her husband used to own one in blue.' Edwards tilted his head. 'Parked outside right now.'

'I need a name, Hugh. A name that fits the registration.'

Edwards sipped again. '*Jesus*, that's good!' He noticed a chip in the goblet's crystal and picked at it. 'What you're asking for is time. Right? Before we go marching all over someone's reputation? How come it's only spooks, diplomats, and politicians whose reputation has to be protected? If a cop goes off the rails no one grubs around trying to get him back on the tracks?'

Sam raised his glass. 'Cheers.'

'I didn't say I'd give it to you. If this were *official* you wouldn't be sitting down with me in Henri's place. And you wouldn't be casting gloom and doom over my pension rights by me being here. So who's calling it, Sam?'

'The woman said it.'

Edwards stared down, miserably, into his glass again. 'I don't like surprises. I may have been boring and predictable all my life – but I'm here and there's many who aren't.'

Sam stood up.

'I didn't say I wouldn't,' complained Edwards.

'You didn't say you would – and I don't have all night.'

Edwards took a print-out from his breast pocket. 'Your car or mine?'

Sam read the details. 'You've done all you need to do, Hugh. Go home and watch TV.'

'You kidding? TV? Goddamn world's gone crazy. Listen, you're too old for this. I know you're the man's buddy – but tell him to sort out his own problems. You've retired and all you've got left to do in the Puzzle Palace is warm the new guy over. Let's get drunk.'

Sam leaned over him. 'The black plastic bag you just filled got its contents from my pushing. You understand me?'

'So suddenly it's personal.'

'I'll call if I need help.'

'Call *before* you need help, you'll live longer,' advised Hugh Edwards.

John Cornell arose from his chair in the Oval Office. 'Archbishop, it's good to see you. Now don't misunderstand me, a visit from you is always a pleasure, but I hope you're not bringing bad news? There's enough of that on television. Have you been watching that lunacy tonight!'

Ricardo Marchionni smiled thinly. 'With all respect, Mr President, this *is* America!' The smile slipped away. 'You expected bad news? The assassination attempt? I've heard nothing more. I'm probably less well informed than you. Tragic.'

'The priest always knows first with death,' said Cornell, heavily Irish. 'My old grandmother taught me that! However, it's not entirely tragic if he still lives.'

'And according to *that* will continue to do so?' Marchionni indicated the murmuring television set. 'I've heard the advice he's giving you – and his play on the prophecies in the Book of Revelation. He would do well to take equal note of the words of the final verses: "I give warning to everyone listening to the words of prophecy in this book: should anyone add to them God will add to him the plagues described; should anyone take away from the words of this prophecy God will take away his share in the tree of life."'

'Maddox is a cheap hood. I know. I've seen examples of his accounts. I plan on doing something about him and those like him who exploit people's susceptibilities.'

'Mr President, you underestimate the power of television. Without it, yes, perhaps he is nothing more than a *cheap hood*, but with it he is a threat. A very potent threat. As is being demonstrated tonight.'

'I have to admit I'm shocked by what's going on across the country. And Austin! That's almost unbelievable. I hope they keep that situation under control.'

'Were you surprised by the events in Iran when the Ayatollah Khomeini had the people whipped into religious fervour and out on the streets and – forgive me – inside your Embassy?'

'Hardly the same thing.'

'Because that was Iran and this is America? Or because they were Muslims and we are Christians?'

'Somewhere between the two, I'd say.'

Marchionni's meagre smile returned. 'Spoken like the consummate politician you are. But realistically there can be no in between. The matter is too serious to be pushed sideways, or worse, ignored.'

'It certainly isn't being ignored. The situation is being monitored by the hour.'

'I'm pleased to hear it. I shall inform the Holy Father upon my return.'

'He's aware of what's occurring?'

'Wouldn't you be informed if there were anti-American demonstrations across Italy?'

'Of course. But this isn't—'

'Anti-Rome?' Marchionni interrupted. 'Not at present, but the nonsense being spouted can easily lead to a backlash when nothing *miraculous* occurs. The Roman Church has been a standing target for anti-establishment and fundamentalist groups of one form or another for centuries.'

Cornell leaned forward purposefully on to his carved desk. 'You said on the telephone you wanted to speak to me – confidentially – as one Catholic to another? I have to be frank, that sort of distinction – *separation*, if you will – bothers me.'

Marchionni indicated the Oval Office. 'Naturally so. You are responsible for the needs of all Americans.'

'And responsible *to* all Americans, Archbishop,' reminded Cornell.

'This was in my mind when I called you, Mr President.'

'Coincidentally, I was about to call you when yours came through. You haven't lost an itinerant priest, have you?'

'You mean Father Kolchak? Not lost, found. He is in my care now. Almost total collapse. Overwork, of course. He doesn't understand moderation – and rest for him is not in the language. You may have seen his efforts reported in the press? Forgive me, I'm being disingenuous – I know you have, he was coming to see you. He told me. Perhaps it was meant to be confidential?'

Cornell said nothing.

Marchionni continued. 'This intended meeting was real? Or conjured up by his stressed mind?'

'My wife had arranged it. She becomes enthusiastic about certain matters – develops pet projects, good works, that sort of thing. Whether I'd actually have had time to speak with your Father Kolchak is doubtful. The way things are I've barely had time to think clearly. Madelaine felt I should meet with someone working – as she puts it, at *ground level* – in the real world and the Eastern European refugee problem spilling on to our doorstep is as real as anything . . .' Cornell paused. 'It's easy to become cocooned in here. *Caged* is probably a better metaphor because of the heavy security and, well, the truth is there's always the danger of being fed only what some might want you to eat. I imagine the Holy Father suffers in the same way.'

'Vatican intrigues subsided after the Borgias,' smiled Marchionni. 'However, he is very well informed of the outside world.'

Cornell glanced at his watch and said bluntly, 'So what's all this about, Archbishop?'

Marchionni's finger aimed directly at Cornell's heavy gold Rolex. 'Precisely that. Time.'

'I don't understand.'

'With respect, I think you do. Or perhaps you may not *realize* you understand?'

Cornell laughed. 'When I was young listening to you priests at mass, it struck me that the reason you're all so ambiguous, so prone to speaking in riddles and metaphors, was because you thought we were all stupid peasants. Now I know you talk that way because it's impossible to explain in plain English an abstract like God to beings who can't exist without the materiality of flesh, blood, and bones.'

'But *faith* in God is not an abstract concept – it is far too tangible, indeed demonstrated in very real human form by human acts – by human beings giving all.'

'Like Kolchak?'

'I meant *literally* giving their lives. Martyrdom. But you are right, sometimes it is harder to *live* for the Church, the Faith, than die for it. To obey its impositions may be harder still. So hard, in fact, as to be impossible for some.'

'Are you here to question my faith, Archbishop?'

Marchionni studied him briefly. 'I'll give you a parable. It was Christ's way and perhaps we both need his guidance now.'

Cornell raised his eyebrows. 'Very well.'

'There was a man who sought power: more power than he already had. He was, shall we say, rising in his business. One day he was offered the chance to achieve his ambitions. *Why not?* he thought, although the offer entailed certain risks and the technicalities involved were not within his expertise or experience – nor indeed that of others he briefly consulted. Thus, by accepting, he would be placing himself in the hands of the seller, a move sometimes fatal in his business. And there was a further consideration. The offer – entailing information and certain claimed expertise of an extraordinary nature – came directly from employees of his deadliest enemy.'

'Sounds like one heck of a risky venture?'

'Nevertheless, let us say our man succumbed; allowed his ambition to make his decision for him and acted positively and immediately without sufficient preparation, approaching others in his field, partners, even superiors, making promises, offering deals or favours. Or was it was quite the reverse? Perhaps he warned – even threatened – these associates before offering them . . . *silence*?

Keeping the claims made by – shall we call them defectors from his enemy's camp – utterly secret. Buried, for good. You're following me?'

Cornell said: 'Go on.'

'In exchange our ambitious man is given all he desires. Or perhaps he is offered more? He had potential for higher office back then and some may have recognized this in him.' Marchionni's black pupils rested deliberately on Cornell. 'But he is told he must wait for this greater prize. The time is not quite right. *Patience*, they say, it will come.' He shifted, smoothing his robes, and smiled. 'He is human. Perhaps he becomes impatient? Or curious?'

Cornell interrupted. 'Or perhaps, Archbishop, something happens to him that takes away his chance of this higher prize? Making him bitter? A virtual recluse? A serious accident, say?' He leaned back. 'But it's your parable.'

Marchionni studied his rings for a moment. '*Whatever* his reasons, he decides he must look at what he has bought. Will it work? Were the claims of the defectors all they purported to be? Soon he is totally, utterly, hooked by this thing and can't let go. He becomes obsessed, so obsessed that although he has made promises to the contrary, he orders work carried out; expensive work needing special facilities, research, experiments; he spends more money than he is allowed, then must explain this expenditure.'

'And he cannot.'

'Indeed he cannot. So he hides these costs from those who have power over him and does so successfully. Then a change occurs – at the highest level. Someone is appointed who does not care for his autocratic, secretive, even cavalier attitude. He finds himself under scrutiny. So there's a growing crisis, he can no longer juggle or invent figures, his source of funding is dry, he must look elsewhere, perhaps even sell assets?'

'Assets?' Cornell repeated, trepidation barely masked in his voice. 'What assets?'

'His company's greatest asset is its knowledge. There are many prospective buyers – too many in fact – to whom that knowledge would be priceless. They would be willing – eager – to pay whatever price was asked. A complete seller's market.' Marchionni hesitated. 'The problem is, in the wrong hands, this knowledge is deadly.'

Cornell eyes fixed on Marchionni's pampered face. 'Saving your cloth, Archbishop, you want to walk out that door you better give me all of this. Now.'

Marchionni spread his long, almost feminine fingers. 'That's why I'm here, Mr President.'

Madelaine Cornell watched Marchionni's limousine draw away and made immediately for the Oval Office, determined to know the outcome of the meeting without delay. She had never felt so out of control of her life – *their* lives – and the feeling was unendurable.

Cornell sat, facing the Washington night through the bay window, not turning as she entered.

She sat across from him, feeling ridiculous; a visitor, an underling: she wanted to reach across the desk and strike him but even reactive anger seemed futile. He hadn't changed; circumstances had. 'Well?' she demanded.

'Seems you were right. According to Marchionni, Kolchak was Kent's man. Once Kolchak discovered what they intended and Kent arrived in Jerusalem in answer to his distress call he made straight for Rome with his story. He explained he had become involved for humanitarian reasons: helping refugees seek political asylum, said he'd been told the Markarovs were scientists wanting to defect – his people – Ukrainian Catholics, forbidden to practise their faith. You have to remember when this was. This story was perfectly reasonable then.' He shrugged as if to say the past was not his responsibility. 'This couldn't have been further from the truth – according to Kolchak's report to the Vatican. He said he was with them for a week – and by the end of it was convinced they were atheists and probably Fascists too. They seemed unable to keep their mouths shut. You were right, they taunted him – seemed unable to resist it, crowed about what they could do to Rome, Islam, America – to anyone not prepared to help them. He said if he had not been a priest he would have killed them in Jerusalem without hesitation.'

'Who did kill them?'

'Wait. The Vatican needed someone inside NSA. Someone who could reason with Kent or block what he was doing but first had to find out all he could before showing his hand. Clair Morrison was their man. He told us much of it himself – showed us, through the video – but hid Rome's involvement; hid the heart of it behind the lie of his own thwarted ambition, behind apparent envy and jealousy – none of it genuine – which I accepted as real. I felt pity for him, wanted to make things right, I even promised I would. He was in a tough dilemma: Church or country? So he walked me right down the middle-line of half-truths hoping he wouldn't be tripped up. He nearly tripped *himself* up, admitting he almost became a Jesuit himself.'

She shook her head in exasperation. 'John, who killed them!'

'As far as Rome is concerned – Marchionni speaking – their hands are clean. They asked Morrison for what we'd term Threat Assessment and were handed a *fait accompli* instead: threat terminated. Kolchak ran to Marchionni today, fearing – after your questions about Jerusalem and Russian recordings – that I'd began an investigation into the Makarovs' murder. In his position I might have come to the same conclusion.'

'All right, I was heavy-handed. So Morrison took matters into his own hands. But *who* did it? Who in their right mind sets a car alight then drives it at another!'

'Religion moves people as nothing else does.'

'That means you know but won't say.'

'It means Marchionni's not saying and I'm not asking.'

She fell silent, angry, distrusting, watching his eyes.

After a moment he said: 'Bungled assassination or suicide – whichever – it was done.'

'And Kent? What were Rome's plans for him if he *hadn't* listened to reason?'

'As far as they were concerned, once the Makarovs were dead, their work was dead also.'

'They really believed that?'

'Kent was appallingly burned. Hospitalized for months. And according to Kolchak the Markarovs had made it clear that everything they knew was in their heads.'

'What about the equipment in the church?'

'Abandoned when they bolted, apparently. It had nothing to do with what they were offering Kent. One of those pre-*glasnost* exchange projects Moscow was big on at that time. The

Markarovs' ticket out of Russia, I guess. Their field – paranormal studies, energy levels from religious artefacts or something equally crazy.'

'So Kent survived, thrived, Rome solved nothing, and we're here fighting him now? Do they want you to take up cudgels for them? "Fight the good fight but don't involve us"? Is that it? Is that why Marchionni was here? Reminding you of your Catholicism? Your duty to Holy Mother Church?'

Cornell watched the lights of rushing vehicles and worried about Sam. He wondered how it felt to love a woman completely then lose her completely – to death. How hard was it to go on at Sam's age? Christ! At *his* age.

'John, I want answers.'

He remained turned away. 'Genesis. In the beginning Kent heard – we don't know how – that the Markarovs wanted to defect. He heard too they had something big. Probably he was given a taster – results of experiments, whatever. Collateral. He saw the potential and certainly the dangers in the concept. He talked with the people *you* cultivate so well – those who influence decisions, who are capable of nudging me – or the next candidate – into the White House with the size of their bank-books and the depth of their power. The ones who rely on stability in this nation to remain what they are and retain all they have.'

He glanced at the TV. 'You see what's happening on there tonight? Maddox and his cock-a-mamie claims? Imagine that multiplied a millionfold? *Multi*-millionfold? Kent did, and saw the consequences. Chaos. So he warned them: it's dangerous enough as a concept *without* research and development – I'm guessing, but that's how I would have made my pitch in his shoes. Then he offered to buy it and bury it – for a price. I believe *this* is what Morrison knew and was hiding from me. He hinted at it but fell short of saying it out loud.'

'What price?' she demanded, because this was her world.

He turned and spread his arms, expansively. 'This? NSA first, then the White House? Why not? George Bush had CIA before he got the vice-presidency, then the presidency.'

'Kent is a burned-up *cripple*!' she objected, furiously. 'He'd never get the nomination. He couldn't do the job! The travelling? The banquets? *Television*, for God's sake!'

Cornell nodded. 'But promises would have been made *before* what occurred in the desert.'

'Now he's reneging on the deal? That's what you're saying?'

'Not according to Rome. Marchionni closes the book. It ends with the killings and Kent staying silent afterwards because at least he survived *and* got NSA.'

'You believe that?'

He paused. 'I believe he's still working with whatever the Markarovs gave him as collateral.'

'I don't understand why Marchionni admitted to anything?'

'Something triggered his decision. Most likely Morrison reported my visit. Then Kolchak turned up claiming you called asking pointed questions that could easily have come from me. Kolchak is a wreck apparently. I'd guess Marchionni couldn't be sure what he might have given away coming to see me alone. I see Marchionni's visit as Rome conducting damage limitation. Controlling the flow of information, the degree of admission, of guilt, of blame if any.'

Madelaine Cornell felt exhausted. She wished she had never forced the issue of Kent. She wanted everything to be as it was: comfortable, safe; the first term secure and a better than good chance for re-election in a second. But now? Now might have been a different world. And she hated it.

'I don't trust them,' she stated. 'Rome.'

'Madelaine, there's more. Marchionni suspects – probably *knows* – their Intelligence capability is quite extraordinary – there's a scandal bubbling inside NSA. He's afraid it could break very soon and really fears the consequences. That was made plain. Kent before a Congressional Committee – worse! a Grand Jury – is Rome's nightmare.' He paused. 'And not a rosy dream for me.'

'I don't want to hear.'

'Remember that night I returned from the Mojave? You suggested Kent could be siphoning money from other legitimate authorized projects to fund whatever he had hidden under the desert?'

'For once I wish you'd told me to mind my own goddamn business.'

'Marchionni believes Kent had run out of options and for the last year has been getting funds from other sources.'

She no longer wanted answers. 'Don't tell me, I don't want to hear this.'

'NSA has a lot to trade. Their eye is on the world – everywhere. What they can see, certain people would pay millions for.'

'Oh my God, the Arabs!'

'It isn't limited to them.'

She crushed fear with anger. 'This could finish you. He's *your* man. Inherited or not, *you've* kept him in place. It was your weakness that allowed him to do this. You fool, you've ruined everything I've achieved! God damn you!' She was pale and close to tears. 'What are you going to do about it? You're fighting for your political life! *Our* existence!'

He shook his head and gave a weary smile. 'Hardly our existence? No one ever got this job for life.'

'You can't believe we'd remain accepted in society?'

He chuckled. 'Richard Nixon seemed to get along well enough.'

'Listen to me. There's no way I'm crossing the lawn to that helicopter for the last time with the entire goddamn world watching! I don't care what you have to do to spare me that – just do it!'

'That's easy, Madelaine. You can go out the rear, I'll do the lawn walk alone.'

Her eyes flared with hope. 'Lester Stansfield? As Secretary of Defense he's Kent's direct boss, right? Dump this on him. He's after the presidency anyway – so kill his chances and save your own hide at the same time.'

'I could ask for Lester's resignation but he could plead ignorance, refuse to resign, and throw it back at me.'

'Then fire him!'

'If I fire him for being unaware – essentially for incompetence – the same charge can be levelled at me. I should have confided in him. It would be said I mismanaged the investigation – though of course it never was that . . . just a series of events that turned into what we have now: an explosion waiting to happen. No one's going to accept excuses, Madelaine, least of all Congress.' Cornell looked at his telephones, his mind momentarily elsewhere, then added: 'And there's always the danger that when you fire your own appointee you're displaying your own deficiencies. I could call in the cabinet but there's every chance I couldn't control the meeting

– and certainly not the decisions. There'll be severe differences of opinion on how to deal with this. Some won't want to keep it under wraps – they'll be scared of a leak, and rightly so. I'm afraid the issue would be too sensitive for the usual loyalties.'

'So forget the cabinet, forget Stansfield, Kent's the enemy, deal with him.'

'How?'

'Any damn way you have to!'

CHAPTER
EIGHT

The guard standing by the lift of Robert Maddox's television ministry was reduced almost to stupor by the sound emanating from the mass of disciples crammed into the rooftop studio, filling seats and stepped aisles, even spilling into camera areas and out through jammed-open doors into the entry lobby, which, with its icons, careful lighting, closed-circuit screens, and hi-tech donation-collection points was both marketplace for and shrine to the TV evangelist – with a nod to Christ.

The sound was loud but not strident nor discordant; harmonious yet discrete: and above all, unworldly.

Greg Lewelyn had never hear *tongues* in such magnitude, such force. The effect was extraordinary, even hypnotic, his mind instantly rebelling as he sensed himself being sucked into the maelstrom of energies and emotions being created by the swaying crowd.

He saw Maddox, multiplied on the screens, slumped in prayer, renewing his energies, his distinctive, strident voice temporarily silenced by exhaustion – though his marathon live telecast went on.

Standing behind him on the set, eyes closed, arms outstretched upward, lips moving rapidly with unintelligible sounds, was Carolyn.

The guard laid his hand on Greg's shoulder, his grip unyielding, his head bent close against the noise, his breath nicotine-tainted, his voice an un-Christian growl. 'Where'd you come from, hoss?'

Grey didn't fight the grip. He pointed at one of the TV screens. 'Bubba sent me up. That's my wife.'

'The mountain gal?'

Greg nodded.

The guard frowned. 'You sure don't look like you came down from any mountain?'

'Her name's Carolyn Lewelyn, right? Here.' Greg showed his driver's licence.

The guard studied it, still frowning, then released his grip. 'OK. There's no seats left. Just stand at back and don't give me no problems.'

Greg joined the edges of the crowd at the entry doors, waited for the guard to sink into a chair and lose interest then started through the crush, the rapturous state of the congregation allowing him to shoulder his way forward almost unhindered.

As if by some unseen signal the noise reduced, perfectly co-ordinated, to a rustling murmur, then silence, as Maddox stood from his praying.

He opened his arms, his smile wide and dentally perfect, his hold on the people relentless, his oratory messianic.

'Why are we here, my friends? You all, in person, and across the nation many thousands more watching right now, standing with us in spirit, in prayer, in the love of Jesus and, soon, God willing, in deed? Why? *Because the signs promised by the Lord are upon us.* Can anyone truly believe the events happening in the world today were not foretold in the Holy Bible? Is it just coincidence that the Book of Revelation describes – *in the events leading to the final days* – the woman upon whose head is a crown of twelve stars? Where do we see that emblem today? On the flag of the European Federation. And the woman? Revelation seventeen, verse nine, is clear: "The woman sits on seven hills." Rome sits on seven hills! Rome the whore, Rome the idolater, Rome who spawned the new Europe. A new Europe potentially more powerful, economically and militarily, than anyone in the entire world. More powerful even than *the United States of America!*'

Maddox slumped as though all of his strength had deserted him, then pulled himself up wearily, as if for a final battle. He pointed at suspended large-screen TV monitors.

'We know the head of the new Federation has been struck down. We have seen the pictures on our television screens, in bloody detail. We have seen them on these very screens here tonight. I remember the time of the Kennedy assassination, watching those dreadful pictures from Dallas and thinking, dear God, no one can survive that! I was right. I knew I was right. My common sense told me that was true no matter what the news said about attempts at revival at Bethesda.

'There were false prophets then who maintained the President Kennedy's wound had been foretold, that these were events of Biblical proportions, events heralding the time of *Rapture*, but John Kennedy died and the false prophets were shown to be practising their deceit on a gullible world.

'My friends, we all know now that John Kennedy was no saint. He was a sinner. He was a man. He was not the Beast. The events foretold in the Book of Revelation were yet to come three decades later. That time ran out yesterday. We saw a wound inflicted on a man which no mortal should survive. Yet, he has survived. He lives. And he will grow stronger. Revelation states absolutely clearly, "The head-wound should be fatal but that the receiver will survive." The wound belongs to the Beast. Revelation, sixteen, eight: "The beast that thou sawest was and is not, and shall ascend out of the bottomless pit and go into perdition and they that dwell on the earth shall wonder." What does this mean? Those who shall wonder are those whose names were not written in the book of life from the foundation of the world. They shall be deceived when they behold the beast. Deceived by that old serpent which is Satan.'

He drew himself up and brought both hands crashing on to the rostrum before him, sweat spraying from his streaming face.

'*Now* is the time of *Rapture*! Those whose names were written in the book of life, those who have stood beside the Lord will stand with Him today on high. Those who have cast Him from their lives, who passed on the other side, who ignored, who scorned His Holy Word, will today surely be cast aside and left to corruption in a world irredeemably corrupt with sin and disease. Hear the words of Revelation: "Outside the dogs, sorcerers, whoremongers, murderers, and idolaters, and whosoever loveth and maketh a lie." Does that sound familiar?

'But not for us such vileness! We are the Chosen Ones. All our lives we have prepared for this moment, and, finally, it is here. Our bodies will be perfect, fit to sit beside our Lord Jesus whose own perfect body arose from the dead into the air to sit on the right hand of God, His Father in heaven! I ask you now: *Who among you will go back down to the filth, the corruption, below?*'

The silence was complete, the intense pressure of his exhortation distorting the flushed, rapt faces of his followers as his eyes sought out the weak and the faithless.

The silence had halted Greg's progress forward; he stood now head bowed as if praying, feeling the weight of intimidation like a crushing sea above him. He closed his eyes to change the image, to swim to the surface and the light of reality; to escape this madness.

Maddox began again, arms raised high, index fingers extended in a clear message, praising God that his challenge lay unanswered, firing up the congregation which ignited immediately with spontaneous glorious shouts, affirming their faith, urging him onward.

Greg took his chance and started forward again, reaching the nearest wall and moving along as near as he could to the stage area. His foot caught in thick electrical cable and something fell.

Carolyn had him in her immediate line of sight. He raised a hand. She stared at him.

'Quit that!' hissed a floor manager, viciously.

She doesn't know me. Jesus, these bastards.

He tried to calculate his chances of reaching her, getting her off the podium, into the lift, and out of the building, when he couldn't even be certain she would go with him. He felt helpless.

At Maddox's direction two fit-looking men in grey blazers bearing the Maddox Ministry logo opened doors on to a balcony with a low balustrade, the sudden rush of cool night air rescuing the near-defeated air-conditioning.

'Who will be first to step up to the Lord?' Maddox asked.

Greg's heart contracted as if ice had touched it.

The cries of affirmation were terrifying.

He saw Carolyn's mouth open and shouted, 'No!' But his cry was lost in the roar of rising insanity.

Do it now or it's over, the still lucid part of his stunned mind told him.

He heard the voice of his dark angel.

Greg, I have seen wonders you would never in your wildest imagining believe possible. Lives given up as lightly as dry leaves shed from an autumnal tree. Children marching hand in hand with their fathers into the steel teeth of machine-guns, eyes filled with rapture, for their belief is greater than death. Death is nothing if one step beyond is paradise. And paradise, Greg, is only a promise. A promise made by one man to another. Be he prophet or saviour or liar. How can you win against these people? Give up the fight and tell the world how weak you truly are.

Go to hell! he had retorted, then. And now too; knowing the reply would be the same.

Hell is where you are, Greg.

Maddox proclaimed: 'To step up to the steady hand of the Lord is to take the sweetest journey of your life. Let me choose first the ones who know love early in their lives and have joined together in the Lord's eyes.'

A young couple pushed forward eagerly, the boy extending his bride's hand to show, proudly, the gleam of a new wedding ring.

'Step up to the Lord!' cried Maddox, urging them forward.

They walked on to the balcony and Greg saw, briefly, as the two looked at each other on the edge of the parapet, a stark moment of doubt, then terror. But for Maddox there was no doubt, no turning back, and those who answered his call heard his voice above all reason.

From below came the sounds of commotion.

'Step into the safe hands of the Lord,' called Maddox. '*Rapture is yours!*'

They stepped out and were gone, any cry lost in the shrieks from the street far below.

'Don't be deceived!' cried Maddox, hearing this. 'The rejected ones below see only what the Lord wants them to see. We know that our brother and sister had disappeared into the air as did our glorious Saviour Jesus Christ Our sweet Lord.'

The rapturous roar in response was overwhelming.

Greg squeezed his eyes shut. *Sweet Jesus, where are you now? Your children are being butchered and you stand above it, uncaring!*

Order seemed to be breaking down, people pushing out from their seats, climbing over them, filling the aisles to bursting.

Greg pressed himself back against the wall in stark terror, realizing that no one was making for or even turning toward the exits – that every eye was on the open doors to the balcony!

Lemmings, he thought wildly and forced himself away from the wall toward the podium, prepared now to kill to stop himself being swept headlong into space if the insane rush began.

Even Maddox seemed to realize the imminent danger. 'Wait!' he shouted into his microphone as a television camera crashed down followed by the crack of an electrical explosion.

His amplified voice restored control, the heaving congregation faltering in their push forward. Urgently, he signalled the choir who began the first rustling murmur of *tongues* again, their sound building as it was taken up by the massed congregation, swelling higher as more voices joined.

'Jesus is waiting for us *all!*' Maddox roared into his microphone, his eyes blinking away stinging sweat. 'We must go to Him in pairs – just as the Lord commanded Noah to show the animals of the world the way to the ark and their salvation.'

Greg had forced his way through to within a few feet of the stage. He called: 'Carolyn!'

She looked at him and recognition seemed to gleam in her eyes. He darted forward, pushing a technician away, reaching her side, holding her.

'*Let's go!*'

She stood, rigid, as if held.

The men in grey blazers moved forward.

Maddox waved them away turning to them, clasping both to him like children, beaming.

Carolyn said: 'This is my husband.'

Maddox smiled for her alone but his words were for his followers: 'The Lord's *first* chosen are already with Him. Taken up from the mountains as a sign for the *Rapture* to begin.' His soaked shirt was transparent against his skin, the collar stained by make-up running from his exhausted face, his pupils dilated by drugs that had kept him going, switched unblinkingly to Greg. 'It is time for their children to step up to Him.'

Carolyn moved to him without demur.

Maddox's gaze remained fixed on Greg.

Greg's voice seemed locked in a vice that no force could release. He looked at Carolyn. She smiled and said something he could not hear. He felt dreamlike and detached. He thought she had said: *It's all right.* And perhaps it was?

Now the noise was a storm, and his sense of being in the heart of it out of control was overwhelming. He saw himself on the parapet, leaning outward, unable to pull himself back . . . and in his cubicle under the Mojave with the sound filling his ears . . . Chaos . . . the sound of chaos . . . all around him. . . everywhere . . . he could almost touch . . . something . . . knowledge . . . he had to live . . . He tightened his mind as he had done against his dark angel and walked to Carolyn.

He held her close bringing her head to his shoulder, his lips pressed as if in a kiss to the damp hair laying over her ear. 'There's no way I can believe what you believe so I have to prove to you it's wrong in the only way you'll understand. I'm sorry.' He took her hand and walked her out on to the balcony, keeping back from the parapet. He turned, aware cameras were fixed on him.

'When's *your* turn, Maddox?' he called back over the noise.

The evangelist's lips were dry and flecked with white spittle, his eyes seemingly focused on some other reality. 'My place is here until all who are chosen have gone!'

'You *walk* down from this tower, you'll be torn apart,' Greg called in anger and turned to Carolyn, taking her hand. 'Close your eyes.'

'I'm going to stand with Jesus,' she told him but earthly fear was already tearing the edges of her voice.

'Stand with *me*,' he said, pulling her up on to the parapet to face him. 'Don't look down. I love you. I'm doing this for you.'

He kissed her then pulled her neck down into his, grasping her head firmly with one hand and enveloping her body tightly with his other arm, pinning her own arms to her sides. 'I love you,' he said again and pushed outwards into space, the stars a whirling spiral above, then sickeningly, below him.

He had stood by the grilled window of the room they had thrown him into, looking up at the stars, waiting for the air-raid to begin, damning them for their callousness at moving him to the top of the building yet grateful for sight of the sky, even a hostile sky lit increasingly by a barrage of high-explosive shells and tracer as invisible attacking aircraft neared.

He knew the smart bomb was imminent because he knew the signs so had moved away from the window to the centre of the room, rolled himself in the foul mattress they had tossed in – laughingly wishing him a good night's sleep – and waited, body relaxed as the survival-training manual ordered, for the inevitable.

He fell four storeys as the smart bomb took out the ground floor of the building, his entire level crashing down, collapsing each beneath, until the top story was all that remained, all that was immediately survivable.

When the roar was over and the rumbling of the settling masonry had ended he opened the mattress, shook the concrete dust from his eyes and saw the vast, open, Arabic sky above.

He found his wrist was broken and from the rubble made a rough splint bound with strips torn from his mattress.

He stumbled downward, picking his way perilously by meagre starlight, for the moon was a thin scimitar turned against a lost crusader journeying home.

There were other surivivors, but by the hopeless sound of their voices they were buried deep – and anyone at basement level in an air-raid was enemy. Even if his humanity had prevailed he knew he could save no lives with one good bare hand. It was time to run.

He ran through the fires and away from the military station finding his thoughts concerning his torturer strangely perverse. No hate, no teeth-grinding desire for vengeance. No blood as payment in kind. To the contrary: he could not have killed him if he had crashed headlong into him in the dark. Not unless he intended taking him back. And if he had formed his thin white smile and said, 'Run, Greg,' in his soft lilting way, it would have been hard not to turn and wave goodbye. He remembered Byron: 'My very chains and I grew friends, so much a long communion tends to make us what we are.' Such is the way between men who have shared the worst in each other, he decided.

Then he was in darkness, and deepening sand, and the flames were behind him as a memory. He knew everything would fade. Except the dark angel who would always live in his mind.

'Holy *shit*!' the fire-chief bawled. 'You people gone crazy up there?'

Greg rolled down off the air-bag, pulling Carolyn, white-faced and shocked with him on to the road. 'You better get someone up there fast or you'll have bodies piled high on your sidewalks. Hear me?'

'To hell with you! Sonofabitch! You just *jumped*!'

'Hoping you'd set the air-bag up in time after you lost those two kids! Don't waste time arguing, do something before your worst nightmare starts happening. He's got maybe five hundred hyped-up people bent on making it to heaven in one leap – and screw gravity. Ask my wife, she was one of them!'

'They'll do it,' Carolyn sobbed. 'Oh *God*.'

'You wait here and talk to the police,' ordered the fire chief.

'Fuck you.' Greg straight-armed him aside and walked, his arm tight around Carolyn's shoulders.

'Smoke!' someone yelled.

She turned looking upward. 'Forget it,' Greg told her, moving her on quickly now.

From behind came shrieks and the sounds of impact, like falling fruit.

The fire chief's voice yelled: '*Jesus!* Get another bag under there! *Move!*'

Carolyn threw her hands over her ears and broke free from him, sobbing, running, stumbling, away from the escalating carnage. He caught her, grasped her hard and shouldered savagely through the crowds who now were breaking down police barriers to get closer to the scene.

He pulled her into a doorway for safety, keeping her face turned from the building as flames licked the summit, silhouetting dark shapes before they plunged, limbs flailing.

'Can you make it?' he asked her.

Her voice was small, defeated, lost. 'Where are we going?'

'To find your folks.'

'Yes,' she said and believed him. She decided she would tell him about elusive angels and the smell of gas they had left lingering in the mountain air.

CHAPTER
NINE

Sam Lewelyn peered out at the Washington back-street auto-restoration shop. He could see a small glass office at one end of the premises directly by a raised hydraulic ramp which held aloft the brutal low-browed shape of a classic Facel Vega HK500. He drove the Lincoln in under a half-dropped roller-door, its big V8 booming in the echoey, enclosed space.

'Hey! We're through for today, all right? You want work done call first!' A bald head appeared from the glass booth and a squat man with heavy shoulders and a solid belly stepped out, then came over. 'Say, that's a beauty. That the factory paint still? Don't ask for no re-spray – I gotta say no.'

'Too busy?' asked Sam, switching off.

'Take a look around, what you see is what I got. Not everybody can afford good restoration work any more.' The man shrugged bull-like shoulders. He shook his head. 'That Continental don't need no work.'

'You don't care to make money?'

'You kidding? Look, I get some great cars here, OK? See that Facel on the ramp? A killer. Over there – see the Bentley? Graber body, best ever; terrific. I got real job satisfaction. But I don't do work on cars that don't need it, OK? That's like sacrilege.'

Sam saw the break-down truck at the far end of the garage, backed up against a second, shut, roller door. He stepped out of the car. 'Let's talk.'

'Cars? Sure, any time. Right now I got paperwork, OK.'

Sam kept a snub rubber-gripped Colt Python in the Lincoln's glove-box. He reached inside for it. 'Not cars. Trucks. Talk about that one.' He pointed.

The man's eyes examined the gun. 'You want it, take it, it's yours.'

They walked toward the truck. Sam bent to the grubby registration plate. It matched that written in his notebook.

'You used it tonight?'

'I rent it, evenings.'

'Got a name? Address?'

'*Cash*, OK? I don't make records. So it's a scam? Who doesn't cheat the IRS some? You a cop?'

'I'm a friend.'

'Not with that Magnum in your hand you're not.'

Sam shook his head. 'Not yours.'

Something touched the man's eyes: perhaps understanding, perhaps resignation – but not fear. He said: 'I don't want any part of it, OK.'

'Of what?'

The squat body shifted, the blunt hands thrust stubbornly into the pockets of the surprisingly clean green cover-alls. 'Like I said, the truck got hired, I stayed here and did the books. Hate the job but it's got to be done.'

'Name?' Sam repeated.

The man sighed.

'Over there,' said Sam indicating the office.

'Easy with the paperwork, OK? I just spent three hours sorting that mess.'

Sam stopped by the ramp and studied it.

The man stood before him, waiting, apprehensive now.

Sam punched a button, the ramp groaned, hissed and began descending. He stopped it half-way. 'Sit,' he said, pointing where.

'You crazy?'

Sam said: 'There was this guy I remember – master-sergeant, Vietnam, back in the sixties – ran one of the big NCO clubs. You did service?'

'Sure, Navy. Engines.'

'You're Franco Bernardelli, right?'

The man licked his lips. 'That's me. People call me Frank.'

'So, Frank, this guy was doing the business and no one could hang anything on him. Skimming the slot-machines sixteen hours a day every day; kept a sea-going yacht and some clean girls off the coast to sweeten the inspectors – and for *in case*. He was real smart. Get the picture?'

'Sure, he was an operator.'

'I was visiting town, enjoying the club, buying a few things from the PX. I needed the break. I was in one of those outfits that no one talked about much then and never now. They want to forget. Know what I mean?'

Sweat had beaded in a vee across the slight scalp indentation where Bernardelli's widow's peak hairline had once been. He nodded. 'Yeah, no parades.'

Sam smiled. 'That's right. No parades.' He placed a big hand on Bernardelli's solid shoulder, easing him down to the green-painted floor and dropped to his haunches beside him. 'Stretch your legs a little, Frank – out front, that's it. Good. Anyway, I was asked – as a favour, nothing official – to see if I could communicate with this guy. So I met him in a bar, tried to make him see sense, be reasonable, you understand? Nothing rough.'

'I see you as being a reasonable kinda guy,' Bernardelli offered hopefully and looked up at the underside of the HK500 on the ramp.

'He wouldn't listen. So I had to move things on.' Sam reached up and pressed the drop-mechanism, the ramp heaved and jerked, stopping inches over Bernardelli's outstretched legs. 'I persuaded him he needed to spend time in the army motor pool with me. They had one of these rigs with a truck on it. Big sonofabitch. He changed his mind pretty quick, Frank. Put in his papers and made for the coast. That's after he got out of hospital. The truck was just that bit too heavy for the ramp so when I stopped it, it kept on going. Only a couple of inches but . . .'

Bernardelli's face was grey. 'Listen, I know you mean it – you got personal reasons so, OK, I believe you'll do it but I gotta tell you it ain't gonna do you any good. Sometimes you have to take what's coming.' He crossed himself rapidly then his hand came up, quick and hard like a boxer's jabbing upper-cut, except it went for the Colt, not for the chin. Then, deliberately, and so fast that for Sam realization was too late and the horror had already begun, the bald head was thrust hard at the gun and a pink mist appeared to hang in the air for long moments before Sam's stunned eyes –

though in real-time it barely existed as vapour on the edges of the red storm which broke over the Facel.

The thunderclap seemed to come afterwards.

Sam knelt, ears ringing, staring at the smoking gun and Bernardelli, who was thrown back against the Facel, his head destroyed. He turned away. He wanted to gag but had given up any pretence to physical reaction years before. His vomit was in his mind and cleaning it up would take a while. He knew from experience.

He stood; achingly tired.

You crazy sonofabitch, I'd have pulled you out of there!

He went into the office, lifted the telephone and dialled, seeing the opened diary on the desk. That day's only entry read 275GTB CALL. No registration number, no owner's name. He looked out into the garage as the line buzzed mutedly in his half-deafened ear, seeing no sign of the rare coupé nor any current worksheet for the vehicle with the others on the wall.

'How many Ferrari 275GTBs do you think there are in Washington?' Sam asked.

'I'm watching America going crazy and you want to know about exotic Italian metal?' complained Hugh Edwards. 'You should see this stuff!'

Sam flicked on the small cheap black-and-white portable fixed on a bracket above him, punching the news channels. Pictures of reporters appeared hazily behind bad interference, talking earnestly and animatedly in front of gawking crowds. One channel showed what he thought at first was the Capitol building then saw the skyline was wrong and recognized the Texas capital.

'Is all this down to Maddox?' he asked.

'Up. Austin's the new gateway to heaven.'

'My boy Greg flew down there tonight.'

'Found Jesus?'

'Lost his wife.'

'You OK, Sam? Sound shook?' said Edwards, alert now.

'He's dead, Hugh. Bernardelli.'

Sam could hear Edwards breathing. 'You?' Edwards asked, finally. 'Or did you find him that way?'

'Did it himself.'

'Any note?'

'No time.'

'You sure you're OK?'

'Pulled himself on to my gun. Just now. Nothing I could do.'

'Called the cops yet?'

Sam breathed out staring out at the garage and not seeing a thing. 'I thought maybe you make house calls? They'll be here soon enough. That shot must have been heard a couple of blocks away the way this place echoes.'

'Don't do anything, don't touch anything, especially don't say anything to the officers when they arrive. Leave that to me. Show your Agency ID, make like whatever went down was spook business and you're not talking. Wait there for me. Where's the gun?'

'Right in front of me.'

'Registered to you?'

'Of course.'

'Leave it be. Stay right away from it. These days, first cops on the scene at fire-arms incidents figure for the first few seconds they're on borrowed time. I'll stay on the line till they arrive. Keep you alive. Talk to me about the Ferrari. You made a connection?'

'Diary listing, today's date. The only one. No sign of the car, no worksheet I can see. Reads 275GTB CALL. Can only be a Ferrari with that designation.'

'The breakdown truck there?'

'To the right of me. Registration confirmed. Bernardelli told me he rented it out today. Cash deal to side-step the IRS inspectors so no records.'

'Sam, someone who can afford a Ferrari 275GTB keeps it in a heated garage with strict security and calls out expensive help when he needs it. He doesn't rent breakdown trucks. Unless you're saying he's the hit-man? Are you?'

'I think Bernardelli wrote the car's description to avoid using a name or telephone number. Could be nothing – but all I've got apart from that is a dead man.'

'I'll check. Can't be many listed. What's that kind of metal worth these days?'

'A million dollars on a bad day.'

'Shoot! That separates the men from the boy-racers.'

The wail of sirens arose, closing in.

'Should have been a faster response than that,' grumbled Edwards.

'Hugh, I think we've been pointed in the wrong direction.'

'You said that at Henri's. It could have been a faked mob hit. So who? Your people? They better have damn good reasons.'

Sam could see the ruined head against the Facel's lower stainless-steel door panel. Under the harsh white strip-lighting the red pool was an astonishing crimson. 'Not the Agency. God.'

'What?'

'I was threatening heavy pain. Bernardelli believed me. He decided he couldn't handle what I said I'd do so he took the other option. Viet Cong did that sometimes. I used to be prepared for it back then. Watched them real close for that look in the eye. Acceptance, resignation. I should have realized. Getting old. Slow.'

'Sam, listen, I'll come over as soon as the black-and-white arrives, OK?'

Sam might not have heard. 'Fear doesn't do it. Commitment, dedication, the motivation is in those. *Faith*. The mob doesn't get near it nor does the Agency. I'm not in shock, Hugh, I'm trying to make sense of it.'

'*Sense* you're definitely not making. What's going on? I thought at best we were talking laundering the Agency's dirty linen . . . at worst with the – with *his* involvement, National Security? Where'd *God* slip in?'

'He was in right at the start.'

'Freeze!' a voice yelled.

'Put them on,' said Edwards. 'Call them over slow. Sam, I'll see you soon, OK?'

Using his secure, direct line, John Cornell called the director of the Central Intelligence Agency at Langley.

'Still at your desk, Hal?'

'Aren't you? Mr President.'

'You spying on me, Mr Director?'

'No, sir, experience of your working habits is all.'

'How's Laura? The boys?'

'Just fine. But you didn't call to discuss family.'

'No. All right, Hal. If you wanted to know about the Russian old guard who'd you go to over there? Who'd give you the most co-operation – and ask the least questions?'

'By old guard you mean those holding power pre-*glasnost*?'

'I'm not quite sure who I mean – but, yes, I suppose that category fits what I have in mind.'

'What *do* you have in mind, Mr President? If you want straight answers you're going to have to be straight with me . . . then let me bend the questions unrecognizably out of shape.'

'I want you to find out if there were ever any high-level meetings with, or concerning, two Russian scientists: brother and sister, twins, named Markarov, Ilya and Irina.'

'High level? You mean the *very* top or . . . as high as KGB? Not that there was much difference.'

'I don't know. Start at the top and work down. It's your field.'

'Do I get a hint why?'

'At this stage I think not. This involves another Intelligence agency and my bringing you in could, later, be awkward for you.'

'I should be told whether we're talking foreign or domestic, friendly or otherwise?'

'Domestic.' Cornell paused. 'I hesitate to confirm friendly – unless there's been a thaw in the air recently?'

'I see.' Ellis chuckled. 'No, still chilly but we've got used to that over the years.'

'I need this done immediately, Hal.'

'Even as you speak my fingers have been at work.'

'Technology stopped for me at vinyl albums.'

'If you have some, keep 'em, they're practically museum pieces now. The problem we have here is that the old guard – and that term covers a heck of a lot of people, high and low – were all more or less involved in the abortive ninety-one coup. Which means they're now dead, damaged, or CTCs.'

'What the hell are CTCs?'

'Converted to capitalism. Same as Nazis were used to keep Germany functioning after World War Two, old Communist bureaucrats have had to be used to keep things moving – after a fashion – over there. Nobody else was ever trained for running the country.'

'Do what you can.'

'How important is this, Mr President?'

'I told you, I want it done immediately.'

'No, sir, I meant as in any consequence thereof?'

'Hal, there may never have been anything quite as important. As far as what the consequences might be if I don't hear what I want to hear . . . ? Well, just say I don't even want to think about that.'

'I'll stay with this until I have results, Mr President. Personally.'

'You know I might have to fly to Rome tonight – the Sazarin business. Call me on Air Force One if necessary. After that, at the embassy. Whatever the time is. Any word on who the assassin might be . . . or worked for?'

'Nothing. Cleanest job I've ever come across. We had the details – what little there were. I've watched some CNN coverage we worked on. What saved his life was he seemed surprised the Pope had come down to meet him – they don't exactly have a lot in common except they share the same address: Rome. He does a kind of short mocking bow and the bullet whips into the back of his head instead of—'

'I get the picture, Hal.'

'Sorry, sir. Insensitive of me.'

'That's OK.'

'Anything else you need, Mr President?'

Cornell swung around to his favourite position at the window. 'Hal. If you had to make a judgement about the old USSR – would you say they lied most of the time? That just about all of it was a sham? That there was little substance beyond the lies of old, frightened men, hanging on to power, afraid of their own down-trodden masses as much – if not more – than the outside world? In retrospect, that's how it seems to me. They ran out of lies. Or the truth became too evident – piercing the fabric of their deceit until their positions became untenable.'

'Any real judgement, Mr President, should be made not on the basis of their lies but of their interpretation of *truth*. Truth was what *they* decided it should be. As you know *pravda* means truth and was also the complete, powerful, irrefutable, unchallengeable organ of their lies. In my opinion they lied all the way to the wire.'

'Yet, despite their *knowing* they were going under, there was apparently never any attempt to bring the rest of us down with them. A Soviet *Götterdämmerung*? A botched coup is hardly that?'

'Sir, it's my – and I'd say informed – belief that if they'd gone for a final nuclear throw, at least half if not considerably more of their missiles would have never left their silos because of malfunction, lack of spares, or plain deterioration. Many might have detonated where they stood. However, with respect, may I say it's important to understand the vital difference between Communists and Nazis.'

'Go on.'

'National Socialism is like lust: full of sound, fire, and passion. Orgasmic. Watch the old film of Nuremberg rallies. It was always in danger of burn-out and final deflation. Communism, to the true believer, is love. Love for ever. Even when marriage between people and state fails or turns brutal. Realistically – and I'm talking for starving Third World millions and not comfortable full-bellied over-educated Western intellectuals – Communism is stronger than religious faith. God if you will. God promises nothing in this world and never will – that's written in stone!'

'You sound like you didn't believe President Bush when he said we won the Cold War.'

'We won the war but the victory was hollow. We just don't care enough about anything to sustain our own beliefs. We stumble from day to day, make another buck, get out of or go into recession, what the hell?'

'While all the defeated Marxists work for a new tomorrow. That's what you're saying?'

'They don't even have to work for it. All they have to do is *believe* strongly enough. Ragged little Oriental men and women with black pyjamas and a palmful of rice daily taught us that. Belief is all, Mr President.'

Cornell sat quite still, gazing forward, seeing nothing – and everything.

'Mr President?'

'Hal, to your knowledge did the KGB ever attempt any religious disinformation plots?'

'You mean destabilization? Sure, Salvador was good for them, half the priests were Marxists.'

'More profound than that.'

'I'm not sure I follow, sir.'

'I'm not entirely clear myself. Just bear it in mind. Please be in touch as soon as possible.'

He replaced the receiver and stared at it. Would they . . . he searched for words, then remembered from somewhere . . . *stamp God's own name upon a lie?*

Belief is all. It was reason enough.

He looked out at the night and saw in his mind the great blocks of stone and glass in Baltimore which contained the marvels of technology that made NSA the awesome power it was.

With spirits lifting he thought: I don't understand the magic your silicon-sorcerers work but though my ignorance may be my weakness it is also my weapon, for I'm not blinded by your science. I believe in human beings. In their best virtues and their worst deceits; in good and evil in equal measure and with defined lines. I believe in liars and that liars conspire, that conspiracy is easiest wrought upon those who have placed their faith in what may be achieved materially.

He stood. He would go to Rome. Ostensibly as a political gesture to show solidarity with the new, vastly powerful European Federation at a moment of crisis, but in truth, to be at the side of the old, frail, failing Holy Father who must at that moment be fearing that the great prophecies foretelling the catastrophic fall of the Roman Church were both true and imminent – not in any physical sense with the massacre of priests, nor the crashing down of great monuments and holy places, but by the reduction of the greatest mystery known to man to a few electronic impulses and, ultimately, to meagre human stature. As Marchionni had uttered, when what had to be said between them was said: *The voice of God, of Christ, reproduced through man's inventions, no matter how clever, how advanced they are, will make him – merely a man.*

Cornell looked at the silently running television news and the growing chaos across the nation. God as media event, he thought. And tomorrow? Forgotten. Yesterday's news.

He would fight the Good Fight. He must. For even it were all a lie – a conspiracy by old, defeated ideologues determined to do the most damage in their death throes – the result could be the same: the end of mystery and the victory of materialism.

And – perhaps from beyond their graves – the old cynics would have won, defeating us with the weapons we used to defeat them: our commitment to, our total belief and achievements in, advanced technology. The irony did not escape him.

He lifted his telephone, called the State Department, and announced his decision to travel immediately to Rome.

Hugh Edwards shook his head. 'You're sure?' he asked.

'I'm sure,' replied Sam, and walked away from the body, as the police photographer began work.

'He could have been trying to get the Magnum away from you?'

Sam turned, pointing upward. 'Then the round would be up there and not in his brain.'

'It's not in his brain – it's in the Facel. *I'm trying to make life easier for you!*' Edwards yelled over the reverberations made by an ambulance being reversed into the garage.

The engine cut. Edwards moved quickly to Lewelyn's side. 'I'm trying to make life easier, Sam.'

'I heard you the first time. So did they.' Sam glanced toward the two officers who had been first on the scene, standing now under the roller door, heads together.

'Fuck them, this is out of their league. Well?'

'You want perjury?'

'At least say it's open? *Maybe* he was going for the gun? It's not like the old days, Sam. Even spooks are accountable now. Some.'

'Some spooks? Or some accountability?'

'This is serious.'

That's what Bernardelli decided, thought Sam. 'OK, Hugh: *Maybe he was going for the gun.* There, I've said it. I still don't believe it and I'll never convince an inquest. He killed himself. It's that simple.'

'Simple it ain't. Killed himself on *your* gun, with *your* finger on the trigger?'

'Give me your gun.'

'Why?'

'Come on!'

Edwards took his Smith & Wesson .38 from his shoulder holster, dumped the rounds, and held it out butt first.

'Cock it.'

'You want me to be you?'

'Finger inside the trigger guard, easy but ready.'

Sam squatted, legs outstretched. 'Down here,' he said. 'On your haunches.'

Edwards obeyed.

'Talk to me. Anything. Say you love me.'

'I want a divorce.'

Sam's hand flashed for the gun barrel, jerking it toward him, at the same time thrusting his head directly at it.

There was a sharp, loud click.

'You're dead,' said Edwards.

'*He's* dead,' said Sam, woodenly, nodding toward the saw-edged sound of a heavy-duty zipper being dragged closed. 'I thought I was all through with black bags,' he murmured.

'OK, so it works.'

Sam nodded. 'Every time. I told you on the phone, it was a Cong trick: when they'd given everything they had and giving up their comrades was too high a price to pay for their own weakness. He'd seen it too. Bernardelli. He said he was Navy. I'd say gunboats working the delta, maybe moving special forces units upriver on snatch-and-run raids. He'd have seen it more than once. Nobody ever got used to it. Nobody was ever really ready for it. It was outside our understanding. Or maybe our understanding of their commitment. We sure as *fuck* didn't have that kind of commitment – or anywhere near it.'

'So why *God*? Or has Maddox got to you too?'

'You don't know what all this is about, Hugh.'

'Am I about to find out?'

'Maybe. I need to make a call.'

'Your lawyer?'

Sam smiled. 'Actually he was, once.' He went into the office and dialled the White House.

'You checked the files here for the Ferrari?' asked Edwards.

'The President, please. Sam Lewelyn. He'll be expecting my call.'

Edwards said: 'I'd like to do that. Just once.'

Sam said: 'Oh.' He looked at Edwards.

Edwards shook his head. 'I don't want to know.'

'I see. One moment.' Sam wrote two telephone numbers in his notebook. 'I'll do that. Goodnight.' He put down the receiver.

Edwards shrugged. 'Flown the coop just as the country's gone crazy. Wise. Nero with brains! He's not that Irish after all.'

'He's gone to Rome.'

'Irony too? Well! I suppose now we should call Big Brother at the Puzzle Palace and have him talk us out of putting you in the slammer.'

'That's one thing you can't do, Hugh.'

'Great.'

A woman police officer with wide hips made huge by gun-belt and stick waddled over and thrust a sheet of paper at Edwards. 'Vehicle trace, sir.'

Edwards read and looked at the battered filing cabinet. 'You did check that?' he asked.

'You said don't touch anything.'

'You took notice?'

Sam grinned. 'Nothing.'

Edwards folded the read-out. 'I'll give you a choice.'

'How many?'

'Three. Four if you count a drophead.'

'Don't, that's a GTS designation, not GTB.'

'OK, here's what you have to be to own a million-dollar automobile. You choose. I'm not taking bets and I sure as hell am not involved. Hear that last part? One: supermarket king; uses it for promo work. Two: investment house; car's mothballed for ever in Georgetown. Three: his well-heeled holiness, the Archbishop Ricardo Giancarlo Santino Vincenze-Marchionni.'

Sam looked at him.

'Rome, you said? Right? The Man's gone to Rome? We're talking coincidence here? Or what's that other fashionable word? Synchronicity? How about *conspiracy*?'

'He's gone to Rome because of Sazarin. That's where the hit took place – you know that! Sazarin is in intensive care at the same hospital two miles north of Rome where John Paul II was taken after the assassination attempt on him in eighty-one.'

'That's fine. So there's definitely no connection between an attempted hit on a world leader in Rome and the murder of a retired spook and violent death of an old-car restorer in Washington? Not one that you know of anyway? Not, say, the fact that the President of the USA happens to have just left DC for Rome?'

Sam looked out of the glass booth. He saw an officer shovel sand on to the pool of blood and wondered irrationally if that was why some deserts were red and how many lives it had cost over the centuries to make them so. He felt cold, and surprised at the realization that shock could still get to him.

Edwards held up two small transparent evidence bags. Each contained a gold crucifix. 'Sazarin wear one of these around his neck, Sam?'

'You know damn well what Sazarin's view of Christianity is. Christ doesn't pay! It's been reported enough. That's why the Italians call him *La Bestia*.'

Edwards tossed the bags on to the battered narrow desk between them. 'Morrison and Bernardelli. Both wore one. Wouldn't think twice about it if it weren't for the rest of it.'

'You made your point the first time.'

'I'm not interested in making points. I'm interested in justice. I'm also interested in my own welfare which means knowing whether I should do my job or take off for the weekend because there are things going on which maybe don't concern small fry like me.'

'I have to speak to the President.'

'But you can't speak to your boss?'

'The President is my boss. Yours too, in the final analysis.'

'Jesus, I really hate this town sometimes! A cop needs real protection to survive.'

Ricardo Marchionni poured himself a cognac, took a long Havana cigar from its humidor, rolled it in the flame from a solid gold Cartier lighter, his lips lightly around it, barely drawing smoke, then watched it burn in a jade ashtray. 'Doctor's orders,' he said with a thin smile. 'The nose has to do the lungs' job now.' He sniffed appreciatively. 'Wonderful! Horseshit and heaven rolled together by a woman's hand. You should be in bed, David.'

'Tell me what is happening?'

Marchionni's eyes, so black they might have been all pupil, turned, concerned, upon Kolchak. 'The difference between us, my poor friend, is that I believe absolutely that God absolved me, you, and the poor brave soul who drove the car, from the mortal sin of murder. I begin to wonder, David, if you truly still Believe? Or did those odious Russian Jews put just enough doubt into your mind for your faith to be slowly eaten away? Such self-destruction as you have embarked upon since then has roots deeper than – forgive me – plain, and in my view, justifiable, homicide.'

He went to his Louis XIV desk and took out a dull-looking automatic made from state of the art ceramic composites. 'If someone with evil intent – murder for gain or pleasure say – broke in here right now and I knew this was in this drawer, loaded, my choice would be to use it or die. As simple – and for us as servants of God as complicated – as that. Let me give you *reality*, David. My work, my influence, my wealth, does more good for the world in one year than a homicidal maniac could in his entire lifetime – assuming there's *some* goodness in him in the first place which actually comes out in deeds? Believing otherwise is foolishness. Complications arise because of the basic Christian precept that both I and the maniac have souls and that our souls are equal. Equal above all other considerations. However, in my opinion, there are occasions when that precept does not hold. Examples? My scenario just now and what occurred in the Mojave desert years ago. One does what one *must*, David, trusting that God, even if He doesn't smile down beatifically, at least nods approval – however perfunctorily. There is another school of thought on the subject; medieval but still valid to our fundamentalist brethren: mindless evil comes directly from Satan and is therefore a legitimate target.'

'The Markarovs were hardly mindless.'

Marchionni smiled. 'You don't need me to tell you that another of Satan's names is the Lord of Chaos. You don't create chaos with brainless fools. Their intellect however does not negate their evil intent – you spent enough time with them to know that. God isn't hounding you as He did Cain, David. If you've been driven into the wilderness, that is your own doing. You took no part in the deed.'

'I virtually delivered them to you. And I *wanted* them dead.' Kolchak's eyes were fevered, tortured by guilt. 'But I couldn't kill, even for Christ.'

'The question you must ask yourself now David is not whether you could kill for Christ but will you kill Him by not doing anything? The truth is that you were prepared, then, to be the messenger bringing the bad news but nothing more. Your real torture lies in that inadequacy. All it needs it that admission and you are half-way to release.'

Kolchak stared at him as though mesmerized.

'This must be stopped, David. You knew it had to be that day you came to me in Rome. You knew in Jerusalem before you abdicated responsibility and boarded that flight. Nothing has changed. That was only the beginning. You were correct. It didn't die. It was contained.'

'Contained?'

'Sometimes it can be more effective to let a child exhaust itself with a toy than to take it away. Kent didn't die, David. He burned. But he survived. And now he burns inside, desperate to unlock the secret that Markarovs left him. He's run a secret programme for years, blindly, without success, costing millions. You remember what the Markarovs told you? The depth, the breadth, of work that would be needed?'

'And the technology. They hadn't the technology,' stated Kolchak almost desperately.

'The technology exists – now. All that is required is money. More money. Kent has bled his own resources for years. We knew that was occurring and that it contained him, even imprisoned him in his obsession, because he dared not reveal his funding sources. His manipulation of his own budget. Now he can't raise more funds in America without risking revealing the criminality of what he has been doing, so he must find it elsewhere. America's practically bankrupt anyway and this is far bigger than America.'

'*Where?*'

Marchionni allowed himself one pull on the abandoned cigar, coughed, smiled, swallowed cognac, and sighed. 'As wealthy as I am, even I couldn't afford to finance such a project. That kind of money cannot be sought from an individual, nor even a consortium; too much even for a single country. A group of countries could find it. A *federation*, David.'

Kolchak stared at him, his skin cold. 'Sazarin? Dear God, *you*?'

Marchionni's black eyes held him. 'We are only pin-points of light in a billion stars, you and I, but if we didn't exist then neither would the universe. Our *being* is necessary for everything to exist.'

'What are you saying?'

'I'm telling you how important we are.' Marchionni laid the gun on the low table between them. '*Opus dei*, my dear friend. It is God's work.'

David Kolchak shut his eyes tight as if darkness was his last hiding-place.

CHAPTER
TEN

Air Force One was no longer the Boeing 747, but that company's new 2707 SST, a three-hundred-foot long supersonic delta with a massive tailplane and four underslung General Electric engines.

For all the SST's speed and undoubted prestige, John Cornell preferred the spacious, and in relative terms lumbering, jumbo, thoroughly enjoying the old-style air-travel appeal of that great aircraft with its double decks and its club-like ambience – if he ignored all the communication and other more deadly hi-tech equipment aft.

He particularly disliked the SST's take-off angle which tilted him too far back and pressed him too deep in his seat. Too Buck Rogers, he had thought on his first experience of it, inadvisedly making that observation within range of the Secret Service officer who decided presidential identification codes. Since then and for ever onward – though not within his own earshot – he was Buck.

He could live with that, he thought, accepting the Scotch-rocks he had asked for: better an out of date American hero than some of the names they could dream up! Nevertheless he worried over how much awareness of, or disdain for, his out-dated scientific knowledge was reflected in the choice of name. You're too sensitive, he scourged himself: lighten up. He looked out of the small, thick port at the dark world miles below. You don't truly realize what you are, that's the heart of it. If you did, you'd act more decisively – and this situation would never have arisen. William Bradley Kent wouldn't be toying with history, he would be history.

'You're spilling your drink,' Madelaine Cornell said, from the wide beige glove-leather armchair in front of him.

He brushed the wetness off the loose dressing-gown he preferred to wear when flying.

'Where were you?'

'Flying with a rocket back-pack.'

'What?'

'Doesn't matter.'

An aide came up. 'Excuse me, Mr President. A call from CIA Director Ellis.'

'I'll be right there.' He arose, avoiding the enquiring look from his wife, and walked down the long narrow aircraft to the communications centre.

'I wish all your reports came in this fast, Hal,' he said into the instrument he was handed.

'We could have ourselves a contact, Mr President.'

'Can you say whom?'

'You wouldn't believe me if I told you, sir.'

'I'd believe anything these days, Hal. Doesn't matter who it is as long as it's someone who would have known what was going on at decision-making level.'

Cornell could hear the smile in Ellis's voice. 'I can guarantee that, sir. You couldn't really get any higher for that period. He's in New York for another lecture tour. You've actually got him on your White House social calendar during his stay. Anyhow, I thought I put out a feeler and got firmly kissed on both cheeks – figuratively speaking. There'll be a price but it could be worth paying.'

'It will be. I hadn't thought of him. All right, ask the question and let me know as soon as you have anything. Is that all?'

'No, sir. I've remembered an incident which perhaps comes in the area of your secondary enquiry? KGB religious disinformation plots?'

Cornell's aide moved quickly forward and lit the cigar he had taken from his gown. 'Go on, Hal, I'm listening.'

'We have on record an incident in December 1964 which might fit. An Australian writer named Donovan Joyce was offered five thousand US dollars at Lod Airport, Tel Aviv, by a man claiming to be a professor of semitic studies at an American university to smuggle an ancient parchment scroll out of Israel. The export of antiquities being illegal, of course. The man called himself Professor Max Grosset.'

'You say *claiming*. Grosset was a fake?'

'Subsequent enquiries found no one of that name at any US university.'

'Go on.'

'Joyce played along and demanded to know more before he would consider the proposition. The "professor" took him into the men's lavatory, where he took the scroll from a black cabin bag. He told Joyce: "Compared with this, the best of the Dead Sea scrolls is an unimportant scribble." Joyce handled the parchment, managed to turn back one corner, and saw neat rows of writing in a language Grosset claimed was Aramaic. He asked for details of the text. Grosset said the writer identified himself as Yeshua ben Ya'akob ben Gennesareth; said he was eighty years of age, the last rightful heir to the Hasmonean throne of Israel and wrote his testament the night before the Romans launched their final assault upon Masada. Grosset then told Joyce the most fantastic story, the conclusion of which was that the scroll had been written by Jesus Christ. You understand what I'm saying here, sir. What they were trying to pull – assuming they were the KGB?'

Cornell turned away from the row of uniformed technicians in AF1's Command Centre, sitting watchfully at their consoles monitoring defence and spy satellite signals. He wondered if Kent was listening to him now, either plucking his telephone conversation out of the ether or from bugs strategically placed in the aircraft. The latter was not improbable, NSA having unlimited access because of their on-board equipment, and although the aircraft was electronically swept for bugs on a regular basis, Cornell had no illusions that the agency had devices which could prove undetectable even to experts. The hardest thief to protect against is the one in your own house, he thought.

Ellis said: 'Are you there, Mr President?'

Cornell lowered his voice, feeling slightly foolish, even paranoid. Neverthless his tone was earnest, even grave. 'I understand exactly what you're saying, Hal. If Jesus was eighty at Masada He couldn't have died on the cross at Calvary. If He didn't die on the cross He wasn't resurrected. if He wasn't resurrected Christianity has no foundation. Hal, what happened to "Professor" Grosset?'

'According to the preface of a book Joyce wrote about the encounter called *The Jesus Scroll* he may have "defected" to the Soviet Union. I have no facts to back up that conclusion but if it were true it certainly smacks of KGB involvement.'

'Involvement before or after the incident? In other words, was it a KGB plant or a KGB purchase?'

'I can't answer that, sir.'

Ellis fell silent.

'What is it, Hal?'

'Mr President, may I ask you a direct question?'

'You usually do.'

'This craziness going on back here right now? Maddox? There's some connection isn't there? Your line of enquiry can't just be coincidence? I've heard it said coincidence has a long arm but this is really stretching it.'

Cornell drew on his cigar. 'I'd like you to fax me as much detail on this story as you have. And, Hal, when I'm more informed I'll discuss this with you fully. That's a promise. Goodbye for now.'

'Mr President, wait! One more thing. Will you make sure you heed the advice of your Secret Service people when you're over there? There's a possibility the Sazarin business was not down to a loner with a need for a place in history.'

'Some terror group?'

'Maybe deeper.'

'Political? *Officially* political. Who?'

'We have assets checking that out, sir, but it's going to take time. Be careful.'

'I fully intend to be, Hal. Thank you for your concern.'

'I'll get that material on Grosset to you right away, sir.'

'Fine.'

Cornell put down the instrument and returned to his seat.

'What was it?' asked Madelaine Cornell.

'The usual terror scares.'

She shuddered.

'You should have stayed behind,' he told her.

'And let Rome make decisions for you? You're a Catholic – practising or not – and they'll put pressure on you to do whatever they decide is right for *them*. Make sure you do what's right for *us*.'

'Us?'

'America.'

'There's a few million American Roman Catholics who would disagree with that view.'

'No man can serve two masters,' she quoted.

He sipped Scotch silently, thinking, there's more: *You cannot serve God and Mammon*. He turned away to the black window, seeing his own tired face staring back at him. Are we thus already severed from Him? Visions of the confusion and violence occurring across the country came to him and he regretted leaving. He shook the feeling off.

His aide returned and placed a typescript on the table before him. 'This came through from Langley, Mr President.'

Cornell nodded and began reading.

Summary of Lod Airport incident as discussed, taken from published material not secret sources, CIA or otherwise:

In December 1964 Australian writer Donovan Joyce was offered $5000 by a man calling himself Professor Max Grosset (who said he was a professor of semitic studies at an American university) if he would smuggle out of Israel an ancient parchment scroll. According to his own account, Joyce demanded to know more before he would consider the proposition, and the professor took him into the men's lavatory at Tel Aviv's Lod Airport, where he took the scroll from a black cabin bag, telling Joyce, 'Compared with this, the best of the Dead Sea scrolls is an unimportant scribble.' Joyce handled the parchment and turning back a corner of it saw neat rows of writing in a language he was told was Aramaic. Grosset divulged some details about the text of the scroll, though not many. The writer, he said, identified himself as 'Yeshua ben Ya'akob ben Gennesareth' and said he was eighty years of age and the last rightful heir to the Hasmonean throne of Israel. He wrote his testament during the night before the Romans launched their final assault upon Masada. The professor, writes Joyce, then proceeded to tell him the most fantastic story, the conclusion of which was that the scroll had been written by none other than Jesus himself.

Donovan Joyce tells this story of his meeting with the professor, who he believed may have defected to the Soviet Union with the scroll, in the preface to his book *The Jesus Scroll*.'

Analysis of claim that the scroll was written by Jesus Christ based on research published by Donovan Joyce:

Question: *Could Yeshua ben Ya'akob ben Gennesareth have been the figure we know as Jesus of Nazareth?*

The name *Yeshua ben Ya'akob Gennesareth* translates as: Jesus son of Jacob of Gennesareth. Although this may seem paternally and geographically incorrect – Jesus Christ's father being recorded as Joseph and Nazareth as his birthplace – some biblical scholars claim that Joseph divorced Mary and that she married a man called Alpheus. It was the custom of the time for male Jews to adopt a Greek name for public use and keep their Jewish name for family use only. The word *alpheus* in Greek means *successor* and its equivalent in Hebrew is *Ya'akob* – or *Jacob*.

Gennesareth is another name for Galilee and is used as such in the gospels. The name Nazareth is not found in writings of the time excepting in the gospels and derivative writings. The first-century historian Josephus Flavius, who was the Jewish military commander in the Galilee area during the Roman war of AD 66–70, names every town he fortified and never mentions Nazareth, despite its present-day site being of strategic importance.
Note: In Hebrew the word *gen* means garden and if dropped from Gennesareth confusion could occur with Nazareth.

Question: *The gospels proclaim Jesus of Nazareth to be the son of a carpenter while the author of the scroll, Jesus of Gennesareth, claimed he was the heir to the Hasmonean throne of Israel?*

The gospels also claim Jesus to be born of King David's line – though David had ruled one thousand years before. During that period the Hebrew aristocracy had been broken up and exiled to Babylon so the royal line was hopelessly lost. The undisputed Jewish ruling family in the previous two hundred years BC was that of the Hasmoneans who had driven the Syrians from Israel. After this victory they fell to fighting among themselves, giving the Romans the opportunity to conquer Israel.

The Romans appointed Herod I (the Great) as king, who then began a campaign to liquidate all Hasmoneans, knowing that despite his own elevation to the throne they were traditionally entitled to it. He appointed his son Herod Antipas as governor of Galilee where the families of Jesus and John the Baptist were. Jesus and John were cousins and John's father Zacharias was a priest in the temple. Zacharias could have been one of the Hasmoneans murdered by Herod Antipas which might have made John the Hasmoneans' heir until he too was killed by Herod. The gospels record without explanation that on John's death Jesus left Herod's territory immediately. With John dead and the Hasmoneans' massacre virtually complete Jesus may have been the only surviving heir to the Hasmoneans' throne.

Question: *How did Christ come to be at Masada?*

There have been many suggestions that Jesus survived crucifixion or that conspiracies existed to elevate his position even to the extent of falsifying his death. Assuming he did not die on the cross and lived to old age, why was he at Masada, under siege by the Romans?

One theory is he escaped the tomb and went to live with the Essene community at Qumran, living there until the Romans attacked the monastery-city, then escaped thirty miles south to Masada. If there were truth in his being genuinely the last claimant to the Hasmoneans' throne this might answer the historical puzzles as to why the Romans attacked Qumran in the first place, why they put such enormous effort, lives, resources, and time – years in fact building an earthwork ramp – into the conquest of Masada, and why the Zealots retreated there as soon as the war began in AD 66. Accepting the fact of Jesus being *genuinely* King of the Jews gives reason to the Romans' extraordinary commitment. His writing the scroll the night before he died at Masada was perhaps his testament to the world of that.

Question: *How could Jesus – assuming he was Jesus of Nazareth – have been eighty in AD 73 at Masada?*

Matthew's gospel tells how Herod sought Jesus's death when he was a child. According to historian Josephus Flavius, Herod died in 4 BC so Jesus could not have been born in the year AD 1. The traditional dating was the result of miscalcuation made by a sixth-century monk, Dionysus Exiguus. Some biblical scholars give the date of Jesus's birth as not later than the early months of 4 BC, but in an article on the chronology of the Bible in Hastings' *Dictionary of the Bible* the date of Jesus's birth is given as between 7 and 6 BC which would indeed have made him eighty years old when Masada fell.

There was a closing note from Hal Ellis:

If Max Grosset was a con-artist hoping to suck in Joyce (a newspaper man with connections, able to publicize the story and maybe make big bucks for him) he does seem to have known his biblical history – or was able at least to put forward an interesting interpretation of events as bait. The fact that he *offered* money to Joyce to smuggle out the scroll, to my mind, disposes of the con-man theory. Because of this I'd guess this was KGB or some other organization or service attempting to damage the Christian Church. There is one other possible explanation: i.e., the scroll was genuine, Grosset wanted its contents revealed but for personal or professional reasons did not use his real name, then subsequently lost his nerve and abandoned the deal. In the event, for whatever reason, he never followed through; he and the Masada Jesus scroll both disappeared and neither have been seen since. H.E.

Cornell sat back, thoughtfully.
'What is it?' asked Madelaine Cornell.
'Fantasy.'
'Oh?'

'Or theological argument.'

'Oh.'

'Don't you want to read it?'

'Does it solve our problems?'

'You expect miracles, Madelaine. Life isn't like that.'

'We need a miracle.' She reclined her chair further and pulled a sleep-mask over her face, shutting him out.

He watched her wondering why he had always blocked out the obvious raw ambition in her. Was it because it fed his own so well, back in the early days, or just plain weakness? Was his ambition exhausted now while hers remained voracious? He gave a firm shake of his head. This was above ambition. *Shut up and sleep, this rocket will be landing at Fiumicino in a couple of hours.*

A gentle nudge at his shoulder woke him.

'I'm sorry, sir, but we have reports coming in of a tragedy in Austin. There are very many dead, I'm afraid.'

He struggled to get out of the reclined seat.

'Let me, sir.' The aide worked the lever to straighten the back. 'We've got pictures from CNN. It's a bad situation.' He moved away, pulled down a large screen and worked controls.

'What's happening?' Madelaine Cornell demanded, ripping off her sleep-mask.

'Curb your temper,' he upbraided her sharply, his eyes on the screen, horror growing in them. 'Turn around and *look*, damn it!'

The aide moved away swiftly but remained within discreet summoning distance behind them.

'My God!' she gasped at the sight of the plummeting bodies. 'What are they doing? Some of them seem to be *jumping*!'

'You said Austin?' Cornell turned backwards to the aide.

'Yes, sir. But they're jumping all over the country. There's more here of course because of the fire.'

'But there's hundreds here alone!'

'I'm afraid so, sir.'

'We'll have to turn back!' she hissed at him. 'Tell them to turn around! Order it now!'

'No.'

'You *son of a bitch*, they'll crucify you if you're out of the country with this happening!'

Apt analogy, he thought. This was terrible, yes, but he had a greater cause to serve, a greater duty to fulfil. 'Turn it off,' he ordered. He felt fraught, yet strangely detached.

'*Off*, Mr President?'

'*Off*.' he closed his eyes and offered a silent prayer.

Madelaine Cornell wept with frustration. She looked at her husband, the face she could normally read so easily suddenly – and purposefully – closed from her.

She had wanted triumph but felt diminished. The Markarovs' theory of recorded, retrievable, time was too great. Her conspiracy, her planned destruction of Kent, made petty. Even the presidency seemed smaller: the pomp, the trappings, deflated; its power, frail. Still, her natural instincts, her fight, hit out: *It wasn't possible. How could it be?* She wanted proof. She wanted Father Kolchak there in front of her swearing his Christ existed, that nothing had changed, that the old order had not faltered, that the world was still spinning and the past was as dead as the bodies that rotted beneath its soil. That what had occurred in the Church of the Holy Sepulchre in Jerusalem was of no importance and all she was dealing with was a scarred, bitter man whose grandiose ambitions had been thwarted. William Bradley Kent.

But Kolchak had not arrived and that had changed the world. Her world. Until that moment she had been in control. If he had come to her instead of Marchionni she would have had all the ammunition needed to destroy Kent utterly. Instead everything was out of control and spinning wildly. It seemed as if the whole world had gone mad. She hated Kolchak. She hated the Catholic Church. And right then she hated her husband.

The aide returned with a portable telephone. 'Sam Lewelyn, sir, from Washington. Not scrambled, you can take it from here if you wish?'

Cornell nodded. 'Sam? They gave you this number, good.' He paused, listening, his brow creasing. 'I don't understand? What are you saying? Yes, I know that Morrison was the Vatican's man – I had a meeting with Archbishop Marchionni from the Vatican Delegation. *What!* Sam, I can't believe that. I *won't*. Coincidence. Has to be coincidence. You can't base that kind of accusation on an entry in a garage diary! OK, you don't need to tell me about the power of Roman Catholicism but you're barking up the wrong tree on this. Marchionni is – Sam, listen to me!' Cornell's eyes were dark with anger, he swung around to the window, his voice dropping to a harsh whisper. 'You're implying this could go as high as the Pope? Forget it! I won't have it. We're not dealing with some fanatical Islamic mullah here!'

Madelaine Cornell watched him in bewilderment and heard Sam Lewelyn's voice say, clearly: 'Rome has had its fair share of blood over the years and you know it! You may be a Catholic, John, but you're not blind to history!'

Cornell saw a dark, bearded priest caught in mid-stride, face tight with anger, eyes like ebony buttons fixed rigidly ahead – perhaps with murderous intent. And Kent ignoring him, his eyes only for the bizarre hermaphroditic twinned faces of the scientists who promised him time itself. And above everything the high, hanging, broken figure of Christ. He saw too, the image of a speeding car trailing flame in the desert and a dedicated, perhaps lost, soul at the wheel, eager to be at one with his God.

Sam might have read his mind. 'A Moslem who drives a truck filled with explosives into a building to blow up two hundred US marines is promised paradise . . . it's not inconceivable that—'

Cornell exploded. 'Rome wouldn't kill! Not now. Not today. This isn't the time of the Inquisition!'

'We'd all kill to survive. Rome too, if the matter needs it. Excommunication is spiritual murder, isn't it? If Rome's enemy was outside the faith and that weapon was useless – would it turn the other cheek and watch the Church crumble?'

'Sam, I want you to forget all of this. Perhaps Kent has done the right thing? Perhaps he *has* kept the Markarovs' work suppressed all this time.'

Madelaine Cornell gasped in astonishment.

Sam barked: 'You don't know that! Kent's an atheist. He wouldn't care *shit* if the whole of Christianity was dumped in the dirt. But that's not the issue here. He's doing *something* in the Mojave – and you ought to be told what it is. That's why you started all this, why you called me in!'

A dead calm seemed to fall over Cornell. 'He's doing what he says he's doing: tracking deep-space radio signals, a test programme for a new breed of advanced computers. Perfectly legitimate. I want it left alone. That's an order, Sam.'

Sam voice returned like the thrust of a jagged saw: 'You're

making a mistake. Running scared from something won't make it stop haunting you.'

'Some things have to be left alone. There are things in this world we're not supposed to tamper with. I sincerely believe that to be true. No matter how strong anyone's faith is, the concept of truth would be a double-edged sword few believers could handle. Christianity vindicated or destroyed by a few inches of magnetic tape? Christ Himself reduced from being a deity to a media event overnight? Can you imagine the media circus following the revelation of the Markarovs' work – whether possible or not? Sam – even if it were possible – *you can't have God played on TV*! It would be over. Centuries of Mystery – *Eternity* – destroyed in minutes. It's simply too *big*. Too terrible even to contemplate. It stops right here, Sam. I mean it.'

'All you've said is true – but that's not what you're scared of. You're terrified that this leads to Rome. John, that's a price which might have to be paid. You're an advocate, you know better than most that truth has a price. Remember what I told you when we first discussed this in your study at the White House? When you light the fuse you won't have any control as to where the rocket will fly and what it might destroy? You're finding out now, and it doesn't suit. You can't haul it back in, John. You need to get Kent to open up that special section he's running. This is about control. About power. You can't let him have either – unleashed. You're the President.'

'Sam, listen: you know the story of Pandora's box? The dangers involved in opening it? The catastrophic effects on the world from what was let loose? Leave it be. I'll handle this in my own way. I'll call you.'

'You'll call me when you begin to wonder if Kent kept the lid on the box for your reasons or his own. Power sits comfortably on some men, John – on others it has to grow and keep growing or they're left naked. You're the first kind, we both know which kind Kent is. I can't let go of this and you're going to have to make a choice. Goodbye.'

'Sam?' Cornell stared at the telephone, a cold weight in his stomach.

'What's happened?' his wife pressed.

Cornell shook his head wearily. 'Clair Morrison is dead. Sam says murdered. He's not making a lot of sense. He says he traced the possible killer who pulled himself on to his – Sam's – gun. Obviously Sam's in a state of shock. The police seem to believe his story but . . . well, it's messy. I'll deal with it when we get back.'

She glanced fiercely at the aide who retreated fast. 'That wasn't all, was it? What was that about Marchionni? And Rome? They're involved, aren't they? I told you I didn't trust them. You tore Sam's head off! What are you hiding? Aren't things bad enough already?'

Cornell gazed out of the window. 'Leave it be. We do nothing. Absolutely nothing.'

She flared. 'I heard your arguments. Damn you, John! What do you care about religion? Or faith? You practically disowned your Catholicism the second you stood for president! When was the last time you were in a Catholic church? Your last confession? *When!*'

'This isn't about Rome – it's about us. America, Europe – the West. Listen to me, Madelaine, I'll never say anything more important than this. The balance of power has shifted completely in the last few years. Political ideologies have shown themselves to be what they really are: weak, temporary, transient. That decline has made true belief the greatest power on earth. There are two great opposing faiths in this world: Islam in the East, growing, thriving! Christianity in the West – dying by the hour. There are others of course but they are lesser and not in direct conflict so they don't count. Hear me, as God as is my witness: *I will not go down in history as the president who destroyed God and let Allah stride unopposed across the planet.*'

She stared at him and the truth was frightening. He no longer needed her. He had given himself to God and there was nothing left for her. For the first time in her life she felt the barren woman she was and turned away from the window in case the withered heart of her stared back.

'I'd say you need a drink,' said Hugh Edwards, rising from his chair as Sam put down the telephone. 'Or three.'

They were in Sam's Baltimore home: in his den, a portrait of

Elizabeth Lewelyn looking disturbingly royal, gazing serenely down on them from above the fireplace.

Edwards leaned forward, gloomily, on the small bar. '"I can't let go of this and you're going to have to make a choice." Even between friends – maybe specially between friends – that sounds like a threat?'

'It wasn't.'

'You're going to have to answer questions, Sam. I've got two dead bodies and you placed at both locations. I need something. Background at least?'

Sam ducked his head at the telephone. 'I can't say anything unless he says so.'

'From what I just heard, you and he aren't talking?'

Sam accepted the beer Edwards held out, not responding.

'You ever dealt with Catholics, Sam? I mean committed Catholics? My wife's one. They march to a different drum. Understand what I'm saying?'

'He's the President. He has a responsibility to see justice done. He took that oath. He must uphold the law above any other consideration, even above his faith. He'll be worrying over that right now, I know him. Anyhow, he's far from committed. Maybe in the early years . . . but that faded. Politics – and Madelaine – took over. Rome never had a chance.'

'That's not how it sounded to me.'

'He was shocked. I gave him news he didn't want to hear.'

Edwards sighed. 'I'll tell you how I read this. Something happened. Maybe made him see the light? Then you call with the bad news that maybe the light's not so pure. So he kicks the messenger's ass?' He drank and wiped froth from his thick black moustache. 'So what's happened?'

Sam heard Clair Morrison's words: *Something happened to him. Changed him irrevocably. Saul on the road to Damascus.* Morrison had been talking about Kent, but had John Cornell fallen on the same road? He drank, silently.

Edwards said: 'Nothing I can do then, is there?'

'You can investigate Marchionni. At least have him watched?'

'Because he owns a Ferrari 275GTB and there's one listed in a diary where an unlawful killing took place?'

'Suicide.'

'Don't expect the DA's office to go along with that story without kicking.'

'Then advise her who she could be kicking against.'

'No, sir, not me. She can find that out herself.'

'So you'll do nothing on Marchionni?'

'Sam, Marchionni holds diplomatic status. That doesn't save anyone on a capital charge but it sure as hell makes it harder to bring one.'

'You forgot to say he's worth about half a billion bucks.'

'Right. And has a family name going further back than the Borgias. Serious old money, Sam – which translates into heavy long-term influence. Investment of the past in the future. That's how it works. *Power*. Trust me. I worked those corridors as a bullet-stopper in my rookie days. You never get over the knowledge that you're being employed on the premiss that your life isn't worth as much as the one you're guarding.'

'So that's it?'

'Unless your man in the White House gives me a reason to move, yes, that's it – for now. I've no evidence against Marchionni. All I've got is you playing hard to get.' Edwards emptied his glass in one long gulp. 'Call me if there's anything I should know.'

Outside, by his car, he said, 'I'm not forgetting what you told me at Henri's earlier.' He tilted his head in the direction of the looming blocks of NSA headquarters. 'Big Brother's gone off the rails? Want to talk about that or is all of this part of the same runaway?'

'I'll call if I need help.'

'You did that once already tonight and suddenly I had two bodies on my sheet.'

'I'll call, OK.'

'Don't leave town,' Edwards growled in passable Bogart and started the engine.

'Hugh.'

'What?'

'He's your man in the White House too.'

Edwards put his head out. 'I didn't vote for him.'

'You told me you did.'

Edwards gave a cadaverous grin. 'I lied. That's what friends are for.'

Sam watched him go then returned to his den and slumped down heavily in a huge, overstuffed, battered leather armchair.

He needed solid proof. Nothing else would satisfy Edwards – or John Cornell. His telephone rang. He snatched at it, hoping it might be Greg. Or Cornell in a more reasonable frame of mind.

The weeping voice at the other end fought to get words out.

'Easy, Georgia,' he told her, his heart feeling like ironstone in his chest for he knew the only reason she ever called was for, or about, Greg, and Greg was in Austin where people were leaping off roofs to be with Jesus. *Dear God, no.*

'I just saw Greg and Carolyn jump off the Maddox Tower,' she blurted, laughing through tears. 'They landed on an air-bag. He just fell outwards with her! What if the bag hadn't been there! He's crazy!' She wept again.

'Georgia, the bag was there, that's all that matters. Are they safe? You saw them walk away from it?'

'Walk! He punched his way through those lunatics, dragging her behind. You wouldn't have believed it was Greg. Then the cameras came off them and that was it. Gone.'

'OK. Good. That's better than dead. Are they still showing pictures?'

'Don't watch it. Any of it. It's the worst of what we are. What's happened to us?'

'I don't know, Georgia. Maybe we just ran out of things to believe in. Real, not junk.'

'If he calls, tell him call me? Sam, will you do that?'

'I will, sweetheart. Don't worry, I'll make damn sure he calls you. Georgia, you're a good friend.'

'Sure,' she said dully.

He put down the receiver. Some things he could do nothing about.

He stared at the answering machine by the telephone, cursed his stupidity, and swung around to where his tweed jacket lay, feeling the weight of the small recorder he had discovered concealed in Clair Morrison's home.

He set it on the bar-top, poured himself bourbon, and listened to himself speaking to Morrison, the two of them sounding drunk: Tuesday night, he remembered – he'd called around right after his Falls Church meeting with Cornell. Then Morrison, John Cornell, and himself – the early hours next morning, watching the Jerusalem videotape. Then Morrison dialling a telephone number – identifiable as local from the number of digits. Sam sipped his bourbon, wound up. Just say your name, he urged silently, knowing it would not happen.

'I had to tell them I was there,' slurred Morrison straight away as if continuing a conversation begun earlier.

'That doesn't matter,' assured a mellow, cultured voice in that kind of accentless American that stops just short of British. 'What else?'

'I said I saw the burning car. I let them think Arabs. Nothing about Bernardelli.'

Sam stared at the machine.

'No names,' the voice reprimanded.

'He's dead,' complained Morrison, very drunk.

'Enough,' snapped the voice.

'The President was kind to me.' Morrison was weeping now. 'He told me I'd be looked after, that I'd served my county. That it should repay the debt.'

'Listen to me. Go to bed. Sleep. I'll speak with you tomorrow. You are not alone. We are with you. God is with you. Sleep now.' The call ended.

Sleep for ever, thought Sam, with cold anger.

Then came a sound like a book being sharply closed.

Sam stiffened.

There was no way of knowing how long after the telephone call it occurred. It might have been hours or seconds. The recorder was sound activated and without decoding equipment to unlock the time-code audio-markers he would never know. He did know he had just heard Clair Morrison die.

He poured another drink and took it to the bedroom where he lay, still clothed, on the vast bed, his arm stretched out to the pillow where Elizabeth's head had lain.

He knew he was drunk. But not so drunk that he could fall gratefully off the edge into oblivion. Not so drunk that the hunter in him would leave the pressing question alone: if Bernardelli had died in a blazing car in the desert, who was the man who had jerked the Magnum to his forehead earlier that night?

He sipped his bourbon, then put the glass aside. Ignoring

Georgia's advice he flicked on CNN and for a few moments watched reports of hysteria brought on by Maddox's telecast around the country. In disgust he switched off and closed his eyes, feeling wretched, very lonely, even abandoned. He slept. But not before he took a snub Beretta automatic from the bedside drawer and held it in his big fist across his chest.

CHAPTER
ELEVEN

The former leader of the defunct Soviet Union was amused. He toasted his wife with chilled Dom Perignon as he put down the telephone in their sumptuous suite in the New York Waldorf Astoria hotel.

She turned from the television coverage of events which had, in succession as the evening progressed, enthralled, amazed, and now shocked her.

'What is it?' she questioned, pleased to see him so, for after his downfall they had been through difficult, degrading times and while for some years now dollars had rolled in liberally – his three hundred roubles a month state pension, once a grievous insult, was now merely a bad joke – it took, nevertheless, a great deal for the famous smile to break as it did now on the cherubic face.

He looked down on the lights of bustling traffic on Park Avenue far below. 'What a country! They pay *me* to lecture them on *their* victory – now their spymaster wishes me to report on my old enemies and name my price for doing so! If he had allowed his interpreter time to take breath I'd have given him every damning word of their confessions for nothing. For my own pleasure!'

She peered at him over fashionable, costly spectacle frames purchased just the day before – though as a good Russian keeping her old ones for the possible return of hard times. 'Learn from them, *mili*. Everything has a price. Your memory is a vein of gold – but it won't last for ever.'

He drank deeply and refilled his glass.

'And your liver could go first,' she warned.

He nodded. 'After tonight no more champagne until the tour is over. I must keep my senses clear for all those eager, clever young minds.' He dipped his head at the horrific events portrayed on the monolithic TV set. 'If any remain alive! Why is it Americans are addicted to excess?'

She muted the sound. 'What did he want – their spymaster?'

'Who.'

'Well?'

'Two scientists: Markarov, Ilya and Irina – brother and sister, not husband and wife. Twins. The crazy thing is that they're here already. They defected in' – he shrugged – 'eighty-six, I think.'

'What kind of spymaster can he be if he doesn't know what spies he has bought?'

'New. The only one surviving from our time is that black bat, William Kent, at their National Security Agency.'

'*Black bat?*'

'KGB named him.' He put hands by his ears, making them huge. 'He hears everything there is to hear. Electronic Intelligence. No one can touch the Americans in that field. He is a genius, which is why he is still there despite the change in the administration. Without him the Gulf War would have been a disaster for the Americans, Britain would have lost the Falklands, and the Israelis would be face-down in the sand or treading salt water. Without Kent I might still have been in power.'

'He is negro?'

'Burns. Bad burns. A KGB joke. An aircraft accident. A genuine one, I was told – not of our making.'

'He is not the one who called?'

'This is CIA. Director Ellis, Cornell's man. Presidents here appoint their own people to key posts – Kent is the exception.'

'As did *we*,' she retorted. 'But our spymasters would know precisely what had occurred – even a decade before.'

'Because our presidents were appointed for life,' he reminded, frowning at bitter memories.

'Forget the past. It is done.'

'Yes.'

'So if these traitors are here already what information can you add?'

'This is the mystery.'

She let him fill her glass and sipped, frowning at the bubbles.

'Perhaps they failed to live up to their promises? How do the Americans say it – failed to *deliver*?'

'I'll call Voroshilov at the prosecutors' office.'

'What can he do?'

'The name Markarov might mean something to those who see little daylight these days. I didn't know everything that went on.' His eyes hardened. 'I didn't know enough.'

'You're thinking of a ploy? These Markarovs were KGB?'

He pulled himself up. 'I think the Americans suspect this and need to know for certain.'

She considered this for a moment. 'Which means they've acted embarrassingly or expensively on the information the Markarovs supplied.'

He nodded. 'They wouldn't pay for a service and not use the product. That wouldn't be countenanced over here. Even in Intelligence their ethos is value for money – and results.' He paused, thoughtful. 'Or they must hide it,' he murmured.

She pressed on. 'If the Markarovs' product now seems suspect then perhaps you can save their blushes – or at least turn off the money tap?'

'Perhaps.'

'My darling, you must consider your price most seriously, here.'

He consulted his watch, calculating time difference with Moscow.

'It's Saturday morning there, Voroshilov's office will be closed,' she reminded.

He lifted the telephone. 'Prisons never close.'

In Washington a Rolls-Royce Phantom limousine pulled alongside the Gates Lear jet bearing the discreet gold-leaf Vincenze-Marchionni family crest as the sleek aircraft was readied for take off from the exclusive private air facility west of the Potomac River.

David Kolchak limped out into a chill wind, silhouetted in the white glare of the Lear jet's glaring lights.

'There is no question of failure, David,' Marchionni said, not alighting, leaning forward from the cushions through the opened door. 'You understand that?'

'I've always understood that,' replied Kolchak, heavily. 'I've never lost sight of that—' He looked away. 'Since Jerusalem.'

'May God be with you.'

'God *is* with me. I feel Him. It's whether He'll stay with me.' Kolchak knelt, quickly, as though afraid.

Marchionni blessed him and for a long moment let his hand remain on the worn, prematurely grey head, his slim fingers gripping the skull before releasing their hold.

Kolchak arose, turning away in silence, face grim and set, eyes streaming as if from the wind, then stiffly mounted the steps lowered from the private jet, not looking back.

'Goodbye, David,' Marchionni murmured, feeling hollow sadness and a dreadful sense of inevitability. And more. Though crushed.

He could see Kilchak through the porthole, staring forward as though his vision was fixed on the deed. He reached for him with his mind. *David, within the larger dimension everything else is peripheral. On this world's level, what we do now – what we must do – could never be understood. Even the Holy Father could not understand. Not completely.*

He felt the prick of tears and sought solace in purpose. He, Ricardo Marchionni alone, had the vision for the achievement of a greater destiny. He had been granted riches, position, power; all for this moment. Those he had sent before had failed. Now his most trusted soldier was setting out to do what must be done, leaving him bereft. But not without purpose.

He had one dictum which he followed scrupulously. Never expect others to do what you would not do yourself.

With Kolchak it had always been that way despite the enormous difference in their circumstances. That had been the strength of their friendship.

He had a sudden memory of himself, heir to millions, and Kolchak, the hired help, both barely seventeen, in soap-suds up to their elbows, laughing, cleaning two cars together, a scarlet Ferrari 275GTB owned then by his father, and a beaten-up fifth-hand Mustang Kolchak had just bought. And his mother coming down from the mansion, scolding him for such a breach of social mores.

Neither of them told her they had decided together that God alone was their judge.

As He was now.

He smiled, fleetingly happy, and touched a button at his elbow, the limousine surging forward just as the sound of the Lear jet's twin turbo-jets rose to a scream which he knew, with certainty, would be echoed in Kolchak's tortured mind.

Hold on, David. My dear love, hold on just long enough to kill. I know you have the courage to die.

In Moscow, Dimitri Sergeyovich Voroshilov was proud. Proud to have been called upon to perform a task, a delicate task, for his former leader.

Voroshilov's opinion was firm – though in such treacherous times for former Party members, necessarily discreet: he should still be their leader. Not leader of the raggle-taggle patchwork of states with broken economies now left with no cohesive head – but supreme leader of all from the Baltic to Bering seas as he used to be. Voroshilov would do anything to serve that goal, though in low moments he admitted this was now impossible and he was living in the past. How many weren't, he wondered now, sighing.

He made his way in the cold morning to the dilapidated prison where the dogs who had brought him down – those who had survived the aftermath – spent their dark days. He believed he had chosen the correct target, the one who in the high times had slithered along the corridors of power, watching, listening, remembering, storing all for later use.

'Good morning, Comrade Antipov,' greeted Voroshilov, sliding open a panel and peering into the gloomy cell.

'*Comrade* is forbidden,' growled the slovenly guard who hadn't a complete uniform to his name and had not been paid for six months.

This was the forgotten end of town where the discarded trash of the new revolution ended up – along with the debris of the old.

Voroshilov shuddered to think how the guard put money in his pockets – other than from occasional hand-outs he offered himself and something, perhaps, from prisoners' relatives. If anyone admitted to being their relatives?

It wasn't that their crime was being Communist, he reflected; there were thousands of party members still running the creaking departments of bureaucracy – for who else could do it? – no, they hadn't been *strong* Communists. If their coup had succeeded the people would, inevitably, have knuckled under and life would have gone on much as before. But they had failed and so they were pariahs, unloved by political victors and losers alike.

Voroshilov closed the panel and smiled at the guard. 'Where is your humour, my friend?'

'What's funny these days?' the man growled, omitting even his usual *your honour*.

Voroshilov nodded gravely and held out his hand. The guard palmed the foreign-currency bill of which Voroshilov had many differing varieties and denominations from various sources who all believed he served them exclusively.

The guard unlocked the door and slouched away to a wall seat where he slumped, gazing dejectedly at the filthy stone floor.

Voroshilov stood looking deliberately at him, until, with a groan, he arose again and trudged away to the upper level.

'What do you want?' demanded Antipov, lying inside the cell on a mean cot, hands clasped comfortingly over his abdomen.

'Like your guard you have poor humour today, Arkady Mikhailovich?'

'If you had my arsehole you'd be in poor humour.'

'Ah! The diet? It could improve, you know.'

Antipov looked up. In his condition anything that offered hope, even improvement, had his complete attention. He would have sold his soul or his mother – probably both – for food which didn't run straight through him like liquid fire leaving him sore, weak, and half suffocated by the stench of it.

'Good,' said Voroshilov, wiping off a stool with his handkerchief and sitting on it. 'Very good, I need your complete concentration on the matter in hand.'

'What matter in hand?' Antipov ventured, warily. 'You've had everything I remember out of me already.'

Voroshilov smiled. 'I want what you have forgotten.'

'I don't understand.'

'Names: Markarov, Irina and Ilya?'

Antipov shook his head, shoulders slumped from disappointment.

'Come, come, Comrade. You must try harder.'

'Never heard of 'em.'

'Then *see* them.'

'What d'you mean?'

'Their names perhaps were never used?'

'You have pictures?'

'Regrettably no.'

'Then how do I fucking see them?'

Voroshilov tapped his temple. 'They were Jews. Scientists. Also they were twins, identical twins.'

A light ignited in Antipov's defeated eyes.

Voroshilov placed his jaw upon his fist, prepared to wait, prepared to endure the stench of this wretched creature for the man he admired so. 'What do you remember?'

'I must think.'

'About your stomach?'

Antipov jabbed a dirty finger, the nail bitten to the quick. 'Anything that goes in my stomach ends up in that bucket, or worse, on the floor. You'll need to get me out of here, it's ridden with infection. What good is the best steak if I shit it on to the floor in minutes!'

Voroshilov lifted his head and frowned at his own scrupulously cared-for hands. 'I need something – an *hors-d'oeuvre*, shall we say? – if I am to improve your conditions even one jot.'

'It was a long time ago,' mumbled Antipov as if making up his mind.

'Dzerzhinsky Square?'

'Kremlin,' Antipov stated more firmly.

'In whose time?'

Antipov told him.

'Who was present?'

'Party theoreticians, the die-hards, the old *doctors* – the fathers of the revolution – those still living anyway. God! They were *old*. There was *history* in that room, Voroshilov. Real history!'

Voroshilov felt a tug at his own bowels. He knew the feeling: he had it often when, in the middle of some apparently insignificant case, something arose which changed the entire picture. In the old days that usually meant the case was rapidly closed. Now he felt the same mixed sense of urgency and unease – but also excitement.

'Why were they there, Comrade?' he asked. 'I swear to you your days are already growing brighter.'

'Because he knew we would be where we are now and needed to convince the others. He'd done the arithmetic, debated the probabilities. There were plans for the struggle to continue.'

Voroshilov pondered this statement, apparently unmoved – though his mind was spinning. 'And the Markarovs?' he asked after a moment. 'What was their place in this?'

'They were faces, not names. No names were offered. Twins, as you said. Strange, one could have been the other easily, even with the difference in sex. *Unnatural*. Know what I mean?'

'Go on.'

'Not here. I'll give you all of it. But out of here.'

'How can I be sure I can trust you? You might feed me nothing but lies.'

Antipov's eyes were like caged animals, they flicked fast in his face, sensing freedom, yet desperation was there too.

'Take it easy,' warned Voroshilov, regretting sending the guard so far away.

'There were tapes made,' blurted Antipov. 'Everything was always taped, you know that. They should have been destroyed.'

'But they weren't?'

Antipov's sly eyes calculated the price of his answer. 'No.'

Voroshilov leaned forward. 'Who knows about this?'

Antipov suddenly felt exposed, fear touching his infected eyes. 'I don't know who has survived? They're probably all dead – old age and . . . what's happened out there.'

'The tapes? Destroyed, I suppose, after the coup? So much was.'

'Perhaps not.'

Voroshilov stared long and hard, searching for the lie and not finding one.

Antipov moved close and the stench from him was sickening. 'Freedom, Voroshilov. Total, complete, never to set foot in this stinkhole hell ever again freedom. And some sort of start outside. I may never see daylight down here, comrade, but I hear damn well what a mess it is up there. I want a start and it has to be a good one.'

'A fair one,' countered Voroshilov.

Antipov nodded. 'A fair one.'

Voroshilov stood.

Antipov said: 'Find Nikolai Nikolaevich Kozlov. He's out there somewhere. Starving, I imagine. Who has work for a scientist specializing in the study of the paranormal these days?'

In Baltimore Sam Lewelyn awoke with sweat streaming from him. He glanced at the luminous bedside clock, still seeing the shattered head that had dragged him, screaming silently, from a dead sleep.

Not Bernardelli's head: Cornell's.

It was four o'clock. He fumbled for the light and switched it on, the glow doing nothing to dispel the awful certainty that gripped him like a live thing: Cornell was flying at supersonic speed into the guns of Sazarin's would-be assassins. No logic, no reasoning, behind it; simple gut-think brought on by shock and booze and exhaustion which he should discard as he would the dead beer cans from the night before. But he couldn't. This was as real as his sitting there on the edge of the bed feeling like death – if death was jangling nerves and zero energy. He heaved himself up with a huge grunt, practically throwing himself into the bathroom and the coldest shower he could survive. What are you doing! he wondered, gasping as the icy needles bit. Four in the morning craziness at your age? Go back to bed, sleep off the booze and the bad dreams. But there was no going back.

He towelled himself hard, flicking on CNN to be faced with the floodlit, charred, skeletal remains of the Maddox tower and terrible pictures of hoses playing on stained sidewalks, and a verbal stream of statistics all of which pronounced death on someone, somewhere – anywhere that night's madness had taken hold.

He shut down the set, stabbed digits into the telephone for a Balitmore number, and heard the rasping sandpaper voice of William Bradley Kent gasp hello.

'They're going to kill the President,' Sam said, butally. 'Rome. Or their Believers. Because you've given them a reason, you son of a bitch.'

'Who is this?'

'Sam Lewelyn. I've figured it out. You've made it work. You've got something Rome can't allow to come out. What is it, Kent? Why's John Cornell suddenly running scared? He wanted you out and suddenly you don't matter. Rome does. Rome matters to him very much. Above everything. Maybe even above the presidency. Marchionni went to see him. Fed him some story. You know what it is.'

'Ask Cornell.'

'They'll kill him. They'll kill anyone who threatens them. They've got too much to lose.'

Kent's harsh whisper changed to rasping reasonableness. 'You have to understand what all this is really about. It was a set up. Moscow's set up, years ago. Except the Markarovs changed the game. Sam, hear me, they came out of that church with Christ. Believe what I'm saying. *They had the voice of Christ*, I swear it. They were killed for it. They almost killed me too.'

Sam sat on the bed. He felt sick. A deep dreadful sickness. 'No,' he said.

'That's what I said, back then.'

'I don't understand.'

'I had it in my hands, Sam. I played it. Once. Then it was gone. Leaving noise. Terrible, awesome noise.'

'You listen. It never happened. You said it yourself: it was all Moscow.' Sam could hear his voice rising, anger bubbling, and there was nothing he could do to stop it. 'Hearts and minds, Kent. Our policy was always positive, they always, *always*, ran theirs negatively. Kill the heart and the mind dies, leaving them jelly to play with, that's how they used to win. Moscow suckered you and you've spent half your life trying to make up for it. They're finished over there but they've won. You're *it*, Kent. The best there is. Who is more powerful than you? Cornell? I'm beginning to doubt it! And they've had you running chasing your own ass for years! You're still doing it, now.'

'*No! I heard it!*'

'No one hears the voice of God, except maybe in their heart. If they did it would become nothing.'

'*Now* you understand.'

'What are you playing with in the desert, Kent? What's my boy doing?'

Kent's breathing was tortured: air passing over scarred tissue. 'They have to find it. It was there – it still is. It must be. They gave me a maze, Sam. A maze that's taken my health and probably what's left of my life. They let me hear the truth, then they drowned the truth in a babble of lies. It's a noise that spawns madness. They drowned Him in there.'

'You don't believe, Kent. Except in yourself.'

'*Credo quia impossibile*. I believe because it is impossible. You know who quoted that at me? Clair Morrison. The words are true, Sam. There's nothing in the possible for us to believe in.'

'Did you have Morrison killed?'

'You know I didn't.'

'Marchionni?'

'Sam, hear me: walk away. Lift even the corner of the cover over this and what you saw on television tonight will spread like a plague across the world. They're simple people out there. They need food. Food for their bellies and food for their spirits. Cut off the first and you kill them, cut off the second and they'll kill you because there's nothing to keep them in check any more. It's happening already: walk any city street.'

'I want it to stop. To stop *now*.'

'Nothing will stop the work. Chain lightning, Sam. It goes on, one flash of energy igniting another and another. Your son will tell you that. You want the truth. It was there on the television tonight – except a fool like Maddox can't see it, can't interpret it. He was right, it was in Revelation but he has no idea where. He was looking for heaven when what's here is hell. Listen to the words: "Then I saw an angel coming down from heaven with the key of the abyss and a great chain in his hands. He seized the dragon, that serpent of old, the Devil or Satan, and chained him up for a thousand years; he threw him into the abyss, shutting and sealing it over him, so that he might seduce the nations no more till the thousand years were over. After that he will be let loose for a short while." Sam, the dragon is all we've ever known. Hell is all around us: it's everything we ever were and it's there now, waiting for us to face it. Satan is us, the evil that men do – there behind a veil as thin, as transparent, as time. Sam, I have the dragon by the tail – there under the desert – *and I can't let go*!'

'You're insane, Kent. I'm going to get Greg away from you whatever it takes.'

'You've lost him. And I suspect you've lost Cornell too. He wouldn't listen, would he? His mind is set. That's how the madness begins.'

'Damn you!' Sam smashed the receiver down and in fury looked around him. He went through the house in a blind rage, tearing it apart, finding the bugs and crushing them with a hammer. He remembered his warning to Cornell in the White House – it seemed like a hundred years before: *He has powerful friends and a long reach. Right into this room if he wants. You can sweep for bugs as long as you like, won't do you any good, he'll get you from outside; you wouldn't believe what can be done these days. You know that scary future world people use to write about? It's here.*

Calm down, he ordered himself. Or his insanity will infect you. Kent was insane, he had no doubt of that. Lucidly insane. The most dangerous kind. The years of isolation, the need for revenge on Moscow who had destroyed him, slowly, from beyond the grave, the obsession that had tipped him over the edge into crazed religious mania.

He had two priorities: warn John Cornell of his fears – if he could get him to listen – even if that meant travelling to Rome, and get Greg away from Kent's heavy influence, the signs of which were already, ominously, evident in his open defiance of the President. Anything else was unimportant. Including disobeying Hugh Edwards' light-hearted but mean warning not to leave the country.

He gave himself black coffee and telephoned Edwards' number.

'Yes?' A voice used to early-hours calls answered.

'Listen,' he said and played the recording of the bugged telephone conversation between Morrison and the man he guessed might be Marchionni.

Edwards sighed when it was finished. 'You forgot to tell me about this before or you've just found it?'

'Forgot.'

'Sure about that?' Edwards yawned and a woman's voice complained in the background. 'Stay on the line. I'm moving before I become *another* homicide victim you're involved with.'

After a moment he came back on, the bedroom extension going down hard. 'Going to be a great day,' he muttered. 'OK, I guess it was shock that made you forget?'

'Must have been.'

'Because it's you, I believe it. So?'

'I found more bugs and another voice-activated deck – here in the house – the same as the one I discovered at Clair Morrison's. I smashed the bugs but the deck's OK. I haven't played it back but I imagine you're on it.'

'Tonight?'

'Yes.'

'All right, this obviously couldn't wait until morning – I mean normal-people morning – so you've got bad news for me. I'm waiting?'

'You heard the tape. Who died tonight in the garage if Bernardelli died in the desert?'

'There's more than one Bernardelli in the world, probably more than one in Washington. Look for the simple answer first, Sam. I'll check if the deceased had any male family also deceased. Died how?'

'Car wreck. Mojave desert 1986.'

'So I'm getting dates and locations now? Hey!'

'Hugh, listen. A Catholic priest was involved in this from the start. A Father David Kolchak. You need a direct connection between Marchionni and the two deaths tonight, Kolchak could be it?'

'Why couldn't you have called to tell me what *all* of this is about? I hate serials.'

'I called to tell you I'm leaving the country. I think Cornell's next. Next dead.'

Edwards fell silent. 'OK, why?'

'Gut,' Sam admitted. 'But listen – I had the same feeling when Sazarin got hit. Events running wild, yet, right in there somewhere, a sense of their being controlled. I even told Cornell – then – that I felt uneasy. He dismissed it. Why shouldn't he? Hell, he's the President, he is in control. If there was something going on he should have known, should have been told. That's why NSA exists. Why the Intelligence community exists. Maybe that's the crunch? He's being sidelined. The players in this believe he doesn't have it.'

'You're not making sense, Sam.'

'I know. But I do know the last place he should be going right now is Rome.'

'Because of what happened there to Sazarin?'

'Because Rome is at the heart of all this. You made the

connection yourself – the crucifixes – back at the garage. You even thought Cornell was involved. He is – he's the next hit!'

'Sam, I'll bet a year's pay when you get there Cornell tells you to turn around and head back. I heard that conversation you had with him. He wasn't long-arming you, he was cutting you out. And he was serious.'

'I still have to warn him.'

'If you feel that strongly, try calling the man again.'

'I've got no facts to give him – and that's all a phone-call is good for. I need to be there.'

'Leaving me with an unsolved double homicide and trying to explain away a witness – some might say suspect – who gave me advance warning he was walking? Why the hell didn't you just walk? You going to take any notice of my objections?'

'No.'

Edwards sighed. 'So how? Alitalia? My wife does that trip every year. Plane doesn't leave until five tonight – out of New York, JFK. Which gives plenty of time for me to be chewed out by the DA and a warrant issued to put you in irons on sight.'

'I'll hitch a ride out of Andrews with my NSA ID. The Air Force always has something heading for Europe early. Frankfurt, probably. I can connect from there.'

'If you're really feeling edgy about this don't you think you ought to let someone know? I mean official? Like the Secret Service. Call them.'

'And tell them what? First thing they'll do is contact Cornell. And as you say, right now he's not receptive.'

Edwards paused. 'You and Cornell go back a long way.'

'You know that. Why raise it?'

'Because if he doesn't feel the way you do about the past – above other loyalties, I mean – you could be in deep shit over this. There's one dead man in the morgue with your bullet in what's left of his brain, another with you down as finder – and John Cornell's the only one who can back up your story of his involving you in all this.'

'I know it.'

'You better know it!'

'Hugh, Cornell's scared of the past.'

'Is that supposed to make sense to me?'
'It will do. Drive me to Andrews and I'll explain.'
'All of it?'
'All I know.'

CHAPTER
TWELVE

Greg Lewelyn had dozed erratically on the airport seat, repeatedly awakened, while Carolyn, fallen across him, slept restlessly, as those retreating from the Texas capital poured into the airport throughout the long night. Waking now, facing an inhospitable morning and another day of hard travelling – with who knew what conclusion at its end? – Greg felt stiff, raw, and hostile.

He saw a pay-phone become free, eased Carolyn's unconscious head off his thighs, and made for it before another of the exhausted, dishevelled, and disillusioned crowd which filled every available seat and most of the floor space at Austin's Meuller airport could get to it.

A man stumbling from a heap of sprawled bodies headed for the same booth but seeing the uncompromising look in Greg's eyes slowed and hovered by another.

Rapidly, Greg tapped in his father's Baltimore number, seeing the flashing digital clock by the departure-board ahead of him click to 5:45 dead.

He heard the message-tape bleep. 'Come on, Dad, wake up,' he breathed.

Over the public-address a tired voice called the first flight out that day – American Airlines to Dallas, which he had bought seats on immediately they reached the airport after escaping the horror of the Maddox tower the night before. From Dallas they could connect to a Roanoke flight with time to spare.

He left a hurried message on the tape saying all was well and he'd call later then returned to find Carolyn sitting up, looking drained and exhausted.

'You can sleep all you like on the plane,' he cajoled, easing her up, practically carrying her toward the boarding gates while around him his situation was repeated: men supporting women, women carrying floppy-limbed children, and even elderly slack-jawed men with glazed, spent eyes supported by their womenfolk.

Greg moved faster, straight into the sudden glaring lamps of TV news crews poised like predators at the boarding gate.

He straight-armed one closing camera-operator away.

'Hey!' a voice bawled but the surging crowd behind swept them through the gates before any retaliation occurred.

On the jet he strapped Carolyn in firmly then leaned his head back wearily on the seat, feeling he was in a time-slip, that events could not have occurred within twenty-four hours, that he had stepped into some other world.

Exhaustion and too much adrenalin, he rationalized; gritty, burning eyelids drooping, consciousness fighting valiantly – but he was already falling face-down into the sand.

> The approaching truck was a tremulous star reflected and magnified on the black floor of the desert basin and, for him, just then, more magnificent than any of the billions, light-years above.
>
> He had to capture that star. There was no other way.
>
> There was one other.
>
> Do nothing.
>
> Die.
>
> Lie where he was until he felt nothing, then let the desert make him nothing.
>
> That was no option. Not for him. He had not survived the attentions of his Dark Angel to dehydrate and shrivel in the sand.
>
> Stop the truck or die. No other way.
>
> He ran blindly down the soaring wave of the dune, falling, tumbling, keeping his eyes open so he wouldn't lose the star and the galaxies threatening to engulf him at any moment.
>
> He had no idea how he would stop a hurtling truck. He simply had to. Just as, unarmed, he must kill the driver or himself be killed.
>
> If he still had the heavy gold sovereigns which had been part of his survival kit he might have bought his way out, but those were in his former captors' pockets, or, more likely, already traded and spent.

Luck, fate, God, or an uncomplicated random event settled the matter, for as he ran suicidally at the vibrating headlights, the driver, asleep at the wheel, was shaken back to heart-stopping consciousness by a tyre thumping hard into the bomb-cratered road and the hurtling spectre, arms raised like claws, in the ghostly tunnel of light ahead.

With a wail the Iraqi took his hands from the wheel and passed his fate and all control of the truck's careering, undirected path to the will of Allah.

The sand saved the truck from obliteration, building up under the axles into a growing solid buffer and for a few short moments saved the driver too until the clawed hand burst through the crazed windscreen and grabbed his throat. With the demon's wild, hot eyes inches from his own he silently paid all debts his soul owed in this world and gave himself up to the next with his last choking acclamation, *Allhua-al-akbar!* God is great.

I didn't kill you, Greg thought through raging fever, staring at the lifeless terror-struck face. *Allah killed you. Or submission to Him did.*

He climbed through into the cab and began stripping the body, gagging at the stench from the man's voided bowels and the thought of putting on his soiled djellaba, yet not faltering for a second. Survival offered no options.

He heaved the body out, covered it with sand, then, watching frantically for lights of other vehicles which – there – could only be Iraqi, or possibly Jordanian, he began inching the big vehicle backwards until he was back on the cratered black-top.

Freedom, he thought, shutting out everything but the night. Or trying to, for his Dark Angel rode beside him as pervasive to his mind as the lingering stench of the driver was to his nostrils.

How long before I'm free of you?

You don't understand, Greg, we are brothers in war, pain, survival, in life, in death. Without me you are the nothing you were before you entered my world and I, yours. I have changed you and thus made you.

Go to hell!

Hell is where you are, Greg.

The stench suddenly changed to exquisite perfume and he was sure he was dead.

'You have to strap yourself in, sir,' said the flight attendant, bending over him. 'We're about to take off.' She bent closer, concerned. 'Are you all right?'

He saw stretching ahead the tightly packed human wreckage from Maddox's soaring eloquence and crashing fallibility and for one stark moment no longer knew which was reality and which memory. Nor even if the memory was real, or fantasy. Or the strident overture of insanity?

'I'm fine,' he said.

The jets roared, then speed and the lifting palm of flight had him and he slept in nothingness.

Hugh Edwards left Sam Lewelyn at Andrews Air Force Base and driven back, troubled in the early morning gloom to Washington. He checked the dash-clock, shrugged, and called a number in the suburbs from his car-phone.

'Aileen? This is Hugh. Sorry to call so early. Jim there?'

The unhappy, sleepy voice mumbled negatively.

He pressed harder. 'Aileen, wake yourself up, I need to get hold of Jim.'

'He pulled Air Force One duty,' Jim Bentley's wife moaned.

'Got a contact number?'

Aileen Bentley was awake now: awake and disturbed. 'The Rome Embassy. Hold on, it's right here. What's wrong?'

'Routine.'

'Don't bullshit me, Hugh Edwards. You don't call at six in the morning trying to contact a presidential bodyguard in Rome and call it routine.'

'It's nothing to worry about.'

'Are you kidding? Do you have any idea what it's like waiting out each day? It's bad enough here in the US – but the President goes to Europe I get put on the rack. They're *killing* politicians over there!'

Edwards pulled on to the highway shoulder. 'All right, Aileen, here it is. Jim drove the President somewhere using his own car. The car was later ID'd near a homicide scene. We're eliminating it from the enquiry is all, OK? That's it.'

Her voice was subdued. 'He told me he took the President

somewhere in the car. OK, maybe he shouldn't have done. What else is he going to do? Let me scream the neighbourhood down at three a.m.? I thought he'd been fooling around. Still did until just now. I told him: What's the President of the United States doing riding in your Ford past midnight? Would you believe him? *Shit!* I let him go away mad. I said I'd never do that. Oh, Hugh!'

'OK, listen, I have to call him – I'll tell him you're feeling bad which should make him feel good. When he gets back you can show him how bad you really feel.'

'*Hugh Edwards!*'

'Go back to sleep – and sleep peacefully.'

'I will – now.'

Edwards knew how Aileen Bentley felt – he'd seen his own wife go through it when he worked diplomatic protection – and hated having to lie but he had little choice. Besides in this kind of situation a lie did more good than the truth. She would thank him later.

He called the Rome number, rapidly working out it should be around midday.

'He's resting,' said a twangy female voice after he announced himself and his business.

'Wake him,' said Edwards.

'Is this necessary? They flew in overnight from Washington.'

'Police business. This call is costing the tax-payer – just like your salary. Do it.'

'Yes, sir.'

A surprisingly bright voice came on. 'What the fuck? What've I done? Illegal parking? I got immunity. Get outa here.'

'I just talked with Sam Lewelyn. You know that name?'

All banter vanished from Bentley's voice. 'I'm listening.'

'You met him. He just told me the circumstances. Told me more than that.'

Bentley paused, cautious. 'He must have had a good reason. I don't think those meetings were meant to be discussed outside of the people involved. Not the way I read it.'

'He had a good reason.'

'This is an embassy line, Hugh. Everything's recorded.'

'It's OK, this is police business.'

Bentley remained silent.

Edwards said: 'Verify. No names. There were two meetings. The first at a woman's house, the second, a man's.'

'Affirmative.'

'The man is dead. Homicide. Gunshot: single bullet, .22 calibre soft-nose – probably silenced – behind the ear, target sleeping. Last night.'

'Shit.'

'Don't jump to conclusions.'

'Who's jumping? I *know* what kind of a hit that is.'

Edwards heard the sharp rasp of a starched bed-sheet being thrown off.

'I'll tell the President,' said Bentley.

'He knows.'

'How?'

'Lewelyn called him on Air Force One. Look, there's more here than I can say. Lewelyn is flying over to see the President.'

'You calling me for the reason I'm thinking, Hugh?'

'Talk to Lewelyn, he needs someone close to the President he can trust.'

'When's he ariving?'

'Soon as he can.'

'He knows about this call?'

'No. He has no idea I know you and I didn't offer the information – in case your position was compromised. He described the Secret Service baby-sitter for the meetings as young, black, six three, skinny, and permanently worried. That's you.'

'I'm ageing. The last part is for sure – now.'

'He'll make contact when he gets there. In the mean time . . .'

'I hear you. I knew something stank right away.'

'Watch yourself. Oh, Aileen says sorry. I just spoke with her. She believes you now.'

'Crazy! I don't have time to fool around – even if I had the energy or the inclination!'

'Take care, Jim.'

'You bet.'

Edwards put down the hand-set and moved off on to the highway again.

Was that a good idea? he pondered. Even if he could have explained everything that Lewelyn had told him would Bentley have believed any of it? Over a phone-line? And if the President himself was dismissing Lewelyn's fears what could one member of the Secret Service do? For that matter what could one Washington detective do – chief or not?

He gloomily fingered his thinning wiry hair, feeling the cool betrayal of his scalp under his fingers. Time moves on, buddy. He went back over the explanation Lewelyn had given him on the way to Andrews. From anyone else he would simply have said 'Bullshit', stopped the car, leaned over and pushed the door open. Not with Sam Lewelyn. Not when the President of the United States showed all the signs of a man faced with the one issue in his life when he turns and says: No.

History? Until now it was something to forget. For him now was real and the future was hopeful. The future was important. Screw Rome and their problems. There would be problems enough nearer home if there was even a glimmer of truth in Sam's story. Hell! No one was going to want the treatment of his race confirmed in full gory, painful, destructive detail. Move forward, don't look back – that was the way out of the ghetto – and you don't have to be a Tom to make it. You just had to be you.

He remembered something from James Joyce. 'History is a nightmare from which I am trying to awake.' It seemed there were people determined to keep the world sleeping in the comfortable bed of delusion.

He drove faster, heading for police headquarters downtown on Indiana Avenue. He was a cop and thought like one, which meant taking things step by step, allowing the big picture to form around him until everything was clear – though he knew that in Washington some things were never really clear and the big picture was often more than a little blurred no matter how close you got to it. Or maybe you just weren't allowed to take that necessary step back to focus?

By nine thirty he had given himself breakfast and enough black coffee to stave off the feeling that the only place he should be on a Saturday morning after being roused at four thirty was in bed getting comfort from – in his very personal view – the undoubted expert in that particular field, his wife Gina.

He drove across the city to a street where a row of modest brownstone town-houses nestled dependably together. He had the information he wanted, acquired with little delay and absolutely no effort from himself, on the car seat beside him. He glanced wonderingly at the read-out, still prepared to marvel at the extraordinary feats accomplished by computers even though he relied on them on a daily basis.

Bernardelli. Augusto, Benito. More often known as Benny the Bet or, increasingly, as time had moved on, the Loser.

Edwards ducked his head and peered out. So, OK, this isn't the high end of town but it's levels above where Benny started, according to records – and stratospherically above the one-room walk-up listed as his last known address which would have been barely big enough for him alone, never mind his family of six.

He drew up outside one brownstone with overdone too-pink frills at every window. He didn't need to check the number.

The woman who answered his ring on the triple-chime door-bell had the eyes of someone waiting for the worst to happen and had been for some time. He showed his gold shield and saw her crack wide open in front of him.

'Let's talk about it, Mrs Bernardelli,' he said, as gently as he could, for he had an Italian wife himself.

In the living room Maria Bernardelli, seated herself on a burgundy velour settee, crossed herself, and whispered, head down and slightly tilted, one ear upward as though God Himself was listening at that moment. 'They will kill us. All.' She wept quietly. 'The children!'

Edwards made a sympathetic noise and switched to fluent Italian, seeing her relax a little even as she glanced up from his handkerchief with surprise.

He explained Gina.

'Ah!' said Maria Bernardelli.

'So? Who are they who would do this terrible thing?'

She blinked like a doe, the fright in her alive.

He murmured. 'Cosa Nostra?'

Her eyelids dropped.

'This house, *Signora*? It belongs to them.'

She rallied, her eyes indignant. 'The house is mine. Mine and for my children when I am here no more. OK!'

'I am pleased for you. It is important in these times to own property. One needs the stability. The roots.'

'Of course.' She blew her nose violently.

He took out his gold shield again, lazily, laying it on the table between them. A reminder.

She stared at it.

He spread the computer print-out beside it. 'Your husband was not lucky with his investments,' he stated. He glanced around him. 'Yet you have a fine home. One I myself would be proud to own. I imagine you have friends who wonder the same thing?'

'What thing is this?' He saw the jaw harden. He might have been watching his own wife.

'How, with a husband – now sadly dead, and I am sorry for this, *Signora* – how you have managed to live in this style?'

'He made one fine investment. An investment for his family. An investment in his own life. Yes!' She drew herself up with pride, her bosom suddenly full.

Edwards wanted very much to be at home in bed. 'Insurance? Life insurance.'

She nodded.

'Benny took out life insurance?' Edwards could barely suppress his smile. 'He found someone who would cover him? *Signora*, with all my respect, I have to tell you I know that there were some very dangerous people with some very dangerous ideas concerning your husband's life expectancy. Life insurance for him would not have been easy to find. Such companies have serious businessmen, they check on things.'

She wept again.

'All right,' said Edwards. 'Let's say he got cover. Where from? Can you find the policy?'

She clucked her tongue as though only a fool would expect her not to be able to lay her hands on such an important document in an instant.

He had it in his hands within the minute.

'Telephone, please?' he asked.

She nodded, warily, at a lacy object resembling a bonnet.

Edwards lifted it and saw an ivory-white telephone with gleaming gilt fittings. He called headquarters and read out the name of the company which had issued – and paid out on – a policy on the dubious life of Augusto Benito Bernardelli in the sum of one quarter of a million dollars.

'Fine,' he said after a moment of waiting. 'Now check who owns the company.' Again he waited, smiling easily at Maria Bernardelli. He frowned. 'Not what I wanted. What chance of getting names of stockholders?' His eyes blinked. 'What? That's the bank back in the eighties that—' He shot a glance at her.

She arose, quickly, frightened.

He waved her down.

She sat, the quivering doe again.

'OK, maybe that's all I need,' he said and put down the garish instrument. He looked at her. 'No one is going to take anything away from you, *Signora*. And no one is going to kill you or your children.'

She glanced, bewildered, at the telephone. 'Benito – he made this investment for the family?' In her uncertainty she had lapsed back into English.

Edwards kept with her. 'Like you said, he made a fine investment for his family. How is it paid, *Signora*? This is important.'

'The money comes regularly – it is better this way, I was advised. After the house was paid we get the money, every month, always, no problem. A cheque, every month. The money is safe?'

'The money is safe. Safe as—' He was about to say houses then saw a calendar on the wall by a crucifix and pointed, watching her face carefully. The calendar portrayed the dome of St Peter's Basilica in Rome.

She clasped both hands to her ample bosom. '*Grazie. Molto grazie.* Then it is very safe.'

'Why do you fear the Cosa Nostra, *Signora*?'

'Everyone fears the Cosa Nostra,' she answered dully. 'Even you.'

He smiled thinly. 'But you fear them for a reason. Benny owed them money, correct?'

Again her eyelids drooped affirmatively.

'A lot of money, right?'

She shrugged, her heavy breasts moving – disturbingly for Edwards. 'Too much money,' she whispered.

'And you settled the debt from the insurance.'

Her eyes flitted with fear. 'No.'

'But it was settled?'

Again she shrugged and Edwards definitely wanted to go home to Gina.

'You know the Cosa Nostra don't forget debts, Signora Bernardelli? Never. Never ever. They extract payment however they can. Money – or blood.'

She chewed the handkerchief as though she were silently screaming.

'But they let Benny off the hook. Even with a quarter of million in life cover coming to you. They let *you* off the hook, *Signora*. Or are you afraid they didn't – not really – and they're waiting for some reason before extracting payment? Who came and comforted you when you heard Benny was killed in a car wreck. Someone offered to settle all the problems? Maybe family?'

'Franco.'

'Franco is who? Brother to Benito? No, I checked. Benny was born a loner and died that way too, family or no family.'

She wailed.

'I'm sorry, but I need to know the connection.'

She was back to Italian. 'Cousin to Benito. Franco was cousin to Benito.'

Edwards held up a photograph of the man Sam Lewelyn had shot involuntarily.

She shrieked and two teenage boys, in expensive trainers and designer casuals, burst in.

'Out!' Edwards barked, his free hand holding up his shield. '*Now*. And close the door.'

They obeyed, though he suspected they were just outside again.

'Franco died last night, Mrs Bernardelli,' he stated brutally in English. 'He killed himself.'

'*No!*'

'Bad news for a good Catholic. Suicide.'

'Never! He never would do this thing. Franco was for God, yes – for God. Very strong. Kill himself? It is impossible!'

'He killed himself all right – though he got someone else to do it. Maybe that way he gets to heaven and not stuck in purgatory for ever. And he gets buried properly, right? Hallowed ground. He died a good Catholic – technically. But he pulled himself on to the gun, Mrs Bernardelli. For sure. I know the man who held the weapon and he doesn't make mistakes. So why?'

'I don't know why you say this?'

He studied her. 'You didn't know he was dead?'

She shook her head, violently, her English disintegrating. 'Who could tell me this? Franco is not married. Mother, father, dead. I don't know anything from Franco.'

'Except he came and sorted out your life when Benny died and told you you had a stack of money coming.'

'He was family. And friend.'

'And lover?'

She shrieked. 'Not lover! I told you, Franco was for God. He gave himself in this way to Jesus.'

'What way?'

She clucked impatiently. '*This* way.' She coloured.

'Sex? You mean celibacy? He was celibate. Like a priest?'

'Franco not a priest.'

'Not a priest – but some . . . what? Society?'

She shrugged.

'Give me *something*, damn it!'

She made hand gestures, eyes wary.

'Masons? A Masonic order.'

Her eyelids dropped.

Oh, shit, thought Edwards. This isn't just a can of worms – it's a serpents' nest that's going to keep on multiplying. He reached for the telephone and called Andrews Air Force Base, asking for the colonel Sam had talked with there.

'We stuffed him into a real high-flying bird about *your* colour a short while ago, chief. Not that you heard me say that.'

'Flying time, Colonel?'

'Fast. Can't say more. Not on this line, not on any line.'

'OK. Sam said he'd call when he arrives. Thanks, Colonel.'

'You bet. Us short-timers have to stick together.'

Edwards put the lace bonnet over the telephone, gazing blankly at it, then arose.

He said goodbye to Maria Bernardelli and left the brownstone with the teenage boys glaring hard. He wondered how long before he was glaring at them across a hard interrogation desk, downtown. Two more losers, he wondered – or would lifting them out of the jungle make human beings out of them?

He drove home with unpleasant thoughts spoiling the promise of Gina. Edwards hated conspiracies because he knew that there never was a definitive answer at the end. Not for his ears, for sure.

He sighed. God, how he hated this town sometimes. He decided when he finally handed in the badge he and Gina were heading for New Orleans to party the years away in the French Quarter and when he couldn't hack that any longer he would watch the rest of the world do it from the veranda. What the hell!

In the mean time he had to tell Sam that the man who died in the garage on his gun, and the man driving a burning car in the desert some ten years before, were very much connected.

Not just by blood.

Both had been suicides that weren't meant to look that way.

Sam Lewelyn decided it was time. He moved forward to the two-man crew of the twin-tailed monster known as the Blackbird – officially the Lockheed SR-71 supersonic electronic warfare and reconnaissance aircraft – this version the 71C dual-controlled trainer version with an extra projecting cockpit.

'Cramp?' asked the nearest officer, leaning back, head twisted, his big helmet filling the view forward.

Sam showed his small black automatic. 'I'm sorry.'

The man's eyes locked with his and saw flat determination. 'We have a problem, Chuck,' he said.

The pilot, in the forward seat, said: 'Talk to me.'

'I think we just got hi-jacked.'

Laughter crackled inside Sam's helmet. He said, quickly: 'Major, if you've got a panic button in this bird leave it alone, please. The skin may be titanium but it won't stop a bullet – even a small .32 like this one. I don't need to instruct you on the effects of explosive decompression at this altitude.'

'Do you see the gun, Kris?' asked the pilot's impressively cool voice.

'Affirmative. Thirty-two, S&W auto. Hammer's back.'

'I'm not doing this from choice, Major,' Sam said.

'I need to say one thing before we go any further. If what you've got in mind is having me fly someplace where they can take the airplane and the EW systems apart then you may as well start firing now because it's not going to happen. Kris, sorry, but you know how it has to be.'

'Sure, Chuck.'

'I'm not after the plane, Major – just the ride. You take me where I need to be and I'll hit the ground running.'

'Let's talk about that a little.'

'There's an Aeronautica Militare Italiano base at Pratica di Mare, near Rome. NSA have links there – it's an ECM and radio calibration facility. You know it?'

'Yes.'

'Is the runway long enough for the Blackbird?'

'Never tried it. It'll be on computer, Kris. Check it out.'

Sam watched the big helmet in front of him dip. 'With the drag chute popped early . . . yes.'

'Can you take off again without endangering life?' asked Sam.

'Does that make a difference to your plans?' enquired the pilot.

'I'm afraid not. Under the circumstances.'

'You must have something burning to do?'

'Just get me there, Major.'

The pilot enquired, drily: 'How do I explain the change in flight plan? Why do I want to land there? They ask these minor details.'

'You figure it out. But do it quickly.'

Stubbornness crept into the voice. 'Sir, I have the stick, so for now we'll do this at my pace. You have to be genuine NSA to have got a berth on board this bird – and you seemed to know Colonel Baldwin real well – so what's going down here?'

'I have this friend whose life is in danger. I need help, badly. The problem is getting people to believe me, so I have to act myself – fast. I'm sorry, this was the fastest ride I could get.'

'You usually go out on such a limb for your friends? This is a multi-million-dollar top-secret military airplane!'

'When he's the President of these United States and his life is in immediate danger, yes.'

Sam listened to the whispering silence of the upper atmosphere, at Mach 3 the sound of huge twin Pratt and Whitney continuous-bleed turbo-jets left far behind. Through the thick glass of the small observation port he saw the midnight blue of near-space and, below, the curved edge of the world haloed as if a fire-storm raged beyond the horizon.

The voice in his helmet said: 'Kris, lose all outside communications for five minutes. OK, sir, maybe you better share your problem?'

John Cornell heaved himself out of bed feeling like he was climbing out of his grave. He coughed and cleared his throat, turning to his wife who stirred behind him in the ornate four-poster bed.

He glanced at his watch. It was well past noon. There was much to do.

He stood, too quickly, his head spinning, sharp stars piercing the sudden darkness. *Christ.* It got worse after every flight. He would have to get himself thoroughly checked out and this time admit there was something wrong.

He felt a hand claw at his naked buttock and turned.

She was propped on one elbow, saying something, but he couldn't hear her.

He said: 'Sorry?' but nothing came out except a fuzzy murmured moan. Or at least it sounded that way.

She seemed to yell at him and now he heard something. He sat on the bed, refusing to panic, swallowed hard a couple of times and waited for normality.

'What's wrong,' she said, right beside him now, her breast against his arm. He felt aroused and wondered if there was any truth in the – probably wishful – theory that the bridge between life and death was orgasmic. If so, how close had he been just then to dying?

'Jet-lag,' he said and this time he could hear himself. The relief was like the wash of tepid rain head to toe across him, light and as frail as mist.

'You looked bad enough to be—' She shut her mouth, tight.

'I'm OK now. You know it gets me that way.'

'Don't tell me, tell someone who knows what it means. Doesn't matter how many times you get examined, if you don't give them information they can't help. Your problem is you equate illness and weakness together.'

'In a president they are precisely that. You want for instances?'

'No. Just do something about it. Where are you going?'

'To do what I came here to do.'

'Sazarin? I thought the ambassador said he was still unconscious.'

Cornell crossed to the window and looked out across Rome, a sense of history sweeping over him like a tide. He shook his head. 'To find the truth,' he said.

Or perpetuate a lie? asked his silent heart.

'This is Skunk Four. We have an emergency situation here, Beale,' announced Major Chuck Milton.

'We lost communications for a while there, Skunk Four,' said a relieved voice bounced off a USAF communications satellite from USAF 9th Strategic Reconnaissance Wing at Beale Air Force Base, California. 'State your position and nature of the emergency.'

'Ah, Beale, you have our altitude, we're approaching the Italian coast, west of Rome for emergency landing at Fiumicino. Over.'

'Negative, Skunk Four. You have an AMI NATO facility at Pratica di Mare, south of Rome. They will have a secure situation for you. We will authorize and arrange. Repeat: advise your emergency, over.'

Milton turned and drew his finger across his throat.

'Gone,' said Lieutenant Kris Paterson.

'Is this the safest way to handle this?' asked Sam, doubtfully.

Milton answered: 'The only way. They have our position down to a pin-head, all we can do is ignore them and go ahead with what we want to do. They don't have any choice but to go along.'

'You knew they'd suggest Pratica di Mare?'

'Breathe *civilian* with this bird and they scream like they've had their nuts squeezed. Relax, they'll be talking serious business with the Italian Air Force right now. Like you said, that base is half-way to being a NSA spook-hut which suits Beale fine. They'll have a blanket ready to throw over this bird the minute it's down.'

'But you didn't give a reason?'

'Sir, you know what the SR-71 is? A mass of electronics set on top of a couple of engines that generate enough heat, vibration, sound, and fury to make Dante's Inferno seem like a candle blowing in the wnd. We fly so high and so fast that that sooty titanium skin out there glows red hot. Beale knows all that. When the time is right I'll tell 'em we had systems going haywire and I had the choice: head on down or lose the bird. Hell, they *told* me where to land!'

'I thank you, Major. Both of you.'

'Just make sure the President's OK. And tell him if the Air Force decides – after this – that we're a couple a mavericks who need grounding we'll be knocking on the Oval Office door, hard.'

'Count on it.'

'OK, Kris. Let's do it.'

CHAPTER
THIRTEEN

Victor Garnett was an attorney-at-law whose services were impossible to buy. *He* chose his clients. All, without exception, from his
own background of very old Catholic money.

Garnett claimed, and few doubted him, that he could trace his
own family line back to the Norman conquest of England in which
his ancestors played a leading, probably violent, part – for they
soon became land-owners on a vast scale in the newly occupied
territory.

Until the reign of Henry VIII.

Henry's declared independence from Rome and his establishment of the Church of England cost the heads and the estates of
many Catholic Englishmen, the Garnetts no exception, their
profound Catholicism and refusal to renounce Rome's pre-
eminence costing them dear. In fact, costing them everything.

Centuries later, despite the revival of the family fortune, Victor
Garnett was doing all he could to redress that ancient wrong
whenever the opportunity presented itself, and, with the level of
funds available – via his sole power of attorney for aged, generally
uncomprehending, clients – he was able to finance certain actions
which he decided aided that end.

One damaging method was funding sophisticated large-scale
drug-smuggling operations into Britain – with the benefit, after
suitable laundering, of good financial returns for his client and
naturally himself.

Another was aiding the brave young men, as he saw them, of
the Irish Republican Army – never through the infiltrated organization NORAID – and whilst this gave him particular satisfaction
he would have been forced to admit – of course he admitted

nothing – that there was no financial gain to be had from this funding, only loss. However, when the need arose, he reminded troubled clients that all financial speculation involved risk – sometimes loss – and was usually able to smooth their wrinkled brows and calm their erratic heartbeats by assuring them that, via creative accounting, certain benefits might be gained from the vagaries of the US tax system.

Involvement in such illegal activities meant that Garnett by necessity had certain – carefully buffered – connections with people and organizations in the business of arranging these matters both financially and operationally. His forays into this twilight world between – as he had it – the vision and the deed were undoubtedly aided by his membership of the powerful and exclusive Masonic lodge, Imperio Parent – They Obey The Command – whose sole purpose of existence was to further the cause of and the protection of those dedicated to Roman Catholicism. Naturally, given Vatican pronouncements on matters Masonic, the lodge was utterly secret. And more effective for this.

That Saturday morning as he moved forward to greet the member of IP who exited that morning from the elevator of his elegant penthouse into the balmy roof-top orangery which through sweeping glass panels allowed the finest architectural features of the United States' capital to appear as backdrop, Victor Garnett's confidence in the protection promised him felt decidedly tested.

Garnett embraced him in the prescribed manner.

'You look dreadful, Victor,' observed Ricardo Marchionni. 'You mustn't blame yourself.'

Garnett murmured agitatedly, 'It's not just Sazarin! I've hardly slept at all with those lunatics chanting through the night.' He pointed at a towering office block. 'Can you believe people *stepped off* that? I saw it and I still couldn't believe it. There's madness out there. I haven't dared step out on the streets this morning, although Oscar' – he indicated his hovering manservant – 'swears they're back to normal. Whatever normal might be these days! What are your impressions of down there? Is it safe?'

'Safe? It never was safe, Victor, you know that. The mood? Stunned. Anti-climactic. They *need* something, that's why Maddox grabbed hold so easily.'

Garnett clicked his fingers and Oscar gently popped the cork from a bottle of pink champagne and poured expertly into chilled glasses.

Marchionni walked away along the marble floor of the orangery, examining, touching, then reaching high to pull fruit from a gnarled branch before settling into the painted peacock-tailed back of an enormous wicker chair. 'You're concerning yourself too much, Victor,' said Marchionni.

'It's *my* finger that was on that trigger.'

'Don't dramatize. It was your hand that passed over the money, nothing more. And unless you're very foolish – which of course you are not – there is no way that payment can be traced back to you.'

'That's easy for you to say. We're not discussing some drunk in the street here! This was – is for God's sake, he's still alive! – the most powerful politician in Europe.'

'Do you understand the *why*, Victor?' asked Marchionni, peeling thick skin from the satsuma.

Garnett sat opposite on a pure white unpolished marble bench. He pulled his narrow shoulders back. 'Doesn't matter what I do or do not understand. I accept what must be done.'

Marchionni sucked, closing his eyes with delight. 'Exquisite. Now listen to me—'

'Is this for me, Ricardo? This explanation? Or yourself?'

'You think I came here for confession!' Marchionni smiled, beringed fingers trailing dismissively. 'The danger is escalation. The *great* danger. It is also, I fear, inevitable.' He bent, laid the peel at his feet, then wiped his fingers on a crisp linen handkerchief.

Garnett watched him in silence, then said: 'Why let it start in the first place? That's what I can't understand? You're prepared, now, to take whatever action is needed, however repugnant to your calling – *multiple* action it seems – yet you could have ended it at the start with one decisive action.'

'I tried and failed. Kent should have died in the desert.'

'There must have been other occasions? It isn't that difficult – not when we have people willing to . . . to give total commitment.'

'Die, is the word, Victor. Say it, don't hide behind euphemisms. I find that insulting to those prepared to do as we ask.' Marchionni's eyes were ebony-hard. He sighed. 'You don't understood just how difficult it was to get near him after that first attempt. Now of course it is impossible. He won't leave Fort Meade under any circumstances. No matter what a man is willing to sacrifice, he must still be able to get *close* enough. Clair Morrison was close enough. He failed, then, in the desert, and he would have failed again now – if Kent could have been persuaded or tricked into meeting him, which I doubt.' Marchionni stared at his ring.

'He was one of us,' stated Garnett, dully.

'He was unstable. A liability. He failed his own vows. He knew the cost. I believe he welcomed the end. Anyhow, that is history.' Marchionni leaned backward to the surprisingly blue sky, the sun hot on his upturned face. 'After the desert it seemed the best course would be to allow Kent to continue and drown himself in his own obsession, as he was bound to do. The signs were all there as clear as this gorgeous sky. I really envy you this place, Victor. If you ever consider selling . . .'

'So you're a psychologist too?'

'A child could have predicted it. The man was a thief. Every spy is a thief. He was presented with an opportunity and he took it. You know that old monkey-catcher's trick? Fruit in the tied-down jar, the opening big enough for the animal's hand but not once the fruit is grasped. Monkey won't let go. Stays trapped. Self-entrapment, of course.'

'And is Kent trapped so? Still?'

'Certainly. The problem is we are trapped with him. His enemies have become our enemies. If he is indicted for – you're the attorney, misappropriation of government funds, minimum? – we shall have done everything for nothing. The true nature of what he had been given will come spilling out. He won't be able to help himself. He will feel it necessary to tell the world what – he believes – he has.'

'And you? Don't you want to know? Not even a little?'

Marchionni smiled. 'There cannot be a *little* knowledge in this. Can't you grasp that? You may as well offer a raindrop to a man dying of thirst. Don't you see, that is precisely what happened to Kent? He's still out in the rain, running in circles, crazed, his mouth open and still dying of thirst.'

'So what must we do? Protect him?'

'We have no choice.'

'And the work continues?'

'Not for much longer, God willing. His source of future funding is about to end. Sazarin will die. Very soon.'

Garnett looked disconsolately at the veined marble floor. 'I'm sorry. I failed you. They should have made certain.'

'To be certain, an assassin has to be close enough to hear the breath die in the body. Those you chose did it for money. Money for their own cause, not ours, no matter how devout they claim to be. Because of this they did not – would not – get close enough for the kill to be certain.'

'You've found someone else?'

'Found and dispatched.'

'Who isn't doing it for money?'

'He's barely aware of money, in any personal sense, that is.'

'For the Faith, then? One of our number?'

'Not one of us.'

'Why then?'

'Must you always have motive? Doesn't the lawyer in you ever rest? For the greatest, the surest, even purest, reason, Victor. For love.'

'I don't think I understand.'

Marchionni gave a small smile. 'No. Because, apart from God, you only love yourself.'

Garnett smoothed the material of his costly silk suiting. 'I don't think that's fair.'

'Accurate.' Marchionni arose, picked another fruit, and tucked it within his robes. 'For later,' he said. 'Come.' He linked arms with Garnett and walked to the gates of the elevator.

'So it's done? You no longer need my help?'

'Your help is always needed. And valued.'

'I know. I meant for now, in this matter?'

Marchionni turned to him, the gilded metal gates between them like a cage. 'You've forgotten your *Hamlet*, Victor. "If it be not now, yet it will come: the readiness is all."'

'I don't give a fig for *Hamlet* – I just hate the *waiting*. Cornell? What is the position with him?'

'I went to the White House last night. He knows – now – what is at stake. Cornell isn't the worry.'

'Someone else is?'

'Cornell admitted he had recruited someone – a friend, better you don't have a name – to help him in his enquiry into Kent. He wouldn't name him but I know from Morrison who it is. It seems he is retiring from a senior position within NSA – their internal security arm – so knows much of what occurs in that closed society. That's something Cornell needs because of Kent's . . . domination . . . of their relationship. He also has a son involved in the Mojave.'

Garnett frowned. 'That sounds like a bad combination of circumstances. Even bad coincidence?'

'I think not. A son following a father into the same organization is hardly a rare occurrence. According to Cornell he had no idea the son was involved with NSA. He saw his name on a personnel list in the Mojave – which became the catalyst that moved him to finally act against Kent.'

'So the President will have his friend halt his enquiries? From his former position this man sounds like he could be an expert in investigation. That's the last thing you need.'

'Cornell has every reason to be quite brutal in ordering the man to end his involvement. I told you, he now knows what is at stake. He is a Catholic, he can't escape that.'

'And if this man declines? I know these investigative types very well, I use them, they don't let go easily – if at all.'

Marchionni pressed the elevator button. 'I will call on you if the need arises,' he said, descending.

Victor Garnett decided he might be – urgently and unavoidably – called away for the next few days.

The TV in the transfer lounge at Dallas Fort Worth airport was showing CNN's coverage of Air Force One's hurried departure the night before, the big screen showing the angry burn of the SST's four massive engines like smouldering holes in the black sky.

Greg returned from a call-booth. 'No reply,' he said.

'You've called twice. It's almost ten o'clock?'

'He's gone out.'

'It was six o'clock when you called from Austin?' she reminded. 'Seven in Baltimore? Why would your dad be out at that time – on a Saturday morning?'

He nodded and sipped coffee silently.

She nodded at the TV. 'Maybe he's gone with the President? He left for Rome last night. It was just on CNN.'

'I'll call Georgia.'

'Why?'

'Have her go to Baltimore and check the house.'

'Saturday – she'll have better things to do.'

'Maybe, but she'll still do it for me.'

He made for the telephones again and punched in Georgia's number. 'It's Greg.'

'Greg! Oh, God! Where are you?'

'Hey, take it easy.'

'Shit! Listen, don't you know your goddamn leap off that building last night made TV nationwide!'

'Did it look good?'

'It's not funny! God *damn* you, Greg!'

'You sound like you've got a hangover.'

'I've been up all night is all! Watching you and your crazy woman trying to kill yourselves.'

'Georgia, I'm fine. We both are.'

'Yeah. Maybe you should have let her fly solo. I'm sorry, I didn't mean that. Maybe I did. So why are you calling? To tell me you're OK? Suddenly you're considerate?'

'Dad's not answering his phone. I need you to check him out.'

'I called him last night – he was OK then.'

'Will you get over there? See if the Lincoln is around – he never walks anywhere. Carolyn thinks he may have gone with the President.'

'She's wrong. The President had already flown out when I called last night. I'll go right now. Where are you going? Back to work?'

'They're calling our flight, I'll call when we reach Raleigh Durham – around . . . quarter of three EST, OK?'

'Don't say that if you're not going to.'

'I'll call. Listen, if Dad's not at home you can let yourself in with a key he keeps out back—'

'Greg, I *know* – I lived next door for nineteen years, remember?'

'Sure.'

'*Sure* to you too. So when do I see you?'

'Carolyn's parents are still missing. I'm taking her back to the mountains. We'll overnight there and come up to DC tomorrow. I have to go, Georgie, I'll call you.'

'Greg!'

'What?'

'Don't jump off any more buildings.'

'I won't.'

'Or get snake-bitten.'

'Count on it. You take care.' He replaced the receiver and turned to find Carolyn beside him.

'Flight's boarding,' she told him.

He clutched her to him and started toward the departure gate.

'You'll get plenty of rest between here and Raleigh,' he told her.

'Sleep, maybe, Greg. No rest. Not until I find my folks.'

Somewhere the muffled roar of jet engines arose, like an animal caged deep below ground.

Dimitri Voroshilov saw the entrance ahead, two columns and a heavy rusting gate sunk a little into the solid phalanx of trees which seemed to have marched in an unbroken column for the last few miles the Zil limousine had covered on the dreadful road. For Voroshilov the gloom outside seemed intimidating and for no good reason he felt apprehension at leaving Moscow's deteriorating streets far behind.

'Kozlov? We are here?' he questioned the small, defeated-looking man with the straggling grey beard facing forward in the fold-up occasional seat.

Kozlov nodded without turning.

Voroshilov spoke through the tube to the driver beyond the Zil's glass division. 'The gates. Drive inside,' he ordered. 'Break the lock if necessary.'

The driver halted the big, outdated, and now virtually springless limousine and stepped morosely from his cosy glassed-in compartment to do his master's bidding, heavy bolt-cutters he had been ordered to acquire readied.

Beside Voroshilov, Arkady Antipov leaned forward clutching his abdomen, neck craned, straining for a sight of the deserted dacha at the end of the rutted drive. 'I hope the lavatory works. What I'm going to do to it is nobody's business!' he promised. 'Jesus, a real solid pot to sit on!'

Voroshilov winced in distaste, appalled at how quickly a man he remembered as having decent manners, if not any real culture, could turn within so few years into an animal preoccupied with bowel movements.

He had fed Antipov too well earlier – after having him temporarily released for 'questioning' – allowing him a glass or two too much vodka to keep him talking and pliable enough to reveal the location of the safe-drop where the tape-recording of the allegedly secret Kremlin meeting was kept.

The effects on Antipov of decent food and alcoholic drink after years of thin prison fare and total abstention became only too evident – and audible – as they set out on their long journey on bad roads, forcing Voroshilov to lower the windows repeatedly, despite the growing cold. He consoled himself by recalling his initial interrogation of Antipov which he had passed on by telephone immediately he had left the prison early that morning – obeying his former leader's firm instructions to the letter and ignoring the lateness of the hour in New York. The immediate result of that call was urgent action leading directly to their presence, now, almost one hundred hard miles from Moscow.

'There were tapes. This was an historic occasion, however secret. Speeches were made. We taped everything. Insurance, for upstairs: in case.'

'They didn't know? Those at the meeting?'

'Of course they didn't know!'

'And you'll tell me all of it?'

'Get me out of here and I'll tell you every word I remember.'

'The tapes? Destroyed when . . . ?'

'Perhaps not.'

Voroshilov smiled, expecting much but still completely blind as to what – neither of the two men offering a word to ease the suspense.

It had been easy enough to find Nikolai Kozlov. The police always knew where to find broken men and were always keen to aid *his honour* the prosecutor.

Kozlov was broken all right, with haunted eyes in a wasted face, the result of the crushing loss of everything: work, status, possessions, creed, even his wife. His patchy, straggling grey beard seemed to make his utter failure manifest. Yet Voroshilov had noted the hint of steel at the back of the eyes and hoped that this worked for rather than against him when the time came. Perhaps he had not become entirely soft like so many, ready to give in to flabby Western thinking too easily, too completely.

The former Soviet scientist had barely spoken from the time they had picked him up from his dreadful shared room in a run-down apartment building on the hard belt of the city but now, as though the sudden presence of the dacha was a cue, he turned and said: 'You have survived well, Comrade Prosecutor – since the Fall. Is it true, do you think – taking the Darwinian view – that only the fittest will survive this calamity we are living through?'

'I believe Darwin yielded to Spencer as the originator of that viewpoint?' offered Voroshilov, lightly.

Kozlov's pale eyes glittered opaquely. 'A lawyer must score his points. Very well, Spencer, then. The question still hangs?'

'"Without victory there is no survival,"' Voroshilov quoted, with conviction, despite these being Churchill the arch-reactionary's words.

'Ha!' guffawed Antipov. 'The revolution is already in the sewers – not waiting, armed to rise again, but washed down into the shit. That is unless the West gets sucked up its own arsehole and we're left to crawl back up to daylight.'

'Shut up!' snapped Kozlov. 'Your mind is so clogged with your own excrement it's coming out of your mouth.'

'The Comrade Prosecutor sees himself in the role of the Robespierre of the counter-revolution,' slurred Antipov. 'We are here for a reason.'

Kozlov studied Voroshlov. 'I think not. I am beginning to believe that the reason we are here may not be entirely hostile. And perhaps not even official?'

'We are many,' said Voroshilov, leaning forward, voice eager, earnest. 'But we have no torch, no hope to search the skies for. I have the task – am proud to have it – to find this light. To recharge it.'

Antipov laughed again. 'If they can't get enough electricity to light up even half of Moscow what do you think we can do! Words! We have as much chance of being revived as a naked whore thrown out overnight in Siberia. Look at Kozlov! He hasn't eaten properly for months. Years! And he's been on the *outside*! Come on, the only one who's alive here is you – because you saw it coming and got your footwork right.'

Voroshilov slapped him, hard. 'The way of survival, you weak pig! That's how it is. Not meekly handing yourself over to the first band of brigands who tell you they've taken over the government. You were KGB but you had no *face*, you could have played down your role, you weren't so important – a bureaucrat – you could have talked your way around the difficulty and kept yourself in a job. They need people like you now. There are thousands like myself serving the counter-revolutionaries so that in time we can reverse their actions and return to the true course of history. One does whatever is necessary in the struggle. Even change from dogma if necessary. History is *made* – it does not simply happen!'

The Zil had halted outside the deserted dacha, the motor still running, heavy and lumpily, like an old marine engine.

Kozlov thrust his narrow jaw at Antipov. 'What has he told you? I can resurrect Lenin?' He looked out of the window at the dead house. 'Better if it were Stalin. Stalin would have more success. The people aren't interested in dialectics. They turn away or shout down anyone who starts all that. All they respond to is a heavy boot – or rifle-butt – between the shoulders. Simple solutions. We Russians have been the same from time immemorial. We'll put up with any amount of broken heads and whipped backs just as long as whoever is doing it puts bread on the table and vodka in our raised fists. *Perestroika, glasnost* – such words! The reality is that words don't buy bread.'

On another occasion Voroshilov would have enjoyed the argument but now his only interest was what Kozlov *knew* – not what he thought. He, too, gazed out at the neglected, sprawling house. 'I heard, Nikolai Nikolaevich, that you were able to do some amazing things with your experiments.' He paused. 'Some things perhaps not entirely of this world? Beyond our experiments with parapsychology? Certainly you were given enough money to take this – alternative – route? I have seen the budgets for these studies of the paranormal. I heard the laughter when some of your papers were read in committee by the counter-revolutionaries. They couldn't believe Marxists were involved in such matters. I admit I was surprised myself. Certainly it runs against orthodox doctrine. I have to say their laughter became gasps when they learned how much had been spent.'

Kozlov was silent. He appeared like a bird, perched, legs tucked in, on the small seat. Finally he jerked forward attackingly: 'Marxist doctrine denies the existence of anything connected with the spiritual world, yes, and certainly the study of psychic power had always been considered counter-revolutionary – but that changed when it was reported the Americans had had success with thought-transmission. The 1960 experiments on the US submarine *Nautilus* with such transmissions being sent from shore and received successfully underwater – whether true or untrue – put an end to that blinkered view in the Kremlin. So under Leonid Vasilev the programme began.'

Voroshilov felt disappointed. He had heard the *Nautilus* story before and always suspected it had been simply that: fiction, a CIA disinformation exercise to rattle the Kremlin and make them waste money on similar experimentation and – perhaps more fundamentally damaging in the long term – cause a revision of hardline Marxist doctrine. Every chink in the ideological wall was important to the Americans. If this were the case they had succeeded. At the height, spending had reached twelve million dollars per year – dollars which later could have saved the revolution.

Voroshilov sighed. 'So that was what you were doing here? ESP experiments?'

Kozlov looked at him almost contemptuously. 'That was for others. I was asked to greet the devil! Do you *understand*? Of course you don't.' He shook his head and pointed vaguely westward. 'If the West was as they constantly bleated all that was good and we were all that was bad then perhaps, on some other level than the one we are able to perceive, there was a power we could tap into which was not of their God – presuming their God exists and actually has power? They scare themselves to their graves with superstition, do they not?' His voice rose. 'Why! if we could only tap into a fraction of that power we could bury them in them! Can you see the logic?' He seemed weakened by his outburst, or perhaps embarrassed by his passion. 'Don't ask me who thought up the idea – dared to think it, because to investigate such forces implies belief in them. Probably some Party *Nachalstvo*, late at night looking into the dark shadows while his mistress snored.' He shrugged small shoulders. 'But we did as we were ordered.'

Dusk had settled, the car silent now, the driver waiting stoically for orders, facing forward, the worn shiny back of his uniform like a solid block of coal.

'Did you succeed?' Voroshilov asked, unsure of how seriously to take any of this. He felt severely deflated.

Kozlov's fingers explored his beard, as if surprised by it. 'What is your definition of success, Comrade? The discovery of knowledge? Or the application of it?'

Antipov complained: 'Do we go inside or sit out here all night?'

The driver had either been listening or his patience failed for he stepped out and opened the Zil's heavy door.

Inside the barren dacha, with electric power restored, the air was so chill Voroshilov saw the mist form from his mouth. He shivered, not entirely convinced the lack of heating and the creeping cold outside was responsible – nor that he wanted to be here at all. His comfortable Moscow apartment seemed very far away. He dearly wanted the light, the warmth of it.

'What precisely did you do here?' he asked, his voice hoarse, the dry cold acting like an astringent on his vocal cords, his question, unintentionally, coming out as an exclamation. He felt decidedly uncomfortable and being neither superstitious nor a Believer this infuriated him.

Kozlov smiled, knowingly. 'What did we do? We played games.' He walked to a door leading off the large entrance hall and opened it. Inside, on the floor, professionally drafted and painted with careful regard for geometric accuracy – evidenced by mathematical and algebraic symbols still visible at each of its five points – was a pentagram.

'This is simply superstition,' objected Voroshilov.

'Superstition perhaps, but not simple. We had the best minds, the best equipment – and most importantly, we were given *time*. We were left to our own devices – no one interfered, no one bothered us, no one visited or inspected.' Kozlov's smile twisted his narrow jaw. 'In the beginning people were sent but they felt the atmosphere of this place – as you did, Comrade Prosecutor – and never returned. We talked via the telephone or through written reports after that. We used to joke that it was a little like the Creation here. We were begotten, then forgotten.'

'You play with words, Kozlov. You have not answered with any gravity as to what you were doing?'

'*Gravity*, Comrade? *We were knocking on the gates of hell!*'

Voroshilov pulled up the collar of his overcoat and thrust both hands into the pockets. 'But you are an eminent scientist?' He pointed a finger at the five-pointed star. 'This is something to terrify peasants.' His eyes flicked sharply at Kozlov. 'That was the true motive? Some bizarre scheme to silence them if they became too vociferous? That I can understand. The fear that we could not control some outer regions of the satellite states was growing at the time. Yes, that makes sense.' Voroshilov felt relief.

'Perhaps that was in the minds of some of our masters,' conceded Kozlov. 'But I believe the real motive was wider. Not domestic but international. The possibility of tapping a power source that might, potentially, be greater than anything the West for all its – proven – superiority could ever find. The West, you see, would be incapable of approaching the subject with open minds. The whole ethos of their society rules out serious research into this *dark* side of the supernatural. They have difficulty enough coping with even the concept of the paranormal. Only those they term *cranks*, or in some medieval sense, *evil*, would dare take that step into darkness. Darkness being *their* term, their fear. That view hasn't changed for centuries. For all their advanced technology they are still crippled by a fear of the dark.'

Voroshilov drew a breath and deliberately stepped into the pentagram. He smiled wanly at Kozlov. 'It feels no different.'

'The protection is not complete,' answered Kozlov, quite seriously.

Voroshilov's smile broadened. 'Holy water? That kind of thing?'

'There are rituals one must follow. Laid down over centuries. One needs instruction manuals to operate a computer successfully, agreed? You can be in great danger from an electronic machine if you are not protected suitably. You must be earthed, insulated. Otherwise—!' Kozlov's hands flew upwards. 'There is little, if any difference with so-called *supernatural* ritual. Ritual is no different from a standard set of instructions. The terminology, the character, of such ritual make these matters appear sinister. Put into context, into a scientific frame, so to speak, one strips the blackness – superstition, doubt, irrationality, call it what you will – away.'

'And brings forth light?' quipped Voroshilov.

Kozlov gazed at him with haunted eyes. 'What it brings forth,

Comrade, is the mystery we were unable to solve. Though we glimpsed things . . .' He smiled, dismissively. 'We ran out of time. Or perhaps we ran out of nerve? I wonder about that sometimes – in the dark – so you see even I, a scientist, suffer from human fallibility. The shadow of the primeval falls across all our genes. Anyhow, the revolution ran out of money. Our work was shelved – I do not like to think of it as being wasted.'

Antipov, returned from the lavatory, had been standing in the doorway behind them. 'Pay the piper. Time to tell him of the Markarovs,' he said.

'Defectors to the West in eighty-six,' prompted Voroshilov. 'You knew them, I understand.'

Kozlov looked bleakly at Antipov.

'What did they steal?' Voroshilov pressed, knowing the thing of greatest value – and potentially of greatest subsequent loss – to the state was rarely the person of the defector but the secrets they stole.

Kozlov said. 'The past.'

Voroshilov frowned.

'Come,' said Kozlov. 'I'll play you history.'

Voroshlov stepped from the pentagram, feeling the tingle from the very base of his spine through to the tinted roots of his carefully groomed hair.

'It began with the Big Bang,' said Kozlov, pulling dust-sheets away to reveal the electronic equipment and banks of reel-to-reel tape recorders on heavy-duty steel frames. He pushed down a mains switch and everywhere needles sprang violently to their right, dials suddenly illuminating. He pointed upward. 'Within the roof-space is a satellite receiver dish – primitive by present-day standards but in the eighties, absolutely state of the art.'

Voroshilov nodded, though lost on technical matters.

Kozlov moved a calibrated lever and a grinding noise came from overhead.

Voroshilov glanced up in alarm.

'Just the dish moving,' Kozlov reassured, adjusting controls. A powerful hiss came through big angled-downward speakers bolted to the walls.

Voroshilov's hands instinctively reached to cover his ears.

Kozlov cut volume. 'Thermal radiation from the Earth –

transmitted as that loud hiss. The dish is pointed at the ground.' He raised the volume high, shouting: '*If we move the dish upward toward space the hiss decreases!*' He lowered the control. 'There. It still exists – but faintly. What you are hearing – our theory – is the echo from the so-called Big Bang. Thermal radiation – formed *ten thousand million* years ago.'

'This is what you mean by listening to the past?' asked Voroshilov, expecting more; the magnitude of the noise and Kozlov's staggering interpretation of its origins notwithstanding.

'What I and my colleagues meant, certainly. Not what the Markarovs meant.' Kozlov worked the lever and the satellite dish moved above. 'Ether, the clear upper air: a medium, not matter, assumed in the nineteenth century to fill all space and transmit electromagnetic waves. The Markarovs believed that all sound exists for all time in the ether, a sort of . . . whirlpool . . . swirling around the Earth for ever, as if the atmosphere were a sea and all language spoken from the start of time a vast build-up of flotsam on its surface.'

'Verbal pollution,' observed Antipov with an insolent drunken smile.

'Be quiet,' snapped Kozlov. 'Their theory propounded that sometimes turbulent air whipped into tornadoes, or even small swirling eddies, was caused by sub-sonic sound vibrations reaching critical or unbalanced levels, as you get in conflicting harmonics. They showed us results of experiments with crop-circles as proof but . . .' Kozlov shrugged.

'Crop circles as cosmic argument!' laughed Antipov.

Kozlov ignored him. 'They believed these natural phenomena could literally be tapped for sound waves – as if the circling downward motion were some sort of "earthing" process.'

'Similar to lightning strikes?' asked Voroshilov.

'There is a similarity though they were theorizing on a *negative* force. They were not seeking anything destructive, Comrade . . .' Kozlov hesitated. 'Not in any military sense.'

'Destructive in some other sense?' Voroshilov pressed.

'*Absolutely* destructive.' Kozlov held the prosecutor's eyes. 'The lies of history could be laid bare overnight. Not a welcome prospect for those who write our history? All those books having to be revised?'

Voroshilov gazed thoughtfully at him. 'I'm not surprised they defected,' he said quietly.

Antipov had settled himself on a steel bench, knowing he hadn't the luxury of sitting on the sidelines any more. He seemed depressed by the fact – and sober. 'They didn't defect, they were bought – then sold. What they had in their heads was too dangerous to allow experimentation on – for obvious reasons. If word ever got out – and we all know in Russia word always does – that someone had the *definitive* version of Soviet history' – he pointed at the tape-recorders – 'and could prove it . . . ! It's the old kindergarten story of the Emperor's New Clothes, isn't it – with the Markarovs yelling: *Naked!*'

Voroshilov suddenly seemed bright-eyed, as if awakening: 'So if they, the Markarovs, could potentially be that dangerous . . . don't shut them up, don't liquidate them . . . use them – because no society is completely free from its past and no past is completely free from lies. And who wants to face those? With the rest of the world watching? Condemning? *Certainly* not America.' He turned to Kozlov. 'Did you know about this?'

Kozlov's eyes were dead. 'They disappeared. We heard they had been taken to Moscow. Then they had defected.'

Voroshilov watched him now as he watched witnesses, his eyes sharp points ready to pierce any lies. 'You believed that story?'

'We were not unintelligent people working here, Comrade. We knew the possibilities of such a . . . weapon? Yes, the word *is* "weapon" because truth, definitive truth, is a sword which cuts down mercilessly. Like a nuclear bomb which destroys the heart of the target completely but doesn't stop there, strike at the heart of a lie and you can take the body of truth with it. Lies perpetuate lies while truth kills.' Kozlov suddenly seemed impatient. 'Forget the philosophical argument. The simple fact is, they didn't *need* to prove they could do what they proposed – they simply had to suggest it was *possible*.'

Voroshilov stared at him. It was perfect. A brilliant long-term penetration and disinformation operation. A time-bomb set in the past, ticking away for the future, somewhere. Where? He was made almost breathless by the audacity, the simplicity, of the idea. The days of bellowing the Big Lie were over. Now, simply whisper you knew the truth. All truth. No one was safe. All, at some time in their past, were guilty. As a prosecutor he knew that unreasoned – even irrelevant – guilt in the accused, or a defence witness, was a lethal weapon placed in his hands. The beautiful irony was it could be all a colossal magnificent lie and still achieve the same results: status quo, to chaos in no time. Not measured in historical terms. Which was, undoubtedly, the measure here.

'I want to know everything,' he said. 'I want to know verbatim what was said at that meeting. The tape, Antipov. I want to hear that tape, *now*.'

CHAPTER
FOURTEEN

In New York, the former leader of the Soviet Union heard the modulated trill of the telephone as he worked on the opening address of his lecture tour in his Waldorf Astoria suite. Lifting it he confirmed the caller's identity then pressed the receiver into position within a custom briefcase packed with electronics and inserted a small earpiece in his right ear.

Voroshilov's voice was hesitant and subdued; he seemed shocked. 'Excellency, I have the tape recording from Antipov.'

'You obtained the equipment I mentioned?'

'I have it.'

'When you are ready, then.'

'Excellency, may I say I have always been loyal. I shall perform any further task you wish – whatever you decide.'

The former Soviet leader frowned. This was the delivery of a man bearing bad news. 'I know that, and you have my grateful thanks and affection, Dimitri Sergeyevich. If necessary, I shall call you again.'

'I am at your service.'

'Very well. Begin the process, please.'

The micro-cassette of the DAT recorder built into the briefcase began turning slowly as the scrambled signal was received. The former Soviet leader watched the tiny spools turning in silence, resisting the urge to smoke until they stopped, then removed the hand-set, replaced it on its receiver, lit a cigarette, drawing smoke deeply, then pressed the descrambler.

The reproduction of Voroshilov's voice on the digital recording with all background noise removed was remarkably clear – as was his nervousness.

'Excellency, the following was recorded in the Kremlin on November 19th 1983. You will, I am certain, recognize the voices of all concerned.'

There was an empty pause before an urbane, cultured, instantly recognizable voice began: 'Comrades, we are here for one reason. We are looking at the future and it isn't ours. Forget war. Our forces are so poorly equipped we could never keep up the momentum of attack, we will be defeated by their technology and their industrial base. No matter how good our morale or our training, battles are won by superior weaponry. These they have – with the means to continue efficient production. Our technology is only as advanced as the obsolete computers they let us have and will remain so whilst their restrictions remain. Be in no doubt that while Communism rules, those restrictions will hold. I need say nothing on the condition of our production lines. The hard truth is we're out of date, going backwards while they surge forward.'

A deep military voice, angry, confident, without fear, growled: 'Vietnam? *Peasants* defeated them – with *our* weapons.'

'Vietnam was a war fought hands tied in the wrong place at the wrong time. Fought in an Asian cesspit of corruption at a time when Western youth desired hedonism not sacrifice and politicians – *elected* politicians – had votes to harvest.'

'We must take immediate measures,' said another.

'We can try. But I fear the past has already defeated us. Corruption, mismanagement, waste, foreign adventurism we could not afford, former leaders too scared to change, too proud to admit failure, too conscious of history and completely blind to the future.'

'But you can't wipe out almost *eighty years* just like that!' the general's voice whipped.

'The *people* can and one day might – in their own bloody way. That is how *we* got here, is it not? Everything we accept as our right could be swept away. Without radical change I see no alternative and if we institute radical change we destroy ourselves. This is our dilemma.'

'You're predicting chaos,' said the aged, worn voice of the then Party Theoretician.

The former Soviet leader believed he could identify, blind, virtually all in that echoey chamber. These were the king makers. They had made *him*.

The answer to the question was firm: 'Chaos is our greatest weapon. From failure, from collapse, new leaders will rise, new freedoms – a new order. We prepare ourselves now to burrow deep into that new order. It is inevitable we become as the West. We will never defeat their technology, so we must become as them. They are willing even now to help that process because it flatters them. But competing with them – and remember that is the basis of their system – will gain us little reward. They are already too far ahead, have too much advantage. They know this, which is also why they are so eager to help. They know they can always keep us as second-raters. To them we are no more than another market and perhaps in time simply another asset.'

'This is defeatist talk,' the belligerent military growl returned. 'If all this is inevitable, what can we do? Wait for the counter-revolutionaries' tumbrils to cart us away!'

'The art of politics is not to react to events but to shape them.'

'In an ideal world, yes,' came the theoretician's quaver. 'This – *assessment* – sounds far from being so. How do you intend shaping events under such circumstances?'

'We appoint someone who will take us down the route to chaos. We know there are many who would gladly follow a more liberal policy. One of my protégés in particular would suit this purpose very well.'

The former Soviet leader felt the first cut of betrayal and knew why Voroshilov has sounded apprehensive. Sick cold formed in his belly as the tape rolled on.

'And we let him ruin us?' cracked the general's voice, hard.

The theoretician replied, cognisance steadying his voice. 'Better *he* be at the helm when the ship hits the rocks than the Party be blamed for the catastrophe. There will come a time when they crave its strength, its authority. When that time comes they must associate failure with his liberal policies and not with the Party.'

The deep growl rumbled: 'And that's all? We submit? All negative, nothing positive? Where is the fighting spirit of Lenin? Dead in the mausoleum? In your vision of the *inevitable*, Comrade, does the West with its decadence flying like a pirate flag strip our wreck bare?'

'Not all,' came the patient reply – but strained now; pain and terminal illness barely concealed. 'While they rescue us we weaken them, attacking their very heart, slowly, but fatally.'

The former Soviet leader could almost see the beads of sweat on the high pale forehead above the Western-made gold-rimmed spectacles.

A crisp bureaucrat's voice objected: 'The heart of their power lies in their financial institutions. If you predict correctly, we will need those to save us whether we like it or not. Attack them and we'd be injuring ourselves – even halting our progress to recovery!'

'Try and see them more clearly. There's more to them than greed. More than materialism. Yes, in a crisis they panic, sell stocks, draw savings from banks but in a real crisis – life or death – they sink to their knees in their homes, crawl to their churches, believe every word of salvation the merchants of God sell them – whether the one in Rome or the millionaire charlatans on their TV screens. They believe they have souls: the final currency to save them from eternal damnation.'

'We've already infiltrated their churches. Deeply infiltrated. Years of effort.' This from the cold, offended, tones of the KGB chairman.

'Not enough.'

'So what must we do?'

'We destroy the basis of their faith. We cut out their souls. What is left is ours.'

'Marxism has no soul,' observed the aged theoretician.

'Precisely,' said their leader.

There was a lengthy silence, broken only by someone's hard cough.

'How?' came the question, finally.

'Bring them in,' came the order.

There was the sound of double doors being opened and shoes echoing on marble.

'What can these offer us?' demanded the general.

'The past,' answered a woman curtly, cool, unafraid, confident, even superior.

'The past caused our problems,' said someone, flatly. 'What we need is a future. Any future.'

'Whoever controls the past controls the future,' said a male voice so close in inflection and timbre as almost to be the woman's, though the arrogance was muted – or carefully veiled. There was however that same surety, that same knowing quality: two children with secret knowledge they enjoyed possessing. He continued: 'You shape the minds of the future by what you feed it of the past. Past fabricated or past fact. But you can't make them believe.'

'The peasants believe anything,' growled the general.

There was a small *cluck* of impatience from the woman – despite the awesome power assembled in that chamber. 'The most stupid accept readily – but they are easily controlled. The intelligent *always* question. The intelligent rebel, the intelligent lead. Make them believe that history is *truth*, is unquestionable . . .'

The former Soviet leader listened intently as the woman went on, his expression stony, any astonishment he felt from what he heard killed by what had gone before.

When it was over he removed the small ear-piece, pressed it carefully into its moulding in the briefcase, lit another cigarette, gave himself a stiff measure of Scotch whisky, and moved to a tall window.

He imagined himself there in the Kremlin all those years ago – in such different times – watching the cabal rise from the long table he himself had presided over later. He could even feel what they must have felt, faced with unpalatable truths: faced with the possible end of all they had worked for. Faced with what, then, must have seemed inconceivable: the end of the Revolution.

He had travelled that road himself.

Some, he knew, would be content their conspiracy would survive the coming new dawn – and if they personally did not it mattered little, for they were idealists, utterly committed: the future belonged to their ideals, not to them. Two were dying even as they spoke – and undoubtedly knew it.

Others like the general would fight, ineffectually, at the very end when the predictions became reality – and lose everything, their lives included.

Were there any survivors from that long table? The ones whose faces he could not see, who trusted no one, who, suspecting the presence of hidden microphones, held their silence? He would probably never know.

He sighed now in resignation, but anger was apparent in the sharp creases of his narrowed eyes. It had been like listening to his own obituary before he had even been born. Or perhaps a closer analogy: the announcement of his birth when he was already dead.

He felt used. Soiled. They had not trusted him with the hard facts. With the truth that was his right. He had, instead, to find out the hard way – and was always going to fail. And they knew it. The dire warnings he pronounced to the people were mere echoes of what he had just heard. He was their fool, their puppet, the catalyst for their new order; not ruler, not revolutionary, not history-maker. Dupe.

Somehow worse, they knew he would not survive. Knew he would fall even as he soared above the world, adored. That really hurt; that devalued the deepest, the most worthy, part of him.

Was the bungled half-hearted coup a curtain-raiser for the next stage in the decline into chaos, or had the general genuinely attempted to reverse the overwhelming tide of history? Whichever it was, he had to go first, a child could see that. How? Kidnap him for a period and let the street factions throw up an alternative. Then release him and let the new leaders dispose of him at their leisure. Simple. Effective. Acceptable. Acceptable to the West who would accept those circumsances in a way they might not had the Party been seen to wield the axe.

And he had fallen for it. Every blind stumbling step of the way into humbling failure.

He understood their motives, of course. They were fighting for survival. As he had. Except they had known and had prepared for the coming storm. Now, he was history and they had designed the future. Or thought they had. Did the old guard really hold – even if they had not yet pulled – all the strings?

Did any of it matter any more?

He looked down on Park Avenue far below, seeing tiny figures scurrying, scattering between miniature automobiles, while others streamed forward in fluid lines on aggressive collision courses, seemingly mindless – excepting perhaps with some basic instinct to keep moving – without direction, without hope?

He remembered the chaotic scenes on television the night before and the evangelist with manic eyes staring out from a drenched, waxy face, who had orchestrated all of it from a glass tower that placed him above reality. And they, the avidly watching, mindless, directionless, hopeless ones had built it for him.

He shook his head, wearily. They don't need a conspiracy to convince them God never existed. They've decided that already and created their own.

He went to the telephone.

'CIA Director Ellis on the line for you, Mr President,' advised the telephone operator in the United States' Rome embassy.

'Put him through,' ordered Cornell.

'Ah, sir, you'll need to use the secure line in the ambassador's office for a Langley number.'

Cornell shook his head, disorientated. 'Of course. I must be jet-lagged. I'll be right there.'

He made his way down wide, sweeping stairs to an imposing panelled door, nodded at the high-buttoned Marine's crisp salute and urged a polished but nervous young diplomat in the outer chamber through to the ambassador's deserted office to unlock the secure line.

'Hal?'

'Good afternoon, Mr President. Weather good?'

'Pleasant. You have some news on my enquiry?'

'I received a telephone call a short time ago from the Waldorf. The matter he had set in motion yesterday resulted in a recording being played over the line to him from Moscow. Scrambled, thank God.'

'Scrambled! You mean it passed through official channels over there?'

'Negative. They used commercial security attaché cases. You know the sort. Basic but effective enough. I had a courier from the New York office pick the tape up from the Waldorf and sent down the line here to Langley. Don't worry, no one cuts through our spinach. It was in Russian, of course. I've had a fast translation made. You should know right away what was said – especially considering where you are.'

'I suspected that might be the case, Hal. I'm listening.'

Ellis hesitated. 'I can't vouch for the authenticity of the recording – though he seemed to believe it was genuine. He must feel gutted, right now. If I knew your own source in all this I might be able to make an evaluation. If even half of this is genuine—!'

'Just read it, Hal. Wait. One question: did you have to promise him anything in exchange for the recording?'

'I offered. Interpreted, his reply came out as: "Tell the President thirty pieces of silver would either be too much or too little depending on one's view of the veracity of recorded history."'

'Did it now? Well, he's probably right. Go ahead.'

Ellis cleared his throat. 'An alleged meeting of an inner group of Party élite, purportedly in the Kremlin, November 19th 1983. He identifies the main speaker positively as the then Secretary-General Andropov. I'm awaiting definitive results of a voice-print for confirmation. The others are power-brokers. All old guard. Andropov needed every one of them. You'll hear what I mean. We name them according to his identification as it rolls.'

'Andropov,' murmured Cornell, as so much fell into place for him. 'Yes, it would be. I want all of it, Hal. Every word.'

'You've got it, Mr President, but afterwards you may not.'

'I believe I'm aware of that already.'

'I am so pleased you have asked for this informal meeting,' said the Pope, his gentle eyes resting on John Cornell. 'You asked for privacy; there is nowhere more private, more alone, than this. Come.' He led Cornell to within a few feet of the large three-cornered window overlooking St Peter's Square where, elevated by a simple wooden stool, he was presented to the world.

'Alone, your Holiness?' questioned Cornell, looking out but keeping back from view. 'I would have said this was the least alone place on Earth. There are hundreds below at this moment watching this window in hope of catching even a fleeting glimpse of you – and there are days when those hundreds swell to many thousands.'

The Pope smiled. 'The more that gather, the more alone one is. There were crowds gathered at Calvary yet Christ was never more alone.'

Cornell turned to him, surprised. 'Holiness, they love you – you're hardly being crucified up here?'

'Am I not?'

Cornell moved closer to him, in need of the extraordinary peaceful aura emanating from the man.

'What troubles you, my son?'

'Holiness, you are Peter, the rock upon which Christ's Church stands. I am afraid for those foundations. I need your help, desperately.'

The Pope nodded. 'I am here.'

Cornell glanced at the window. 'All those people out there? How strong is their faith?'

'Only they, and God, know that.'

Cornell shook his head frustratedly. 'When you proclaim the Word of God to the world from that window, do they truly believe what you say – or do they believe *you*?'

'To believe in someone is to believe what they say, my son. That in many ways is the essence of Christ's teachings.'

'Holiness, if I as a politician go on TV and read from the Gospels some might accept I am a Christian demonstrating my Christianity but many would say I was a politican gathering Christian votes.'

'The modern world is steeped in cynicism. One must rise above it.'

'The point I'm trying to make is that the words I speak are *irrelevant* to their judgement of me or my motives.'

The Pope nodded in understanding. 'And because I am Pope my words are incontrovertible? My utterances infallible? That also is what you are saying?'

Cornell said: 'Acceptance of truth is restricted by the medium by which it is spread.'

'Or enhanced by it. A lie will always be a lie but it can be believed as the truth if it is produced, directed – shaded – to that end.'

'In politics we call such adepts spin-doctors.'

'But we are not discussing politics,' stated the Pope.

Cornell leaned forward, urgently. 'Holiness, we are discussing God and His existence for those ordinary people out there.' He struggled to find words. 'The ones who will never get the chance to sit where I am now and feel that He must exist because nothing that has existed for so long with such strength, such devotion, as the Holy Catholic Church could be an aberration of history – or, of man deluding himself for his own comfort. Unless one feels the ... *womb* ... of all this around you – one is still outside believing, not inside, convinced. Their faith is fragile, not because of any lack of strength in their belief but because they are too much in contact with the material. I fear soon it may be shattered.'

'The material has always been Lucifer's domain. God-given . . . for a time only.' The blue eyes moved easily to the window. 'We don't live in God's world, my son. Surely that is obvious? Chaos is the blood that feeds the Beast.'

'I trust in God to control the devil. I am more afraid of man's propensity for self-destruction – and his disregard for the lives of others.'

'You speak of the terrible events in your own country we have seen on television?'

'Robert Maddox is no Lucifer. He's a misguided fool at best, and a cynical manipulator at worst. He is not the danger.'

'I am listening, my son.'

Cornell's mouth was dry, he reached for the glass of wine on the silver salver between them and sipped. It tasted like dry chalk in his mouth. He missed Sam suddenly, seeing him at college, slouching in tennis whites, a sweater knotted loosely over wide shoulders, talking easily to one of the beauties who habitually hung around him. He recalled some words and felt desolate. 'Friend of my better days. None knew thee but to love thee!' He said: 'Holiness, do you believe that man's presence in this world is limited to the time he spends – physically – upon it.'

The Pope smiled. 'Are you asking me if I believe in the soul?'

'Much less than the soul but, like the soul, intangible.'

'Some might say you are talking of so-called *lost spirits* . . . but I don't think so?'

Cornell was earnest; for him, suddenly, everything was urgent. *This* more than anything. He spoke swiftly: 'Holiness, there is a very dangerous theory abroad that maintains everything we utter remains in the ether for ever. A catalogue of history from the start of time to the world's end. The grunt of the first caveman, the cry of the last child yet to be born, the whisper of the last to die. It's all out there now – or will be.'

'And the cry of Christ on the Cross?' asked the Pope, his hand resting gently on Cornell's own, easing him.

Cornell sighed with relief. 'I knew you would understand.'

'Any theory, however dangerous, is only so when men put it into practice.'

'I am fighting to stop this, but I feel I am fighting a war on too many fronts, against too many factions – even that I am pitching my Church, my faith, against my country. I fear that, inevitably, I shall lose.'

'You can't lose, John,' said the Pope, quietly, almost a whisper. 'You can be defeated, but you can't lose.'

'I don't understand,' Cornell murmured and felt a hand on his bowed head.

'You will, my son.'

Cornell felt numb, frozen in his chair. It was as if the weight of the world pressed him down and nothing, nothing, could relieve the relentless pressure.

'You're unwell,' said the Pope, reaching for a bell-cord to summon aid.

Cornell got unsteadily to his feet. He felt a heart-beat away from dying. No pain, just bone-deep exhaustion – and a heavy tilt to his world. 'I'll be all right. Forgive me, I must go.'

The Pope drew him close and held him.

Cornell felt strength flow into him. 'It began in Moscow—' he started but the words were too much for him, the task too great.

He heard a voice say: 'It ends in Rome, John.'

He replied: 'I know.' But it might only have been inside his head.

He lay against the cushions in the limousine, wondering if it had all been a dream. Only the small white calf-bound Bible embossed with a cross in gold leaf grasped in his hands as evidence of his ever being in the lonely room high above the square. He swung around, too fast, seeing – or thinking so, through his dizziness – a white clad figure like a ghost gazing down from the window.

'Easy, Mr President. We'll be at the hospital real soon.'

He looked at Jim Bentley's black face.

'Probably just jet-lag, sir, but we're going to get you checked out, relax. We'll get hold of Mrs Cornell.'

'I didn't pass out back there?'

'No, sir, you walked out – with a little help from me and the

Holy Father. He made sure no one saw any of it. They've got ways out of that place you wouldn't believe!'

Cornell looked at the Bible. He couldn't remember being given it.

'He signed it for you, Mr President.'

Cornell opened it at the front and read the penned Latin inscription *Summum bonum* – 'the highest good' – followed by the signature and below, a gospel reference. The velvet bookmark already lay at Mark: chapter V. He read verse 9.

My name is Legion: for we are many.

And he saw it all clearly.

They had done precisely what his own State Department would do with any dangerous regime. They hadn't tried to destroy it, they had aided it so that when the time came they could kill it. Moscow had spawned it, Kent had bought it, and Marchionni with whoever else had a vested interest had clandestinely funded it – and in doing so kept it buried underground for as long as they wanted. Until Kent wanted more. And had found Sazarin rising. Sazarin, with a power-base as strong as Cornell's was ailing; who had the lifeblood to feed and unleash the Beast of Chaos they thought they had chained beneath the Mojave. The frightening vision of Kent offering NSA facilities to the highest bidder Marchionni had warned of in the Oval Office was exactly that – a frightener. Their thinking, their message, was clear. Poor old Cornell wouldn't dare blow that kind of story – and if he doesn't blow *that* he won't the rest.

They thought him weak, even doltish. Figured it was plugged, sealed tight by raising the terrible spectre of what might come out. *They?* He had a moment of cold reality and felt foolish: had he become so paranoid he saw vast conspiracies? Yet the moment retreated and the gentle face with kind blue eyes was before him again. *My name is Legion: for we are many.* It didn't matter who they were. Those who had the most to lose. Those with the most to fear from an increasingly unstable human race deprived of its fix of God.

He shook his head in dismay. If he was right, then their efforts had given Moscow's lie credibility. He felt a chill finger pierce his heart. Had the lie been dangerously near the truth? He looked out at the crowds flashing past. He saw the Coliseum come up, then was gone, and modern glass blocks reflecting the long black shape of his own passage as if in time itself.

The androgynous heads of the Markarovs, who had started all of it with their experiments, seemed to appear before him, smiling, warning mockingly: *Whoever controls history controls the future.*

Whoever wants to control it.

He knew why he had come to Rome.

'Which hospital, Jim?' he asked, his throat tight, the cords feeling like razors.

'The same one that treated the Holy Father, sir. He called ahead himself.' Bentley smiled. 'I heard him do it. He's tough. The Ospedale Gemelli couple of miles out of town. We'll be there soon with the outriders.'

'Where Sazarin is.'

'Yes, sir. That'll make two presidents they'll have checked in. Some kind of record, I'd guess.'

Cornell leaned back and closed his eyes, preparing himself. He hadn't managed to tell the *Papa* any of it, he thought wearily. Not of the conspiracy. Not of Moscow. Not even of Marchionni who was in his own way nailing Christ once again to his cross. It didn't matter. He suspected the Holy Father would have smiled indulgently – yet kindly – in the way of a man who knew the irrefutable truth. Even when that truth was hidden from him. •

CHAPTER
FIFTEEN

Sam Lewelyn drove the borrowed '62 Maserati Vignale Spyder warily, unused to the hard ride and taut handling after years with the wallowing, marshmallow-feel of the powered-everything Lincoln Continental. Better his life in his own hands than at the mercy of one of the slouching boys manning the small line of taxis beyond the guard-post at the Aeronautica Military Italiano base at Pratica di Mare, he decided.

He caught the rising wail of sirens early because the 3500GTI's canvas top was broken – thus down – even before he spotted the flashing hazard lights of the motorcycle outriders and the swirling blues from the cars. The splash of vivid colour from the Stars and Stripes streaming from the Lincoln's right fender was like seeing a dear friend over a distance – or like his first step down to US soil from the C130 after too long in too many jungles.

He yelled *Hey!* and smacked his foot to the Maserati's floorboards, giving chase – certain he would see fluttering on the left fender the blue gold-bordered presidential pennant with its shielded eagle clutching branch and lightning bolts – only to be hauled in after barely half a mile by a motorcycle patrolman who came out of nowhere and swung hard into his path, removing his white-gauntleted hand from the handlebars with a flourish to wave him to a weaving, screeching, halt.

Sam clambered from the car, furious. 'Goddammit, you want to give me a speeding ticket do it *after* I speak to the President of the United States.' He pointed agitatedly at the fast vanishing motorcade.

'American?' asked the patrolman.

'Hell no! I speak this way because I got adenoidal problems. *Jesus*, son, can you see anyone else around here with a crew-cut and weighing two hundred and fifty pounds! Hey, I'm sorry, that's rude, I apologize, OK? But I need to see the President. You understand?' Again he pointed. 'I'll pay whatever fine you say – just let me catch that Lincoln.'

The officer shook his head.

'What's that mean?' growled Sam.

'No Presidente Cornell.'

'The hell you say – I just saw his car.'

'He is—' The patrolman tipped his helmet in the opposite direction to where the Cadillac had gone then pointed at a road sign. 'Gemelli? Ospidale Gemelli. Presidente Cornell sick.'

'Sick! How sick?'

The patrolman shrugged. 'Sick. Ospidale Gemelli very good. Presidente Sazarin here. Before, when the *Papa*' – his gauntlet formed a pistol – 'he Ospidale Gemelli.' He frowned, suspicious. 'Why you want Presidente Cornell?'

Don't say it, thought Sam, or for sure you'll end up in the slammer: people who go around blurting the president's life is in danger are the ones cops look at the hardest. 'Friend,' he said. 'I am friend of Presidente Cornell. *Capiche?*'

The patrolman looked doubtful and walked away, examining the car. He pointed at something on the windshield. '*Militare?*' He removed his gauntlet and made a give-me motion with his fingers. 'Licence,' he ordered.

Shit, breathed Sam. 'US,' he explained. 'American licence, not Italiano.'

'Passport.' The hand beckoned again, impatient now.

'I didn't come through any passport control so there's no stamp, OK . . .' Sam sighed and handed the document over, feeling like he was wading through treacle.

The patrolman scrutinized it, glanced up at Sam's face, then began flicking through the stamps. 'Where you come Italia?' he frowned deeply. 'When?' He made the motion of a stamp being applied and shook his head sharply. 'Where?' he demanded.

'I just told you. Wait – here's my NSA identification. Official, OK?' Sam's big finger pointed. 'See? That's how I got here.' He

223

looked at the sky and mimed wings. 'Military. All right? Pratica di Mare.' He pointed at the Maserati. 'Automobile from *commandatore*, OK?'

The patrolman frowned again and said, slowly: 'Na-a-sa?'

'Not NASA,' Sam fumed. 'N-S-A. Not space, not rockets, satellites. Spy satellites?'

'*Spy!*'

'Oh, Jesus.'

The patrolman pointed at the car making a quick circling motion with one hand for Sam to turn for searching, the other unclipping the flap on his belt holster.

'Sorry, son,' breathed Sam, knowing the small hand-gun lodged in his sock guaranteed his arrest. He stepped in close and jabbed a short, measured upper-cut under the strapped jaw – the only area unprotected by the motorcycle helmet – then dived into the Maserati and drove off fast, tyres burning and engine screaming at the revolutions, horns blaring angrily in the background, though whether at his reckless driving or his violent act he did not know. In his mirror he could see the patrolman sprawled unmoving by the roadside, a car already halted behind and people running. He shook his head with regret. 'I just don't have time to argue,' he breathed.

As soon as he had made some distance he swung into a side street, grabbed his small bag from the passenger seat, and abandoned the Maserati, then strode quickly to the first bar he could find, entered and ordered a cold beer and a taxi.

'American?' asked the barman.

'Canadian,' said Sam. It wasn't much but it could make the five minutes' difference he might need when the dogs started running.

The barman shrugged. 'Where you want to go?'

'Vatican. Vaticano.'

The barman smirked and polished a glass. 'You want nice girl.'

'Not right now, thanks.'

'You come back. I have nice girlfriend.'

'Sure.'

'You check with God first, OK!' The barman laughed and made a comment to the sole other customer who joined in.

A lopsided Fiat wheezed to a halt outside. Sam paid for the beer and climbed in, the driver turning and pointing at the other end of the rear seat. Sam moved over, his bulk righting the weary springs.

'Drive,' he said, as the barman came out on to the steps to see them off.

'Vaticano!' called the barman as the Fiat pulled away.

'Hospital Gemelli,' Sam corrected and held up dollar bills. 'Just as fast as this heap will go. *Fast*. OK?'

'OK,' nodded the ageing driver. 'Afterward Vaticano?'

'Anything you say. Right now, Hospital Gemelli. Fast.'

The driver pointed at his flat-down accelerator foot, smiling. 'Fast.'

'Sure,' murmured Sam and lay his head back on the seat.

'Sick?' enquired the driver, worriedly.

'I've felt better.'

'American?'

'Do they go together?' growled Sam and closed his eyes, wondering if he really had left the rails. He couldn't remember going so crazy-mad over anything – except as a big lanky seventeen-year-old over some girl with a pony-tail who for once hadn't done the chasing. Except this could be long-term hurt – if the whole thing was just indigestion from Henri's way underdone steak the night before.

What the hell, John needed someone like him to keep the bastards at bay. Anyhow, with Elizabeth gone, a couple of years in the slammer was no big deal. He felt sorry for the cop though – and hoped he'd judged the blow well enough. At least the kid had the helmet to protect him when he hit the ground – which was mainly how the ones that ended up vegetables got theirs in that kind of hard-play. He knew too well.

'Presidente Cornello in Ospidale Gemelli,' said the driver, very proud.

'Cornell,' corrected Sam with a small, grim smile.

The driver held up two fingers. '*Due presidente! La Bestia.*' The two fingers became a gun aimed at his head. '*Pah!*' He ducked his head into his shoulders as though caught out at something, his eyes flicking warily backward, Sam seeing the fear in them.

He had a brief mental picture of Maddox and wondered if his Book of Revelation madness had reached this far – then cursed himself for being so American: Maddox wasn't the start of it. Here.

This was the heart of it. Rome. With its centuries of intrigue, barbaric cruelty, and idolatrous superstition. It was almost possible to believe – deeply, not in some sensationalist, hysterical way – that Lucifer could walk these streets in human form.

He asked: 'President Sazarin is still alive?'

No answer.

'Sazarin? *Morte?*'

The old man turned. '*No morte,*' he said firmly and drove onward, hunched forward over the wheel, shutting Sam out.

Aldo Morello moved away from John Cornell and stood back studying him as Cornell reached for his shirt and tie draped over the railed end of the hospital bed.

'I suggest you stay until morning at the very least,' advised Morello. 'Our facilities here provide complete privacy and security. Your people can arrange the necessary temporary communication links.'

Cornell shook his head. 'And prompt the kind of press speculation I don't need?'

Morello smiled. 'Mr President, with respect, this isn't America, where you can keep such matters under wraps. I'm afraid that's started already.'

'I've only been here half an hour!'

'In Rome a rumour spreads within seconds. Half an hour is an eternity.' Morello glanced at his wristwatch. 'Actually the examination has taken almost an hour.'

Cornell sighed.

Morello said, cautiously, 'I assume you know your condition?'

'No. And I don't particularly want to.'

Morello nodded. 'There is always that dilemma.'

'I can guess. I can tell by the way I feel that . . . well . . . that things aren't as good as they could be.' He pulled on his shirt, stating defensively: 'However, my own physician hasn't identified any problem.'

'I know you politicians,' rebuked Morello. 'I doubt if you've given anyone time to really check you out.'

Cornell knotted his tie. '*Professore*, being sick – or admitting to sickness – is terminal for a politician. If as you say you treat them, then you already know that.' He glanced up. 'Actually I've been feeling pretty good lately.'

Impatience crossed Morello's classically Roman face. 'The hush before the axe falls. I'll be brutal with you, Mr President – you have to know the cause. At the risk of stating the obvious, you're no ordinary man – you're the leader of the most powerful nation on Earth and as such I consider it my duty both as a doctor and as a citizen of this misguided planet to ensure that you know what you're dealing with.'

'What you're really saying is you feel you have to tell *someone*. Well, tell me first.'

'You may be suffering from a brain tumour. More tests are needed, of course, but I must warn you I am rarely wrong in my diagnosis.'

'Even after such a brief examination?'

'The signs are there. One can't ignore them.'

'How long?'

'I need more time to answer that.'

'But it could be any time? It could have been today?'

'Perhaps? It is too early for such thoughts.'

Cornell moved to a mirror and adjusted his tie. 'You're treating President Sazarin?' he asked.

'I'm heading the team, yes.'

'What are *his* chances?'

'A bullet in the brain is usually terminal. When he arrived I said he needed a miracle to survive. Now . . .' Morello shrugged. 'He's not by any means out of danger but I have to confess his continuing recovery has little to do with my expertise or my staff's care. Some people are just destined to live. If he does recover, the gutter press are going to have a field day – as will your American TV preachers. We already have a group of very vocal Christians encamped in our car park. Their message is very basic – and very unchristian too. *Kill the Beast!*'

'How do you rate his chances of complete recovery?'

'That depends on what you mean by complete. Able to function at the level he had been prior to the assassination attempt? Doubtful – but not entirely impossible. He was lucky, the bullet actually *bounced* off his forehead – but took a chunk of him with it. However, it's not unknown for a full recovery to occur in such cases. There have been injuries in wartime when a considerable section of the skull has been blown off yet the victim made – essentially – a full recovery. Not just motor functions: reasoning, intelligence, have remained at pre-trauma levels.'

'Presumably he's still unconscious?'

'Hard to say quite what state he's in. *Floating* is perhaps the best description. His eyes are open, yet whether he actually sees is undetermined. We've tried the usual tests but they're inconclusive. There's no movement or reaction but he could be watching. Or blind.'

'Where is he?'

Morello pointed to the connecting door in the pastel-shaded wall behind him. 'Next door. We only have this one special section, opened a few months ago, commissioned – a touch *eerily*, I have to admit – by Brussels over two years ago because the first Federation President when elected would be officially resident in Rome. They needed no lessons in how violent the modern world can be. Of course it was really only ever meant for one major figure at a time. You and Sazarin are overfilling it at the moment. He has the intensive care unit – this is the recovery room.'

Cornell turned. 'Perhaps President Sazarin might care to share his source of miracles?'

Morello smiled: 'You're surely not making the mistake so many great Roman rulers succumbed to? Heeding the crowd? Many of them are nothing more than superstitious peasants at heart. No! Perhaps it goes deeper than that: they are pagans still; the old gods hover in their peripheral vision, dark forms, eager to step out of the shadows at the slightest opportunity. There's no evil presence, no mysticism, in the room next door, just a gun-shot man, very lucky indeed to be alive. The rest is best left to the imaginings – perhaps even the subconscious desires – of the peasants and the Born-Again Christians or the Pentecostalists or whichever group believes such rubbish.'

'You're wrong, *Professore*. There *is* a form of mysticism. It's called charisma and we both know what *that* can do to the crowd. Mussolini wasn't that long ago in Italy, Hitler had a European dream, did he not? And Sazarin has greater power than either of those – greater, even, in the long term, than perhaps any president of the United States will ever wield again. Federated Europe is more than a superpower. It will be, in its final form – with most of the former Soviet bloc succumbing through sheer necessity – the greatest economic force on the planet. Combine that with a charismatic leader and you've got one hell of a brew.'

'You're frightened of him,' said Morello, surprised.

Cornell's eyes were steady. 'I'm terrified. Terrified by what he might become. He's already an outspoken atheist who's displayed little evidence of humanity to make up for that. He says he's a pragmatist and so he is: he deals in the practicable rather than the ideal course – he orders mass arrests of refugees who break border controls. And the people of Greater Europe cheer him for it, whether rich, comfortable, or downright poor. Of course they do! They've all got something to lose. But what will be the next stage when the camps are full and the starving Third World heads in uncontrollable numbers for Europe's replete borders, as they are certain to do? Shoot them down at the frontiers? *Thin down* the camp population to take them? We've witnessed that final solution before. Who could hold a man with so much power in check? The United States?' Cornell shook his head. 'We'll never fight another war in Europe, I'm certain of it. We've enough problems of our own. The American people are sick of your internal squabbles which inevitably involve them – and cost American lives.'

Morello smiled drily. 'All they want to do is make money?'

'They want to live – and have a reasonable quality of life. No sin in that.'

The telephone by the bed rang. Morello lifted it, said *pronto*, listened for a moment, rang off and said, smiling, 'Your wife will soon be here – there was some difficulty in locating her. I regret she was found at one of our most famous fashion houses.'

Cornell had a hand to his forehead. He sat back on the bed. 'I think I'll heed your advice and stay overnight. I feel a little shaky still.'

Morello checked his pulse. 'I suggest you change into pyjamas and get some rest. There are various sizes in the wardrobe.'

'Thank you for your concern, *Professore*. I'm very tired. I'll sleep a little until my wife gets here. Would you inform the Secret Service detail of my decision, please? And perhaps tell them not to disturb me unless it's a national emergency.' Cornell gave a weary smile.

'It is an honour to have you here, Mr President. I only wish the circumstances could be different.'

'I'm grateful for your honesty.'

Morello turned at the door. 'Not honesty. Pure self-preservation. I've seen what aberrations may be caused to human behaviour by the condition you have. Frankly, I wouldn't want you within a thousand miles of the White House if final tests prove positive.'

'How many miles away are we here?' chuckled Cornell, playing the Irishman, his big-toothed smile spreading – but never quite reaching his eyes.

With Morello gone he arose from the bed and tried the connecting door.

It opened.

The black Cadillac bearing US Embassy plates swept past the wheezing, tilted taxi and swung on to the hospital concourse. Inside the limousine, Madelaine Cornell saw massed cameras behind a solid phalanx of police and more heavily armed *carabinieri* and applied a final touch of powder to her face, totally unaware of Sam Lewelyn's heavy form spread uncomfortably across the Fiat's rear seats.

The Cadillac pulled up with a slight squeal from its heavy tyres, two secret-servicemen immediately closing in on either side of her as she alighted, moving her swiftly through the camera-flashes and yelled questions into the reception area.

'Wrong entrance,' barked one, over the pandemonium, pushing people back from the First Lady. 'There's a new VIP section.'

The receptionist stood up from behind her VDU and indicated the glass doors of the entrance, then right.

'We're not going back out there again,' the second bodyguard snapped. 'It's bad enough in here!'

'Isn't there a way through inside?' Madelaine Cornell demanded.

The receptionist pointed her pen in the direction of a corridor. 'Follow the line coloured dark blue – this will take you to the VIP suite. They are expecting you, Signora Cornell. I will page Professore Morello. You understand?'

'Sure we understand,' said the nearest secret-serviceman,

backed-up very close to Madelaine Cornell. 'Mrs Cornell? Let's go. *Please.*'

They set off quickly, a group of people following some yards behind.

'Who are they?' snapped Madelaine Cornell, glancing back.

'Rubber-necks. Those cops should have a presence *inside*. We've got it under control, ma'am.'

The second bodyguard turned and waved them back. They faltered but started forward as soon as his back was turned. At the rear of the group a limping priest, greying head down to his rosary murmuring what might have been a prayer, kept pace, his face glistening with the effort.

Sam had barked: 'Hey!' rapidly tapping the driver's shoulder as the limousine flashed past. '*There.*' He pointed after the Cadillac. He waved dollar bills.

The old man leaned back. 'You come for Presidente Cornello?'

'Yes!' Sam jabbed a finger at the limousine. 'There . . . Signora Cornello.'

The old man shook his head pointing to a road on the left and turned around enquiringly. 'Presidente Cornello.'

'You sure?'

The grizzled head nodded vigorously.

'OK, do it.'

The Fiat swung left into a subsidiary road leading to a new-looking low wing, lurching to a halt with a wrench on the hand-brake. A gnarled finger pointed. 'Presidente Cornello.'

Sam fed dollar bills on to the front seat. 'OK?'

'OK.'

Sam added a couple more, got out, and looked around.

The old man leaned out of his window, tilting the car even more. He barely whispered: '*La Bestia,*' then gestured over Sam, touched both fingers to his own eyes, crossed himself swiftly, and reversed down the road, hard, the worn transmission juddering and whining in protest.

Sam decided he had just been given protection against the evil eye and right then was grateful for anything.

He stood indecisively on the paving by a long brightly lit

window, noting in a professional way the texture of the glass which made it bullet-proof and confirmed he was where he ought to be.

He saw Madelaine Cornell first, chin tilted up haughtily, above the mêlée behind, bodyguards tight as they should be, one half-turned toward the excited gaggle further back along the long corridor, mouth opened in a rebuke silenced by the thick glass.

The crowd came up behind milling directly in front of Sam, slowed by fire-doors, pushing at each other before starting off again almost at a run to catch up.

Jesus, thought Sam. Where's security?

Then he saw the lowered greying head and black cassock, inches from him, the face slick with sweat and sick with pain, a kind of madness in the eyes. The face lifted to him then away, the broken body picked up its jolting gait once more.

Sam saw, vividly, the Church of the Holy Sepulchre, MOSSAD's silent video, dark murderous eyes, the same jolting gait marching from a woman's mocking smile. That unmistakable gait. One soldier's quiet recognition of another's pain. Sam had seen the results of wounds from high-velocity ordnance too many times: single entry smashing bone; multiple exits slicing nerves and tendons, leaving a whole but inflexible limb.

He began running, heart pounding, already wishing he was ten years younger even before he took the first step.

Father David Kolchak had arrived in Rome by the Lear jet just before noon that Saturday. Ignoring Marchionni's strict instructions he had taken a taxi to the south of the city, taking a meagre room in a small *pensione* chosen at random. There, he slept for five hours, despite the bed-bugs.

When he awoke, washed in the cracked bowl, and stood naked before the mirror, his body appeared to have been struck by some disease. He stared at the bites, grateful for them, for their constant irritation kept other, worse, things from his mind. Yet he was fearful too, for their appearance upon his flesh was like the eruption of his mortal sins, past and future. He did not consider the present. He was too detached from it. But the moment would come when reality returned. That, he knew, was as certain as death.

He had forgone all food and drink and, leaving the *pensione*, walked to St Peter's Square to face his God, but once there could not enter His house. Instead, he stood weeping for himself – with no tears shown to the world – until it was time.

Again he walked. This time two miles to the North and the Ospidale Gemelli, his leg jolting hard into his body with each stiff swinging movement, until the sweat poured in warm rivulets down his face, feeling like blood.

With each step forward the light of God seemed to lift from him and the heavy claw of Satan embed itself deeper, drawing him on.

He heard divine words of comfort inside his head as he walked, then intoned them aloud, repeating them over and over until only they existed and all else was shut out for ever.

> *The beast that thou sawest, was and is not; and shall ascend out of the bottomless pit and go into perdition.*

He was now only one step from eternity, though forgiven and seated with God or cast into the pit, he could not know. Despite Marchionni's promises of absolution he knew that only Christ could promise him salvation. Ricardo Marchionni could guarantee one thing only: knowledge gained by his legion of committed contacts, of Sazarin's precise location inside the Ospidale Gemelli. *Where the Beast lay.*

He had arrived at the concourse of the hospital in a state of near-total exhaustion; crippled by pain from his leg and the burden he carried.

Seeing the US embassy limousine arriving with Madelaine Cornell almost finished him, bringing his heart to his gasping mouth and causing him to turn sharply away, before what remained of his reasoning told him that here was the perfect opportunity – using the apparent confusion – to enter the hospital and successfully perform the deed.

After that was done, nothing mattered.

Shutting out the pain he limped forward, entering the reception area in time to be swallowed in the clamour, then attached himself to the group following America's First Lady with Marchionni's state of the art ceramic automatic lying coldly against his bare stomach like fear.

*

John Cornell found himself in a small interconnecting room that seemed to be a rest area for medical staff manning the special VIP unit. He walked between comfortable armchairs, noting an array of monitor screens displaying vital signs and other medical information he did not recognize – and the interiors of two rooms: his own and he presumed the one beyond the door ahead of him.

He tried the handle and opened the door.

Sazarin lay staring at the ceiling, his eyes unmoving. Cornell moved closer until he stood almost over him with only the transparent tent which hung completely over the raised bed between them.

Cornell looked away. *I'm not a killer.* He gripped his head, feeling the tight band – like harsh iron – grip him. *I can't leave this world with a mortal sin dragging my soul down to hell.* He knelt beside the bed, the plastic of the tent cool beneath his clasped hands. He glanced at Sazarin's handsome face. *Can't you accept God?* he asked in silence. *If you could I would walk away from here, the murder in my heart defeated.*

He prayed briefly for Sazarin's soul and his own, knowing that there was no escape. Here was the man who would and could destroy his Christ. For Sazarin Christianity was an irrelevance. He remembered Sam's term: *Godless mediocrity.* That was Sazarin's vision of the future at best. At worst it could be hell – without any aid from the Book of Revelation or Lucifer.

Cornell rose heavily to his feet looking down at the still, staring figure. Sazarin's unlimited funding of the Markarovs' work could not be allowed. Reduce God to the level of man's own puny technology? Whatever it took, he would stop it. His eyes sought the power supply for the respirator.

Sam came around a corner fast and saw a long glass corridor, the small lit ornamental garden beyond distorted by the thickness of the material. At its head he spotted a tall security arch which couldn't stop an assassin carrying a weapon through but would he knew warn the hell out of whoever guarded the area.

He saw Jim Bentley at the furthest end of the corridor, where the glass ended and a suite of rooms began, sitting on a chair outside one of two doors on the right, alone, reading a magazine in the flat silence. Sam felt relief. If the bodyguard was relaxed the body was still alive. Obviously he had reached here before the crowd. Before the priest.

Perhaps it was all a form of madness, he thought, suddenly feeling foolish and wondering how he would explain his presence to John Cornell.

He was quite unprepared for the sudden appearance of Madelaine Cornell and the two bodyguards from an adjoining corridor by the security arch.

He called out but his voice was drowned by shouting as uniformed men ran out of a side room, bawling abuse at the unruly, following crowd which now seemed to include photographers.

The arch clanged an alarm as the two secret-servicemen stepped through, the hospital guards swinging around from their yelling to see the men turning, nonchalantly displaying their weapons. Someone yelled, 'OK.' It might have been question or affirmation.

Only then did Sam see the priest break from the clamour and step through the arch, limping stiffly down the corridor.

Sam charged forward, using his heavy shoulders to barge through the throng. The alarm clanged immediately he passed under the arch.

He yelled: '*Madelaine, that's Kolchak!*'

Kolchak turned and appeared to shake his head as though something was wrong, then made straight for a door to his right.

Sam crouched, fast.

Madelaine Cornell had stopped at Sam's shout, her two bodyguards swivelling around, eyes alive, hands poised like serpents coiled for the strike, unsure what was happening but seeing a Catholic priest half-way down the glass corridor – faced unthreateningly away from their charge – and, just before the crowd, a very big, purposeful-looking man who must have activated the security arch, crouched, his hand coming up with a small pistol from his sock.

Behind them Jim Bentley had leapt to his feet, horror on his face, knowing what was going to occur and knowing too that his warning yell would be too late.

Madelaine Cornell screamed as the secret-servicemen's guns blasted.

Sam felt the cold marble against his hands and wondered how the hell he had slipped. He could see the sky through the glass ceiling of the corridor. A dark aircraft passed overhead, noisily, it might have been the Blackbird heading home, and he said: *Thanks for the ride*. Or thought he did.

David Kolchak had an advantage over all of them. He knew precisely where to go. Stunned at the sound of his name being yelled, he recovered fast enough to see – and close enough to reach, even half-crippled – the door he must enter before the bullets took him down. He took two great jerking strides, hauled it open and stood inside, backed against it, fingers working the lock, blinking in the sudden gloom, ears roaring from the eerie silence. A sharp detached *blip* from the life-support system machine brought him back fast, his hand fumbling inside his cassock for the automatic.

Two heavy bangs sounded from outside.

John Cornell stood up quickly from where he was crouched on the far side of the bed. 'Father?'

The gun-shots were thunderous in the enclosed space, scarlet blooming instantly on the pure white sheets.

Cornell fell back, throwing up his hands in self-protection but the gun kept on firing steadily, like measured hammer blows, until the door crashed open and rapid gunfire from outside silenced it. Then strong hands clasped his shoulders and he saw black skin.

'It's OK, sir – this is Jim. Are you hit?'

He had no voice at all. He shook his head sharply.

'You're sure about that, Mr President?'

Cornell tried to haul himself up but the weakness was enveloping him. 'Help me,' he said, nodding at where Kolchak lay with another secret-serviceman beside him, gun readied, looking bewilderedly into the grey face.

'You can put that away now,' said Cornell.

'He's still alive, sir. You never know with fanatics.'

Cornell knelt very close beside him. He murmured, 'Father. Thank you. *Thank you*.'

The secret-serviceman looked at Jim Bentley, perplexed. Bentley gave a small shake of his head.

Kolchak's eyelids fluttered, he flexed momentarily then gave a deep sigh.

'That's it, sir.'

'Go away.'

'Mr President?'

'Go away. I don't need you any more.'

'He just tried to kill you, sir, you're shocked.'

Cornell turned to the bed. 'Not me.'

Madelaine Cornell stood in the doorway. 'That's David Kolchak,' she said.

Cornell hadn't noticed her. Hadn't felt for her at the moment he thought it was over for him. He had nothing to say to her.

'Sam's been shot,' she said, brutally.

He looked up at her sharply, tried to rise. '*Sam!*'

Jim Bentley caught him as he toppled. 'Easy, sir. Take it slow. You can't go out there, not until the area is secure.'

A crisis team burst into the room, immediately setting upon Sazarin, Aldo Morello bending quickly beside Cornell, automatically taking his pulse. 'You're not hit?'

'Not a scratch.'

'Dear God, what is all this? I was conducting an operation—! Why were you in here?'

'I needed to see him.'

Morello gazed at him for a moment then said, briskly, 'We need this room clear – you men take your president through into the recovery room – through there. Let him rest, I'll check him thoroughly later.'

'Sazarin's dead,' snapped Madelaine Cornell. 'Look at him! See to my husband now. He needs your attention. He's ill, can't you see!'

Morello fixed her with a baleful gaze. '*President* Sazarin is not dead, Mrs Cornell – but he will be if you don't leave here immediately.'

Cornell felt hopelessness slip blackly over him. He could do no more. He felt consciousness slide and had one bitter thought before the darkness. He had only been given enough time to fail.

*

He awoke with Sam – big left arm in a sling – beside him, soft bedclothes around him and the feeling that perhaps he had been given a second chance. His last.

Sam smiled. 'Hello, John.'

'Sam! You're all right.'

'Just fine. I've been winged before. One round hit – nothing anyone could do – all happened too fast. My head hurts more – from the marble floor.'

'Thank God.'

Sam paused. 'The priest was Kolchak – the one we saw on the Jersualem videotape.'

'I know.'

'I thought he was here for you. Hell, I thought *someone* was here for you. I spotted Kolchak and the coincidence . . .'

'He wasn't here for me.'

Sam nodded. 'Local cops figure all they've got is a flipped priest. There's a parking-lot full of Jesus Freaks out there – they're rounding them up right now, *hard*. Rome's not too good a place for Christians right now. I've done some listening as they patched me up . . . Sazarin's got some powerbase here! Cops out there love him. Figure he was going to give them the go-ahead to get some order on the streets.'

'How is he?' asked Cornell, carefully.

'Holding out. Must have some constitution. Word is he might make it.' Sam looked down awkwardly at his sling. 'John, I hijacked a Blackbird out of Andrews to get here. Held a peanut gun on the crew. Up there it might have been a cannon. Crew had to co-operate. I told them I thought that your life was in danger. Just a gut thing . . . after we had that spat on the phone. Took me over, I guess. Maybe you could make sure the guys don't get into a disciplinary problem? It was my brain-storm.' He paused. 'And I hit a cop here – but they're going to forget that . . . under the circumstances.'

Cornell took his meaty hand and grasped it. 'Listen to me. Jim Bentley has a tape-recording of a call I had from Hal Ellis at Langley. Get it from him and take Air Force One back to Edwards – you'll be there in three and a half hours. I'll authorize the flight as Jim drives you to Fiumicino. By the time you arrive you'll have heard the tape.'

'What do you want me to do, John? Just say it. Anything.'

'Make Kent understand he's got to quit. Right now. No announcement. I'll deal with the formalities when I return. Assure him I'll see he's OK. If we have to cover funding discrepancies we'll do it. The main thing is he has to pull the plug on the Mojave project.'

'John, I've talked to Kent. He's not going to listen. He thinks he's got the voice of Christ bottled up under the Mojave and he wants it *heard*. He's crazy. I mean really crazy.'

'Sam, this thing is bigger than Kent – bigger than you realize, believe me – but he's the key. Play him the tape. Make him realize what's at stake here. Do whatever you have to do. Stop him. You understand me.'

Sam stood. 'I hear you.'

CHAPTER
SIXTEEN

Greg drove the hired Dodge off-roader into the small mountain community, the powerful headlights picking out the darkened, empty clapboard houses.

He saw the heavy darkness of the mountain ridge ahead and the solitary light at its foot. He reached across the seats. 'Someone got back here before us.'

Carolyn struggled awake, her voice hoarse. 'No one here has a car fast enough.'

Greg indicated the light.

She sat up. 'That's the Jackson home. I don't understand?'

'Maybe they didn't leave?'

'I thought everyone left.'

'Didn't you see them in Austin? On the flight there?'

'I don't remember.' She looked at him, perplexed, even panicked. 'Greg, I *don't* remember.'

'Take it easy. Let's find out what's going on.'

'They're not the most neighbourly people.'

'I don't feel too neighbourly myself. Maybe they're hiding a couple of snake-bitten people in there?'

'You really believe that's what happened?'

'You bet I do.'

'I can't forget the smell of gas.'

'OK, say it was gas you smelt. Could have been used to knock out the snakes – afterwards?'

'Greg, they don't need gas to handle snakes here.'

No, he remembered, vividly.

He pulled up outside the dilapidated, slightly leaning house. 'Their car's here,' he indicated.

She frowned. 'That's new. They've had an old Chevy as long as I can remember. He kept it going, she kept it shining, my dad used to say. Never had kids. Mom always said that old Chevy made up for it.'

'Maybe they traded up?'

'Folks around here don't trade up cars.'

He stepped out. 'You stay inside.'

'Why?

'You know why.'

'They won't influence me.'

'I thought that yesterday – until we arrived.'

She looked away.

He walked to the house alone, stopping to peer into the gleaming sedan, seeing factory protective polythene on the seats and door panels.

'What're you looking at, son?' demanded a gruff voice.

'Latest Chevy. Nice car. Just delivered?'

'Not your business.'

Greg indicated the sloped shot-gun. 'If that's loaded, Mr Jackson, I'd appreciate you pointing it somewhere else.'

'It's loaded.'

A woman appeared, behind, gasped, and drew Jackson's head down to hers, whispering urgently.

Jackson growled, 'I know that.'

'Something wrong, ma'am?' asked Greg.

Jackson said: 'How come you're not dead?'

'You saw TV last night?' Greg kicked the car's tyre.

'Cut that out!' barked Jackson.

Greg turned. 'I guess we're lucky to be alive, Mrs Jackson. You didn't know? Maybe you switched off the set when things turned bad? Conscience troubling you?'

Jackson lifted the shot-gun a little. 'God-fearing folks don't suffer from bad conscience.'

'When did you buy the Chevy, sir? Just a neighbourly question. It *is* yours, isn't it?'

'You're no neighbour of ours!' snapped Emily Jackson. 'You corrupted a decent child. Took her out *there*! *Sodom!* 'She spat the last words, a thin arm flung out at random.

Greg ignored her. 'Maybe you won it? TV game show? Casino?

You got lucky in Austin? But you folks don't hold with gambling, do you? And I don't think you ever reached Texas. I don't believe you ever even got on that plane.'

Jackson growled: 'We saved. Kept the same Chevy since fifty-six – the girl'll tell you. It was time. You just quit talking about the car, y'hear.'

Greg glanced up the mountainside. 'The Pritchett home's up there, right? My wife's folks? They just floated up to heaven, you say. How? What did the Lord use? A balloon? Gas lifted them up?' He watched their faces carefully, seeing Emily Jackson pale even in the meagre porch light.

Jackson's grip on the shot-gun tightened. 'Don't you start mocking the Lord's will.'

'Jesus! How can you carry on with that crap after all that happened? The Lord's *will*? The Lord had nothing to do with it.'

Jackson raised the gun to his shoulder. 'You're close to meeting your Maker, son. If I were you I'd get in that car of yours and drive.'

'No, sir.'

Jackson shifted the gun sideways a little and fired.

Buckshot whipped into the trees on Greg's left. He felt a tug at his arm and looked down to see a small rip in the sleeve of his loose-fitting leather jacket.

Jackson came down the porch steps and jabbed the smoking barrels into his chest. 'You're living dangerously, son. Move.'

'No, sir.' Greg side-stepped, turned, jerked the barrel upward, and jabbed his elbow into Jackson's nose.

Emily Jackson shrieked as her husband slumped on to the dirt path with muffled cries coming through his bloodied fingers.

Carolyn leapt from the Dodge.

Greg held her back. 'That's a brand-new car. They've been paid for doing something – or covering up something. I want to know what?'

'*We saved for it!*' screamed Emily Jackson, bent over her husband, a handkerchief to his face.

'Bullshit.'

Carolyn struggled. 'Maybe they *did*, Greg?'

He indicated the dilapidated house. 'They couldn't raise the down-payment.'

Jackson hauled himself up, swaying, looking murderous, tears streaming from reddened eyes.

Greg released Carolyn and turned the shot-gun on the car. 'One left,' he said.

Jackson yelled, spraying blood.

'Who paid? Maddox? Did Maddox set it all up? For the *collection* plate!'

'Reverend Maddox had no part in it,' wailed Emily Jackson. 'Don't you say anything bad about him.'

'I'll let the law do that, ma'am.' Greg laid his hand on the roof of the car. 'Talking about the law, kidnapping is a Federal offence. This should be as out of date as your old Chevy by the time you're free.'

Carolyn protested: 'I've known the Jacksons all my life, there's no way they'd let my folks get hurt.'

'Isn't there?'

'Leave them be.'

He turned on her, exasperated. 'They might have your parents inside – or dead somewhere around here! Don't you want the truth? Don't you care?'

'Of course I do! But I'm a Christian. I don't believe in brutalizing people to find them!'

Angrily, Greg heaved the shot-gun into the brush. 'OK, ask them where your parents are. Yesterday they went to *heaven* – what's today's story?'

Emily Jackson sobbed: 'We just wanted something new for once. We *deserve* something new.'

'Who paid?' snapped Greg.

'It doesn't matter,' Carolyn told him. 'I just want them back safe. Where are they, Mrs Jackson? Please?'

'They took them Green Bank way. Where they've got those telescopes,' growled Jackson.

Greg felt a chill touch him.

Emily Jackson said, tearfully: 'I told Josh to follow . . . with his lights off . . . just in case.'

'In case of what, Mrs Jackson?' pleaded Carolyn.

'She wanted to be sure they'd bring them back OK,' snapped Jackson.

'But why Green Bank?' asked Carolyn, bewildered.

Emily Jackson dabbed at her eyes with the bloodied handkerchief. 'They only wanted to ask questions, child. They were kind. *Interested* in us. Not like some who want to drag us into their filth.' She glared at Greg.

'What questions?' he asked, measuredly; fury dissipated and uneasiness setting in fast.

'You leave her be, boy!' Jackson snorted, painfully. 'They said tests. Secret. Just talking, they said. Government people. You have to trust government people!'

Emily Jackson suddenly wailed: 'Then Josh saw them . . . all shining in the dark.'

'Greg, what's happening?' Carolyn clutched him, her eyes fearful.

'Not angels. Protective suits. Gas. Sounds like you were right.' He gently eased her from him and gripped Jackson's arm firmly. 'Show me.'

Jackson protested: 'Where you taking me?'

Greg swung him around, hard. 'Here's how it is. My way you've got my wife to protect you – maybe she'll even let you keep the car out of misguided Christian kindness. That's her business. The alternative is the FBI who'll squeeze you till it hurts and crush the car afterwards.'

'Whatever you say,' muttered Jackson.

Greg indicated the Dodge. 'You lead, I'll follow. That thing is heavy duty and fast. Try outrunning me, I'll catch up, and drive you clear off the mountain. Hear me?'

Jackson walked to the car, head tilted back, his wife holding a towel to his nose. Inside he struggled with unfamiliar controls before finally starting off with a lurch.

Greg followed in silence, the gleaming Chevrolet trapped in his big headlights on the winding mountain road, suspicion creeping up on him like the closing-in mist outside.

'Tell me,' Carolyn said, watching him.

He fixed his eyes ahead, not answering.

'Just say what you're thinking.'

'I don't know what I'm thinking.'

'Tell me about Green Bank.'

'You lived here, you must know about Green Bank.'

'What *don't* I know? Tell me!'

'There's no secrets. It's a Government programme. SETI. "Search for Extra-Terrestrial Intelligence" programme, run by NASA. Started in 1992 on the five hundredth anniversary of Columbus's discovery of the New World. Press treated it as a joke – not least because Dan Quayle was nominally its head at the start.'

'They're serious?'

He glanced at her. 'One hundred million dollars committed over seven years? Someone was serious.'

'Committed to what?'

'Searching the cosmic haystack for a needlepoint of sound is how the Press described it.'

'But that's what you said you do?'

'We don't search, we decipher. Or try to.'

'Who gives you the material?'

'Classified.'

'You mean you won't say?'

'I don't get told.'

She turned, her exhaustion flaring into anger. 'You get it from Green Bank. My mom and dad being taken has something to do with your work, *right*? There's no other connection. That's what you're thinking? Greg? *Tell me!*'

'I don't know.'

'You fought with your dad because he wanted to know about your work. Did *he* know something? What's going on?'

'It wasn't Dad who wanted to know. It was John Cornell.'

She stared at him, stunned. 'The *President*? Greg, what's happening. *Please?*'

'Look, I've known the Cornells for as long—' He stabbed a finger at the Jackson's Chevrolet. 'For as long as you've known *them*! To me they're just ordinary people – they don't impress me. I know the way they operate. Power games. Hers mostly. I've seen her manipulate him more times than I can remember. I was within my rights to refuse. I was going to be asked questions that only the NSA Director should be asked to answer. Cornell and Kent have had a cold war going since Cornell gained the presidency – everyone in the agency knows it. Cornell's decided to hot it up.'

He turned, sharply. 'That snap inspection on Monday? Cornell looking for ammunition. Leverage. He wants Kent out but won't face him down. It's that simple.'

'No, it's not. You're still down on him because of your mother. That's unfair. Your mother died in England. She *wanted* to be there. To die there.'

'They have telephones in England. It's not castles and drawbridges any more!' he snapped.

'Don't get mad.'

'I'm not.' He glared ahead.

'What's going on, Greg?' she asked, quietly; afraid.

'I don't know.'

'I think you do.'

They had descended into a valley. Sprawled along the roadside was a shanty town of tarpaulin tents and near-derelict cars. Rain had begun beating down through the mist, adding more misery to the depressing scene.

'Jesus, is this America?' murmured Greg.

Carolyn wiped condensation from her window, she said, dully, 'Old folks here tell when the Great Depression lifted it came to rest in the mountains. Liked it so much it decided to stay.'

'They've got a real sense of humour.'

'Living like this you can cry or get mad. Get mad, you go to jail; cry hard enough you end up in a pine box. Either way you lose. So they laugh. TV people came up here and called this America's Third World – right there on the screen. No one gave a damn. So they had to be wrong, didn't they? People care about the Third World.'

Greg said: 'You got out.'

'Sure, I left my folks and walked down the mountain. I'm the exception everyone can point at when they blame the rest for being *wasters*.' Her eyes filled with tears.

'We'll find them,' he said gently. 'There's a reason for what's happened.'

'I didn't hear you say a good reason.'

Headlights on full beam blasted the flooded windshield, the approaching car moving slowly on the narrow muddy road, wipers flailing at high speed.

Greg pulled two wheels on the dirt shoulder, allowing the low, glistening shape of a Jaguar coupé to slide by, glimpsing the blurred profile of the driver fixed arrogantly on the road ahead.

He swore, hit the brakes, and swung the Dodge hard round, spraying mud in a great arc.

Carolyn fell across him, her seat-belt snatching at her. '*Greg!* You'll lose the Jacksons! What's wrong?'

'Forget the Jacksons.'

'Greg!'

In silence, face set, he hammered the Dodge up the mountain after the cautiously driven Jaguar until he was close enough to confirm the registration, then swung alongside, forcing the car on to a low earth bank.

He was around the car's long nose, had the door hauled open and the hand going for an automatic in the locker gripped firmly by the wrist in seconds. 'Leave it,' he ordered.

Cardus saw his face in the glow from the interior light. 'Greg! For God's sake, I thought I was being robbed! What are you playing at? You could have killed me!'

Greg reached in for the gun, checked the load, released the safety, and pointed it.

'What are you doing?'

'Get out.'

Cardus protested but complied, struggling over the high transmission tunnel and out on to the churned-up earth, blinking uncertainly in the steady rain. 'What about my car? I can't leave it like this?'

'It's off the road. Park lights should last the night.'

'The *night*!'

'How long depends on your answers to my wife's questions.'

Cardus turned to the Dodge.

'Where did you think she was, Cardus? Still in Austin? Or dead?' Greg gripped his arm and marched him to the Dodge. 'Carolyn, you drive. Go back to where we left the Jacksons.' He took her seat as she moved over, turning to the rear, watching Cardus's face under the interior light, the gun resting threateningly on the seat back.

'Your parents are unharmed,' said Cardus, addressing Carolyn's eyes in the driving mirror. 'They're very comfortable. Their accommodation will be better than at home, I'm sure.'

Carolyn glared at him.

'No disrespect intended. I'm just trying to reassure.'

'She's not reassured. Why, Cardus?'

'You understand it would have only been a matter of time before you were fully appraised of the background – the realities – of the project.'

'I thought I had been.'

'You were told all you needed to know – at that time. Circumstances have changed.'

Carolyn snapped: 'If my folks are so damn comnfortable how come you had to *gas* them to bring them here?'

Cardus ran his hand over his swept-back fair hair. 'I admit the method was harsh but we had no choice. This involves the highest level of national security, I can't say more than that. The Director will explain. I don't have that authority.'

'Kent's here?' Greg reacted with surprise.

'Of course not. He never leaves Fort Meade. There's a direct link to Meade at Green Bank.'

Carolyn said: 'I just want my parents back safely. I don't care about the rest. Any of it!'

'It's not as simple as that,' Greg told her. '*Is* it, Cardus?'

She swung around. 'But they are at Green Bank? The Jacksons said they were taken there. They followed you.'

'The Jacksons are nothing,' said Greg. 'They were paid to look the other way. Right, Cardus? Was the *Rapture* story planned or did the Jacksons panic when they found out Carolyn and I were coming up here? That was the last thing you expected, wasn't it – knowing my feelings about the community?'

Cardus sat in silence.

Greg drew back the hammer.

Cardus sighed: 'They're confused people, they barely know the difference between reality and fantasy. The whole thing snowballed. Utterly stupid. Greg, that gun really isn't necessary. It's also dangerous.'

'What is the *noise*, Cardus? Green Bank supplies the tapes? Is that it? SETI's actually picked up something? There *is* something out there? Is that what you're hiding?'

'I told you, I don't have the authority. Director Kent will explain.'

Greg shifted but the gun remained steady. 'The President hasn't been told everything either, has he? That's why he wanted answers from me.'

Cardus could not conceal his alarm. 'You've spoken with him!'

'I chose not to. Obviously I was wrong.'

'No! You were absolutely corect. Cornell's not the man for this. I tried explaining that to you before you left the station. Anyhow, going by the news from Rome perhaps we won't have to worry about him for much longer.'

'What news?'

'News flash says he's been taken ill. Some reports say he was shot. The situation is still confused. It's something to do with Sazarin.'

'We haven't used the radio.'

Cardus shrugged. 'We're better off without him.'

'He's the *President*!' Carolyn snapped and turned on the radio. A finger-picked banjo's sharp tangled notes blasted out.

Greg reached back and switched it off. 'Worry about Cornell later,' he told her.

'*Greg!*'

'Right now your folks need all our concern.' He looked hard at Cardus. 'You asked a lot of questions in your office a couple of days back but I was so tied up with my work and Carolyn needing a break from the station I didn't really listen, did I? You weren't talking about my father's relationship with the President, you were talking about *mine*. You thought maybe I was reporting directly to Cornell? You couldn't have been more wrong. I was ordered to answer Cornell's questions by my father in Washington – he was actually driving me to the White House – and I refused. So what gives Kent the right to withhold vital information from the President? Hell, from the *people*! What makes him so special?'

'You don't understand what we're dealing with here. This is far more important than you can ever know. Maybe more important than you can understand. We're talking about history here.'

Cardus looked at Greg's face.

'I said you wouldn't understand.'

'I'm still listening. History, you said?'

'Civilization.' Cardus's eyes were alight. 'Everything we are and ever will be could all be lost in little more than a moment. Our light in the heavens, shining for generations, gone in a blink. That's the consequence.'

Greg looked at him astonished. 'You're a scientist? You sound more like Maddox. The consequence of what?'

'Of there being *nothing*. Of that empty truth becoming the *only* truth. Of people knowing they have no purpose beyond temporal existence.'

Greg felt his scalp crawl. 'What has SETI picked up, Cardus?'

Carolyn screamed.

Greg barely saw the sudden blinding flare of headlights, too close, approaching too fast, before the massive *bang*, the lurch, the nauseating, hanging moment as the world fell over, over again, then upended and stayed that way, leaving silence broken only by the far-off whirr of wheels and the tick of hot metal cooling in the rain. Then nothing. Darkness, that was not the wet Appalachian night.

The vast convoy of fast-moving vehicles caught him completely by surprise. They were upon him, driving without lights at a suicidal pace, before he knew it, only his fighter pilot's reactions saving him as he swung blindly off the road into the desert.

Then he knew why.

The RAF Tornado attacked so low it seemed to pass through the fire cloud above the first vaporized tanker-truck like a screaming black bat. Then the world became hell, and fire consumed air so fast he gasped with the shock of it, sucking in raw heat and believing that somewhere some fool had used a nuclear device and he was in the eye of a fire-hurricane.

He threw himself from the truck he had killed for, the driver's stolen robes smouldering, ready to ignite as he dug madly in the sand as if it were the sea and he could dive deep enough to escape the fire, the heat, the carnage.

Then in that part of his mind which still remained sane he heard the unmistakable scything whip of helicopter gun-ship rotors and knew there was no nuclear explosion – only high technology decimating an enemy whose greatest mistake was to exclude truth from their strategy.

He gave himself up to the sand. There were worse graves.

*

He stared upward, blindly, still stunned but recollection returning fast, smelling two distinct odours close enough to breathe: perfume and cordite. Rain swept across his face, obliterating them. He moved his head and felt the automatic fall away from his neck then, pushing away the strands of hair hanging over his face, found the head above him.

'*Carolyn!*'

She groaned.

He moved cautiously, crunching on a bed of crystals, testing his body for broken bones and finding none. Reaching upward he fumbled for the ignition, found it, switched off, and withdrew the key.

'*Greg?*'

'Thank God. How do you feel?'

'Nauseous.'

'You're hung by your seat-belt. Before I try getting you down, can you feel anything broken?'

'I don't know. There's no pain. My head hurts. *Greg, I can smell gasoline!*'

'Gas tank's probably ruptured. It's not reached us yet but we need to get out right away. Can you make it?'

'*Just release me!*'

'Don't panic. I'll try and support you. Release the belt. Ready? Do it. '

She slumped down heavily beside him, gasping sharply.

'You OK?'

She struggled frantically to right herself, her breathing frantic.

Please God, no sparks, he thought, and reached upward for the door handle, pushed it and kicked out with both legs, the door screeching on the road.

'Go!' he snapped.

A liquid moan came from the rear and he turned to it.

She gripped him, hard. 'Where are you going!'

'Cardus.'

'No!'

'He knows where your folks are. Get out, for God's sake!'

He pushed her off and crawled back along the roof-lining to the dark twisted shape.

'Cardus?' He found a fluttering pulse, and seeking a heartbeat, blood; too much of it, pumping from the bullet hole at the centre of his chest. He could not remember the gun going off. He swore and searched rapidly through Cardus's pockets, found keys and the heavy gold lighter he liked to flourish for others though Greg had never once seen him smoke.

Cardus's hand gripped his with impossible strength, pulling him close, gasping something.

'Kent? What about Kent?' Greg urged.

'*Tell him.*'

'What?'

'*Babel.*'

'Cardus, where are her parents? For God's sake!'

'*You understand. Tell Kent.*'

'Understand what!'

'*Babel.*'

'Cardus?'

Carolyn shrieked: '*Greg! There's gasoline everywhere.*'

Cardus sighed for too long, then shuddered like a man entering a cold place.

'Sorry,' Greg murmured and crawled out on to the road.

Carolyn stood in the darkness, wet and shivering violently, arms clasped around herself, shock setting in fast.

He held her. 'You have to make it. You understand?'

He caught her crooked, trembling smile in the moonlight.

'He's dead, isn't he?'

'Worse.'

'What?'

'Shot dead. The gun went off in the crash.'

'It wasn't your fault,' she told him, trembling violently now.

He stripped off his leather jacket and wrapped it around her. 'Get into the trees. Move.'

'What are you doing? *Greg!*'

'Do it.'

He pushed her away from him and crouched, backing up, testing the ground, tasting the wetness on his fingers. He worked the lighter in cupped hands until it flared then touched it to the ground and ran, arms pumping, for the trees.

'It's not going to take,' he breathed beside her, the eerie pool of blue fire on the road barely alive.

'Why are you trying to burn it? *Him?*'

'We need time. The autopsy won't miss the bullet-hole in a burnt-up body but a cop wanting to get out of the rain might.'

The blue pool had spread now and the roof-lining material inside the Dodge flickered dull yellow, billowing dark smoke.

'Come on,' breathed Greg. 'This goddamn rain!'

He tensed and she grabbed him. '*Don't!*'

The heat was a furnace door opened suddenly, the blast a searing fist buffeting them despite the protection of the trees.

In the light from the flames Greg could see the rear of the car that had hit them, its front buried deep into a tree, something lifeless sprawled across the wrecked hood.

Carolyn leaned against the tree, turned away from the wreck, head down, her wet hair straggled. 'That's the Jacksons' new car.'

'I know. Wait here.'

She watched him sprint through the rain, the flickering flames making his movements appear stroboscopic, like old silent film. He leaned over the hood of the Chevrolet then ducked inside the wreck before running back, slower now, his body language confirming what she already feared and even in her own way, knew.

'I'm sorry,' he said, panting.

She closed her eyes, forgiving them for what they had done and wishing their souls well. Right then she wasn't too clear about God.

He held her. 'Let's get out of here.'

'How?'

He showed her Cardus's car keys.

They started walking in the rain.

The Jaguar started immediately, the smooth pull of twelve cylinders easing the powerful car off the muddy bank, a throaty rasp coming from one slightly damaged exhaust.

Back on the road, Greg stopped. 'We can't go to Green Bank, not in this, they're bound to have some kind of security. The car's too distinctive – they'll know something's happened to Cardus.'

She closed her eyes. 'I don't know what to do.'

'We can try and get close. I could go on by foot but I don't know where to look. I don't even know the layout. They're bound to have security. If anything goes wrong that leaves you outside on your own and you're not in good shape.'

'I'm OK.'

'Not to drive to DC and try and explain any of this to someone powerful enough to do something. If Cardus was telling the truth you can't go to the President.'

'I wouldn't leave you with *them*!'

'You'd have no choice. Besides, can you explain any of this?'

'Greg, my parents have been kidnapped – that's all I have to explain.'

He shook his head. 'You've just been seen on TV with a bunch of hysterical religious fanatics half of whom are probably dead – jumped, fell, or burnt – but dead. I'm sorry, but that's how it is. Who's going to listen to you? They'll just think you're in shock and tell you to get treated.'

'Tell me what to say. All of it. Tell me something they will listen to.'

He shook his head wearily.

She nodded at the car-phone. 'Try your dad again.'

'We've been calling him all day. God knows where he is. Anyway Cardus's calls are almost certainly monitored by Meade.'

'Why?'

He crossed his arms over the steering-wheel and rested his forehead on them, every part of him aching – he supposed from the crash. He hadn't smoked since college but he longed for a cigarette now. The smell of gasoline on his clothes blunted the sudden craving. 'Why? Because it's possible. Because it's too easy with computers. Because he'll have been using their satellite link. Because we're in the middle of something which makes people disappear and die.' He looked at her. 'I'm sorry, I didn't mean that the way it sounded.'

Her head was thumping and muzzy. She let it fall back against the seat-rest. 'It might be true.'

'Cardus said they were unharmed. I believed him. If they were taken alive, they wanted – *needed* – them. There's no sense to it otherwise.'

'But *why*?'

'I'm guessing.'

'I don't care. Guess.'

'Because of me. And you. The programme you saw me working on was based on language. A special language.'

'*Tongues?* That's why you recorded me?'

'Yes.'

'I don't understand.'

'It's not understandable. That's it. Chaos. For years they've been looking for order. I went in completely the opposite direction. I hadn't revealed any of this to them – though I told Cardus I was working in a new direction. I wanted results first. I wanted to be the Boy Wonder who'd cracked the puzzle. I wanted the accolades.'

'But they knew?'

'They must have bugged us. Maybe they bug everyone in the station? Or they copied data off my computer?'

She shook her head, dazedly, eyes closed. 'It still makes no sense to me. I just want my folks back safe.'

He lifted his head sharply. 'Wait,' he said, switched off the ignition, took the keys, and unlocked the trunk, returning with a notebook computer and a matt-silver metal briefcase protected by combination locks.

Greg tossed the case on to the back seat, switched on the Compaq and waited for the password prompt. He tapped in: BABEL.

'How did you know that?' she asked.

'Because Cardus's ego was too big for him to die without telling me how clever he was – how important his work was. He was giving me his genius to take to Kent.' He smiled, ironically. 'His genius – my inspiration. Larry Maine warned me Cardus used people.'

Data filled the screen, Greg scrolling and reading fast.

'What does it mean?'

'It's ways through a maze. *Failures*, rather. There's too much here, I need time to go through all of it. Looks like years of analysis.'

'A maze?'

'A sound-maze. Ah! here's something.' He paused, freezing the display. 'They're working on a specific source. It isn't SETI passing on signals on a regular basis. There's one specific recording. These results are all from the same sound source. Maybe from one signal – heard once and never repeated. That would certainly explain their obvious obsession with it.' He leaned back. 'They can't break it, that's clear.'

'And you can? Your theory?'

'Wait.' He stopped scrolling. 'I don't think your parents are being held at Green Bank.'

'Why? Where then?'

'This is a flight plan. Green Bank has an air-strip built for the SETI project.'

'But why should it be them?'

'Two passengers, right date, more or less the right time if they'd moved fast. It all works.'

'But that airstrip could be used all the time? That flight might be taking anyone from there?'

'Carolyn, wake up, this is not a SETI computer – it's Cardus's personal machine, I've seen him use it a hundred times. I just got it from the trunk! He wouldn't log flights that didn't concern him.'

'But that flight is to England!'

'And the latest data entered is about England. I need to look at detailed maps.'

'To find them?'

'Maybe. Have you heard of ley-lines? Supposed natural-force lines?'

'My parents talked about them. But not that way. They only acknowledged one force. Jesus.'

'I don't see the connection?'

'Glastonbury. A town in England where we – the sect – believe Jesus went between the time he was a boy and a man. With a man called Joseph of Arimathea. They believed he was able to communicate over thousands of miles from there. They said there were lines right around the world. Ley-lines. They believed he gave the Apostles the secret – the power – to know and use them to spread the gospel when he gave them the gift of tongues.' She smiled. 'I used to imagine Jesus, maybe sixteen, speaking into a kind of telephone, talking to his family – even talking to Heaven.' She tilted her head toward Greg and smiled again.

'I was at school near Glastonbury,' murmured Greg staring at the screen, falling silent once more.

She lifted her head. 'What is it?'

'Stonehenge,' he said, after a moment. 'Glastonbury would be virtually on a straight line due west.'

'Stonehenge? I remember that from high school. The prehistoric stone circle?'

He pointed at a list displayed on the screen. 'All prehistoric stone circles. And all – supposedly – connected by force lines.' He tapped the screen. 'They know something, heard something, that's heading them in this direction.'

'What direction?'

'Magnetic force lines. Electromagnetism is the most powerful force known to man. Goddamnit! what are they after? What have they *heard*?'

He shut down the computer and started the car but didn't move off.

'Where are we going?'

He turned to her. 'The President's in Rome, ill or shot – maybe even dead. We can't count on his help. We don't know where my dad is, so—' He glanced at the computer. 'We use what we've got ourselves.'

'We go to England?'

He nodded. 'We use some of the money I've been earning. Concorde flies out of Dulles tomorrow morning at quarter of ten. We're not going to get a regular flight out tonight – not by the time we reach DC. Concorde's the fastest way. We should have time to check Dad out.'

She pushed wet strands of hair from her face, almost done. 'I don't know what's happening?'

He reached for her. 'We've been going for two days – hard travelling – with barely any sleep. You can't do that, have what happened in Austin, walk away from a total car wreck, and feel in control. You need rest.'

She flared, angrily. 'I'm not sleeping while my parents are being held somewhere!'

He looked at her. 'Right. So let's do it.' He put the Jaguar into gear, driving cautiously until he was satisfied the car's handling had not been affected then used the power of the suberb engine, driving fast, expertly, his movements precise and minimal, windshield wipers flailing, the angry, broken exhaust note settling to a deep drone. He grinned. 'Won't take us too long in this. Get some sleep.'

'Tell me more of what you were doing.'

He shook his head slowly.

'I'm not stupid. Tell me. Explain it!'

'OK. Chaos. The shape of matter before it was reduced to disorder. They – our people in the Mojave – assumed order existed. They're NSA, that's normal for them. It's how they're used to working. Their natural environment, if you like. Intelligence gathering, codes, analyses, all rely on order to be worth anything.' He stared ahead at the twisting road, the leather-bound wheel squirming in his hands. 'Even if information is sent in scrambled form – complete gibberish – there's a background element of order because there's the knowledge the signal will be received, then unscrambled.'

'But what's this got to do with tongues? With England? Stonehenge?'

'Speaking in tongues is totally chaotic. Neither the speaker nor listener understands what is being uttered. Right? In the same way if a thousand messages were recorded chaotically, then replayed, the result would still be chaos. The first step in deciphering what has been recorded is to understand *how* it was recorded. I don't claim I know how to decipher such chaos but I'm beginning to understand how it might at least be feasible. I believe to decipher chaos you must *apply* chaos. The question is how?' He reached across for her. 'You, and your parents, have a gift. A gift Kent's people want to analyse. To use for whatever purpose. We don't know what. We do know they want it very badly. They've proven that.'

'Greg, if we don't understand *ourselves* what we're saying what's the point?'

'They're trying to find ways to make you understand. Other forces. Do you see?'

'No.'

'Then you'll have to trust me.'

'What will they do to Mom and Dad? What can they do? Don't lie to me.'

'They'll do whatever it takes. You heard Cardus say that nothing is as important as this. Whatever *this* is?'

She turned away. 'There are hundreds – thousands – with the gift of tongues. Will they disappear, too?'

'I don't know how deep this runs.'

'Could they do that?'

'You really mean could they be *stopped*.'

'Yes.'

'That depends on what they've heard – from out there.'

He turned to her. She seemed asleep. The rain had stopped. He switched off the windshield wipers. The stars in the thin mountain air were awesome. He felt an extraordinary thrill rush through him: excitement, exhilaration, the icy razor edge of discovery. *From somewhere out there someone had spoken.* There was no other explanation. What else could possibly frighten so many powerful people? Could drive them so? He believed he had heard part of that message. He needed all of it. Then all he had to do was understand.

He and Carolyn, together.

'The Tower of Babel,' she murmured. 'Chaos.'

He remembered the Maddox Tower in Austin and the vast babble of garbled voices he heard as he had exited the lift. 'Yes.'

'I understand,' she said, and slept.

Joe Neilson located the wreck four hours after a flash in the mountains had been reported by the night-watch at the Green Bank Observatory who at first believed they had witnessed a meteor impact.

He shook his head wearily. Would people never learn? You take these curves *easy* or you end up fighting the wheel, over-correcting and meet someone heading in the opposite direction or fall off the mountain – or both.

He went to the Chevrolet first because there had been no fire and maybe someone had survived, then trudged, mournfully, to the burned-out upended Dodge and crouched, playing his flashlight over the still smoking interior.

He grimaced as he saw the blackened form and instinctively moved the beam away: he'd had his fill checking the wrecks of Iraqi tanks.

The glint of brass in the crystal carpet that had been the windscreen was unmistakable.

He sighed, touched nothing, returned to his ranger's wagon and made his calls knowing now he would be there for hours. A cartridge-case meant a gun, a gun meant a bullet, and the first place to look for a spent bullet was in the nearest corpse. The coroner, he decided, could do the probing.

He sat in his car, just above the mist line, dawn rising, looking out over the blue-green mountains nudging through the haze like stepping-stones in a dream. He sighed with pleasure: he'd travelled the world with the military, fought some wars, seen some sights – but there wasn't any job any place anywhere that offered *this*.

He smiled, enjoying the view and the morning, knowing soon this peace would be shattered by ambulances, coroner, forensic, detectives – the whole shoot! One murder created a whole industry, he thought. What would we do without the first deadly sin?

Joe Neilson waited, content with his mountains.

CHAPTER
SEVENTEEN

Sam Lewelyn walked down Air Force One's gangway, exhausted and hazy. He might have been dreaming. Adjusting his wristwatch back to US Eastern Time compounded his disorientation: the great Boeing SST had lifted off from Fiumicino at 10.00 p.m. Rome time – now he was crossing the concrete apron at Andrews Air Force Base at 8.30 the same evening. He could barely believe he had flown out of Andrews early that morning, hunched in the second, training, cockpit of the Blackbird with a .32 in his sock.

He saw Hugh Edwards waiting by a small group of uniformed Air Force officers and civilians and raised a big hand. Greeting him, he glanced around with surprise: 'Thanks for coming, Hugh. I thought there'd be Press from here to the White House.'

'There's a pack baying at the gate who probably bought a tip-off that Air Force One's call sign had come through. There's no official announcement of the flight. I wouldn't have known if you hadn't called – and I get to hear all the rumours.'

They walked in silence to Edwards' Pontiac parked in the visitors' lot. Inside, Edwards inserted the key in the ignition, left it, and twisted around in his seat. 'What happened over there?'

Sam stared ahead to the brightly lit patrolled perimeter fence and the entry guard-post beyond where steel barriers were dropped against the group of frustrated media people.

'Sam?'

'Give me a minute.'

Edwards lowered a window, watching as the browned meer-schaum was stoked up.

'What have you heard?' Sam asked, finally.

'CNN news flash. President taken to hospital after an audience with the Pope. Then they reported a rumour – they emphasized *rumour* – about a shooting at the same hospital. Since then nothing. Heavy news blackout. Talking heads saying zilch. It's an unhealthy situation, Sam.' He gazed at the heavy face wreathed in smoke. 'So?'

'Cornell is ill. Don't ask me what or how serious, I don't know. But I know *him*. He doesn't lie down on the job for anyone. Especially not for himself. He's got more pride than anyone I know when it comes to his work.'

'So he really *isn't* on that plane.'

Sam turned, surprised. 'Did you think he was?'

'I told you, its a real unhealthy situation. Those Air Force types beside me had it figured a body would come out of that monster's belly.'

'Only me,' murmured Sam, then paused for a long while. 'He sent me back here,' he said.

'Why?'

Sam answered by pressing a tape into the Pontiac's cassette deck.

Edwards asked: 'Do I drive and listen or is this so momentous I sit right here till it's over?'

Sam opened the door, tapped black ash on to the conrete, shut it, and reclined his seat. 'It's either the most momentous – and revelatory – record of any modern historical event, or the most irrelevant. Depending on your view of history.'

The President's voice enquired: '*Hal?*'

Edwards turned up the volume as the conversation with CIA Director Hal Ellis from the US Rome Embassy began – followed by the Agency's transcription of the Andropov meeting with Communism's most committed disciples in the Kremlin committee room.

Throughout, Sam lay back on the reclined seat, unmoving. He might have been asleep.

The tape clicked, dead.

Edwards stared at it. 'You know what we just heard? Communism's Last Supper. *It's all over, guys – but keep the faith and there'll be a better world for all in the next.* It's horseshit, Sam. Someone faked this to get the CIA running around their own tails. You know that?'

262

'I *thought* that. Until Langley verified the voice-print on Andropov. I spoke with Ellis from Air Force One.'

'Then Langley's got it wrong. Or someone has learned how to fake voice-prints. Hell! I've heard you can do anything these days with synthesizers. Come on, Sam, they couldn't have been setting themselves up for the chop that far back. If they knew what was going to happen they'd have done something about it. No one throws the towel in that easily.'

'That's the point, they didn't know in any practical sense. And they didn't quit, they kept on fighting, hard, keeping the screws on. Read any newspaper between then and Gorbachev taking power. Make no mistake about it, Hugh, they didn't give up easily. What they couldn't do was stop the rot. Once a machine that size starts going bad it goes all the way. They knew it. Or some of them did. So they made contingency plans. You think the Nazis didn't do the same when it became obvious – long before Berlin fell – that the Third Reich was over? The real hard-liners? They knew the Allies would have to rely to a large extent on the established order or they'd be dealing with complete chaos from day one of occupation. What do you think the de-Nazification programme was really about? It wasn't about punishment, it was about re-establishment. The same thing is happening to the Soviet Union. The West occupied it, not by military force – by the power of the most potent weapon anywhere. Money. George Bush was right when he said we won the Cold War. Now we're rebuilding the old enemy, just as we did Germany and Japan. And we know the results of those actions: they've dominated and influenced the world's economy for over fifty years and practically crippled ours!'

'They're slipping now.'

'Which leaves a damn great hole to be filled!'

'OK, hold it there. So Andropov figured, if – all right, *when* – all else failed, the West would pick up the pieces and the Party would still run things in the background because there'd be no one else qualified? Sam, maybe you didn't notice but their house didn't just fall apart, it ignited – and the pieces are scattered over the floor, burning up fast! Watch the news any day of the week.'

'It's not over, Hugh. It's only just begun. You noticed how many former Soviet states have applied to join the European

Federation? You ever looked at the Federation's policies – and legislation – closely?'

'Conspiracy theories, Sam? I know your politics, I know your fears, I know they're held sincerely and maybe with some justification. Hell, you're on the inside! I'm a cop. Top of my heap but still a cop. Not some spook who knows, imagines, or, Christ knows, probably *wishes* things which would give me nightmares a heck of a lot worse than the one which sent you flying miles high to Rome this morning with a rocket tied to your ass. I can't live with that kind of storm cloud over my head. I want to live day to day, enjoying it. I want to know what's going on – *now*. And I'm waiting for you to tell me.'

Sam looked at the black face shining in the glow from the stark halogen perimeter lights. 'You mean, what am I doing back here?'

'Hell no! I want to know what you're *going* to do. I don't believe for one minute that Cornell – sick, shot, or as healthy as a newborn babe – would send you back here ahead of him as some kind of PR exercise. You're here to give someone a hard time. That's your line, Sam. Or it was once. Cornell make you the hatchet man?' Edwards gave a long hard look. 'You here to break Kent?'

'I'm here to break Kent's heart. And I don't feel bad about it. His mind has already gone. He believes he's heard – and I do mean *heard* – the word of the Lord. Heard the voice of Jesus.' Sam pointed at the tape. 'He did. It was cooked up in some KGB recording studio. With Kent's power that's one heck of a dangerous delusion. He's gone on too long believing it. God knows how deep into the organization his psychosis has reached.'

'So let Cornell indict him, impeach him, or whatever it is politicians do to dump government high-flyers who've lost it. Walk away from it, Sam. You're out, retired, take the Continental and drive till your backside falls off.'

'I can't do that.'

'And I look the other way?' asked Edwards. 'I'm beginning to wonder if Bernardelli really did pull himself on to your Magnum.' He turned and faced the windshield, angry, blowing out hard, misting it over. 'You want to know what I found out about Franco Bernardelli? Or maybe it doesn't matter any more? You're going to hear it anyway. Franco's some kind of Mason. Was. He had a cousin – also named Bernardelli, Augusto Benito – whose widow

264

picked up a cool quarter of a million bucks' life insurance after that desert "wreck" you told me about. I talked to her. She's running scared. Has been since it happened. So the cop in me tells me maybe I've got *two* suicides here? A big payoff to the widow of the first and who knows what to whoever for the second?' Edwards shrugged. 'Probably no one. Franco was committed body and soul to the Catholic Church, says the widow – and she should know because he sorted out her life when Benny burned, telling her she had a bundle coming from life insurance. Benny the Bet arranging life insurance was impossible. He'd blow the premium every time. She knew it then and she knows it now. That's why she's scared. Benny was a gambler and a loser – but big. Heavily into the mob and about to be wasted, that's how I'd write it if I was writing official reports which – as yet – I'm not! So anyway, Franco pitches to Benny something like: "I've got friends who'll see your family all right for life – all you have to do is give them yours."' Edwards turned back. 'The bank that paid out has heavy connections with Rome and I don't mean the city. All I've got to do now is link Marchionni to Franco's Masonic lodge and the lodge to the bank and we're on a roll. Only first I have to find which lodge! Maybe your good friend the President might know that?'

'Take me home, Hugh. I need to sleep.'

'You mean you need to think.'

'Right now I'm too tired to think. We're not twenty-year-olds any more, Hugh. Either of us.'

Edwards started the car. 'If I were I'd be uptight and eager to fight the conspiracies of government.'

'Now you don't care?'

'Oh, I care all right. But it's like potency, Sam, getting it up at my age is one thing, following through is quite another. Sometimes you just got to lay back and let it happen.' Edwards flipped open the dash locker and tossed Sam the infra-red recorder Sam had given him for safekeeping before boarding the Blackbird at Andrews early that morning. 'That recording could be evidence if you decide you want to use the law.'

'The ravings of a deranged man?'

'You want to destroy someone, Sam, you hit his reputation first. Of course, you go that route you *have* to go public. And that's the last thing John Cornell wants, correct?'

'Just start the car, Hugh.'

Edwards drove the thirty miles from Andrews AFB to Sam's house near Fort Meade quickly, turning the corner just before eleven o'clock to see a brightly painted VW Beetle planted outside with a dark head slouched low behind the wheel.

He nudged Sam. 'Someone waiting on you.'

Sam opened his eyes. 'Sorry, I must have dropped off.'

'Snoring like a train. You know that car?'

Sam struggled to focus his tired eyes. 'Georgia. Friend of Greg's.'

Edwards pulled up nose to nose with the Beetle, seeing the curls rise behind the steering-wheel and the door open. A tall black girl got out.

'Hi, Georgia,' said Sam, hauling himself out. He kissed her. 'You never got to meet Hugh Edwards? Careful, he's a cop. Heavy duty.'

Edwards leaned on the car roof and reached over, hand extended. 'Right now I'm *off* duty.'

'So be even more careful, Georgia,' advised Sam.

'He means for all the more pleasurable reasons,' grinned Edwards.

'Is this a rehearsed act?' Georgia asked. 'Or are you two just naturals?'

A telephone rang. Georgia snatched Sam's keys from his hand and ran towards the house, calling back: 'That's got to be Greg, I've waited all day for him.' She stopped at the door, fumbling through the keys. 'I missed his second call at my place – I knew he'd call back here.' She inserted a key and turned it. 'Hey, I couldn't find your spare key, Sam!' She opened the door and ran inside for the insistent telephone still sounding in the hallway.

Sam just saw her lift it before orange flame engulfed her – only experience and what remained of his once phenomenal reflexes saving him from the almost instantaneous, devastating blast.

He knew Georgia was gone long before the debris stopped falling and could only pray that Edwards – on the wrong side of the car – had somehow escaped. He pulled himself off the road and saw the lifeless body sprawled brokenly over the car's roof. He had learned long before that prayers never beat high explosives.

He blinked at the sudden cold dreadful emptiness, allowing tears to surface which Elizabeth had strictly forbidden him to shed for her.

He reached into the bloody mess of Edwards' jacket and found the heavy Colt .45 automatic he knew his friend always carried, and, not wiping away the blood, jammed the heavy weapon into his belt.

'What happened?' asked a shaken voice, urgently.

Sam gazed blankly at the gathering crowd, seeing faces he had known for years and not recognizing them.

'Are you all right, Mr Lewelyn?' asked a neighbour.

'We've called the fire department!' exclaimed another running over, illuminated by the flames, gasping as he saw the splayed body.

'Bomb!' barked Sam, shaking now. He waved them away furiously. 'Keep back. There could be more explosives!'

The effect was instantaneous.

'I'll call the police!' someone yelled, running into his house opposite.

'Get an ambulance,' a voice called after him.

Sam stood, leaning on the Pontiac, swaying as if drunk. 'No point,' he murmured, then heaved Edwards off the roof and laid him gently on the roadside turf. He kissed the lacerated black forehead then left him and climbed into the Pontiac.

'You're not driving, Mr Lewelyn?' a woman shouted. 'Mr Lewelyn, you're not fit!'

Sam couldn't hear any of it. The blood pounding in his ears would have drowned a thousand voices.

The seat of William Bradley Kent's empire lay to the north, half-way between the nation's capital and Baltimore, off the Baltimore-Washington Parkway, amid miles of rolling tree-covered Maryland countryside. The surrounding secure town, known as SIGINT City, is composed of almost twenty buildings including shops, medical centre, post office, telephone exchange, college with an enrolment of eighteen thousand, TV station and production studios, and an independent electric power station producing 106,668 KVA – enough to run a city of fifty thousand with every kilowatt needed and used by the most powerful and influential Intelligence organization on Earth, the United States National Security Agency.

Security at SIGINT City is fierce. The entire complex is surrounded by a ten-foot high Cyclone fence topped by multiple rows of razor wire. Beyond this are five strands of lethal electrified wire supported by wooden posts driven into the ground in a bed of green pebbles. The final barrier is another towering Cyclone fence with, for the truly determined infiltrator, Federal Protective Service armed guards with attack dogs. Above all of this, on the roof of the complex – around the bizarre antennas which swarm spikily like insects around the two gigantic eggs of the radomes – closed-circuit TV cameras with telephoto lenses aim downwards, slowly rotating, continuously scanning the area surrounding the main buildings.

As Sam Lewelyn made the right turn off the Parkway on to Savage Road he had no illusions that while he might get in to Fort Meade peacefully, coming out was likely to be something he would know little – or nothing – about.

He had only the respect and trust that came with his former position working for him. If that was blown he was going in naked. All he could hope for was that he was presumed dead – and that the gate guards had not yet been told his ID was void. Time was on his side. His only delay had been to drive through a coin-op automatic car-wash to spray the dust and blood from Edwards' sedan.

At the main gates he had to explain the car to the blue-uniformed FPS guards who were so used to seeing him in the massive Lincoln they were openly shocked by his appearance in an up-to-date sedan.

'Say, you didn't go and sell the old Continental, sir?' scowled one.

'Not hardly. A few problems needed fixing. Getting old, like me.' Sam's big hand patted the door skin. 'Friend's car. Not the weight in the metal, but it's just fine.'

The man ran his palm over the roof and looked at his wet palm.

'Just washed it? Shoulda done it here, it's cheaper.'

'You saw it you wouldn't have waited. Kids from a burger joint. I'd like to smear the stuff over them.'

'Tell me about it!'

The second said, 'It's too small for you, Mr L. You'll have medical bills if you have to stick with this for too long.' He peered in the harsh lighting at the windshield, bored by the night-shift and wanting to jaw. 'Hey, your friend's a cop?' He indicated a pass.

'That's right.'

'Never knew a cop who lent his car to no one,' said the first.

'You didn't know enough cops,' grunted the second.

'I was a cop – I knew plenty.'

'Then you knew the wrong ones.'

Sam wore a hard smile which seemed to be frozen in the barrier-lights. 'Director Kent not broken out for the big ball-game?' he asked, knowing it was nerves talking, instantly regretting his crassness.

The nearest guard's eyes deadened as did every NSA employee when the spectre of their autocratic ruler was invoked.

Sam smiled broadly and shrugged to indicate as poor joke.

The other guard said, 'Never saw him leave here ever. I once waved the President through to see him.' His eyes held awe. 'President came *here*.' He glanced towards the lights behind the sealed windows of the Headquarters Tower. 'You planning on seeing him? You know I gotta call that in.'

Sam shook his head, using a resigned expression to shroud his lapse. 'My days here are over, Pete. Just spinning out the hand-over so I can use the barber shop regularly. Can't get the same cut anywhere else.'

'Won't get one tonight, Mr L.,' chipped in the other. 'He's long gone.'

Sam shook his head. 'Tonight I'm here to check some equipment back in from the house. It's overdue and tomorrow's Sunday.'

'I'll need to see that,' said the nearest guard.

Sam offered the small infra-red recorder Edwards had returned to him.

'Those things good as CD?'

Sam smiled. 'You know how much performance information is worth?' He jammed a thumb backwards. 'Out there?'

The guard gave a grin, said: 'Yeah, well . . .' and logged the sedan's registration, affixed a permit, and waved him through as one of NSA's salmon-coloured police cars rolled into the area. Sam waved casually at the two FPS occupants and kept moving, considering how quickly the familiar and the safe became hostile and threatening. He had driven NSA's secure streets, walked its secret corridors, for thirty years. 'My nearest and dearest enemy,' he remembered from a moment of glory in a high-school production of *Henry IV*, as he closed in on the tan-coloured Headquarters Tower with its new twin hundred-million-dollar nine-storey towers connected to the green Operations Building.

All monoliths are grey in the dark, he thought, parking the car in a vacant slot. *Go on thinking this way and you won't make anywhere near the ninth floor*, he cursed himself angrily – most of him barely there, and what was hurt so bad he had dragged down the shutters and locked them. Summers over, winters here, and the only thing between you and the cold is *you*. So march, no one's going to do this for you, few could get this close and only a handful could get within breathing space of Kent. I am my President's faithful soldier and his enemy is mine.

March.

He stepped from the car; the big Colt .45 felt like a twenty-pound lump of pig iron in his belt as he walked – and about as conspicuous. He'd wiped it off in the car-wash but to his embattled mind the dark steel was still crimson stained. Detergent and water couldn't shift Hugh Edwards' blood. *Fire might.* He buttoned his jacket over the powerful weapon.

'Who's going to search that big bear Lewelyn?' he murmured to himself, mimicking the night shift at the desk inside. 'He's been here so long you don't even see him.' *The rooftop cameras do*, he warned himself. And Kent, right now, could be watching the monitors and looking at the face of a dead man – or what he believed was a dead man – and reaching painfully for the telephone.

The irony crept up on Sam and he smiled, coldly. A man, burned and half-crippled, waiting for another who – but for the grace of God and a lump of General Motors' steel – should be.

Sam walked through the main doors.

Maybe he's just sitting there in his softly buzzing electric wheel-chair, quite still, only his eyes moving, scanning documents.

I feared him too, Sam realized with surprise. Kidded myself all this time. But fear of the man, or the power he wielded? *The man.*

And the death mask with which the plastic surgeon had blessed him: blessed, because the taut, white, seemingly brittle skin hid all pain, fears, guilt, or weakness which, displayed, would have plunged William Bradley Kent down into the ranks of normal men.

Sam shook his head. Kent could never be normal. He saw more of his kind than any other mortal. Only God could see more – *if* God had eyes which could see from the edges of space if one of his creations had developed dandruff! He saw his country's enemies move in the dead of night, heard them speak in their most secret conclaves, could predict their hostile actions before they planned them and perhaps was edging ever nearer to God by knowing their thoughts. Nothing, or so the legend had grown, was impossible for William Bradley Kent, whose mind had been greater aged twelve than those of the men and women who dared teach him.

A mind in a scarred body pretending it had come out of the horror unscathed? Was that the heart of it? Sam wondered. If I were forced to inhabit that tortured frame I too might search obsessively for the voice of Jesus. And if it were offered me? If I believed I truly heard it? Would I relinquish that *Rapture*?

Sam mounted the familiar one dozen steps of the rectangular building and walked through the glass doors leading into Gatehouse One, the only one of four gatehouses around the complex which led directly into the Headquarters Tower.

From now his life was as frangible as a dry fall leaf on a crowded sidewalk.

Straight ahead the two duty Federal Protection Service guards gave him the big welcome and his legs felt strong enough to carry him toward their checkpoint where, perfunctorily, one checked the laminated security badge hanging from around his neck for visual ID, colour coding, and correct computer information.

'It's you all right, sir.'

'Be trading this for a Visitors' soon,' grumbled Sam.

'Don't worry, we won't give you a hard time.'

'After all these years, I hope not.'

Sam turned.

'Sir! There's blood on your pants?' exclaimed the second guard, further away.

Sam stopped, his heart in free-fall. He looked down to Edwards' bloodstains at his waist where he'd jammed in the .45.

'On your jacket too. You OK, Mister Lewelyn?'

Sam swore. 'Ran over a cat on the way. Had to break its neck afterwards. Damn, that's a good jacket ruined.'

'Maybe it'll clean up?'

'Shame about the cat,' said the one who had checked him through.

'Get a tetanus shot – in case,' advised the second.

'I will.' Sam walked on, staying loose, keeping his body language familiar for them.

He walked the corridor past the long mural showing Agency employees at work – ignoring this because he'd seen it a million times before and in a less heightened state it would be just wallpaper – fixing his gaze instead on the fiercely protective eagle grasping an ancient skeleton key in its talons set at the shimmering centre of a mosaic of the Agency's seal made up from twenty thousand hand-cut cubes of Byzantine smalt glass which dominated the end wall. White letters on a sparkling cobalt blue backround warned him he was in the secret heart of the NATIONAL SECURITY AGENCY.

Is this how you see yourself, Kent? The stern protector of the key to knowledge?

'Goodnight, sir,' said someone young, hurrying past, male or female he would never know.

'Sleep well,' he called.

'Last thing on my mind,' the reply floated back to him.

Sam thought that sleep, right then, was about the sweetest thing in creation.

He turned left at the seal and entered the Tower lobby where the faces, in oils, of former Agency directors watched his every move; smiling eyes hiding the knowledge the eagle's key had unlocked for each.

Another armed guard faced him, rising from his position by the six elevators which could take Sam either one floor down – and a century forward – into the future world of super-computers, or nine floors up to Mahogany Row: the executive offices where the real power lay.

Sam raised his eyes upward.

The guard frowned and turned to his desk. Sam moved like the young deadly Special Forces officer he had once been, striking precisely behind his ear with a short two-knuckle blow which had the same effect – without the skull-fracture – as a baseball bat.

Time now was everything. He dragged the guard into the elevator, punched nine, and was there in seconds. Heaving the guard over his shoulder he made straight for the far end of the corridor to the bright blue door emblazoned with the Agency seal, the office suite of the man known within the Intelligence community as DIRNSA – pronounced *Dernza*. Room 9A197: the heart of all NSA power.

He had guessed, correctly, at that time of night and the next day being Sunday, the outer office of executive registry secretaries would be deserted. He dumped the guard in their washroom, removing his gun first, took the key from inside and locked him in, heaving a heavy filing cabinet across for good measure, then walked quickly through the outer office, swung right, and opened the door facing him.

William Bradley Kent sat in his habitual gloom before a smoked-glass desk – quite bare apart from a white document which seemed to float in a pool of pale light.

Sam laid Edwards' .45 gently on the glass between them. He said: 'First thing is you get on that phone and call the dogs off.'

'No need, Sam.' Kent's voice was a ghastly whisper. 'Violence wasn't necessary. My guard had orders to escort you up here without prejudice. You didn't give him time.'

'So you know.'

'One way or another you had to come to me in the end. What happened at your house was just one more reason. I'm sorry about what happened to your friends. I am, sincerely. It wasn't the Agency.'

'No? You know *damn* soon after it happened.'

'Your house is listed with the police department – you know that. The instant they had a call about that address, the lines here rang. You're wrong, Sam. So wrong about all of this.'

Sam slid the tape across the glass desk-top.

Kent gave what in a normal face might have been a smile. On his ruined face it was a tightening of tissue already strained to the limit. 'I know what that contains. Dear God, I know the content of every call the President makes – *and* those made by the Director of the CIA – if I need to. Sam, you don't know the depth of this. I don't believe you could understand even if you had that knowledge. Oh, you're not stupid. I'm not being insulting. It's simply that you're not able to see the big picture.'

'Try me.'

The muted buzz from Kent's electric wheelchair was like an angered hornet trapped somewhere soft.

'No one wants to know the sum of human guilt. That's what we're faced with here. Put it on a completely mortal level. Imagine broadcasting the proven – *actual* – detailed truth – actual *voices*, Sam – of the slave years? Result? Riots? Murders? Mob-rule? Worse. Much worse. *Calamity*. Right across the nation. We would have to react so harshly we could never recover as a nation. Our standing in the eyes of the world would be destroyed. Worse than China after Tiananmen – because we are a democracy.'

Sam slapped the glass hard, the gun bouncing, cracking down. '*It's all a lie* – listen to the Goddamn tape! The Markarovs were a set-up – their work a con-trick, disinformation, call it what you will – and it damn well worked. Listen to yourself. You've let a broken regime, a *dead* enemy trick you.'

Kent reached painfully into his desk and Sam picked up the gun.

'Don't be ridiculous, Sam,' Kent chided. 'By the time I could get at a weapon you could have emptied the magazine of that antique into me.' He placed a metal box on the table and took out what appeared to be a fused spool of wire.

Sam stared at it.

'The sum of our guilt, Sam. Or potentially so.'

'I don't understand.'

'I know.'

'Goddamnit, explain then!'

'The truth lies right there. Burned beyond revelation.' Kent held up clawed hands. 'I salvaged a strand with these. White hot though the container was, I held it and opened it and screamed while I did so, but I knew that if I could have just a few inches of that wire I would be grasping history in my tortured fingers. And then I would know what I had to protect us from. Our greatest enemy is ourselves. Our freedoms are the weapons which destroy us. Given the freedom to use the truth of the past we would destroy ourselves utterly. We do it now, don't we? How many times have we seen children – privileged children – tearing the memory of their parents to shreds? Well, that's what would happen to the nation. Our history is our foundation. Just as the elders are the foundation of the family. Destroy credibility, mock, give reason for guilt – and nothing will be left except anarchy. The hordes are out there, now, right now, waiting to be slipped. All that holds them back from tearing everything down is that we believe in something – and they believe in nothing. Nothing at all. Any one of them will kill for loose change – while I would die for the history which allowed the minting of those coins, for the heritage founded by the head upon them.'

Sam took out the infra-red recorder. 'You want to hear some of the things you said to me on the telephone early this morning? Jesus speaking to you—?'

'I said I had *heard* the voice of Jesus in material form. Not that He had spoken to me in some ethereal sense. There is a significant difference. The first makes me a witness, the second, deluded perhaps, or insane.'

Sam pointed at the melted silver clump of wire. 'On *that*?'

Kent nodded.

'Let me hear it – now.'

'I don't have it.'

'Of course not.'

'If you can't trust me, would you trust your son?'

'Of course.'

'Greg's heard it.'

'What?'

'The problem is neither he nor any of the others who have been working on it can separate – isolate – it.'

'Yet you could.'

'I heard what I heard. Perhaps I was meant to hear it. Perhaps my pain was the price I paid for the privilege. Or perhaps it *qualified* me? There are precedents in Christian history. I don't know. What I do know is that there are some – many – who will kill ruthlessly to keep that voice silent.'

Sam looked at him. 'You must know about what happened in Rome?'

'Of course.'

'Why was the priest Kolchak trying to kill Sazarin?'

'Sazarin had been targeted as I had. You don't think America is the only important nation on this earth?'

'Sazarin would not have suppressed information on the possibilities of this technology?'

'Suppressed? He had every intention of developing it. Sazarin is a confirmed atheist. He is a technocrat who believes in the future with a single-mindedness that precludes all that has gone before. He is truly a child of his generation. For him all that has gone before is worthless – all that is to come is both achievable and worthy of his and his generation's time and effort – with his vision, of course. What he does not realize is that somewhere at the heart of all this is a lie so great it will tear Rome to the ground. Why do you think he was shot the first time? He *can't* be allowed to put European power behind this. Have you any conception of the wealth, the influence and power, the Catholic Church has, worldwide? They can shape government policy. They can even shape governments in some countries. Bring down Rome – even shake its foundations and . . .' Kent moved his clawed hands apart.

'What lie?'

'If I knew I wouldn't have placed myself in the – tenuous – situation I am in now.'

'But you know something?'

'The Markarovs confessed they were Moscow's tools – but that the *basis* of their work had real meaning. Potentially, it worked. In exchange for my promise to fund them and give them access to the technology they needed desperately and couldn't get in Russia, they promised to reveal the lie – the clever knot Moscow had tied for the West to unravel, perhaps taking us years but inevitably bringing us down.'

'But they died before they could do that.'

'As I almost did.'

'Since then you've searched through what you call a maze? You couldn't find what they meant?'

'All we have is a shred of wire. It's not enough.'

Sam sat slumped in the chair, exhausted, defeated – wanting an enemy to strike but losing him as easily as a dream.

'It's hard having no one to hate,' said Kent. 'You're a man of action caught in a cerebral web. Check yourself into a hotel, Sam. Sleep.' Kent's chair buzzed louder and moved a little. 'What have I to gain from trying to kill you?'

Sam watched him. 'I'm an old bloodhound, I don't let go, no one knows that better than you. And you need Greg. I sense you need Greg badly. There was every danger I would reveal everything I discovered to him. Stop me and a lot of your problems ended right then. Even if John Cornell was persuaded to leave matters be, you knew Sam Lewelyn would keep trudging on, nose to the ground. The problem is the wrong people died and the old bloodhound came looking for blood. And you're not worried. You live in a world of half-truths – this whole edifice is about *interpretation* of what your billion-dollar electronic eyes and ears reveal. You could convince anyone of anything with all this behind you.'

'This is beyond you, let it be, Sam.'

Sam's heavy jaw jutted. 'But not beyond Greg?'

'Ah! The father's fear of the son? Your son is one of Sazarin's children – except he has your heart, which this country can be grateful for. His mind might yet unlock the trap Moscow set – and perhaps even more?'

'How can you trust the word of the Markarovs? Have you made their technology work?'

'No.'

'So all of this could be exactly what that tape of Andropov admits it to be – a conspiracy to cause loss of religious faith and confusion in the West?'

'Except the Markarovs admitted the conspiracy. I knew there was something planned – if not precisely what it was.'

'So you have a multi-billion dollar intelligence organization like this one disappearing up its own asshole trying to work it out – for ten years. That's some success! Do you blame Cornell for wanting answers?'

'He'll find none which suit him. He's a man who would give the nation its past as a right. He doesn't know what he's doing. He's set you running blindly while stumbling about in the dark himself.'

'Couldn't you trust him? He is the President, for Christ's sake! He's shown he'll stand by his faith – why shouldn't he have the chance to show he'd stand by his country? You don't have the right to pass judgement.'

'There are some matters even a president – a certain kind of president – cannot be trusted with.'

Sam shook his head. 'Who are you people who rule the world?'

'The ones who can be trusted with it,' stated Kent.

Sam said 'Fuck,' took up the gun, and fired into the taut white mask until only red remained.

Then he ejected what remained of the Colt's magazine, dialled the telephone number of the private VIP wing of the Ospidale Gemelli that John Cornell had given him, and listened, ears ringing, to the unfamiliar tones, heart banging yet infinitely weary and hardly caring any more.

A woman's voice answered in Italian, he guessed a nurse. 'Give me President Cornell right away,' he ordered. 'I'm calling from the United States. This is urgent.'

The voice switched immediately to firm, disapproving English. 'He is sleeping. The time here is just before six in the morning!'

'Then wake him. He is expecting my call.'

'Ah! You are Mr Lewelyn? I see President Cornell left a message he should be woken when you called. Please do not speak for too long.'

Sam put the call on Kent's speaker-phone and leaned back, closing his eyes, aware for the first time of the banging coming from the outer offices where the guard had obviously regained consciousness. He thought he heard, too, the elevator hum and the muted thrum of feet. *Better wake up, John, or you'll be speaking to a dead line. Or a dead caller.*

Now, voices were clear – and he guessed they had freed the guard. He heard a door bang, quick feet moving, and voices laced with uncertainty and fear whispering.

'My gun's empty!' he bawled.

'How do we know that!' barked a voice.

'Take your time thinking about it if you want!'

'We're comin' in ready to use our weapons, sir.'

Sure, he thought. Why not.

'Sam?' a sharp voice cracked from the speaker.

Two blue-uniformed men burst in, pistols extended at arms' length in double-handed grips.

Sam already had his own hands up and clear of his body.

'Hello? Hello! Operator, this is President Cornell, I've lost my call.'

The guards' eyes flicked between Sam and the speaker, perplexity, even panic, on their faces.

Sam said: 'Morning, John. I believe I could use a good lawyer.'

CHAPTER
EIGHTEEN

Greg drove around the corner and saw luminous police tapes stretched across the road further on, flapping in the driving rain. He drew into the kerb, stopped the car, switched off the lights and shook Carolyn awake.

She sat up, startled. 'Are we here already?'

'*Already* is almost seven hours.'

She blinked. 'What time is it?'

'Coming up to four in the morning.'

'I can't believe I slept right through!' She glanced around. 'Why have you stopped here?'

'There's something going on at the house. That's Georgia's car out front. She must be here.' He unbuckled his seat belt.

'Why don't you drive up? It's pouring!' She wiped condensation from the screen and peered forward hopelessly through the heavy rain and the darkness, seeing only the luminous tapes and the garish bright yellow paint of the VW Beetle.

He turned. 'Cardus had the kind of security clearance which didn't allow disappearing room. He was driving up to see Kent when he passed us near Green Bank. Kent never leaves Meade and he never sleeps more than a couple of hours – that's Agency legend. He'd have been waiting for Cardus. Cardus is dead and I killed him. By now this car's a liability.'

'It was an accident!'

'Point a loaded gun at someone, you accept responsibility for accidents. The charge would be manslaughter – minimum. But I have to find out what's going on. What else can I do?'

'I'm coming with you.'

'Stay in the car.'

He stepped out and began walking quickly toward the luminous tape, collar up, head down against the rain.

'Hold it right there,' a voice commanded, very brusque, even angry. A caped police officer stepped out from where he had been sheltering and played his flashlight over him.

'What's happened over there?' asked Greg.

The flashlight lifted to Greg's face.

'Shine it *there*!' snapped Greg, pointing, rain hanging in heavy drops from his hair and eyebrows. 'That's my dad's house! *Oh, Jesus!*' He could just make out great glistening swaths of thick black polythene sheeting in the darkness, the collapsed shape of the bungalow giving away the devastation beneath. He knew, sickeningly, that no one inside could have survived. He felt detached and thought he might wake any moment to the whisper of the chill air-conditioning of the underground Mojave desert station.

'He wasn't in there,' said the cop.

'*You're sure?*'

'Let's see some ID.'

Greg fumbled for his wallet, his relief making him clumsy. 'The girl who owns that VW – where is she?'

'She's gone.'

'Where? That's her car. She wouldn't leave it.'

The torch swept back on to the wrecked bungalow.

Greg shook his head, numbed. It wasn't possible.

The cop shone his torch on Greg's driver's licence. 'Eyewitness across the steet saw her go inside just before it happened. Seconds, she said. Washington chief of detectives caught his outside. Never had a chance, either one.'

'*Hugh Edwards?*'

'You knew him?

Greg seemed bewildered by the question, his face awash with rain: it seemed to hit his eyes yet he didn't blink. He nodded, said: 'Years.'

The officer softened and for the first time the Irish brogue came through. He handed back the licence. 'Didn't know him myself, but he was one of ours. We take that badly. Sorry I was rough on you.'

Greg stared at the devastation. 'How did this happen?'

The cop's jaw lifted, Greg seeing grey eyebrows and crinkled, disapproving eyes in the upward glow from the flashlight. 'Better you ask them.'

Two raincoated men came over fast from a car parked opposite the house, one holding an umbrella aloft over both, the second grasping a miniature torch with a narrow, very bright halogen beam that slashed the darkness like a sabre as they ran.

The cop moved away to the shelter he had found. Greg thought he heard him hiss, *Watch yourself, son*, but it might only have been the rain.

A piercing beam cut into Greg's eyes. He threw his hand up against it. 'Hey!'

'What's your business?' one of the men demanded.

'That's *him*,' snapped the other urgently and thrust his hand into his raincoat, holding the material away from his body as he flashed the torch inside. 'No question.'

Greg felt an arm grasp the sodden leather of his jacket and suddenly he had had enough. The why didn't matter right then. He simply wanted it to stop. All of it. It was exhaustion and outrage and grief and plain red-eyed anger with no regard for the consequences that he hadn't experienced since school days: not even at his worst moments in Iraqi hands.

He stuck at them as if the survival-training manual were open in front of him: fast, disabling blows, silent but for the soft sound of their execution and the muffled, harder culmination. No cries, all over in moments, drowned in the hammering rain.

They both carried hand-guns: lightweight, powerful, and expensive Heckler and Koch automatics. Reluctantly Greg took one as a deterrent for the cop, slipping it inside the soggy pocket of his leather jacket, praying he would not be forced into using it.

He found him smoking in the shelter of an empty car-port two houses down. 'Where's my father?' he demanded.

'I thought that's the first thing the spooks would tell you.'

Greg showed the automatic.

The cop looked at it, then at Greg.

'They're NSA, right?'

The cop shrugged. 'Spooks is spooks to me.'

Greg said: 'I'm having a real bad time – and it's not over.'

'I can see that, son.'

'For Christ's sake – *where's my dad*!'

'Homicide at Meade is all I know. Word is they're holding him there. Won't release him to us. Bad news. Got their own goddamn laws.'

'Homicide? Who?'

'You think their kind blab to beat cops like me? They were nervous as hell so you can count on someone big. How bad you hurt them, son?'

'They'll survive.'

'Your dad drives that big old Lincoln, right? Shame about that.' He ducked his head at the collapsed garage and destroyed house. 'I've seen him around the area. Big feller. Polite. Could be tough, maybe?'

'That's Dad.'

'Son, why don't you hand over that foreign piece so we can talk about this without any iron between us.'

Greg glanced away, back toward the Jaguar. 'I'm tired. I need to sort this out in my head. I don't want to hurt you but I need time.'

The cop nodded, seeing determination and exhaustion, knowing this was one of those times when the sensible ones lay down – in the dirt if necessary – and let their man run. He said: 'Leave me in the dry, OK? I get rheumatism from the damp.' He turned around and took off his cap.

Greg said: 'Tell them, I get squeezed I go to the *Post*.'

'*Washington Post*, right?'

'Don't forget.'

'This something like Watergate?'

Greg chopped hard with the edge of his hand, precisely at the vital point at the meeting of neck and shoulder, grasping the unconscious figure before he fell, leaving him folded double by the garage door on dry ground. There would be bruising and stiffness for a day or two but better that than a fractured skull. He wiped dirt from the waterproof cover of the fallen cap and replaced it on the slumped grey head.

He ran back to the Jaguar and climbed back in, soaked through.

'What happened!' Carolyn gasped, seeing the automatic.

'Didn't you see?'

'I can't see anything through this rain! You just left me here!'

'Take it easy.' He started the car and drove off keeping the revs down because of the cracked exhaust.

'*Greg!*'

He would not look at her, driving tautly, speaking rapidly as if he wanted it all out and over quickly. 'Georgia's dead. Hugh Edwards, too. Dad's friend – cop – chief of detectives in DC. I don't know why, I don't know who. The house is blown to hell. Dad's alive. Been arrested for killing someone at Meade. I'd guess Kent. There's no one else. This whole thing is about Kent. There were two NSA security people back there – not cops, definitely not cops. They wanted to take me in. I had to deal with them. A local cop too. They're all OK.'

'How do you know that?'

'I know. No one's dead. They'll recover. Leave it.'

'I want this violence to stop!'

He rounded on her, savagely. 'You think I *don't*? Those are my friends who just got blown to pieces!'

'But you're just compounding the—'

'What? *Sin?*' Blind rage flared in his eyes. 'What does it take for you people to see reality?'

'Don't call me *people!*'

He slammed on the brakes, the car skidding, swerving, before the tyres bit. His words were like blows across her face. 'You better dump all those Christian *sensibilities* right now because things are going to get as rough as hell from here on in and there's no place for ideals.' He leaned across and pushed open her door. 'Or walk, now, because you're a liability. I want my dad free – and I'll do whatever it takes to do achieve that.'

Outside, lights came on in houses.

He swore brutally, pulled the door back hard and drove off fast.

She sat in silence, he driving, locked in his own thoughts.

'I'm sorry about Georgia,' she said, finally.

'So am I. She was doing something for me and it cost her her life. She was always doing something for me and I did nothing for her.'

'She loved you. I always knew that. It worried me.'

He said nothing, his face tight, controlled.

She felt tears swell and let them spill. 'I'm so sorry, Greg.'

'Listen to me. This is real. It's happening to us. There's no easy get-out. We don't have any choice here but to be as rough as we have to be. I'll do my best to keep you out of it as much as I can but if you want your parents back you're going to have to be tough. I need to get your folks back because that's the only way we're going to get some leverage. They'll have the truth of all this – whatever it is. It's vital we find them. That cop back there – I told him to tell the NSA people they leave us be or I go to the *Washington Post*. Maybe that'll scare them off. Depends on what's being hidden here. It could be so big they won't risk touching us – or so big we're dead already. You understand me? I'm sorry but that's how it is, I've got no soft wrapping.'

She wiped tears from her face. 'Would you do that? Go to the Press? Your work is secret – you've always been so firm about that.'

'I haven't changed the rules. *They* have.'

She looked across at him. His eyes were like cold glass, fixed on the road ahead, vacant of feeling. She was scared of him and scared for him too. For a moment she saw what he had never shown her: what had happened, what they had done to him in that foreign desert, fighting, to her mind, a foreign war. A war for the protection of wealth at the cost of human life. For her, the greatest sin imaginable.

She wondered if she had lost him? If she had ever *had* him? Or was what she saw only what he wanted her to see? The rest – the truth – concealed, just as he concealed the dark secrets of his torture? Just as he concealed ever since – for her? – the medal President Bush had pinned to his chest in the White House with her standing, watching, disapproving, feeling out of place and uncomfortable because for her it was a double-edged ceremony: both recognition of heroism and celebration of death – for his survival had undoubtedly cost other lives. Even one life, even a so-called enemy's life, was one too many. She had not dared ask herself if any of it was worth the cost of *his*. She could not face that terrible question now.

This, now beside her, was the man who had survived. Not the man she loved. But the man she knew she needed. The easy, docile – *tamed* – man was gone. Her creation? She didn't know. She did know it was like waking with a stranger.

She looked away at the highway flashing past, the morning light rising. She had to accept what was. There was no other way. Not if she wanted to see her parents alive. Her voices told her that and she trusted her voices. Whatever *black* – as the sect had it – Greg hid from her, she and her parents were going to need very badly. She would have to compromise her faith even more now than she had already by marrying him and accepting his world's values – though admitting she had, for her own intellect, her own self-respect, sacrificed much before even meeting him. She was no saint. She wanted – and she went out and got. *You walked down the mountain, no one else. Don't think you can climb back up so easily.* Still, it was a gradual erosion of her deepest self and she felt a deep sadness that something more than lives had been lost that night. She prayed it was not her faith. Nor her love for him.

'Where are we going?' she asked.

He shrugged. 'I don't know, yet. We could risk the airport but it won't be long before they're watching it. If we can get on Concorde we have to sit it out until take off at nine forty-five. That gives them too long to figure out it's Sunday and I'm not going to get hold of someone senior at the *Post* easily. They'll have too long – with us sitting there – to work out what to do.'

'Greg,' she hesitated. 'We stayed once at Georgia's – remember? She was away? You had a key.'

He nodded.

'Could you face going there – just for a few hours? You could sleep a little and I can check the flight on her phone if you can't use this one.'

'We definitely can't use this one now.' He nodded. 'OK, that sounds sensible.' He eased his foot down on the accelerator heading on to the Baltimore-Washington Parkway. He wished he could talk to his dad. He wanted him to be all right. He wanted to wipe out the things that had been said between them on the way to the White House. He wished he had never leapt so arrogantly from the car and had told John Cornell everything he had known. If he had, Georgia would still be alive, so would Hugh Edwards – and, if his worst fears held firm, his father would not have killed William Bradley Kent.

They made Washington DC quickly on the near-deserted truckless parkway. He abandoned the Jaguar – stripped clean of all evidence of Cardus, even tearing out the car-phone – on a dump-site on the bad side of downtown, keys in the ignition, knowing there was no more effective way to make the car disappear for ever. It would be out of state with new plates by noon or dismembered and spread across the country on the parts black market within days.

From there they had a wet, edgy walk to where they might catch a drifting cab or hitch a ride, afraid, despite the early hour, that their bags, and Cardus's costly notebook-computer and aluminium combination-lock briefcase glowed like beacons for derelicts or muggers.

They found an all-night diner safely, four blocks away, bought coffee and doughnuts and ate them gratefully, drying off until the cab Greg called arrived. They made Georgia's apartment in Orleans Place on the north-east side with daylight as bright as it was going to get all day. Greg would have given a great deal for a few more hours of darkness.

On the hall table facing them as they walked in was a message. *If you're here and I'm not – STAY. Love, Georgia.* Greg read it impassively, stripped off his rain-ruined leather jacket, and his jeans, fell on to the overstuffed settee, pulled one of the African rugs over himself, and was asleep in seconds.

Carolyn sat watching him for a long while, sleep beyond her, then made herself coffee and dialled British Airways' twenty-four-hour number, booking two Concorde seats with Greg's credit card.

Then she took Cardus's aluminium briefcase into the bedroom and began forcing the locks with a heavy-duty screwdriver she found in Georgia's comprehensive tool-box until they cracked open with sounds like pistol-shots. She checked she had not woken Greg then began searching through the contents.

None of it meant a thing to her – until she played the half-sized cassette in the DAT recorder she had found in the thick lid of the case. She heard herself, babbling and incoherent. Then other voices, knowing them to be her mother and father. She felt the tears rise – and cold fear – and fought both back, forcing herself to listen for something, anything which might be some lead – but understanding nothing. It was the same meaningless babble. *Tongues.* She cursed this useless gift which offered no hope. Then came more voices she had never heard before, more *tongues*, until frustration was close to anger.

Then, quite suddenly, a noise arose which made the hair on the nape of her neck rise, a sound that pitched her out of time, so far back it might have been some primeval animal roaring, yet *knowing* that this was no base animal. She clasped her hands to the headphones desperate to tear them off but unable to. She shook her head violently to escape it but there was none. She heard all of humanity crying out in unison as if it were a single child at the terrifying moment of birth. She felt she would die from the sheer terror, the magnitude, of it. An icy thought cleaved through her confusion. Humanity? Or God? Or—! Her eyes rolled upward in her head. She thought she screamed. She hoped she screamed.

'Hello, Sam. Seems we have a bad problem here.'

Sam Lewelyn leaned against the wall of the high-security cell deep underground in NSA's nuclear-proof zone under Fort Meade, the dead-white overhead lights making dark pits of his bruised, exhausted eyes.

'You've got the problem,' Sam answered wearily. 'All I've got is a murder charge – you've got to rebuild an organization. And from what I understand you could be looking at some deep probing. Those boys on the Hill love nothing more than swinging the axe at a sacred cow – and NSA is as sacred as they come. No dirty tricks like Langley? Clean, antiseptic, just straight intelligence without any *side*? Hell! They going to *enjoy* this.'

NSA's deputy director sat on the bench beside him, waving the security guard out of the cell. 'Oh, I don't think it's as bad as that. I'd go so far as to say we could survive this without the Hill becoming involved.'

'Dreamland. You've all lost touch with the real world. You see too much from out there.' Sam jabbed a finger upwards. 'Space. You can't tell how people *feel* from satellite film. They're going to eat you alive. And you're no Ollie North so you won't swing it the way he could.'

'Your son is – a bit – though. Isn't he?'

Sam glared.

'I mean a bit like Oliver North? Hero? Distinguished Service Cross? You *earn* that. I hear it could have been the Medal of Honour if it wasn't for the question mark over his stability? The attempted brain-washing? You never know with *that* kind of treatment what the recipient is likely to do. Or worse – likely to change into. We found out the hard way after Korea and Vietnam. My, didn't we!'

'What's on your mind?' asked Sam, icily.

'Just making the point, Sam. Someone in his position can't go making bizarre accusations. There's always *doubt*, you see. That's acknowledged. Ask any medico who understands the field.'

'What's Greg doing?'

'Threatening. As yet, not actually doing. We have to sit this one out, I think – for the moment. Watch everyone dance while we wait for the band to play our tune.'

'You mess with Greg and he'll hurt you – he has his mother's ruthlessness and he doesn't give a damn for authority. He'll bring you down and he'll smile doing it.'

'And his career with the Agency?'

'You really don't understand how the young think, do you? They'll take issues they believe in over traditional loyalties any day of the week. Does he know I'm here?'

'He knows you're in trouble.'

'And Georgia? He knows about her?'

'It seems so, yes.'

'Don't sleep easy, then.'

'We accept no responsibility for any deaths.'

'Of course not. So how *threatening* is he?'

'He says he'll go to the *Washington Post*.'

'They have the reputation.'

'But will he? Against national security interests?'

'Is that what you call it?'

'It's what our charter calls it.'

'If he says it, he'll do it.'

The deputy director gazed unhappily at the backs of his hands – the liver spots on them disturbingly prominent under the harsh lights. He sighed. 'We'll destroy him if he does. We can trail out as many head-doctors as it takes.'

'He won't care.'

'You will. His wife will.'

'I'll say it again: what's on your mind?'

'Talk to him. Tell him we're prepared to deal.'

'What are you holding to tempt him?'

'Why! You, Sam.'

'I'm not playing your game.'

'Of course you are, you're slap in the middle.'

Sam shifted, putting both shoeless feet on to the cold plastic floor. 'Hear me: I don't care what you do. I spent plenty of time as a Cong prisoner before the Air Force blew that crap-hole away. You don't have anything worse, I guarantee.'

The deputy director put on rimless glasses and his eyes immediately became quicksilver pools. 'Murder One means the chair in Maryland these days, Sam. Whatever happens to us in any enquiry won't affect that sentence – if we push for it. We can place witnesses on the scene immediately after the crime was committed. Witnesses who saw no other person in the room. You know it's simple to prove no one could escape Kent's office. You'd get the chair and no leave of appeal. It's that tight. Really.'

Sam shrugged.

The deputy director arose. 'Let's see how Greg feels about it, shall we? He's just booked on Concorde to London – two seats – we just had the data from the Airways computer. A telephone booking made from the Rowntree woman's apartment. Flight leaves at nine forty-five – though we can delay it a little if we want. I think we ought to have you two face to face on this, don't you? Family talk. Work things out together in the good old American way? The guard will take you somewhere you can freshen up – you look awful.'

Greg dragged the headphones out from under her clawed fingers and pulled them over his own ears, listening for a few moments, eyes clouded, then tossed them on to the bed.

'What is that?' she gasped.

'The Babel noise. I've only ever heard a small part of it. Selected soundwaves. That's much more than I've ever heard.'

'It doesn't *affect* you?'

'It affects me all right but to an extent I'm used to it. I've lived with it every day for months.'

'How *could* you?'

He studied her. 'You heard more than I hear. Maybe more than I'm capable of hearing.'

'What *is* it?'

'You tell me.'

She stammered. 'I don't want to think about it.'

'You may have to.'

'I don't understand?'

'If you heard . . . understood . . . something just now we might have to use that to get your parents back. They're desperate for a breakthrough. They'll deal. There's too big an investment in this. The Mojave station alone cost millions.'

She shook her head. 'I couldn't face it.'

'Like I said, you may have to.' He emptied everything from Cardus's ruined aluminium briefcase on to the bed, went to Georgia's study, returning with a leather grip he found there, and dumped its contents on to the bed also.

She picked through the discarded items from Georgia's bag: political leaflets, typed minutes from meetings, a batch of notebooks bound tightly with rubber bands. 'She was really politically active, wasn't she?'

'I didn't ask.'

'But you knew.'

He repacked the DAT recorder, computer floppies, and Cardus's notes in the bag.

She showed him an address book. 'When we were here before I saw her with this book, making calls – ten, maybe more.'

'Georgia talked on the phone all the time.'

'She was arranging a demonstration.'

'OK. So?'

'If she was here – now – I think she'd suggest she help you. I know she would.'

'How?'

She told him.

He took the address book.

'I'll make some coffee,' she said.

He lifted the bedside telephone, dialled one number while flipping through pages then stopped dead and cut the call. He dialled the number off the page, glancing at his watch, prepared to let it ring for as long as it took, early Sunday morning or not. Finally an annoyed, sleepy voice answered, changing within moments to alert attention. Next, he began working through other numbers from the book. Finished, he retrieved the DAT recorder from the leather grip, took it into the living room, rigged connections to the regular cassette recorder in the stereo unit there and made two copies from a stack of blanks.

Carolyn brought him coffee. 'I booked the flight.'

'How?'

'Your credit card. No problem with seats.'

He looked up. 'They're permanently linked to the Airways computer on a key-word basis. We'll have been added to that list.'

'You didn't tell me!'

'Doesn't matter.' He sipped hot coffee, writing notes on the cassette sleeves, saw her watching him, said: 'Insurance,' returned to the study, coming back with two large manila envelopes and a thick felt-tip pen. He wrote in big, bold, black capitals that could have been read yards away, placed a cassette-copy in each, checked his watch, drained his coffee and sealed the envelopes. 'Let's do it,' he said.

Rod Straker parked his car and made for the Concorde check-in at Washington's Dulles International, wondering if he'd blown a perfectly good Sunday.

The way things were that week ... European Federation President Philippe La Valle de Sazarin's attempted assassination on the Basilica steps, Texas evangelist Robert Maddox trumpeting biblical warnings from Revelation over the airwaves and swinging the susceptible half of the population from the tops of buildings, and, overnight, strong rumours out of Rome of some bizarre cover-up over a second hit on Sazarin – with US President Cornell lying in the next room of the same hospital for an undisclosed medical emergency ... Straker was prepared to follow up on anything.

At least the caller's identity had checked out – *if* it really was him.

Greg Lewelyn: Gulf War hero. Former USAF Lieutenant. A real MIT whiz. Flew five missions out of Saudi. Shot down on sixth. Captured by Iraqi regulars, handed over to the *Mukharabat* for interrogation; tortured but apparently did not break – no operational secrets known to him being compromised. Rumours of brain-washing techniques being used never officially confirmed. Escaped from detention after an Allied air-raid destroyed the building, made it through Iraqi lines killing a number of crack Republican Guard troopers in the process. Hijacked a moving gasoline truck on a night-time desert highway, killed the Iraqi driver, and struck for Allied lines – straight into the destruction by Allied helicopter gunships of a great column of vehicles fleeing Kuwait loaded with loot. Barely survived. Awarded the Distinguished Service Cross by then President Bush – some said it should have been the Medal of Honour – then drifted out of sight. Rumour was he had been sent to an especially equipped secret government rehabilitation centre to make sure he was straight after the mind-bending, but on the telephone that morning he claimed the National Security Agency swallowed him whole, setting him to work on an ultra-secret sound-analysis project deep in the Mojave desert.

He claimed also that NSA were prepared to kill to stop details – or even the existence – of the project being revealed and that he had contacted Straker because of his stature and proven record of not being silenced by governmental pressure – wanting him to witness his safe departure with his wife via Concorde for London. Straker knew 'witness' meant *guarantee*. Lewelyn promised more, much more – in time – if they succeeded in leaving the US, though expecting to be stopped by NSA's Office of Security or perhaps even the police. To safeguard against this he had threatened NSA he would go public – via the *Post*.

If this is for real, thought Straker, it's going to be an Old West stand-off right in the middle of high-tech Dulles International.

On the other hand maybe there *had* been some bending of Lewelyn's mind – and it had finally snapped.

Straker spotted the photographer he had called immediately the telephone had gone down – pictures to be taken only if a confrontation occurred were the instructions he had, reluctantly, agreed to and would stand by – and fell into step beside her.

'Sunday mornin' comin' down,' growled the photographer as low to Kristofferson as she could get.

'Heavy night?'

'Don't ask.'

'Don't need to.'

'I look that bad?'

'Worse.'

'What's happening?'

'Nothing. If anything does you start shooting. Otherwise, just look as if you're ready.' Straker indicated her hanging camera and lenses. 'Act like a hired gun.'

'What qualifies as *anything*?'

'I'll tell you when it happens.'

'No sneak shots?'

'Definitely not. I want all of this.'

'And all of it is not here today?'

'Is it ever?'

They walked straight into a rowdy banner-waving crowd accusing police of a cover-up over the death of a black activist during the night. Straker recognized the name Georgia Rowntree.

'Damn,' cursed the photographer. 'That's my line of fire gone.'

'He said there could be a diversion.'

'All the political activists I know sleep on Sunday, recovering from Saturday's *après-demo*. Your man must be persuasive.'

'Or he's got one hell of a cause,' murmured Straker. *This was becoming interesting*.

Greg held the manila envelope high on his chest, the bold black lettering declaring ROD STRAKER, WASHINGTON POST.

Sam saw it immediately and gave a low chuckle.

'He's sharp, your boy,' said the Deputy Director.

'I warned you – his mother's genes.'

'English deviousness?'

Sam smiled, coldly.

They were watching from above the concourse, through the one-way glass of a security point.

'Time to get down there,' said the Deputy Director.

'He won't listen if his mind is set on something,' warned Sam.

'Let's give him the opportunity, shall we?'

*

Greg recognized Straker immediately from extensive media cover-age of the investigative journalist's coups for the *Washington Post* – the reason he had called immediately he saw Straker's name in Georgia's *action* book.

'Have you flown Concorde before, sir?' enquired the British Airways check-in clerk.

Greg shook his head, watching around him, barely listening.

'You can go through to the Concorde lounge. There are refresh-ments, magazines, and telephone facilities available.'

He nodded, took the travel documents she handed him, and keeping Carolyn close moved away.

'Your dad!' Carolyn exclaimed.

Greg saw Sam towering above everybody, a battleship of a man, looking worn but determined. Gerg knew from the hard glint in his eye that Sam had been backed into a corner and was ready to come out fighting any time now.

'He's not alone,' warned Greg, feeling the tension rise in her.

'Don't worry, we can handle this.'

He saw Straker position himself prominently on the concourse with a denim-clad woman hung with cameras to his right; they might easily have been covering the demonstration which was now being corralled by a sudden influx of police.

'Hello, Dad. You look beat.'

Sam gripped his arm. 'When's the last time you looked in a mirror? The both of you.'

'Been doing some hard travelling. About to do some more.'

Sam nodded. 'This is NSA Deputy Director Wendell.'

'I recognize you, sir,' said Greg, meticulously correct.

'Best we discuss this somewhere secure,' said Wendell.

'No, sir. We stay public. All the way.'

Annoyance flitted across Wendell's face then vanished. 'Very well – though the noise is going to make things difficult.' He tipped his head at the demonstration. 'Your arrangement? The banners are for your friend, I see. We didn't kill her. You must understand that.'

'Your men were there.'

'Doing their job,' said Wendell tightly. 'You might have thought about that before acting so violently.'

Greg glanced across at Straker who gave a small acknowledging nod.

'I hope we can keep the Press out of this – for your sake,' said Wendell.

Greg said nothing.

'Your father has something to say to you. Sam?'

'I killed Kent,' said Sam impassively. 'Mostly for his arrogance. There are greater reasons of course. I believed he had plans to kill the President. I was wrong but I still believe he saw that as an option if John Cornell began digging too deep. He had too much control. *They* have too much control.' Sam lazily aimed a big thumb at Wendell.

'This is ridiculous, Sam,' snapped Wendell.

'No, it's logical. In this high-tech world the Agency is the presence behind the throne. Eyes, ears, decision-swayer. *Power*. When our major enemy disintegrated in front of us you had to maintain the fear level or lose your justification for being. John Cornell knew that. I was late in seeing it but I sure as hell see it now.'

'You don't understand what's going on here!'

The chanting in the background was growing. Greg had to raise his voice: 'They've picked up a signal. The SETI programme at Green Bank. My job was to decipher it.'

Sam stared at him, then turned to Wendell and saw reluctant confirmation in the worried face. He smiled, then laughed out loud. 'He had all of you running like headless chickens! Kent did. It's wonderful, truly wonderful!'

Wendell coloured deeply, angered, yet perplexed. 'What do you mean?' he growled.

'Kent used SETI funding. That's obvious. I bet he used SETI equipment and personnel. No one realized. Not the truth of it. There's no signals from space. Not of the kind you mean, Greg. Kent was after us – not what's out there.'

'I don't understand?' said Wendell, shifting uncomfortably, disturbed by Rod Straker's obvious attention and deeply concerned about directional microphones or Greg possibly being wired.

Greg looked at Carolyn. 'History,' he said. 'Just before the crash, Cardus said: "We're talking about history here. Civilization. Everything we are and ever will be could all be lost in little more than a moment. Our light in the heavens, shining for generations, gone in a blink. That's the consequence." I thought he was rambling and told him he sounded like Maddox. I asked, "The consequence of what?" He said: "Of there being nothing. Of that empty truth becoming the only truth. Of people knowing they have no purpose beyond temporal existence." I missed the point entirely – as I was supposed to, as we all were. I asked him: "What has SETI picked up?" Meaning from space.'

'And?' demanded Wendell.

'We crashed before he could answer.'

'Us,' said Sam. 'They'd picked us up.'

'I think Dad's right, sir. It's a theory that's been kicked around for years. Some research institutes are playing with it today – apparently without success but we can't be certain. It's a question of wave-forms. Sound vibrating in the ether on frequencies out of our hearing. That's what Cardus meant by *history*. History all around us. If we can pick it up. We wouldn't need text-books, we could play it back, no lies, no bias.'

Wendell said, disturbed: 'Then these signals from the supposed source in space which SETI—'

'Don't exist,' said Sam. 'Never did.' He looked at Greg. 'None of it exists, son. It's all hokum. *Moscow* hokum. Moscow laid out the ingredients and Kent brewed away for years like he had a secret still that would give him the stuff of dreams. He got taken in just as the rest of us have.'

'To what end?' protested Wendell.

'Can't you see it? What do we do when we decide to bring down a government? We undermine their values, stir up the people, and, come the crash, go in, pick up the pieces, and make a buck or two reconstructing the economy. We've just seen what can happen when one lunatic with the power of TV behind him starts proclaiming Jesus is about to call in his markers. Play it another way: announce Jesus never existed – never was crucified, *official*, the grey wizards in their glass towers have proven it. Then every TV and radio station in Christendom runs it. Hell! it would all be over in a week. And we'd wake up wondering if the rest of the day had any purpose at all – excepting those of course who never believed in anything anyway. You need examples of who they might be? You don't have to look east to find them – we bred our own right here in the good old USA.'

Wendell said: 'This is fantasy.'

'You believed messages from outer space – financed the programme with millions of dollars – and you call *this* fantasy!'

'There were budgets, permissions—'

'And secrecy. That's why it worked. Everything you needed to convince you was given you. Put another way, Kent fed all of you just what you wanted to eat and Moscow was the cook.'

'There's no proof of any of this?'

Greg looked hard at Wendell. 'There might be.'

'How? Where?'

'There's a secret facility in England. Near Glastonbury.'

'Impossible. The nearest in that area would be the INTELSAT earth station at Goonhilly Downs, Bude, Cornwall. There's two one-hundred-foot dishes sixty miles north of Goonhilly, but they're GCHQ's, not ours.'

'There's a facility, believe me.'

'How can you be so sure?'

Greg glanced warningly at Carolyn. 'You'll have to trust me. But I'm right. Let us board the flight and I'll come back and prove it to you. You want to step into Kent's chair clean, don't you?'

Wendell's eyes fixed upon him, glacially, then he turned pointedly toward Straker. 'No contact whatsoever with the media?'

Greg nodded.

Wendell said: 'Very well. While you're gone I've a few questions for your boss Cardus. I'll soon get to the heart of this.'

'He's dead.'

'What! The car crash?'

'I'm afraid I shot him. His gun. I was holding it on him when the crash occurred.'

Wendell looked bleakly at Sam. 'My God, if there were any more of your family we'd need a new service!'

'It wasn't Greg's fault,' snapped Carolyn. 'They'd kidnapped my parents – that's why Greg threatened him – why we're going to England.'

Greg said, 'That's what started the rush to Austin – Maddox picked up on their disappearance and cashed in. Cardus mounted the abduction operation – when he realized I was going up to the mountains. Thought maybe I'd uncover something and tell Dad – who'd brief the President. Cardus grilled me before we left the station – I just didn't pick up on it.'

'Uncover what?' demanded Wendell.

Greg looked at his watch, concerned about take-off time. 'Too complex to explain now. Take my word, he really needed those people. If I'm right, watch the Press, there may be reports of others taken from similar religious settlements – maybe even in other countries.'

'You have proof of this abduction?'

'We had eyewitnesses to the kidnap.'

'Had?'

'They were in the car that hit us. They're both dead.'

Wendell passed a hand over his forehead. 'I just hope to God that journalist of yours hasn't got someone pointing a directional microphone this way. This is a nightmare.'

Sam said, 'You've only just stepped into it.'

Wendell looked long and hard at him, then nodded tightly as if decided. 'Sam, they go but you stay. I need that insurance. If this thing can't be buttoned down tight when it's over I'm going to have to show I played this by the book right to the wire.'

'I'm staying right here to meet the President off the plane, anyway.' He glared. 'And don't try to stop me.'

'I'll be next in line. Except it seems I won't be greeting him but supplying – difficult – explanations. You two had better board Concorde,' sighed Wendell.

'If we haven't missed it,' said Greg.

'No fear of that. We've had the flight on hold from the moment you booked your seats. I think as an act of faith, Greg, you might hand the envelope for Straker over to me.' Wendell extended his hand.

Greg hesitated, looked across at the journalist and deliberately shook his head, then complied.

Wendell said, 'It occurs to me there is an Agency facility in the Glastonbury area – but it's no listening post. I doubt there's any major equipment there at all. Basically it's little more than a safe house. Rather grand. Some of our European people make use of it when stress gets too much. Senators on Intelligence committees getting the big tour have found it very comfortable, I understand – though it's not on that circuit any more.'

'Why?' asked Greg.

Wendell shrugged. 'I don't check activities in every property we own. That's operational – not my side. Something sensitive going on there, I imagine. I'll check it out.'

'Don't!' snapped Greg. 'Don't do anything.'

Wendell nodded, wrote an address on a small notepad, and handed the sheet over. 'That's near Marlborough – county of Wiltshire.'

'Greg was at school at Marlborough,' said Sam.

Greg looked at Carolyn. 'Avebury Circle is right there. And Silbury Hill. Ley-lines – remember? It has to be the place.'

'You'd better go now.' said Wendell.

Sam grasped Greg in a bear hug, slipping something into his jacket pocket. '*Genesis*,' he murmured close to Greg's ear, then released him, kissed Carolyn, and watched them go.

'So where was the fire?' asked the camerawoman as she and Rod Straker walked back to the car-park.

'Couldn't you feel the heat?' said Straker, feeling the flush of excitement. His unfailing early warning of another Big One. He remembered the advice of his Pulitzer Prize-winning mentor at the *Post*: *When you think it's over, it's only just begun.*

CHAPTER
NINETEEN

AMERICA'S NIGHT OF LUNACY ran the banner headline on the tabloid newspaper among the depleted pile of that Sunday's publications at the front of the bookshop in Heathrow's Terminal 4. Every one bore a full front-page photograph of Maddox's twisted, blackened Texas tower, with rows of bagged bodies lined on the sidewalk like overnight refuse. More gruesome details and photographs were promised inside. Greg turned Carolyn away, making for the car-rental counter where he signed for a compact 2.8 Audi 80.

He checked the clock above the desk and adjusted his watch to local time. 'Seven fifteen. Using the motorway we can make it to Marlborough in two hours. What's the matter?'

'You sound British.'

He smiled. 'Half of me is.'

'Don't you need to sleep?'

He took the offered documents for the Audi and moved away from the desk.

'We need darkness,' he told her, walking out on to the concourse where the car was waiting. 'You're going to have to accept whatever happens.' He tossed bags into the trunk. 'You understand?'

She nodded.

They were on to the M4 motorway quickly, Greg pushing the Audi to the legal limit and holding it there. He slotted the cassette tape Sam had passed to him at Dulles into the player.

John Cornell's fateful Rome telephone call from CIA Director Ellis, containing the translation of Voroshilov's report of the Markarovs' work and the subsequent conspiracy, began.

301

Miles on, when it was over, Carolyn looked at him, dazed. 'Is it possible?'

Greg was far away, in the dacha outside Moscow, hearing sounds being drawn agonizingly from the ether by scientists struggling at the furthest reaches of their field with inadequate technology that gave them little chance of success. Yet they *had* succeeded. He knew that to some degree they must have. To pull off the deception there had to be at least the basis of truth – or everything collapsed. Kent was no scientist but the people he employed certainly were – and they would soon have realized they were being deceived. Moscow had given Kent a nut to crack and at its centre there had to be a kernel of truth.

Greg could see what had happened. The Babel noise was that truth. The Russian scientists perhaps had a hint of it – enough to realize its potential – but simply could not drag it out with their primitive equipment. Yet all the while it was there: subsonic, latent, potentially overwhelming. Later, American technology had revealed it; revealed, but not explained.

The problems began for Moscow's conspiracy when the Babel noise obliterated whatever disinformation was supposed to be 'discovered' on the tapes the Markarovs provided as proof of the – tantalizingly limited – success of their sound-retrieval techniques. Kent became obsessed by the wrong thing. He devoted his life – and NSA resources – to unlocking the noise, not the *lie*.

So what lay beneath? Greg remembered opening the cassette on Concorde and seeing the words scrawled on the sleeve: *Sam, find Moscow's lie and nail it before the world does – and believes it!* No signature but he knew instantly – from years of receiving birthday cards from him – the hand was John Cornell's.

He blinked, suddenly aware of headlights flashing angrily in the rear-view mirror and pulled quickly into the middle land to let the speeding car pass.

'Greg?'

'Sorry – what did you say?'

'Is it really possible to bring back the past?'

'I think it's possible – I know it's dangerous.'

'Why? Think how wonderful it would be to hear the voice of Jesus! Children wouldn't need to read the Bible to know Him. They could hear him speak! Surely that's good.'

'It's only good if it's true. If He really happened. Happened as the Bible says. You know how legends can be . . . embellished.'

'*Don't!* Don't say that. You can't throw doubt on my faith.'

'Carolyn, you – and those like you – are the exception. You're a minority. Face it, the West long ago lost any pretence to a spiritual foundation. We're in a spiritual vacuum. Only the East is completely unshakeable in its faith and we ignore that at our peril. I don't believe that faith necessarily has to be in God – but any society must believe in *something* if it is to survive . . . if it is to be a society at all. That's what John Cornell was saying on that tape, and he's right. He's also right to be scared, because if we lose what remains of our beliefs we're doomed. We won't so much be overrun as lay down and give up.'

'I never thought I'd hear you say that!'

'Listen, I'm not speaking in favour of God – or Jesus – or any other supposed deity. I'm just saying that without belief in something, there's nothing.' He pointed up at the night. 'We couldn't survive in the vacuum of space but we believe we can conquer it – so we do. *That's* what I mean.'

The tape ejected: a sudden sharp sound cutting through the muted, shut-out sound of wind, road, and engine.

Carolyn stared at it, feeling reduced by the enormity of what she had heard. Her voice, too, was small: 'Why my folks?'

Greg glanced at her, quickly. 'I think they're only a part of it. Maybe they need . . . hundreds, even thousands . . . to conquer the noise. Carolyn, I saw what it did to you. Alone you couldn't handle it – but maybe as a group . . . ? You understood something – I saw that in your face. Perhaps it needs collective understanding? Back near Green Bank when I tried to explain Chaos, you mentioned the Tower of Babel. Maybe that's what they're building – or *rebuilding*? Trying to reverse the process? Genesis states that – once – *the whole of the earth was one language and one speech.* That's perfectly feasible: Dolgopsky in Israel and Shevoroshkin at Michigan are both working on the possibility of reconstructing one mother tongue from which all languages sprang. They've named it *Nostratica*. Something happened to end that period, call it Babel or a series of catastrophes which scattered people across the globe: God or evolution, it doesn't matter, the end result is the same, we don't understand each other any more – not without effort.

'And it stopped us dead in our tracks as far as our development was concerned. Imagine how much further advanced we would be now if we had all conversed in the same tongue from the time of Abraham! Genesis gives this as God's reason for Babel: "Now nothing they have in mind to do will be beyond their reach."' He smiled. 'I'm not converted, I've just read up everything there is on Babel since I started playing with voices. You know my memory!'

'You're mocking me.'

'No. I respect your belief. I can even see why you believe – I can't see how. OK, assume no catastrophe – just God. We know what He did. But why? Did He get scared? Saw from up there we were catching up on Him – so decided to confuse the hell out of us? Genesis: "Let us go down there and confound their language that they may not understand one another's speech"? That makes us a lot more special than He – otherwise – leads us to believe?' He grinned. 'The fallen angels He cast out after the great struggle in heaven? Lucifer and his cohorts? Is that why the Bible calls this world Lucifer's domain? Is that our beginning? OK, maybe now I am mocking, but I have to tell you we're really close to universal communication again. We don't need speech, we have electronics and an information language that's universally understood. Does that fix Armageddon just up ahead and us set for the next lightning bolt from heaven? If that's what you believe then I can see why your people want to be separated from the rest of us! Why you count on being lifted up into the air before all hell breaks loose.'

She said nothing, staring out at the night, headlight beams from speeding cars in the opposite lanes exploding briefly on her pale face.

Greg watched her for a moment, then turned back to the road. 'So, put all the languages in the world in one melting pot – record them that way – and what have you got? *Tongues?* I don't know. I'm guessing. It's probably more complex than that. But I see light now where before there was only darkness.' He paused. 'And not a little madness. I'm certain there were many before me – working on the noise – who cracked completely. Larry Maine warned me. He said he'd found out the rate of breakdown was really high. I think they wanted me, particularly, because I'd encountered certain techniques in Iraq when I was captured. Mind manipulation. Brain-washing, if you like. I think they believed that might offer some form of resistance to the effects of the noise. I think that's why they took me on so quickly, asked so few questions. No one gets into NSA that easily. I thought at first – vanity – they needed me real bad. Underneath I guessed it was to do with Dad being who he was in the Agency and I resented that. I know – now – I was wrong. They wanted me because of what had been done to me. I'm certain of it.'

'You've never talked about Iraq before.'

'I couldn't.'

'Why now?'

'Maybe it's the end of the tunnel. I said, I can see light.'

She looked at him, hopefully. 'You've found Jesus?'

He smiled wryly. 'I wasn't looking for Him.'

'But he was looking for you. To save you.'

'You think I need saving, Carolyn?'

'We all do. From Satan.'

He looked hard at the speeding ribbon of the highway, his face glowing amber in the dashboard light. 'I've seen the face of the devil and survived.'

They arrived on the outskirts of Marlborough just before half-past nine and stopped at a petrol station to ask directions.

'After the circles then, are you?' asked the attendant, topping up the Audi's tank.

Greg leaned out. 'Circles?'

'Corn circles. Don't you read the papers? You're Yanks? Just arrived? I went to Florida last year.'

'Where?'

'Disneyland. Great!'

'I meant where are these corn circles.'

'Where you're going, of course! There's loads up there already. Hippies. Coppers blocked some of the roads. Had to. Up from around Glastonbury most of 'em. Lot of their sort there. Coming from all over now, though. Doing drugs and all that. No wonder they hear all them sounds. Prefer a drink myself. That's ten quid.'

'*Sounds?*'

The attendant peered at Greg's credit card, went to a glass

booth, and came back for a signature, handing over a bedraggled newspaper. 'Tells you the lot. Been going since Friday. You with this cult thing then?' A dirty fingernail pointed at a report. 'See? Says some on 'em are Yanks.'

'Can I keep this?'

The attendant shrugged. 'Sunday. No tits.' He bent and grinned with bad teeth at Carolyn.

Greg pulled away, switching on the Audi's map-reading light. 'Can you read with that?'

Carolyn nodded.

'Savernake House, on the edges of the Marlborough Downs, has been the central gathering point for hundreds of travellers, so-called ATs – alternative types, they hate the term New Agers – who have descended in force in their buses and Volkswagens around the magnificent country house owned, sources say, by an anonymous American millionaire rumoured to lead a religious cult some of whose members, locals say, are currently staying at Savernake. Talk of links with multi-millionaire US TV evangelist Robert Maddox whose broadcasts led to hysteria across America this weekend are so far unconfirmed.

'So far the hordes have been kept out of the grounds proper by extremely unmystical types who are not averse to physically man-handling those who get too close to the main house. The acres of fields around the house however – part of the property – have been completely taken over by what would in the sixties have been described as a Hippy happening. It is in fact these fields which started all of this off. Cornfields which, overnight on Friday, became mysteriously stamped by so-called corn circles. Word of the formation of new circles spreads like wildfire among ATs and within hours groups were arriving to sit cross-legged within them chanting mantras.

'The same scene has been witnessed many times before. What makes this occurrence unique is the *sound*. When it occurs it is extraordinary and . . . alien. Nothing within this reporter's experience could describe it. So deep as to be barely heard, felt certainly – nauseatingly – in the belly; the muscle walls of the abdomen seeming to act as a soundboard, sometimes with disgusting results. Some say they can feel their internal organs vibrating while others swear to involuntary orgasm. There are, too, sudden, apparently excruciating, high-frequency sounds heard only by some of the growing crowds. The effect on these unfortunates may accurately be described as akin to an epileptic fit. There are a few who swear that there is much more than what is being heard by the majority. But that fits with the mood of this extraordinary happening in rural Wiltshire. *Voices* is the nearest description one hears – *confusion*, say others.'

Carolyn gasped: '"Chaotic babble!" Greg!'
'Go on.'

'The feeling among the more way-out types here is that this particular phenomenon – the voices – are "vibrations from the Old Watchers which hover as a kind of protective layer over the earth". A form of mystical geomagnetism is the nearest to any rational description heard in two days.'

'They're almost right,' said Greg. 'Except there's nothing mystical about it. The vibrations are from sound. Old sound, centuries of it. Maybe only the frequencies of human voices? Or the frequencies they shift to – with time. Maybe these frequencies are drawn by magnetic forces: even natural ones, like ley-lines? Why not, we pull in radio signals every day in the same way? This area is riddled with ley-lines, acording to the data in Cardus's computer. The central meeting point is supposed to be Glastonbury Tor but what if they've been experimenting in this Savernake place with your folks – maybe others too – and something happened, something physical? The Russians encountered a similar phenomenon in their experiments. Remember what the translation said on the tape? "Turbulent air whipped into tornadoes or even small swirling eddies . . . were caused by sub-sonic sound vibrations reaching critical or unbalanced levels as in conflicting harmonics." They had results of experiments with crop circles as proof!'

'But what does it mean? Here?'
'I think it's expanding. Not just air-movement – the sound is coming through too. All these people gathering here are acting like a great dish, a huge human receiver!'

'Human?'

They had turned into a narrow country lane. He stopped the car abruptly, jerked up the handbrake and swung around to her in the darkness. 'Yes, *human*. That's it, don't you see? They've tried all the high-tech electronic routes and they're back to the greatest computer of all.' He stabbed a finger at his head. '*Here*, crackling with electronic energy – the human brain!'

A few miles on, the camp-fires were like burning wreckage from some enormous catastrophe. Scattered across the rolling downs they glowed and sparked, large and small, each surrounded by human attendants like lost spirits drawn to the light – which in a greater sense they were.

'There's so many!' Carolyn exclaimed at the sight, seeing behind, in the reflections from the flames, massed half-derelict vehicles parked haphazardly on the grass with lean-to canvas shelters or tents beside them.

Greg pointed away to the east. 'More over there – look!'

A sudden flashing blue light appeared as they rounded the corner of the narrow country road, police in reflective clothing stepping forward.

Greg halted before the barrier and leaned out. 'What's the problem?'

'Sorry, sir,' answered their sergeant, his voice a soft but firm burr. 'You'll have to go back.'

Greg took out his wallet and extracted the address NSA Deputy Director Wendell had written for him and showed it but leaving his Agency ID clear in the torch beam. 'Map says this way.'

The sergeant's eyes lingered on the eagle and key seal, then up to Greg's face and over to Carolyn. 'Better tell your lads up there they shouldn't be so heavy-handed with trespassers – otherwise it might mean a charge. They can't just use force whenever they like it, know what I mean? It's not America.'

'Can't use force whenever you feel like it in America either, Sergeant – but, sure, I'll tell them.'

The sergeant stepped back, ordered the barrier pulled aside, and waved them on.

'Greg, we've got to go in there!' said Carolyn alarmed. 'You heard what he said.'

He nodded, tightly. 'We'll deal with it as it comes.'

'What would you have done if he'd called to check?'

'Savernake House has to be on their special-handling list. He saw my ID. He wasn't going to make any call.'

'You mean they know what's going on?'

'No. But they have to be made aware when security services – domestic or allied – have an interest in a property. Nothing specific. They just know to keep back.'

'Then they can't be happy about all this!' She pointed at the sweep of camp-fires in the darkness.

'Police can't do much if they remain on common land.'

Carolyn yelled: 'Look out!'

A group of young people had leapt out in front of the car, faces painted with Tantric symbols, hair long and wild, the men wispily bearded, dangling pendulums of bright crystals, their colours caught in the headlights like jewels.

Greg braked, swerving violently to avoid hitting them.

'Don't stop! It's bad here!'

The Audi's nearside wheels mounted the bank, the car tilting dangerously, Greg fighting to keep control, losing forward motion as the underside rubbed along the earth, then, a sudden *bang* and the car became a wild thing, engine roaring, steering-wheel spinning uselessly, a shocking grinding rising from underneath. Greg could only suppose they'd hit jutting rock and ripped the underside of the car away. They skewed to a halt, still tilted, the engine-roar uncontrollable. He switched off the ignition fast, fearing sparks and fire.

The silence was like the bottom of a grave, black clouds in the night-sky like earth piled in mounds above, the hazy moon a dull grey lamp over all. The sound filled the air, then lights like flashing static flickered around the car, crackling on the bodywork as if hard insects were attacking the metal.

'Oh, God!' whispered Carolyn.

Greg could see ahead now, his eyes adjusting to the darkness. There were hundreds of them in the field, both sexes, even children, spinning, moving in a great mass within the forming crop circle like dancers – but there was no joy, no ecstasy on their painted faces, only bewilderment and near panic, their long hair standing out and up, caught in the same fine web of current which trailed like blue-white extensions of the hair-strands.

Greg could see eyes bulging now as a glow built up, seeming to come from within the bodies now not from around them.

Then the noise became audible. Deep, like a vast underground river running beneath.

'Out!' snapped Greg. 'Now!'

Carolyn sat transfixed; watching yet not seeing, eyes lost in the middle distance, she might have been blind, listening to a world barred from the sighted.

Greg heaved open the door and leapt out, gasping as the noise really hit him, clamping both hands over his ears, struggling as if against strong wind to the other side of the Audi.

He saw Carolyn's fingers move to the central locking control and bawled, '*No!*' but it made no difference. He stood in front of her banging on the window but she ignored – or could not see – him. Giving up, he turned away and scrabbled for anything hard, anything to break glass. He found a heavy sharp-edged rock, fought his way back to the driver's side and smashed it into the window until it exploded inward. He hauled open the door, tearing her hand away from the central lock then smacked her seat-belt release and, brutally, dragged her out across the central console and on to the road. She fought him and he hit her then carried her over his shoulder at a dead run to where he could see rectangles of light through the dark shapes of trees before the horizon.

Behind him the car exploded and the noise faded. He heard terrifying, agonized screams and felt heat in his internal organs, imagining – and instantly shutting out – what he believed was occurring behind him. He remembered the glow coming from within the spinning bodies. Microwaves. The sound had ridden on microwaves and the bodies had been cooked from the inside out. Crazily, Faustus came to him. 'Hell hath no limits . . . where we are is hell.' He ran onward, blindly, afraid only of what lay behind him: what lay ahead was within the limits of his fear. He stopped only when the heat inside him cooled and the sound, a memory he had already locked away.

Carolyn moved beside him on the grass bank. He leaned over to her and touched her face.

She looked at him.

'I had to hit you,' he said.

She stared.

'You OK?'

'My God!' she whispered.

He had no words.

She reached for him and held him, not breaking, calm, somehow stronger, aware.

'You know something,' he said.

She nodded.

'Can you tell me?'

'You can't tell. You only *know*.'

'Does it help us?' He pointed at the house. 'Help them? Your parents?'

'They know too. By now.'

He looked away, then at the sky. He felt himself trembling. 'I wanted it to be from out there. I wanted life to exist – beyond us. To put things into perspective.'

'I know.'

'It's inside us, isn't it? The control of it.'

'We are it. We don't know it. We lost it. Long ago. We're finding our way back. Everything we want to know is here.' She held his face close. 'We know already. We've been there before and we have yet to go. There's no dividing line.'

He looked back the way he had run. 'We're not ready.'

'No.'

'Do you know when?'

'We'll know when. We're children playing with matches and we could set the world on fire.'

'Is this is a warning?'

She gave no answer.

He could feel the pulse from her and loved her, yet was very afraid he had lost her. 'I love you,' he said.

'I know.'

'Will you leave? Go back to them? Back up the mountain?'

'They're coming down from the mountain.'

'Into this crazy world?'

'*Because* of this crazy world.' She smiled. 'You'll see.'

Savernake House was Georgian, its tall elegant wrought-iron gates a central uplifting point in a seemingly endless stretch of railings backed by thick hedging, running east to west. There was a white gate lodge which even in the darkness was visible from quite far back along the narrow but well-kept road.

Greg wondered where the cameras were – other than the ones mounted openly on the solid ornamented gate-posts.

The gates were open.

'You stay here,' he told Carolyn.

'No.'

He stopped.

'It's over in there,' she said. 'Can't you see that?'

'Over how?'

'They'll be waiting.'

'Your parents?'

'Of course.'

'You know that?'

'Yes.'

He saw the shape behind the right-hand gate. In the darkness it might have been an animal lolled against it.

'Wait here,' he said and moved closer.

The outer clothes were not completely burned, the synthetic shirt a stiff, scorched, melted layer over the charred remains beneath, the jacket holed in places as though burning coals had been tossed on to the body. The face had gone, now resembling old burned wood which would crumble at the touch. Greg remembered photographs he had seen in training of burned pilots – horrors they were shown to make them aware they were not immortal, not airborne gods. This was different. Complete combustion. He felt he could probe with his finger and find only charcoal where once had been a living heart, where, even in an air-crash victim, some tissue would survive the flames.

He was reminded of reports of supposed spontaneous human combustion he had read with his usual scepticism during college days, reading up afterwards on so-called *telluric* fields – the Earth radiating electromagnetic energy which produced phenomena such as static charges and light effects – as a possible explanation. But this was awesome power. No mere static charge could do this. He could not understand what Carolyn *knew* and probably never would but this in front of him was no sibylline spiritual experience – however powerful. Here was destruction. Complete, dreadful and truly terrible. Here, the key to unlock the horrors of Armageddon. If he had any firm belief in God he would say this was how His Wrath would be manifested.

He stood up and wondered how long before the inevitable investigation of BABEL slid into the development of this hellweapon.

We're children playing with matches and we could set the world on fire.

He knew what he must do. Before Sam's feared grey wizards flew in silently – as they surely would, within hours. He dragged the body into the lodge feeling it crumbling even as he did so, laid it in the centre of the beamed sitting room before a twin-barred electric fire, went into the kitchen in search of matches and saw the gas cooker. He closed any opened windows, turned all the gas-taps on full and moved swiftly outside, grabbing Carolyn's arm and running up the gravel drive toward the wide sweep before the porticoed façade of Savernake.

There were two more bodies lying on the steps – they seemed to have been running for the main doors. Greg dragged them inside on to the harlequin-tiled floor of the entrance hall. From somewhere further inside he heard a familiar sound, like the wind whispering in trees, like a thousand rustling leaves, peaceful yet vital, rising and falling, powerful but never strident. *Tongues.*

Carolyn too was taken up in it and he followed as she moved through the house to where the source flowed outward.

They were congregated in a glass-domed hall, the sky visible above. A podium had been erected with a metal frame to support the electronic equipment arrayed upon it. To either side, on high stands were a series of high-frequency speakers and below these heavy bass-bins, all pointing inward to the group. The Babel noise had changed. Changed from what Greg had been used to hearing in his cubicle in the station. Changed from what Carolyn had heard on the tape in Cardus briefcase. No less chaotic, no less awesome, but bearable now. As if mercy had tempered the fury it held. Greg looked at the tightly massed, swaying, group of people: all races, all colours, all uttering the same sounds; the same *language*. All wearing that same look of ecstasy and of something more: revelation

They understand, he realized.

Carolyn understands.

He saw her beside her parents, the three of them weeping, lost in complete joy. They were the chosen and even if he was on the outside he had his part to play.

From somewhere in the night came the deep thud of an explosion.

He knew what he had to do.

He must get them out so he could burn Babel down. Before chaos ruled and uncontrollable horror crept from under its shadow.

He went forward and stopped the tape and was, for that night, their guide.

That role for them was yet to come.

Well after Savernake became a fiery star on a dark horizon.

EPILOGUE

'Hello, Greg,' said John Cornell. 'It's good to see you after so long. Here, wasn't it, in the White House? President Bush's time.'

He sat in a tall-backed armchair in the Oval Office, two long pale settees before him. He indicated the seat closest to him. 'Carolyn, sit next to me here. Greg, set yourself beside your lovely wife.' He smiled at her. 'Take that as a statement of fact and not in the least bit sexist. Forgive me for not rising,' he added, offering no reason, his drawn, pale face reason enough. 'Sam, sit over here on my right where I can see you.' Cornell flashed his big-toothed grin. 'Sounds like a wake! That it is *not*, I assure you.'

He smiled at Carolyn. 'I apologize for Mrs Cornell's absence – she's exhausted after all the travelling of these last few days. These supersonic aircraft may get you there quicker but by God you pay for it a couple of days later. Sam, you've recovered from your ordeal? I know how you hate being caged.'

'There's still every chance they'll do it again,' growled Sam. 'For a heck of a lot longer.'

'Well, that's one reason why we're here.' Cornell shook his head firmly. 'When the head of an organization, secret or not, dies violently after the discovery of some – shall we say – accounting discrepancies, the first hand that forensic officers paraffin-test for traces of gunpowder is that of the deceased. I'm an old criminal lawyer, I know the percentages. The head of a powerful secret organization is no different – after all he has more opportunity than most to divert funds. However, why look for scandal?

'No, the consensus of opinion is that we are looking here at a man who finally cracked. For God's sake, he had enough reason. Those terrible burns, the constant pain! Incidentally, Sam, the tape of Director Kent's tirade over the telephone to you in the early hours of Saturday? Very significant. Much of it was quite undecipherable – because of an accidental coffee-spill I understand – but the experts have done their best and it's quite clear that he was, undoubtedly, suffering from severe – even critical – stress. One might say that it was best that matters were resolved this way. A fine mind like that going haywire is too dreadful to contemplate. You know, with that empire of his I always saw him as a kind of Caesar and indeed he acted like a true Roman – fell on his own sword, in a manner of speaking. An honourable end.'

Cornell raised a hand and silenced Sam then turned to Greg, barely breaking breath.

'What a pity that house in England was destroyed. The electronic equipment the report said? There were some very fine – and valuable – pieces there. I actually visited Savernake some years ago when I was a Senator. Beautiful place, just beautiful. Regency, you know. Wonderful fireplaces. They called it a retreat – and so it was – but of course we all knew whose budget it was marked to.' He paused, all lightness gone from his tone. 'I understand from your father you were able to salvage a tape-recording? You've been working on it? Does it help in this matter? I understand you've been briefed?' He glanced quickly at Sam, who nodded.

'It tells us what Moscow intended, sir,' replied Greg.

Cornell shifted. 'Does it have to do with Masada? Jesus supposedly being there? Dying there? We believe they – KGB – tried to launch that story before. Andropov again – during his time as KGB Chairman.'

'Not Masada, sir. Glastonbury. England.'

Cornell leaned forward. 'Go on?'

'There was a period in the life of Jesus when He disappeared from view. It narrows down to the period from his preaching as a boy in the temple and surprising the elders to his appearing again proclaimed by John the Baptist. The nearest you can get to any hard information is, quoting Luke, "He returned with His mother to Nazareth and grew up advanced in wisdom and in favour with God."'

Cornell nodded. 'That period has often been debated and never fully explained.'

'Historically we're looking at the reign here of two Roman

emperors: Augustus and Tiberius for this period. It was in the fifteenth year of Tiberius's reign that Jesus returned. I mention this because this was a period when extensive travel was taking place. Long journeys were commonplace.' Greg looked again at Carolyn. 'Carolyn's own people – and a number of other similar religious groups – have a long-standing belief that Jesus was taken as a boy from Israel by Joseph of Arimathea – who later sought His body from Pilate – to Glastonbury, England, and remained there in a form of retreat. This could have been as protection – until it was his time. Stories of His Coming were rife and he'd had a fairly high profile as a youth with his preaching. He could have been taken out of the Middle East, easily. England was under Roman rule but his enemies were not truly the Romans but the Jewish religious establishment. The story could have some truth in it. It is perfectly feasible – reasonable – given the circumstances. If you have – potentially – a radical leader, you protect him, even by exile, until the right moment. And Jesus was radical.'

'And the Soviets bent that story? That was the lie we were to swallow?'

'Bent? Mr President, they were offering proof – historical fact – on the basis of results from the Markarovs' work on sub- and ultra-sonic sound retrieval. They did more than bend the story, they reconstructed the rest of Christ's life!'

'Just as they did with the supposed Masada evidence. The Gospel according to Andropov says Christ died in Glastonbury?'

'Lived, married – and died, yes.'

Cornell murmured: 'Never returned, never preached the Sermon on the Mount, never crucified, never resurrected. All gone in three words. Lived, married, died. A mere man. Dear God, the simplicity, the audacity of it is *inspired*.' He looked at Greg. 'You believe in anything, son?'

'I believe we had a doubtful past, a shaky present, and a fragile future. I believe we might make it under our own steam if someone doesn't overheat the boiler and it blows – or we burn all the fuel first.'

'That's a start, and maybe it's appropriate for the times, but you have to believe in something more than that. That's why the Soviets died. Only the very top few really believed in their creed. Everyone else was there for the ride or was cowed by fear. Sam, give your son a drink of that fine single malt we shared the other night.'

'He doesn't touch the stuff.'

'Today he does. Presidential command. Besides I want to steal his wife away for a short while.' Cornell pointed at the desk. 'Try that chair, Greg – see if it suits you. You've got all the qualifications.' He stood, offered Carolyn his arm and led her out through the double doors, under the colonnade and down the steps on to the leaf-strewn lawn of the Rose Garden.

'What a fall this has been,' he said. 'Poor gardeners can't keep up with it. Summer flowers have faded now of course but we have the heliotrope, chrysanthemums, and salvia, they'll provide colour until frost.' He pointed at a bench, led her there, and sat beside her. 'Your parents are well? Recovered? I understand they weren't mistreated – apart from the gas, of course, which was unforgivable. We believe Maddox died, by the way. There's a rumour he escaped and is in hiding but we've had a report from the fire chief down in Austin and he can't see there was any way out. Other than the way you made it. That was some jump!' He glanced at her and saw fleeting terror in her eyes.

'Greg made the jump,' she said.

He nodded then for a while gazed silent and withdrawn at the colonnade of the West Wing then over to the mansion itself, as if weighing the history of it. Finally, he said: 'I have something to ask you. You don't have to answer. You're free to refuse even the President of the United States. You can tell me – if you want to pass the buck – that what I ask is within the bounds of privileged information.' He pointed with a wry smile at the grey afternoon sky.

She looked at him.

He nodded, as though accepting her silence as affirmation. 'Greg told his father what happened over there in England. Sam is my dearest friend and you will forgive him for telling me also. I make no excuses for what you might consider an invasion of your – deepest – privacy. I do have reasons, however, strong reasons, perhaps stronger than those you may have for remaining silent. Like you, I believe unquestionably in the Almighty. I think you know that to be true. In my position – for as long as I hold it, which may not be for much longer, but I intend to carry out what remains with vigour – I am responsible for millions of lives.

'Threats of war and rumours of wars, as the Bible says, are all around us. We may think we have neutralized the big threat but I can never be so complacent as to believe that. I believe we have a major conflict to fight in the East – *still*. I believe we fought the first battle in that conflict in the Gulf War where your husband served his country with great courage. I fear that line drawn in the sand by my predecessor President George Bush cannot hold. I need to know – and I shall pass whatever you say on to my successor and urge him to believe and trust in it completely – *where* we must stand and fight? Fight with no question of retreat and at whatever cost? History has always dictated that there is a line where one must say, this far and no further. I am the one who must make that decision. I must bear the pain, the heartbreak, resulting from that decision – perhaps even more than the grieving mothers and fathers whose sons' lives I spend. I need to know so that we may be prepared, so that, God willing, we may save lives.'

Her sadness was infinite. 'Jerusalem,' she said.

'And will we win?'

'We?'

'America. The allies.'

'God will win.'

'And Man?'

She looked directly into his green eyes and for a moment he saw what she saw and her words were only confirmation of the horror.

'God will confound our understanding once more, brother will turn against brother, seeing only stranger and enemy, and the last battle will be fought in chaos.'

'And then?' he asked, hoarsely.

'Then, *we* begin.'

Madelaine Cornell watched out of the window across the lawns of the Rose Garden to the bench, crushing down envy of youth and jealousy for beauty in its prime. And failing. She wanted to be the young girl again who excelled at everything, who ruled every man within her horizon. Without that power she did not want to be where she was. But she *was* the First Lady. She might have been raised for that role. She had no choice but to play it to the full. Which meant standing beside the President, her husband, whatever the circumstances.

She wished it were as simple as that. She wished she had never uttered a word that morning, just one harrowing week before, when he had returned from the desert exhausted. She wished she had let him slip beside her in the darkness and sleep – or even inside her if he had the strength – allowing William Bradley Kent to rule as he had always done. She wished that day had never begun. She wished for order and somehow to push back the chaos that now engulfed her life.

She watched him walk back with Carolyn Lewelyn, his face set. She wondered how it was all going to end. There would be no scandal, she decided. John would do what had to be done. He was without a devious bone in his body but he was a master in the art of the possible. He would be correct but firm: certain matters required solutions which served the greater good. It was the way of things. Politicians had faced that fact – that dilemma – for centuries. He was not the first and far from the last.

She sighed. And even if now there would be no second term, she knew that widowed First Ladies always received preferential treatment over the spouses of living ex-presidents. It was only natural. And she looked stunning in black. She *must* decide the theme of her White House garden. One was certain to be named for her – just as there had been for Jacqueline Kennedy. Nothing too brash nor too exotic. Good taste was so important.

Especially when one was part of history.

And *that* was so much more important than mere youth.

John Cornell walked them down to the White House limousine that had brought them. 'What are your plans now?' he asked of Greg. 'I know your dad is going to put his feet up and fish – hopefully sometimes with me. NSA still?'

'I believe so. I have a short leave of absence while the Mojave station is wound down – our side of it.'

'Vacation?'

Greg turned on the steps. 'I want to find one missing piece in all of this, sir.'

'Really? What is that?'

'I've seen the video MOSSAD made in the Church of the Holy Sepulchre. The recording machine in shot was running – and other equipment was set up. They were excited – the Markarovs – you can see that in their faces.'

'I think you can put that down to expectation of the good life they believed was to come. Kent apparently offered them Savernake.'

'I still want to find that equipment, sir. It's nagging at me. It didn't leave with the Markarovs. I've seen the police report of the desert accident. There were a couple of burned-up suitcases in the Buick, that's it. No electronic equipment at all.'

'Kent might have had it removed.'

'The trunk was still locked – and melted shut by the flames. I think they abandoned all of it in Jerusalem. Probably sold off or stolen by now, but we're going there anyway.' He held Carolyn to him.

Cornell nodded and extended his hand. 'I wish I could go with you. Well, God go with you. And you be sure to tell me if you find anything.'

'We will – Mr President,' said Greg, firmly.

Ricardo Marchionni pulled himself out of the scarlet Ferrari 275GTB, stepped back and gazed admiringly, even longingly, at the long scarlet nose and swooping rear.

The young priest who had got out from the other side caught the keys Marchionni tossed to him. 'When will you return?' he asked, distressed.

Behind them the Lear jet's engines whined upward.

Marchionni smiled. 'When God – and the Holy Father – decide it should be so.'

'But why so suddenly? What's happened? Rome called you. I heard.'

'Have you been listening to my conversations?'

'No!'

'I'm pleased to hear it.'

'I would never do that.'

'Probably not. Well, keep yourself well, eat properly, don't pine, it withers youth faster than anything else. And be careful in that.' Marchionni pointed his ringed hand at the Ferrari.

The young man lowered his head and pressed his lips to the ring.

'You heard me?'

'I won't drive it again except in the grounds – to keep the engine turned over.'

'Good, you would suffer the worst trials of temptation: I've heard it said that Lucifer rides beside the driver in every Ferrari. Personally I think he hides under the hood.'

Marchionni turned away. It was time to bury the dead. Time also to feel the security of God and Rome and have others take the field against Satan. *You've spent so long fighting him, you know him too well.* He climbed the short steps, accepting the small measure of cognac in a crystal goblet from his personal steward as he stepped inside the jet.

He sat in the same seat that David Kolchak had occupied only the night before. Kent was dead, and Sazarin? Sazarin should be. The enigma lived on. God's hand had been stayed. Or He had His reasons. Marchionni sighed. There was only so much one could do and sometimes none of it was what He wanted. The main thing was that the White House, now, would act in Rome's best interests. Cornell might not be there for very long – according to impeccable Vatican sources – but that was someone else's problem. Anyhow, no incoming new president ever raked over past coals in case he started a fire he couldn't control.

He looked out at the dark young man grasping the Ferrari's opened door, priestly robes blowing wildly in the jet-wash, and it might have been himself waiting for Kolchak all those years before in Rome, set on a road that to his mind must be travelled to the end whatever the cost.

He smiled and touched the cognac to his lips, savouring but drinking none. *Some roads outlive every traveller, while others break you.* He knew the first to be true and expected the second. The art – and to Marchionni all of life was art – was to survive as long as possible, and to regret nothing by seeing only the furthest, shining horizon.

And if in his darkest hour he needed the comfort of justification for his deeds he need only call on Jesus's words in St John – not for the first time in his life, His servant disagreeing with his Master: *And you shall know the truth and the truth shall set you free.*

Marchionni swallowed all the cognac.

Freedom was the first step to chaos. History had proven it.

Riots raged in the streets of Jerusalem and the air reeked with the acrid stench of tear-gas but the Church of the Holy Sepulchre on Golgotha was a haven of peace, its dark, gloomy interior hung with low lights from the clutter of chapels of the various ancient Christian sects – Roman Catholic, Greek Orthodox, Armenian, Syrian, Coptic, and Abyssinian – while scaffolding, ladders, and piles of tools for the continuing, interminable restoration work merged the present with the deep feeling of past alive within the cool walls. Yet, despite all disruption, the sheer holiness of the place was unaffected.

Nothing could affect that, thought Greg – following behind the old Jesuit Father, Carolyn close beside him, her head covered – it's in the stones, the air, the foundations and soil beneath, in the blood spilt on the cross on this Hill of the Skull – if you were a believer – and even beyond, in legend from the dawn of biblical history, for it was Adam's skull which is said to be buried here. Whether from the presence of God or the accumulated faith of the millions of believers who had passed with total devotion through the church's doors he could not know. He simply knew the feeling of holiness was there. And accepted it.

The old priest had the laboured breathing and permanent stoop of one crouched for too long, for too much of his life, in low damp passages.

'Nineteen eighty-six,' he said, holding up the bright white battery lamp. 'Yes, nineteen eighty-six. July. The heat outside was unbearable.' He turned, smiling gently. 'But the church is always cool.' He nodded, for himself. 'Blessed.' He moved on. 'Ah!' He took keys from the belt of his robe and tried two, failing impatiently before the third turned easily in the lock.

The small chamber was arched, seeming to be hewn straight out of rock, filled with broken statues laid flat like white corpses, and icons sealed in plastic wrapping with rounded, holy eyes peering through into this cool tomb, and – like things fallen through a hole in time – electronic amplifiers and speakers, and a tape recorder with reels still connected together by dusty brown magnetic tape made white by chalky dust.

'There! Exactly as they left them,' said the priest. 'Seems a shame really. I've a brother who enjoys music – my, his equipment! Makes *this* look positively archaic. To think this was barely ten years ago. How things have changed. Still, someone might have got some use out of it? Such a shame. We would have sold it but they said they would return and if we can't believe people, who can?' He laughed, wincing from some complaint.

'We'd like to hear the tape,' said Greg.

The priest turned, surprised: 'You're not taking it all away?' He glanced at Carolyn, concerned suddenly. 'Do you feel unwell, my dear? The air – and the thought of the weight above – can be quite oppressive for some. I'm used to it, of course, after forty – almost fifty – years.'

'I'm fine.' She stared at the machine.

'Maybe you won't want it removed,' said Greg, watching her.

'I'm afraid I don't understand.'

'Play the tape,' said Greg. 'Perhaps then we might all understand.'

The old priest frowned. 'Very well. There's electric current in the passage outside. Perhaps you would . . . ?'

Greg unravelled the length of mains cord with the equipment, found a plug socket a little way down the passage, then heaved the heavy recorder on to a wooden crate, switched on cautiously, and heard the motor whirr to life. Carefully, he blew dust away from playing heads and tape then rewound it to its beginning. He turned to Carolyn. 'You're sure you want to hear this?'

'We've come a long way. All of us.'

Greg worked the switch. At first it sounded as if the tape was badly wound, grinding through the gate and over the playing heads. He moved to halt it.

'*Don't!*' the priest barked.

Greg saw the old face, white with shock yet illuminated as light pierced the rock directly over him, tears rolling down his cheeks as they did Carolyn's. Greg backed away from the turning machine, feeling alone, outside whatever was occurring, hearing a long unearthly groan rising like approaching thunder in the dark hush before the storm. There was anger too, explosive, contained, never released. And there was pain. Unimaginable pain trapped in eternity, relived through eternity. He felt sick and part of him wanted to die, the rest of him to run. '*What is it!*' he gasped.

Carolyn and the priest were on their knees but still he stood, for now between him and them was the Serpent, and behind him, so close to be almost touching, felt, yet unseen, was his Dark Angel whispering his relentless message. *Hell is where you are, Greg.*

He called out but his words were lost – if they ever existed.

Carolyn had moved beside him grasping his hand, the priest before him murmuring the words on the tape: the anguished question repeated over and over, trapped for all eternity where they had been spoken.

'*What is it!*' Greg asked again.

She looked up at him, tears flowing freely now, pain and light and joy in her eyes. '*Who,*' she said.

He sank to his knees beside her. The voice of his Dark Angel stilled, the Serpent, behind him.

The fire was extinguished and he dragged himself up from his sandy grave, the air shimmering with heat, the fumes terrible. He turned and saw the horror, the great snaking black column of utter destruction and cruel death behind him while above in the dark haze he could see the shapes moving slowly, their angry sound somehow distant, detached from the deed, as so they were. All he had to do was walk – keep walking toward the sun and the air would clear, the fumes would fade, the morning light would wash over him and he would be, with each step, nearer home. The fiery heart of a new day was on the horizon.

Glover Wright
Eighth Day £4.99

One man knew the secret. He had to be destroyed . . .

MAN'S POWER TO PLAY GOD ...

At the end of the Second World War it was the Third Reich's final
secret – buried for ever in a bunker under the Black Forest.

Yet forty years later the details emerged. Stolen by the Allies, then
developed in a series of experiments that would shock even a cynical
modern world.

On the lonely wastes of Dartmoor, one man running through the night
saw the horror and what was to come.

Adam had to be destroyed . . .

'Chilling, superbly researched and utterly enthralling . . . the work of a
master thriller writer'
JACK HIGGINS

'Tackled with great ease and flair . . . faultless'
SUNDAY TIMES

All Pan books are available at your local bookshop or newsagent, or can be ordered direct from the publisher. Indicate the number of copies required and fill in the form below.

Send to: Pan C. S. Dept
              Macmillan Distribution Ltd
              Houndmills Basingstoke RG21 2XS
or phone: 0256 29242, quoting title, author and Credit Card number.

Please enclose a remittance* to the value of the cover price plus: £1.00 for the first book plus 50p per copy for each additional book ordered.

*Payment may be made in sterling by UK personal cheque, postal order, sterling draft or international money order, made payable to Pan Books Ltd.

Alternatively by Barclaycard/Access/Amex/Diners

Card No.   ☐☐☐☐☐☐☐☐☐☐☐☐☐☐☐

Expiry Date   ☐☐☐☐☐☐

Signature:

Applicable only in the UK and BFPO addresses

While every effort is made to keep prices low, it is sometimes necessary to increase prices at short notice. Pan Books reserve the right to show on covers and charge new retail prices which may differ from those advertised in the text or elsewhere.

NAME AND ADDRESS IN BLOCK LETTERS PLEASE:

....

Name _____

Address _____

_____

_____

_____

6/92